PRAISE

That Blig...

TOM KENEALLY on Mary Bligh: 'I love this stroppy sheila.'

'"Sometimes I hate my father." So says Mary Bligh as she introduces her account of a complex human who was the centre of a storm of personalities and motives, of commercial and in some cases psychotic greed in early Australia. Like no other figure in history, Bligh has been characterised by skilful foes in Britain and Australia as a one-dimensional savage.

'Sue Williams returns us to the true estimation of flawed and well-intentioned Bligh, beloved by ordinary settlers, hated by an unworthy elite, and loved and hated by a courageous daughter. This is a task undertaken by Sue Williams with superb narration and engrossing drama.'

PRAISE FOR

Elizabeth & Elizabeth

'In Sue Williams' hands [Macarthur and Macquarie] become vividly real . . . I feel as if I have lived through these times with these two incredibly courageous women.' *Good Reading*

'Williams skilfully shows how both Elizabeths are moulded, pulled apart and pushed together by the times they live through . . . [*Elizabeth & Elizabeth*] provides a record of the too-often overlooked impact both women had on the early development of the colony.' Meg Keneally, *Weekend Australian*

'Williams draws a touching portrait of a friendship that manages to thrive despite difficulties small and large.' *Sydney Morning Herald/The Age*

'*Elizabeth & Elizabeth* is a fascinating look at how these two remarkable women navigated themselves through difficulties and heartbreaks to leave a legacy felt nearly two hundred years later.' *The Historical Novel Society*

Sue Williams is the best-selling author of the historical novel, *Elizabeth & Elizabeth*, also set in early colonial Australia, and is an award-winning journalist, travel writer and non-fiction author. She has developed a writing style that tells a story as evocatively as possible, with a keen eye for detail. Sue's biographies include *Under Her Skin: The life and work of Professor Fiona Wood*; *Mean Streets, Kind Heart: The Father Chris Riley story*; *Father Bob: The larrikin priest*; *The Last Showman: Fred Brophy*; *No Time For Fear: Paul de Gelder*; *Peter Ryan: The inside story*; *Death of a Doctor*; and *The Girl Who Climbed Everest*. Other books are about travel, true crime and genetics, while she has also had a children's book published in the US.

That Bligh GIRL

SUE WILLIAMS

ALLEN&UNWIN
SYDNEY · MELBOURNE · AUCKLAND · LONDON

First published in 2023

Copyright © Sue Williams 2023

Allen & Unwin
Cammeraygal Country
83 Alexander Street
Crows Nest NSW 2065
Australia
Phone: (61 2) 8425 0100
Email: info@allenandunwin.com
Web: www.allenandunwin.com

Allen & Unwin acknowledges the Traditional Owners of the Country on which we live and work. We pay our respects to all Aboriginal and Torres Strait Islander Elders, past and present.

A catalogue record for this book is available from the National Library of Australia

ISBN 978 1 76106 588 0

Typeset in 12.5/18.5 pt Garamond Premier Pro by Bookhouse, Sydney
Printed and bound in Australia by the Opus Group

10 9 8 7 6 5 4 3 2 1

The paper in this book is FSC® certified. FSC® promotes environmentally responsible, socially beneficial and economically viable management of the world's forests.

For my mum and dad, Edna and Bill Williams,
who have always been so supportive

PROLOGUE

26 January 1808

Three hundred scarlet-uniformed soldiers, with fixed bayonets and loaded firelocks at the ready, are marching through the rough dirt streets of Sydney.

Some passing locals stop to stare at the troops being led by their New South Wales Corps' band, playing a rousing rendition of 'The British Grenadiers' on the fife and drums. Others scatter in terror.

It's the twentieth anniversary of the founding of one of Britain's newest colonies and one soldier's bellow that this will be the most glorious day in the Corps' history is met by a cheer from the ranks.

These men in battle dress, with their colours flying and rebellion in their hearts, are on their way to overthrow the colony's governor, the notorious William Bligh. But when they reach the cast iron gates of Government House, they halt.

Standing behind the bars is the lone figure of a small, slim woman, dressed in a black frock and bonnet. Mary Putland does not move to allow them in; she simply stares steadily into the eyes of the man at the head of the battalion.

For a moment, Major George Johnston hesitates. 'Madam,' he says finally, gathering his wits, 'move aside! We have not come for you. We have come for your father.'

'Well, you shall not have him,' she replies. 'Go back to your own homes and your families. Leave this instant!'

Johnston—commanding officer of the Corps, the first man ashore in the First Fleet, and the celebrated hero of the battle against an armed pack of convicts that outnumbered his men ten to one—again wavers. He'd expected the governor to be here himself, with his guards, his staff or a crowd of his supporters. He hadn't envisioned Bligh's daughter being the sole sentry brave enough to face his troops.

He reaches for the bars of the gate but still Mary refuses to yield. He shouts an order, there's a clatter through the ranks and the men ranged behind their commanding officer raise their muskets to their shoulders. Mary doesn't flinch.

Instead, she raises her furled white silk parasol above her head and, as the soldiers push the gate open and jostle their way in, she rains blows on their chests and their shoulders. 'You traitors!' she shouts. 'You rebels! Get back!'

'That damned Bligh girl,' Johnston mutters, his frustration matched only by his secret admiration of her pluck. 'She'll be the end of us.'

Part One

LEAVING

1

FATHER, DEAR FATHER

Mary Bligh
5 OCTOBER 1803, LAMBETH, LONDON

Sometimes I hate my father. I know how shocking that sounds, so I don't think I could ever say it out loud. I couldn't even confide in my sisters or my mother, although occasionally I notice her looking at Father with a scowl and I catch her eye and she carefully rearranges her face to give nothing away. But I suspect there are times when she loathes him. She must.

My sisters don't feel the same way as me. They regard him with awe, like so many other people. Captain William Bligh is a national hero, they say; he's a symbol of all that's good and upstanding and courageous about England.

I beg to differ.

Of course, he's clever. That's not in dispute. Remember Captain Cook's terrible murder on the Sandwich Islands? Well, Father, at just twenty-four years old, watched the whole thing through a telescope from the ship and was the one who took charge of Cook's ship's navigation and brought everyone safely home again. Ten years later, he ferried his loyal crew back over nearly four thousand miles in an open boat following the mutiny on HMS *Bounty*. They couldn't even make landfall after one man was killed on Tofua and they had no firearms they could use against hostile natives. Both feats were pretty remarkable.

But what of him as a man? What is he truly like in the outside world? Is he kind and caring? Is he a strong leader who carries the hopes and dreams of his men with him? Or is he more of a bullying, blustering braggart?

At home, I find him plainly insufferable and I have no doubt that those *Bounty* mutineers thought the same. And it's not as if they were the only ones to ever stand up to him, either. Later, another crew on the *Nore* mutinied against him, too, over poor pay, calling him the 'Bounty Bastard'—a nickname that's stuck with him ever since. I would have loved to have seen his face as they taunted him, although his challengers paid dearly. The ringleaders ended up hanging from the gallows for their audacity.

But at least I can escape my father. I can go into the bedroom I share with my sisters and hide away from his booming voice and his terrible oaths that make everyone cringe—even the dogs skulk away in terror. I can retreat to the kitchen, where he rarely ventures, and ask the cook to stand aside so I can take out my anger kneading bread. Bread-making is a great way to vent my anger as it silently absorbs all the punishment I mete out.

'Mary, Mary!' Mother says to me when she catches me there, pounding the dough with a ferocity that at times even takes me aback. 'What are you doing? There'll be nothing left of that by the time you've finished. Knead it gently. Look, this is the way.'

I move aside to allow her to take over and pretend to take an interest. 'Thank you, Mother,' I say meekly. 'I see what you mean.'

She frowns as she patiently turns the dough and presses her knuckles into it, rhythmically turning and pressing, turning and pressing. 'I've shown you so many times, but it doesn't seem to make any difference,' she says.

'Sorry, Mother.'

'Are you really?' she asks, stopping what she's doing and looking me full in the face. *'Mary, Mary, quite contrary . . .'* she starts reciting the nursery rhyme that she knows will make me smile.

I can't help myself.

'That's better now,' she says. 'You're so much prettier when you're not glowering.'

'Thanks, Mother,' I say. 'I do try, but sometimes I find it hard . . .'

She nods. She knows me better than I probably even know myself. But after she leaves the kitchen, I seize the dough again and smack it hard with my fist. I don't care about being gentle. I'll often mutter curses as I work the dough, taking care that no one is around to hear. I'd love, one day, to say such things to Father, but I'd never dare. I can't imagine what would happen if I did. The role of dutiful daughter is so much a part of me, I can't conceive of being any other way towards him. I prefer to knead my profanities into the dough, into something that won't answer me back, that won't curse me, that won't deride me or belittle everything I do.

I wonder if those men on the *Bounty* felt the same way. If they did, then really, they didn't have much choice other than to rise up and load him into that little boat and send him out to sea. For I know how ruthless and cold-hearted he can be when he considers himself crossed, and how vicious when he encounters what he sees as disrespect. He's never been a terribly violent man, that's true, but the lashings he gives with his tongue inflict far more long-term pain and suffering than any physical beating. I've seen his wrath and his appetite for revenge first-hand. And it terrifies me, every time.

Once, when I was maybe seven, I remember walking with him, Mother, my younger sister Elizabeth and the twins Frances and Jane in their pram along the River Thames, close to our home in Lambeth, when a vagrant wandered into our path.

'Move over, sir!' Father said to him. 'Let us pass.'

The man looked him up and down, then sneered. 'Why not ask me nicely?' he retorted. 'This footpath is as much mine as it is yours.'

I felt Mother's hand tighten around mine, and I knew what was coming.

'How dare you be so insolent!' Father exploded. 'Do you not know to whom you are talking? Get out of our way.'

'William,' Mother said in a quiet, pleading voice, 'not here, not now . . .'

I don't think Father even heard her. 'You ill-mannered bugger!' he shouted, stepping towards the man and waving a fist in his face. 'God damn you! If you don't move now, I shall make you.'

Standing stock still, the man looked stunned at the crudeness of Father's language, and I wondered, briefly, if he was as shocked as me by how quickly things had got out of hand. He then glanced at Mother and me and the three little ones. 'For their sake, I will,' he said softly, 'because they deserve better.'

He side-stepped us and made off down the path, leaving Father ruddy-faced and Mother trembling. I burst into tears. I couldn't help it. The scene had scared me horribly.

Since then, some thirteen-odd years later, anytime he feels he's not being respected as much as he deserves, Father descends into a fit of rage, and almost nobody is safe from his ever-increasing wrath. But strangely, despite his anger stemming from a lack of respect towards him, he has no interest in treating others with the same regard.

I sometimes wonder if it's anything to do with him being an only child. Although he has a half-sister, born before his father married her widowed mother, Aunt Catherine was nineteen by the time he came along, and had left home soon after marrying a naval surgeon. As a result, my father was brought up as the light in both his parents' lives, and indulged terribly, from what I've heard of his childhood. He never had to learn to cohabit happily with brothers or sisters, or to negotiate fairly with equals for favours. Instead, he became used to getting his own way, and threw a tantrum whenever he didn't. In adulthood, he's not much different. What he wants, he's used to getting. And woe betide anyone who stands in his path.

I often ponder what Mother saw in him—still sees in him—but she hushes any talk around the dinner table, even when he's away at sea, of their relationship. But while he's so harsh towards me, and towards nearly everyone else he seems to encounter, to be fair, I've never seen him raise a hand, or even so much as speak sharply, to her. She's just about the only person I've seen him treat with absolute respect. That's understandable, too. She's brought him love, a happy home, children and, probably the most important thing for him, contacts for his naval career.

My elder sister Harriet, who is two years older than me at twenty-two and married last year, is much more forgiving than me. When she visited us a few weeks ago from her marital home not far from ours in London, she took me aside. 'Why do you get so angry with him?' she asked. 'He's been a good provider, and he started work so early in life. It couldn't have been easy for him being signed for the Royal Navy at seven, when he was just a small boy, to get the experience he needed for a commission later. These days, he obviously makes Mama happy and he's treated like a national hero. If he's good enough to receive praise from Admiral Horatio Nelson—and not even once but *twice*—why not from you? Most would think we're very lucky to have a father like him.'

I rolled my eyes. 'That's fine for you to say,' I replied. 'But since when was Nelson any true judge of men's character? From what Father's told us of what happened in the Battle of Copenhagen, I bet he was just happy that Father was as pig-headed as him and ignored their commander's signals to take Nelson's lead instead. Father demands absolute loyalty from his men, yet he followed Nelson rather than the man really in charge. Doesn't that make him the ultimate hypocrite?'

'Mary!' Harriet sighed. 'You're so unforgiving. Papa was so courageous in that battle and that's one of the reasons England is safe and secure today. Can't you give him a little credit?'

'Of course,' I said, 'you're right.'

But I didn't really believe it. Harriet sees a different side of Father. Like his parents were to him, he's always been terribly affectionate to his firstborn, and has always talked to her and listened to what she says. Since Harriet married, and then named his first grand-child William Bligh in his honour, he's become even more doting. Whenever he's home from the sea and she drops by, his face lights up with pleasure.

By contrast, I can't seem to do anything right. As a small child, I suffered terribly from The Itch, with a rash all over my body that I couldn't help scratching and making worse. Mother used to make an ointment for me by crushing mercury pills, which Father brought back from naval supplies, but he had no sympathy at all. He'd slap my hand away whenever he saw me scratching.

'You'll scar for life if you keep doing that,' he'd say. 'Is that what you really want? To make yourself ugly? You'll have to hide yourself away as no one will want to see you.'

I'd shake my head dumbly, tears in my eyes. 'No, Father.'

'Well then, stop it,' he'd admonish.

I was only about four years old, but I still remember the night-mares I'd have afterwards, of a hideous creature cowering in a cupboard, covered in red scars and pus.

Thankfully, after a couple of years, The Itch disappeared. But Father's criticism never did. He just found other aspects of me to find fault with.

Recently, when he caught me poring over the latest clothing catalogues, he saw red. He despises my interest in fashion and has often ticked me off for glancing at my reflection in a shop window as I pass. 'Why can't you be more like your sister?' he scolded. 'She worked hard at acquiring all the skills she needs to be a good wife and mother, and look what a good match she made.'

'But I spend so much time on my music, reading, drawing and embroidery, as well as learning how to prepare meals from Cook,' I told him. 'I think it's also important for a young lady to study fashion . . .'

Father shook his head with disgust and rolled his eyes. 'What frippery! Ridiculous frippery!'

Now that Harriet is expecting his second grandchild, it's even worse. Every time his eyes fall on me, I know he's comparing me, unfavourably, to my sister. And, stupidly, it makes me only crave his approval even more.

I try to please him, I really do. One day, I cooked him and Mother dinner—pigeons in a white sauce, and chicken stuffed with roast chestnuts. He ate it, but said he'd prefer something much simpler. I was crushed. Then, the next morning he said he couldn't sleep as the food had upset his stomach. If I'd intended that, I would have been happy but, sadly, I hadn't.

Another day, I showed him a sketch of our house and garden in Lambeth that I'd been working on all week. I thought I'd made a very good job of it, as my tutor had always told me I had artistic talent. He barely glanced at it.

'Yes, yes,' he said. 'Very nice, I'm sure. Now, I have work to do. Please don't disturb me.'

As he shut the door of his study, leaving me holding my sketch stupidly and fighting back the tears I could feel burning my eyes, Mother came over and put her arm around me.

'Come on, Mary,' she said. 'Your father's a very busy man. He's got a lot on his mind. He doesn't mean it.'

'No,' I said, turning away. 'He never does.'

I went to my bedroom, slamming the door behind me, and sat at the dressing table staring at my reflection in the mirror. I noted, with satisfaction, how pale and bereft I looked. I understood Father could often be preoccupied with work and his worries about our family. My youngest sister, Anne, is very sickly and not quite right in the head, and I know he frets about what the future might hold for her. His preoccupations have grown worse since he and Mother lost Henry and William, my twin brothers, just a day after their birth. He'd been so happy when he'd heard he had sons, and so devastated by their deaths.

That is still no reason, however, to be quite so dismissive of me.

But I have a plan, and it won't be long before I break it to him. I hugged myself and my secret tight. As Father might say himself so indelicately, he has a hell of a shock coming to him.

1

THE SECRET

Mary Bligh
14 NOVEMBER 1803, LAMBETH, LONDON

The paper is crumpled from having been unfolded, pored over and folded again so many times. I take it out of the top drawer of my bedroom dresser once more, smooth it out and read the cursive ink. Every time I do so, it brings a delicious frisson of pleasure.

My dearest Mary, it begins. I savour those words for a moment, then move on to the now familiar note. I think I could recite every precious word by memory.

I am so delighted to have met you, and on each occasion I find even more pleasure in your company. I smile. The same is true for me. *I know we've only met four times now, but I have been absolutely charmed by everything about you. I haven't been able to stop thinking about you.* Nor me him.

I stop and wait before I go on to the next wonderful part. I want to eke out the anticipation. Finally, I can stand it no more.

I would like, with your permission, to ask your father for your hand in marriage. I know this is unexpected, but I very much hope you will agree. Nothing would make me happier than spending the rest of my life with you.

I hug the note close to my chest. Dear John! The note had arrived just two weeks ago, and we are now preparing, this very evening, to see my father. I have no idea how he'll greet the news; whether he'll be pleased or enraged. But with our liaison so secret, there's no doubt he'll be thoroughly taken aback.

Father has known John Putland far longer than me. It was five years ago that he first mentioned him over a family dinner. A fellow naval man, it seems he had acquitted himself so well during the victorious Battle of the Nile against the French off Egypt, which had curtailed Napoleon's ambitions, that Nelson had personally promoted him from midshipman to the rank of lieutenant. Such a rapid rise from a junior sailor to officer was quite unusual, Father said, and he had been keen to make the acquaintance of the young man.

The opportunity presented itself just a year later, when Father was posted to Dublin, John's homeland, to survey the harbour. There were no good charts of it, and the port had become notorious for wrecking ships on its rocks. With Father such an expert in surveying, the Admiralty asked him to go and make recommendations on how it could be improved. On the evenings he wasn't occupied with his calculations and his charts, he made a point of seeking out John and the two men met on a number of occasions for a meal and a drink and, no doubt, to swap war stories.

Father was in Dublin for three months, and when he came home again he was full of praise for John, saying he was smart and respectful and he had a bright future ahead of him. Father said he wanted to invite John to London, but before he could, my father was summoned back to sea to captain HMS *Glatton*.

There, he experienced his finest hour in the Battle of Copenhagen, as he told us almost every time we sat down for dinner in the following months.

'Look, this is my ship, the *Glatton*,' he'd say, seizing the salt cellar. 'Here is Nelson's ship, this pepper pot, while that plate is the enemy. And then the Admiral signals for us to retreat!' He'd throw up his arms in disbelief. 'Can you credit it? Retreat! From this position!' That, apparently, was the point at which Nelson ignored the Admiral's signal, putting his blind eye to his telescope, and Father had to choose which man to follow. 'I knew Nelson was right. We defeated fifteen Danish warships. And how many did we lose? None!' It was a story he told constantly. Only the props changed.

As a result of Father's loyalty and skill, Nelson invited him onto his ship for dinner, just the two of them. Father still has the invitation displayed above his desk and we all know the words off by heart: *My Dear Sir, Will you do me the favor of dining on board the St. George this day . . . Your truly obliged Nelson.*

Being invited to dine alone with Nelson was a rare honour and apparently both men had a fine evening, reliving their most successful battles. Talk arose of John Putland somewhere around the post-prandial brandies. Nelson was admiring of his new lieutenant and interested that Father had met him and also enjoyed his company.

The next time Father came home from captaining the *Glatton*, he invited John over for dinner. To my surprise, when one of our maids, Jeannie, showed in the handsome officer, I liked him the moment

I met him. He was nothing as I'd imagined. So tall he absolutely towered over me, but quiet and softly spoken with a warm smile and tightly curled dark hair, the young officer seemed embarrassed by Father's boasts of his exploits and promotion. I warmed to him instantly. I could see Mother approved of him, too.

'Lieutenant Putland,' I eventually screwed up the courage to ask him after we'd finished dessert, 'tell us about your life before the navy. Where are you from, and do you have brothers and sisters?'

He smiled that gorgeous smile again that lit up his eyes. 'Well, Miss Bligh, there's not much to tell,' he replied. 'I was born in Bray, County Wicklow, about ten miles south of Dublin. I have seven brothers and sisters.'

'And have you been in the navy long?' Mother asked.

'I joined in 1797 at the age of sixteen. I'd always been interested in the sea.'

I did a quick calculation. So, he was twenty-two, just two years older than me. Perfect!

'Your parents must miss you when you're at sea, and also worry about you,' Mother said. 'I know when William is away, I can think of little else . . .'

Father glanced at her, and obviously wanted to change the subject back to seafaring. 'Now, let's adjourn to the other room,' he told John, 'and leave these ladies to their own chatter.'

I felt a stab of disappointment as I watched him lead John away, but noticed, with some satisfaction, that the officer also looked a little deflated.

The next time John was invited, I made a real effort with my appearance and could see from his eyes that he'd noticed. I wouldn't call myself a natural beauty, but I'm skilled at presenting my finest features in their best light. While I'm short in stature, I have a trim figure that I accentuate with waists pulled in as tightly as I can bear on my dresses, and I wear my long black hair coiled on top of my head. That evening I wore a new pale green gown trimmed with white lace, which I knew set off my complexion, and Jeannie pinned a little lace flower into my hair. She smiled at me as she did it. Nothing was lost on her.

'Oh, Lieutenant Putland,' I said, stretching out my hand as he came in after Father, 'so lovely to see you again.'

'Thank you, Miss Bligh,' he replied, blushing. He caught my tiny hand in his bear-like paw, bowing so deeply that his curls fell into his eyes. It was as much as I could do to resist smoothing them back. 'And very nice to meet you again.'

While we waited in the parlour for dinner to be served, I made sure I was sitting in the armchair next to his and engaged him in light conversation. I told him about myself; how I'd been born in Douglas on the Isle of Man, where my mother lived when her father was the Collector of Customs and Water Bailiff there.

'But it was my misfortune to be born on April Fools' Day,' I laughed. 'That's something my father never lets me forget!'

John smiled at that. 'But I can be sure, Miss Bligh, that you are no fool,' he said. 'In fact, you seem to me to be quite the opposite.'

'Thank you,' I said, feeling a flush creep up through my face. 'I suppose I can't be the best judge of that.' I moved back to safer ground. 'Sadly, I don't remember anything of Douglas, however. We moved away soon after my christening, first to Wapping and then to Lambeth—to this house where we are now. Have you done much exploring here in London? How do you like the city?'

'I like it a great deal more now,' John replied, looking at me so intently I had to drop my gaze. 'Although I find London so very big and noisy.'

'Spoken like a true man of the oceans,' I said. 'Father always says the thing he loves most about life at sea is the stillness, the peace.'

'He is certainly not alone in that,' John said. 'When, of course, we're not engaged in battle.' He then fell quiet and seemed unsure of what to say next, until his eyes alighted on the sketch that I'd been careful to leave in a conspicuous position on the mantle, just in case I needed a prop.

'Is this yours?' he asked, rising to his feet and making it across the room in three strides.

I nodded. 'Yes, it's a sketch I did of this house.'

'I can see that,' he said. 'It's an extremely good likeness. You have a rare talent, Miss Bligh.' He looked over to Father who was reading a newspaper, plainly annoyed that I'd commandeered our guest. 'Captain Bligh,' he called, 'you did not tell me your daughter was so gifted.'

Father looked at me sharply.

I smiled demurely as if butter would never melt in my mouth.

Harriet's husband, Henry Barker, is a professional artist, drawing panoramas of cities like his father before him, and then sketching and making engravings of famous battle scenes, including one of Father's battle in Copenhagen. When I once timidly showed him one of my pictures, however, hoping he might offer me some advice on how to improve, he was just as dismissive as Father.

As a result, I did take some pleasure in the suspicion that, despite Henry's growing fame—and praise from Nelson, no less, for those battle sketches—Father was a little disappointed in his favourite daughter's choice in husband. An artist pales in comparison with someone who's a battle hero. And John is certainly that, and more.

A less welcome regular guest, in my eyes at least, is Uncle Joseph, a man I find an insufferable bore. He isn't really related to us, but that's how Father likes us to refer to him. Sir Joseph Banks, as he's known to everyone else, is certainly very learned in his field of plants and agriculture and landscapes and animals, but he does so love to preach, at great length, to anyone who's prepared to listen.

He's always been a great friend and supporter to Father—he was the one who gave Father the role of captain on the *Bounty*, picking up breadfruit plants in the South Pacific and transplanting them to the Caribbean. The idea was that they'd be cheap and plentiful food for the plantation slaves, and things began well . . . up until the mutiny.

To give him his due, however, Uncle Joseph did take Father's side and helped him through the court martial for losing his ship. Since then, the pair have been as thick as thieves, and Father often invites him to dinner at our house with his wife, Aunt Dorothea, or 'poor Dorothea' as Mother refers to her. When I once asked her why, she put a finger to her lips and said, mysteriously, that Dorothea was long-suffering. Harriet told me later that Uncle Joseph is known for having a number of lady friends. That's something that endears him to me even less.

Father behaves differently around him, too. He tends to defer to Sir Joseph at every opportunity and becomes . . . almost obsequious. I can understand why, though. The botanist seems to have the ear of everyone in power, most importantly the King, and is now regarded as the expert on much of the world's geography, including the far-flung land of New Holland. It was he who, when America stopped taking our convicts, first suggested Botany Bay would be an excellent alternative, Father once told us. Since then, Uncle Joseph has been instrumental in the running of the colony, helping Captain Arthur Phillip become the first governor of New South Wales, appointing his successor Captain John Hunter, and then the current Governor Captain Philip Gidley King.

Despite Uncle Joseph's influential standing, I was much more excited by the thought of John visiting again. He came along to three more dinners, and I took every opportunity to try to impress him and engage him in conversation. One evening I was casually playing the pianoforte and singing when he arrived, and was thrilled when he joined in the chorus. I could see the effect I was having on the officer, and recognised I was becoming very fond of him, too. I'd never had a man pay me such attention before, and I found his gentle manner and his ready praise quite disarming.

Finally, at the conclusion of John's fourth dinner at our home, he'd slipped me a note, *that* note. When I read the missive up in my bedroom at the top of our three-storey house in Lambeth Street, my heart flipped over. I was thrilled. We could marry and set up home together, and I would at last be free of my father and his scorn. The prospect filled me with warmth and a feeling of lightness. I wrote back immediately and had Jeannie deliver it to John's lodgings. I left him in no doubt that I felt the same way and would be happy to be betrothed to him.

I could barely contain my impatience until I received another note back, saying John would be around the next week to speak to my father. I determined we would do it together.

And now the evening has arrived, and I can hear his firm knock on the front door. I almost run down the stairs in my haste to get there so Father won't have a chance to spirit him away. I find John standing at the base of the stairs, a wide grin on his face when he sees me. Father looks puzzled as he notices me behind him.

'Captain Bligh,' John says, 'could we adjourn to the front room? We have something important to ask you.'

Father still looks bewildered but he leads us both through. All three of us remain standing. 'Sir,' John started, 'I have been most grateful for the kindness and hospitality you have shown me. I have enjoyed getting to know your family, but especially Mary here.'

Father glances at me, then looks away, as John battles on.

'Over the last few weeks, I have become more and more enchanted by your daughter. And now . . . and now . . . I wondered . . .' John seems to run out of courage as Father stares at him, frowning. He takes another breath and then it all comes out in a hurry. 'I would very much like to marry Mary.'

There is a silence that seems to last forever. I finally break it. 'Father?' I ask. 'Father? What do you say? I think we'd be very happy together.'

Father sits down heavily on a chair, and we follow his lead and sit down opposite him. He seems to be gathering his thoughts. He glares at me, then fixes his eyes on John. 'Lieutenant Putland,' he says eventually, 'I would be very pleased to give you permission. I only hope Mary appreciates what a fine young man she has in you.'

3

AN UNPLEASANT SURPRISE

Mary Bligh

28 JANUARY 1804, LAMBETH, LONDON

My wedding day on Saturday, 28 January is truly the happiest day of my life. I wear a beautiful full-length gown in a rich burgundy, as is the fashion, with a delicate overlay of lace, and a beaded pearl fringe under the bust. That pearl fringe is repeated at the bottom of the lace, eight inches above the hem of the dress at the front, and along the train at the back where it sweeps the floor. My outfit is finished off with a pair of long black satin gloves and, after Jeannie has brushed my hair until it shines, she pins a lace headpiece with a crown of pearls into my tresses. I carry a bouquet of white lilies.

John Putland looks magnificent in his full-dress naval uniform, with his curls tamed by what I imagine is liberal use of pomade. I think that day, standing on the steps of the grand Church of St Mary in Lambeth, having married by licence since I am just twenty years old—a whole year under the marriageable age—we are one of the handsomest couples ever seen.

A surprisingly happy part of the day is my father. He pats my hand in a very rare show of affection as we walk down the aisle, and beams all the way through the ceremony. By contrast, Mother looks anxious and, although I smile at her reassuringly whenever our eyes meet, she doesn't look happy at all. It doesn't make sense to me. By rights, she should be delighted, and Father should be irritated that I've done so well for myself.

I mention it to John at the reception and he looks pained. 'I'm sure your mother is just sad at losing another daughter,' he says. 'Her *favourite* daughter. And maybe your father has come round at last and is happy for you.'

I giggle. There's no way Mother would see it like that, nor Father. But it's very kind of John to try to make me feel better.

My sister Harriet unknowingly adds an extra level of pleasure to the whole day. I can't help stealing glances in her direction every so often—she looks ready to burst, with her face red and her dress straining over her belly. I know it's mean, but every time I feel John's great arms easily encircle my tiny waist, I take delight, for once, in the favourable contrast between us.

Despite her discomfort, Harriet looks genuinely happy for me, and our four younger sisters, all in their Sunday best, are excited and a little overawed by both the occasion and this new vision of me. Seventeen-year-old Elizabeth appears plainly envious, and I can't blame her, while the twins Frances and Jane, now fifteen, giggle nervously together in that way of young girls. Sweet Anne, poor thing, is now twelve, but seems much younger, and is still very much in a world of her own. My nephew, little William Bligh Barker, is perfectly behaved, even though he's just fifteen months old.

Aunt Catherine sadly isn't here; she's apparently too sick to leave home. None of us were surprised. By my reckoning, she'd now be nearly seventy. The last time we visited her in Plymouth, a few years after her husband, John, died, I was shocked at how frail she seemed, especially next to Father. But I suppose the nearly twenty years' difference in their ages becomes magnified as they advance, and Father has always said that hard work and so much time spent outside breathing in fresh sea air has kept him vigorous and healthy.

I'm very pleased, though, that Catherine's son, my first cousin Commander Francis Bond, is here. I don't know him very well, as he's eighteen years older than me and has spent so much of his time at sea, but I've always felt that it's nice to have a male in the family. He was once a regular visitor at our house, too . . . until Father asked him to sail on his second breadfruit voyage. It was two years after the *Bounty* fiasco and he wanted Francis to be his second-in-command on the HMS *Providence*. We all understood why; he wanted someone he knew he could trust after his closest friend Fletcher Christian, a man whose name we now dare not speak anywhere near my father, turned against him to lead the mutiny. His nephew seemed the perfect choice.

That didn't work out too well, however. On their return, Francis said very publicly that he'd never sail with Father again. I'd been looking forward to his next visit to our house enormously, so I could ask him what exactly Father had done, and what had happened.

Unfortunately, Francis was never again invited for dinner, despite covering himself with glory afterwards for capturing numerous French and Spanish privateers and reportedly receiving huge sums of money in rewards.

Father seemed to have cut him off completely, and it was only Mother's intervention that enabled me to invite my cousin to the wedding. I notice that he and Father diligently avoid each other, and I hope that if I don't have the chance to speak to him, then at least Harriet will have the acumen to pick up some delicious gossip. I knew there'd be no more breadfruit voyages anyway. Apparently, the slaves had refused to eat the stuff, so it was an experiment that hadn't been successful for anyone.

My husband—Oh! How I love saying that!—introduces me to each of his friends and I'm pleased to see from their faces that they feel he's made a fine match. And I feel lucky, too, in having met him. For once, my father has done me an enormous favour by inviting such a good, kind and considerate man into our lives.

'Mrs Putland?' a voice behind me says. It doesn't register until it's repeated, and I realise, with a start, that it's me the speaker is addressing. I spin around, laughing, and find myself face to face with Uncle Joseph.

I'm so happy today that I hug him, and then can't work out who is more surprised, me or him. As well as finding him a pompous know-all, I've always secretly felt that Uncle Joseph doesn't much approve of me. But, today, on my wedding day, he is perfectly civil.

'Congratulations, my dear,' he says, extricating himself from my embrace. 'You look most beautiful today.' Then he turns to John. 'And congratulations to you too, Lieutenant.'

'Thank you, sir,' John replies, bowing his head and clicking his heels together. 'We are very honoured that you could make it to be with us today. It has made this day even more special.'

Uncle Joseph looks pleased at that and shakes John's hand warmly. 'You make a fine couple,' he says, stiffly. 'I hope your futures hold many adventures for you both.'

It's an odd thing to say, but I just smile. I'm sure he means well. Then he sidles back off to Father, and the pair spend the rest of the evening deep in conversation. I wonder, for a moment, what they are talking about, and then am whisked onto the dance floor with my new husband, and never think of it again.

The one person I do miss on this special day, though, is Father's bogeyman Fletcher Christian. In the early days, he spent a lot of time with us at home as one of Father's favourite mariners, almost like the little brother he never had. We all liked him. He was very different from Father—always laughing and joking around. I would sometimes wish he was my father instead and wonder what life would be like if he were.

My parents knew Mr Christian's family from the Isle of Man, where he'd lost his father as a young boy. His mother had squandered the family fortune and only narrowly avoided debtors' prison. Mr Christian had endured a hard life, but you'd never know it to meet him. He was always cheerful and kind to me and my sisters.

He was a clever man, too, despite his lack of schooling. He'd been a cabin boy on one of Father's ships at the age of seventeen and moved quickly up the ranks. He was keen to learn all he could of navigation, and Father took him under his wing, pleased to find such an eager apprentice. He recruited him onto his *Bounty* voyage

27

and wanted to make him master, but the navy objected on account of Mr Christian's inexperience. Instead, Father made him master's mate, and then promoted him to acting lieutenant halfway through the voyage. And then . . . and then . . .

'My love, what are you thinking about?' John asks me, breaking me out of my reverie. 'You suddenly look sad.'

'I'm fine,' I reply. 'I was just thinking of . . . absent friends.'

'Fletcher Christian?' he asks.

I smile fondly up into his concerned face. 'You know me so well already,' I say. 'Yes, I was just thinking how much I miss him.'

'And I wonder where he is today,' John muses.

'Who knows?' I reply. 'There are rumours that he has snuck back into England but, really, he could be anywhere.'

I remember coming upon him one day in Father's library, where he'd been having a lesson in navigation. He was holding a book and studying it intently. When I asked him what he was reading, he said it was about a tiny island in the Pacific Ocean, whose closest neighbour was Tahiti, called Pitcairn. He had a dreamy look in his eyes. He asked me what I thought such a distant place would be like. I said I had no idea, but perhaps it might be filled with dangerous savages. He just laughed at that. He said he imagined it could be the most peaceful place on earth. I found myself thinking back to that day often after my Father returned and told us that Mr Christian had taken off with his ship, along with the other mutineers. I would never tell anyone else just in case, but I sometimes wonder if he decided to take the *Bounty* there . . .

'One day, I'm sure you will see him again,' John reassures me. 'In the meantime, I'm going to do everything in my power to make you happy. I promise you, we won't be staying with your parents in London too long. I just need to make sure my estate in Kilkenny is ready for your arrival.'

'I can't wait!' I say to him, my eyes shining. 'I have never been to Ireland, but I am sure I will love it.'

'And I will love showing you around,' he replies.

I wasn't keen to start out our married life under the same roof as my father, but I was comforted by the fact he was set to return to sea soon after our wedding day. Sure enough, three months later, Father was appointed to another naval ship, HMS *Warrior*.

I was delighted but, typically, it wasn't a happy experience for him, or some of those on board with him. During the voyage, he accused one of his lieutenants of neglecting his duty, and the officer, as a result, called for his court martial, claiming that Father had called him a rascal, a scoundrel and had shaken his fist in his face, and displayed 'a tyrannical and oppressive and unofficerlike behaviour contrary to the rules and discipline of the Navy'.

Mother was distraught. I tried to comfort her, but at a hearing in February 1805, he was found guilty. Thankfully, Uncle Joseph came to our family's rescue and Father was given a warning to be more correct in his language in future.

A few days later, on my way to bed, I spot Father and Uncle Joseph arriving home together. They look rather like guilty co-conspirators, and I decide to stay out of trouble and pretend I didn't see them, but Father stops me.

'Mary, call John for me,' he says. 'We want to have a word.'

'Why?' I ask. 'I can pass on a message.'

At that, Father looks annoyed, and growls at me to do as I'm told. I smart. I'm now a grown woman and a wife, but still he treats me as a child. Still, old habits die hard and I obediently fetch John and stand in the room watching the three men.

'Mary!' Father says. 'I think you were on your way to bed, weren't you?' He says it in a tone that brooks no dissent, so I turn silently on my heel and climb the stairs. For the next three hours, I hear the clink of bottles and glasses and voices growing more boisterous by the minute, but I can't quite make out what they're saying.

I sleep fitfully, and in the morning ask John what they were discussing.

He looks embarrassed and immediately I fear there's something wrong.

'On Sir Joseph's request to the British Government, your father has been offered the post of governor of New South Wales,' he says quietly.

I feel relief flood through my body. I'd imagined bad news, but this is good. It would mean Father would be on the other side of the world, and I'd at last be free to lead my life far away from his scorn.

'That's marvellous!' I say to John, clapping my hands with joy and doing a little jig. 'Thank goodness, I thought you were going to deliver bad news!'

John looks unsure of himself, and suddenly I feel the blood drain from my face. 'What is it?' I ask. 'Tell me, what is it you are not saying?'

'Well, your mother doesn't want to accompany him . . .' John starts, then falters.

'So?' I ask, confused. 'They've spent great periods of their married life apart. I am sure this will be no particular hardship, for Mother especially.'

John smiles weakly at my jest. 'I'm sorry, my darling,' he says, 'you don't understand. Your father plans for you to come as his First Lady and for me to be his aide-de-camp. It is all arranged.'

I look at him, speechless. And then a thought occurs to me, and slowly the picture becomes clear: Father had planned this all along. He'd been plotting this with Sir Joseph and needed a family member—with Cousin Francis now out of the picture—who he could trust to act as his aide-de-camp. I was just the bait. I crumple into the chair behind me. Finally, I understand.

That's why Father was so happy on the day of my wedding. Perhaps that's why he invited John over so many times in the first place.

Now, his plan has come to fruition and I am simply the naïve girl who thought she'd made the best match in the world.

4

PLEADING FOR MY LIFE

Mary Putland
20 MARCH 1805, LAMBETH, LONDON

I've fumed and ranted and raged for the past month, but my father
won't listen. I've appealed to Mother, too, but predictably, she flatly
refuses to take my side against him. The only person who's at all
sympathetic is John. But even he, I sense, is conflicted. While he
swears he had no knowledge of Father's plan and says he understands
my anger, I think he secretly sees the proposition as the adventure
of a lifetime and can't help but be attracted to the idea of going
to the other side of the world to take on a position of real power
and influence.

'But John,' I plead with him, 'you'll be the aide-de-camp to my
father. This is *my father* we're talking about; not some kindly official
who actually values, and pays heed to, the men who work under
him. He will treat you as badly as he's always treated me and all

his other underlings, I'll wager. Will you be the next one to rebel against him?'

At that, John laughs. I don't join him; I scowl.

Seeing the look on my face, he quickly changes his expression and puts his hand on my arm. 'Mary, my sweet Mary,' he says, 'I am sorry. Of course, I understand what you are saying, and what a difficult position this has put you in. I know you don't want to spend more time with your father, and we had our plans to go to Ireland and start our family there ...'

I cut him off. 'And yes, what of those plans?' I ask sharply. 'Are they to be abandoned as soon as someone offers you the chance of personal aggrandisement? What about me, your wife? Do my feelings not count for anything?'

'They count for everything,' John says, and I can actually see the pain in those beautiful blue eyes of his. 'But this is a wonderful opportunity for us and my career. This is a chance to see a new land, one that has been described as most bountiful. It could be a whole fresh beginning. And your father won't be there forever. He will serve out his royal appointment and then be back here with your mother and sisters before you know it.'

'But what about the house in Kilkenny you've inherited?' I ask, fighting back tears. '*Our* house?'

'That's no problem at all,' John answers, shaking his head. 'It's not that I know it well, anyway. I think I've only visited it twice in my life.'

'What will we do with it, though?' I continue my mission to plant doubt in his mind.

'I've had a letter from my cousin John Roberts,' he says, 'who writes that he'd like to live there and is willing to pay me a thousand-pound mortgage for the property.'

At that, I can feel tears starting to slide down my face, and John gathers me in his arms. 'Please, Mary,' he whispers into my hair. 'This is a wonderful chance for us, I promise you. I will be there at every moment of the day to protect you, too. Apart from the ceremonial occasions, where you'll have to be the First Lady, you won't see so much of your father. I will take up all the rest of your time, you'll see!'

I can't help smiling at that.

John rocks back on his heels and looks me full in the face. 'That's better!' he says, cupping my face in his hands, wiping away my tears with his thumbs and kissing me, hard, on the mouth.

I'm still not convinced, but it's hard to find anyone who's prepared to listen. I think Mother feels embarrassed that she doesn't want to go and needs me to accompany Father to assuage her guilt. My younger sisters need her here, she keeps saying, and she is not confident they would cope well with the voyage if they were all to go. She also talks about her seasickness and says it would make her nothing but a hindrance on the high seas.

'But what about my seasickness?' I whine. 'You know I cannot stand the sea either.'

'Ah, but Mary, you are so much younger than me,' she retorts. 'You will recover much more quickly. I imagine you will become used to it sooner and won't feel its ill-effects for long. Besides, you can take Jeannie with you. She will look after you.'

She argues well, but I know she's not telling me everything. Although she and Father get on well, especially with the breaks offered by his long periods at sea, I am sure she would regard the prospect of spending six months closeted together in a small cabin with horror. I feel the same dread and we won't even be sharing a cabin. There's no way she will ever admit that, however. Then there's the fact that Harriet's first son, William, is just two and a half, and his little brother, Henry, will be one soon, and Mother absolutely dotes on them. I know she hopes they will have a little sister next. It's unlikely my brother-in-law, Henry, would countenance even the idea of his family upping and leaving England simply to accommodate Father and his ambitions.

Even more than that, however, I know Mother worries about Father and the consequences of his terrible temper. So far, he's managed to evade real censure but who knows what will become of him in New South Wales? If she stays in London, she'll be able to advocate for him with the authorities and smooth over any problems. She's always been wily and wise. In fact, were it not for her, there's little doubt he'd have nowhere near the good luck and influence he has now.

Mother had a much better education than Father, and she is undoubtedly more cultured and certainly better born. Her favourite uncle was Duncan Campbell, the important merchant and West Indies plantation-owner. He had a number of his old ships moored in the Thames to serve as convict accommodation so the men could be taken ashore as part of work gangs. Those convict hulks helped make Great Uncle Duncan's fame and fortune, especially when, as a close friend of Uncle Joseph's, he had them refitted to take convicts to New South Wales instead.

It was he, indeed, who had Father appointed to naval ships and promoted to lieutenant before the Treaty of Paris saw the size of the navy cut. Later, he introduced Father to Uncle Joseph, suggesting he'd be the perfect candidate for the breadfruit voyages. He even provided the ship—an old coal cargo vessel called *Bethia*—that became the *Bounty*. So, without Mother, Father could well have remained a lowly mariner, rather than rising through the ranks of the Royal Navy, making money on the merchant ships, and now about to be appointed the governor of Britain's newest colony.

Despite my apprehension, I try to reason with Father, too. I pick a time I know he'll be in a good mood—on a Sunday after we've all been to church. He likes to parade around as the perfect family man, basking in the glow of his large familial entourage. I start off carefully.

'Father, I've been thinking,' I say, kneeling submissively beside his chair, where he's reading a new report on the colony.

It looks like it's an effort to tear himself away from the pages, but he sighs and looks at me. 'Yes, Mary?' he asks, although I can see him instantly stiffen. 'About what, pray?'

'About me being your consort in New South Wales. It's just that . . . It's just that . . .'

'What?' he barks.

'Well, I was looking at our former governors there,' I say timorously, trying not to lift his guard. 'Captain Arthur Phillip, for instance. He was married twice, but neither of his wives went to New South Wales. Then Captain John Hunter—'

'He never married,' Father breaks in.

'That's true,' I counter. 'But he took his niece, someone who really loved entertaining, and had all the social graces. You could hardly say that of me.'

Father nods. I can tell he's wondering what's coming.

'Then there's the present governor, Captain Philip Gidley King. He's the first one to take his wife with him, Mrs Anna Josepha King—'

'And your point is?' Father asks, plainly losing patience.

'It's just that the first two governors managed perfectly well without their wives, and so really, I am not terribly necessary,' I say in a rush. 'I know you often despair of my lack of good sense, and I thought you might well be much better off hiring one of the wives of officers already there to fill the role of First Lady.' I'm speaking quickly now so I won't lose courage, and my words are tumbling over each other. 'I mean in terms of receiving visitors and organising entertainments and being diplomatic,' I say. 'You could hardly agree that any of those are my strengths.'

Father raises his eyebrows. 'No, they certainly are not, but I hope you would do your best to learn,' he snaps. 'Now, is that everything?' He picks up his report again.

'No, Father,' I reply, swallowing. 'Please! John and I are just starting out in our married life. We have plans, we have dreams. Please, *please* don't make us do this.'

I see that familiar edge of temper suddenly spark in his eyes, and I steel myself for what's coming. He slaps the report down on the side table and rises to his feet. I can see his hand is trembling with rage.

'Now, Mary, stop this nonsense at once!' he says, his voice sharper than I've ever heard it. 'You are coming to New South Wales and that is the end of the matter, God damn you! You have a duty to your father, and a duty to your country, and I won't stand any more of your bleating. I don't know what on earth is wrong with you. I'm offering you a great opportunity, but you don't seem to realise that.'

'But Father—' I try to break in.

He raises his hand and speaks over me. 'Mary, that's enough!' he almost shouts. 'Your husband appreciates what a chance I'm giving you both. Indeed, it was a condition of my acceptance of the offer that he be my aide-de-camp. He was eager to agree and sensible enough to be grateful. He'll come and he'll serve admirably, and you will do your snivelling best to be a passable First Lady.

'Now, that's the end of it. Leave me to do my work. Go and help your mother or go to your husband and let him talk some sense into you. And be warned: if you carry on like this, you'll lose him before you've properly begun.'

And then Father strides out of the room and slams the door, leaving me stunned and in floods of tears. So John had agreed to this before he told me? And he'd had the power to stop it yet didn't! I feel devastated. It seems I am the last to know about this. I stay kneeling on the floor until Jeannie comes in and discovers me; she wipes my face and helps me to my bedroom. I don't think she's terribly keen on going to New South Wales, either, but she knows her place.

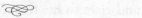

It's a strange period in the house. I mope around aimlessly, with Mother looking discomfited at what she is putting me through, Father seething at my ingratitude, and John, bless him, trying to keep the peace with everyone. He only just keeps it with me. I'm still furious with him for what I see as his betrayal, despite his insistence that he did it for our own good. The only time we all come together as a family is for Aunt Catherine's funeral after she dies at the age of sixty-nine after a long bout of ill health.

I take the funeral as an opportunity to spend time with my cousin Francis. He and Father are still avoiding each other, so it is easy for me to slip into the pew beside Francis at the church service to provide him with some company. I think he appreciates the gesture.

Afterwards, Francis says he's heard that I am travelling to New South Wales with my husband and my father. 'Captain Bligh must be very pleased at the appointment,' Francis says. 'It's a big honour. But I can see why they've chosen him.'

Instantly, I am intrigued. 'Why is that?' I ask. In truth, it had never occurred to me to even wonder.

'It's said they're having a lot of trouble over there, and the colony is close to collapse. Rum is the only currency and officers from the New South Wales Corps have the monopoly on the production and import of spirits. Governor Hunter was under orders to stop the trade, but he couldn't do it, and now his successor Governor King has failed, too. He has, in effect, lost control of the colony to the Corps. The soldiers are all-powerful, and they're running rings around anyone who tries to restore order.'

'So why my father?' I ask, wide-eyed.

Francis smiles at my bewilderment. 'Think,' he says. 'They need someone to sort out corruption in the colony, and to curb the trafficking in spirits. It's going to be a hard task, but do you know anyone stricter, surer of his own opinions, more dogged and more determined to have his way? On his first breadfruit voyage, on the *Bounty*, did you know he wouldn't even allow the crew to have proper time off? He'd order the blind fiddler to play and the men to dance to his tunes on the deck in order, he said, to keep them healthy and lively. Fancy! I've never met a man more bloody-minded in the way he sets out to achieve what he wants. Sorry, I shouldn't have sworn.'

It's my turn to smile. He has my father down to a tee. 'So, they want someone like him?' I ask.

'Oh my oath, yes. Sir Joseph Banks apparently suggested him, saying he's incorruptible, upstanding to a fault and as pig-headed as any man who lives.'

'Well, that's true enough,' I say. 'And, pray, is that why you said you wouldn't work again under his command after that second breadfruit voyage?'

Francis tilts his head and regards me for a second. 'That's *exactly* why I said that. Your father—and I'm sorry to say this, Mary—is one of the most unreasonable, aggressive and belligerent men I've ever had the misfortune to serve under. I think he could either be utterly perfect for this governorship—or he could be an absolute disaster.'

5

THE LONG WAIT

Mary Putland

1 JANUARY 1806, PORTSMOUTH, ENGLAND'S SOUTH COAST

A new year and, by rights, we should have been marking its arrival from somewhere in the middle of the Great Western Ocean. But instead we are still here in the southern port of Portsmouth, waiting for the bad weather to lift. It's colder here than I've ever known, and foggy and icy on the streets. There's no snow—Father tells me that's because of the winds that blow in from the sea—but the bitter chill and grey dreariness of the place are unremitting.

I miss my husband, too. He is still in London and will be joining us later, when our departure is imminent. He has business to wrap up, he says, and paperwork to complete for the estate in Ireland. I noticed a letter from his doctor on his desk the day we left, so maybe he will be seeing him, too. Strange that John didn't mention it, but it was surely a simple oversight given the flurry of activity before my departure for Portsmouth.

At the time we were all still wrapped up in our own grief, anyway. Harriet's firstborn, William, died in October when we were still at home preparing for our voyage. He was just three years old when we laid him to rest in his tiny coffin. He'd had a terrible cough that the doctor hadn't been able to cure, and Harriet would sit up all night at his bedside as his small body shook with the strain, laying cold compresses on his head to try to cool his fever, and then wrapping him in blankets when he shivered. The lively little boy we'd all known and loved shrank in both size and spirit as we watched on, helpless. While he lived, none of us dared voice our suspicions out loud: that it was consumption. It was only afterwards that the word ever passed Harriet's lips.

The day we buried little William Bligh Barker in the family mausoleum at the Church of St Mary in Lambeth, alongside his uncles and my brothers William Bligh and Henry Bligh, was one of the saddest I have ever known. Seeing Harriet so distraught, while heavily pregnant with her third child and insisting on holding eighteen-month-old Henry in her arms the whole way through the service, brought everyone to tears all over again.

Perhaps it will be good for Father, at least, to be away from home and all that female sorrow. Mind you, these are dark days all round. Before we left London, he had received word about Admiral Nelson's death at the Battle of Trafalgar.

'Britain has lost its greatest hero,' Father told us morosely. 'He was the reason we won against the French. He told his men at the start of that battle, "England expects that every man will do his duty," and by God, they did. And that's what we will be doing in New South Wales.' He looked at me sharply. 'Won't we, Mary?'

Now I am in Portsmouth, doing that duty, and trying to make the best of things. The city is interesting, and very busy, with ships constantly docking from all over the world. That's exciting to see, but there are now many vessels, like our flotilla, waiting for a break in the weather to depart. Every day, Father marches from our lodgings to the port and looks out to sea, and then comes back to report that it won't be today, or tomorrow, but maybe the next day. In this, I'm seeing a completely different side to him. Unlike me, fidgeting and exasperated and keen to be off now that we are committed to this venture, he seems to have endless patience with the weather, a patience I've never seen extended to anything or, more importantly, any person before.

Here at the port, he seems much more cheerful and more at home than in London. He knows it well from having spent so much time preparing for previous voyages, and I think being so close to the sea relaxes him. People recognise him, too, and often greet him as they pass, some fondly, and others not so much.

He spends a lot of his time cloistered with his private secretary Edmund Griffin, who is coming with us to New South Wales; a schoolmaster's son from Kent and a man so serious and colourless our family regards him as simply a part of the furniture. He's terribly timid and, despite being tall and thin, he stoops and bends as if he's desperate not to stand out among other people and is apologetic for his very presence. I sometimes wonder if he's always been like that, or whether working for Father for so many years has made him this way. He can't be much older than me, but I've always felt he is one of those men who are born middle-aged. I remember impersonating him once to my sisters, rubbing my hands together in that irritating manner he has when he's nervous, but Harriet didn't laugh. She took me aside and told me not to be so unkind.

'Don't you realise Mr Griffin has always had a soft spot for you?' she asked me. I looked back at her, baffled. She sighed. 'Think how civil he is to you, and how he defends you to Father when you're in trouble. He never does that for any of the rest of us.'

I was about to retort quickly that I was the only one who regularly drew Father's ire, when it dawned on me that she could be right. He'd always been very kind and thoughtful towards me, even though I barely acknowledged him. 'But surely Mr Griffin can't be sweet on me!' I blurted. 'That's . . . ridiculous!'

Harriet raised one eyebrow. 'And why is that?' she asked calmly. 'You're only just married. Before that, it's not as though you were overrun with suitors.'

I glared at her. But from that day forward, even though I still didn't quite believe her, I resolved to be more courteous to Mr Griffin. I'd looked out for any hint of affection, but he seemed to have been avoiding me since the wedding. I wondered if that was a sign, but then dismissed it. I'd have John with me for the voyage, so it would never be an issue.

Some days, Father and I go walking together around the town, and he points out all its maritime sights. He shows me the fortifications to keep it secure from enemy attack, and the castle at Southsea from which, two hundred and sixty-one years ago, King Henry VIII apparently watched his favourite ship the *Mary Rose* sink in the Battle of the Solent against the invading French. Do our battles against them ever end?

We also often visit a site close to our lodgings where the warship the *Royal George* was lost not twenty-four years ago. It had been purposely rolled for work on its hull, Father told me, his face tight, but had then started letting on water and went down with the loss of around eight hundred lives.

'Oh Father!' I say. 'Please stop telling me about these disasters just as we're about to set sail on our ship for six months.'

He looks embarrassed. It has obviously not occurred to him that I might be nervous. 'But so much has been learned from these misadventures,' he replies. 'Don't be silly, Mary. We will be fine.'

Then he walks me around the moats, the dry dock where ships come to be repaired, and the various spots around the harbour from which his past ships departed.

Father becomes unusually animated when he points to the site from which the ships of the First Fleet cast off to settle New South Wales, and the wharf he set sail from two years later for his mission aboard HMS *Bounty*. That ship, of course, is yet to come back.

'Just think, Mary, in a couple of weeks' time it will be eighteen years since Captain Phillip landed in Botany Bay and went on to found the colony,' he says to me, a faraway look in his eyes. 'I wonder what it will look like now. Apparently, Port Jackson is one of the most beautiful harbours anyone has ever seen, good and deep along its length with lush greenery all around.'

'It sounds lovely,' I say meekly. To be honest, I don't have a clue what it will look like. I've only really known London as a place to live, and it will certainly be a world away from that. When I allow myself to think about it, I'm quite frightened by the prospect. I never wanted to go, even though I understand it could be a great advancement for John. I now worry that I'm not up to the challenges that lie ahead. But as my husband advised me, I'm concentrating on what I need to do one day at a time: now making sure Father is looked after in Portsmouth, and constantly telling Jeannie to unpack and repack so we are ready to leave.

'Yes, you're right, it does sound lovely,' Father says. 'Sir Joseph says it is the perfect place for settlement and, with so many convicts now there to work, and more free settlers choosing to go all the time, I cannot wait to see what they've made of it. I think if Sir Joseph were in better health, he would be in half a mind to accompany us.'

I make a sympathetic noise in response but, really, I'm thanking God for small mercies. Being cramped in small quarters with Sir Joseph as well as Father would be my idea of hell. But Sir Joseph is now into his seventh decade and is not well. He suffers terribly, I've heard, with gout; something that makes him even more cantankerous than normal and which, at times, confines him to a wheelchair. He does tend to gluttony—I've seen the quantities he eats at our dinner table—and drinking to excess, and being so overweight can't possibly help his gout. Sometimes, you reap what you sow.

But Father's face has softened. I steel myself for another recount of the wondrous wisdom of Uncle Joseph or a re-enactment of past battles, but when he speaks it's on a subject I've never heard him talk about before. 'I'm also very keen to learn more about the natives,' he says. 'The first time I visited Van Diemen's Land in 1777 with Captain Cook, we'd almost run out of water and wood for the ship's fires, so we went ashore at a place we called Adventure Bay and chanced upon a group of natives, sixteen men and six women.

46

I found all the men had names when we tried to communicate with them, but they were very fearful of us and they wouldn't stay long.'

I am fascinated. I would have thought he'd have no time for natives after Cook's violent death and the voyage after the *Bounty*. 'Is that the only time you met some?' I ask.

'No, the next time I visited Adventure Bay on the *Bounty*—' and his eyes darken for a fleeting moment '—I was most keen to meet them again, but the surf was so rough we couldn't land in our longboat. When we were just off the coast, though, we saw a group of about twenty emerge from the bush, completely naked, making a prodigious clattering of speech and running very nimbly over the rocks. They called to us sitting on their heels with their knees close into their armpits. I threw them gifts of nails and beads and they obviously have a quick eye as they caught them very cleverly. I shall be most interested to encounter more of these natives in Sydney.'

'They are there, too?' I exclaim. Father nods and turns away, and again, I realise how little I know of our destination.

Other days, I go out with Jeannie as Father feels the town is unsafe for me to walk alone, with so many sailors and roughnecks out and about. She has been with our family for ten years, and I am glad of her company. She has been an enormous help, assisting me in deciding which clothes to bring, what household items I will need and gathering a few mementos from home. She also comforted me after what was a very teary departure. My sisters all cried, even Harriet, and Mother wept, too; although, I suspect her sadness could have been mixed with relief that she wasn't the one leaving. Who knows when I will next see them all?

Previous governors have spent four, five or six years in their posts, and I suspect Father is aiming for six as Francis told me he is being paid two thousand pounds a year by the British Government—twice the purse of Governor King—so he might well want to eke that out a bit longer. John, however, is adamant that we might like it so much that we could choose to stay on after Father has gone. I can't imagine that, but you never know, especially if we have children there.

Jeannie was upset as our carriage left Lambeth, too, I could see that, although she tried to hide it. I wondered what she had to be upset about. After all, it wasn't that she had much to leave in London. A maid's work there would be very much what a maid's work would be in Sydney, I imagine.

As the days stretch into weeks in Portsmouth, and there is still no break in the bad weather, I sometimes despair that we will ever leave this town. I feel like we are in a constant state of limbo. One morning I suggest to Father that we return to London and wait there instead, but he won't consider it. Instead, he's becoming more and more concerned with the arrangements for our voyage. It's going to be an elaborate convoy of no fewer than six ships, with HMS *Porpoise* at the front, then the merchant ship the *Lady Madeline Sinclair* on which we will sail, then the *Fortune* for male convicts and the *Alexander* for female convicts, and finally a second merchant ship, the *Justina*, and a whaler called the *Elizabeth*.

But the problem, as Father sees it, is that the Admiralty has put another man, Captain Joseph Short, in command of the flagship *Porpoise*, and thus the whole convoy. My father, a man superior in rank to Short, will simply be in charge of deciding which course

48

we will follow and which ports we will stop at. Father is outraged; he plainly expected to be put in control of the entire expedition, especially with such a wealth of sea-going experience and, moreover, as the future governor of New South Wales. The morning he goes off to meet Short, I have my heart in my mouth all day, worrying how it will play out. One look at his ruddy face and knitted brows on his return tells me all I need to know.

'Damned impertinent fellow!' Father spits. 'The cheek of the man! How dare he speak to me as he did. Does he not know who I am?'

My spirits sink as he vents his anger and frustration. This six-month voyage is going to be bad enough, without Father feuding with the man in charge. And this is before we have even left Portsmouth!

When John finally arrives late in January, I don't think I have ever been so relieved to see someone in my life. I fall into his arms with pure joy. But as he holds me close, suddenly his body is racked with a terrible, hacking cough. He pulls away and draws out a handkerchief to cover his face until he is recovered.

'John, my darling!' I cry. 'What is the matter? How long have you had this?'

'Oh, it's nothing,' he replies. 'Just a chill. I shall be over it in a few days. As soon as we get out into that fresh salt air, I shall recover.'

'Did you see your doctor?' I ask anxiously. He looks surprised. 'I saw you had a letter from him,' I explain. 'I thought you must have an appointment. What did he say?'

'Not very much at all,' John replies, pulling me back into his arms. 'I am sure I will be well soon. Now, tell me about yourself.

What has been happening during your wait? How are you getting on with your father?'

I tell him about Father's clash with Captain Short, the plans for our convoy, and the loading of most of our possessions onto the *Lady Sinclair*—all the furnishings we will need for Government House, my piano and lute, our books, my sketch book, some laying hens, a milking cow and her calf, three little roasting pigs for our journey, and most importantly my array of frocks and bonnets.

In turn, John brings me news of home: the twins also both have colds after playing in the snow when Mother's back was turned, and Harriet is staying well away for fear of catching it, given her baby is due in a matter of weeks. He also brings me two new dresses that Mother ordered when it was first decided I would go to New South Wales, as some recompense for my distress. I unwrap them and try them both on, twirling about the loungeroom of the lodgings as John looks on in amusement at my excitement.

When John arrives, Father decides to board the *Lady Sinclair* early to give us space in the lodgings without him. I am surprised at his thoughtfulness, but then realise he probably wants to be there as early as possible to keep an eagle eye on what Short might be doing or planning to do. We will follow Father onto the ship in two days—two blissful days—as the weather finally seems to be turning favourably. I'm happy not only for myself, but also for John. He looks pale and two days of rest should help rid him of that terrible cough.

The morning we are due to exit the lodgings and board the ship, I enter the drawing room and call for Jeannie, with no response. I go to her bed under the stairs to wake her, but it is empty. Her bag is also gone. Instead, there is a sheaf of paper on the coverlet. I pick it up and read it quickly.

Jeannie is very sorry to let me down, but she really does not want to go to New South Wales. She will miss her parents and her fiancé too much; six years is simply too long to be away from them. She overheard John discussing the possibility of staying on, too, and that would be intolerable for her. Although she is very grateful for the opportunity and for her time with my family, she has left us to return to Scotland to be with hers.

I am devastated. I feel I have lost an invaluable ally, someone who would have supported me through this blasted voyage and someone I could have truly relied on as I navigate this new life on the other side of the world.

I had not known she had a family in Scotland, nor a fiancé, although I realise now, with a start, that I had never even asked her about her own life. I sink down on her bed, my head in my hands. This suddenly all feels much, much too hard.

6

LOST AT SEA

Mary Putland
10 FEBRUARY 1806, AT SEA

We have now been eleven days at sea. Eleven horrific days. Eleven days of wishing I were dead—and that many of those around me were, too.

The sea has been a raging foe ever since we finally left Portsmouth on 30 January. There have been wild winds and lashing rain and the *Lady Sinclair* has tossed and turned and groaned and creaked with every wave that's threatened to tip us all into a watery grave. I have vomited up every single mouthful of food I've managed to eat, and every thimbleful of liquid I've drunk. I must now have nothing at all left in my stomach, but still I sit hunched over my bucket, dry-retching as I slide across the rough planks of the cabin floor, ruining my good blue linen gown as it catches on the nails when the ship rolls from side to side, bucks and rears. I'm past caring. I've never been so miserable in my life. I half-wish for the same fate as the *Mary Rose* or the *Royal George*; then at least this hell would be over at last.

Father has completely lost patience with me. He, of course, seems completely oblivious to the tempest we've sailed into. He has been striding around the decks, inspecting everything that stays still long enough to be inspected, and barking out orders to anyone who will listen. Whenever I come across Mr Griffin he shoots me sympathetic looks that I take with good grace, and then wisely seems to vanish into thin air. He must be well used to Father's fits of bad humour.

'Come on, Mary,' Father chastens me. 'It surely can't be so bad. Accompany me up to the deck and look at the horizon. That will make you feel better.'

Reluctantly, I let him drag me outside, and I stand glumly on the deck, peering at the thick grey mist in front of us and avoiding the curious eyes of the sailors who have barely had a glimpse of me in all the days I've been here, hidden away in the cabin.

'Now, isn't that better?' Father demands. 'We'll make a sailor of you yet!'

I'm now wet through and freezing cold as well as feeling so ill. I try to nod, but instead I feel the familiar bitterness rise up the back of my throat and into my mouth, and I gag again. This time, a stream of yellow bile trickles down the front of my frock. I see a couple of sailors laugh, and tears of shame and anger sting my eyes.

'For God's sake, Mary,' Father says, 'pull yourself together! If you don't get used to this now, you're not going to survive this voyage.'

I turn on my heel and march, well, stagger, with as much dignity as I can summon—which really isn't much at all—back across the deck, down the narrow stairs and along the corridor to my cabin, then slam the door closed, hard. Damn him! Damn this ship! And damn everyone who's sailing in her!

I feel completely, totally alone. And what's even worse was that shortly after John and I celebrated our second wedding anniversary on shore, I boarded the ship only to find that Father had obviously riled Short so much that the captain had transferred my dear John Putland onto the *Porpoise* with him. He said John was needed there instead, but it was a move I suspect was far more about taking revenge on my father. By rights, I should now be with my husband making a home for us both in Ireland, getting acquainted with the society over there and dazzling everyone with my fine new gowns, wit and repartee. Instead, I'm stranded on this accursed ship without John or even a maid to care for me, while my father's foul temper continues to make those around him suffer. John had promised he would remain by my side to protect me, but that was a pledge which didn't take long to break. Despite my anger at his betrayal, I miss him so much I've cried myself to sleep every night so far.

There's a soft knock on the door, which I ignore. But then there is a louder one. 'Mary,' I hear my father's voice call, 'are you in there?' The door opens. 'This is ridiculous,' he says. 'Your mother said she couldn't make the voyage because she would become too seasick, but I thought you were made of sterner stuff.'

'Well, now you know,' I reply wearily. 'I'm sorry to have disappointed you. Yet again.'

He frowns, then obviously decides to let the comment go. 'I'm going to flag the *Alexander* and see if perhaps there's a nurse aboard. You can't go on like this.'

It's a rare moment of sympathy but I feel too wretched to even acknowledge it.

He waits for a moment but when it becomes obvious that I will say nothing more, he turns on his heel and walks out.

I lay down on my berth and try to sleep. If only I could stay asleep until this voyage is over, perhaps then it would be bearable.

A few hours later, I hear another knock on the door, and this time I can hear two sets of footfalls in the cabin. I rouse myself. It's my father again, but this time he is accompanied by a slip of a girl in a coarse grey cotton shift, with an untidy shock of fair hair.

'Mary, this is Meg,' Father says. 'She isn't exactly a nurse, but she's been looking after a number of the women aboard the *Alexander*.'

I look her up and down. I don't really like what I see. She looks rough. Unkempt. Grubby. And she has an angry red weal on one wrist. A sudden thought strikes me. 'She's a convict?' I ask.

'Yes,' Father replies.

'So . . . how can she help me?'

'Ma'am,' Meg says, in a voice so soft I have to strain to hear, 'if you will allow me. A number of the women have been similarly seasick, but I took the liberty of bringing a bag of ginger root with me on the ship. It has proved surprisingly effective.'

I look at her haughtily, then shrug in defeat. I have nothing to lose. 'Then maybe I should try it, too,' I say.

'Thank you, ma'am,' she mutters, then looks at Father. 'I need to use the galley to prepare it. Could you please show me the way?'

They leave, and I slump down on the couch. When they return, she's holding a mug of what looks like hot tea. 'Drink this, please, ma'am,' she says. 'I've shown the cook how to make this, so he'll give you another one in two hours, and then have another cup before bed this evening. You should feel much better by morning.'

I take the mug from her and blow on the surface to cool it. Then I start to sip. It's so peppery and spicy I can feel it burning as it slips down my throat. It's not unpleasant. 'Thank you,' I say, and the girl smiles. I can see, beneath all the surface grime, that she is actually quite pretty. I look away.

I go to my berth as Father shows her out, presumably taking her to the longboat to be rowed across to her own ship, back with her own kind. I doze fitfully, am woken for another cup of stewed ginger root, and then continue to sleep on and off.

The girl was right. The next morning, I am feeling much more like myself again. The sea feels a little calmer, too, with the sun struggling to break through the clouds, and I even eat a little breakfast. Father is delighted; he grins from ear to ear. He sits with me and talks about our poor former Prime Minister, who is due to have his state funeral in eleven days. He never met William Pitt the Younger, Father says, but he deserves our unending gratitude. He steered us through many difficult times during his long spell in office, including to victory against the French. He also decided to found the new penal colony Father and I are on our way to after our Thirteen Colonies refused to accept any more convicts.

Then a cloud passes over Father's face, and he moves on to tell me about his latest altercation with Captain Short. This is why he was so exasperated by my seasickness, I realise. It wasn't my health that concerned him; he was simply desperate for someone to vent to. As he rants and rails, I begin to feel almost sorry for the captain. He must have rued the day he heard we were to be passengers.

'The man's an absolute scoundrel,' Father is saying. 'He has done nothing but disobey my commands, and taking John away with him . . .' He shakes his head. 'He leaves me in an impossible situation. I'll have to write to the Admiralty and explain how this man has done his best to defy me at every opportunity.'

'But he was given the charge of the convoy—' I start to protest.

'And that was their first mistake!' Father butts in immediately. 'They should never have done that. It's an absolute outrage.'

I'm no admirer of the captain after he took my husband onto his ship, but he did say that John could come back if his cough grew any worse. I worry now, with Father plotting more trouble, that even that small consolation might be taken away from me. I take a deep breath. I find it hard to stand up to my father; I always have.

'Maybe they thought you would be too busy drawing up plans for the colony to be bothered with being in command?' I venture timidly. 'After all, you have made this journey, and others just as long, many times.'

'Well, if they did think that, they were wrong,' Father snaps back. 'Completely wrong. How am I supposed to sit back and watch a comparative amateur run this operation? It would be different, of course, if he sought my guidance, but he doesn't. In fact, he seems to do the exact opposite of what I advise each time.'

'But isn't he in charge . . . ?' I try again.

'No, he isn't meant to be,' Father says. 'He's only allowed to command the convoy in my absence. But the miscreant says that given I'm not on the *Porpoise*, I should be regarded as absent. It's absolutely ridiculous.'

'Yet it's in his interests, isn't it, for us all to reach our destination safely?' I ask. 'After all, he has his wife and children aboard with him, doesn't he?'

'Yes, his six children and apparently a seventh and eighth on the way,' Father snorts, disapproval obvious in his voice.

It occurs to me that maybe the captain's wife expecting twins has made it even harder for my father, who lost my twin brothers the day after their birth. That could go some of the way to explaining his fury.

But he hasn't finished. 'The man's clearly an idiot. He plans to stay in the colony with his family and make a living as a farmer. Doesn't he realise that, however hard he makes this voyage for me, I have the power to make his life much, much worse in New South Wales? He's an imbecile if he thinks I won't do that.'

'Oh Father,' I say, 'please don't talk like that. The man's just doing his best. You never know, he might turn out to be a valuable ally over there. Wouldn't it be better if you sat back and did all the other work you have before you, and left this journey to him?'

Father looks at me with an expression of pure scorn, and I instantly regret trying to discuss the matter with him, rather than simply listening to what he had to say and being sympathetic. 'Mary, you know nothing about this and the world beyond yours,' he says. 'I'll thank you to keep your simpering to yourself. This is men's business, of which you know nothing.'

I fall silent. He continues, 'But I have been giving some thought to your lack of a maid on board,' he says. 'I think you could do worse than the woman Meg I brought over yesterday. She seems to have done wonders for your health.'

I'm horrified by the thought. 'But she's a convict!' I exclaim. 'She could be a murderer, anything!'

'Don't be overdramatic,' Father replies. 'That's the kind of typical response I'd expect from you. I have checked the manifest. She is not a murderer.'

'So why is she here?' I ask.

'She's a thief. She stole from her employers.'

'Well then, what's to guarantee she won't steal from me?'

Father looks exasperated. 'If she does, we can punish her,' he says. 'But I doubt that will happen. After all, it's not as if she'll have anywhere to run to. This will be a good lesson for you, Mary. We're going to a new land where over three-quarters of the seven-thousand-strong population are either convicts or ex-convicts, and certainly most of the women. You'll have to get used to their company. Many will be doing important work for the future, building houses, farming, laying roads or working in service at the homes of the settlers.'

'But don't I have any say in who I want as my maid?' I ask, and even I can hear the whine in my voice.

'Don't be ridiculous. The women on the *Alexander* all have good reason for being there. Her crimes are probably a great deal less serious than others. I'll have her brought over, and that's the end of it.'

HUMAN CARGO

Meg Hill
13 FEBRUARY 1806, AT SEA

Whenever the call comes for women to go up and scrub the decks, there's always a stampede of volunteers. But Meg Hill is invariably one of the first to be chosen. The crew in charge of keeping in check the *Alexander*'s forty-nine female convicts and fifteen male convicts—whose wives and children agreed to accompany them for their sentences in New South Wales—know that she'll get the job done, while some of the others will, instead, provide them with welcome entertainment.

Meg tries hard not to judge. Who is she to do so? She's on her way to New South Wales for a crime she committed, just like everyone else. She's no better nor worse than anyone on board. Everyone is simply trying to survive as best they can. And maybe if she were younger, or prettier, or hadn't had such a good upbringing, she would also choose other ways to win favour. She too would pull up her skirt or tug down her top and wriggle suggestively for the mariners in return for a few extra scraps of food or a teaspoonful of rum from their daily ration. Or she'd trade sex behind the lifeboats for favours.

But as it is, Meg simply loves the chance to leave their stinking quarters to go up on deck and feel the sun on her face—or more often so far, to feel the rain—and take great gulps of the fresh salty air. She is happy to work hard, too. At least she gets the chance to fill a bucket with clean sea water, which means she can give herself a quick wash when the guards aren't looking before she starts with the brush on the timber. It's hard work, but she doesn't mind. It feels like a wonderful opportunity to stretch her limbs after the cramped living conditions under the waterline, and it's a rare moment to have time to herself to think, away from the cacophony of noise downstairs: the talking, the songs, the weeping, the prayers, the arguments, the shouting, the moaning and the screaming.

Over the two weeks they've been on this ship so far, she feels as though she's met almost the whole miserable mass of its human cargo. Down below, the air quickly became fetid—the bucking sea left so many women sleeping in pools of their own vomit when it crusted onto the straw mats on their berths, impossible to clean off. The screams of terror were even harder to bear. Dysentery, too, was affecting many, and the open drains along each side of their quarters spread any sickness fast. The single daily bucket of water allocated between four women for both drinking and washing was soon covered with a surface of slime, which dissuaded many women from drinking enough. The rations of brined beef, nicknamed 'salt horse' because it's as tough as old nags—which is what many suspect it might well be—never does much to salve their hunger.

So, when word spreads that Meg has brought on board a bundle of herbs and spices that could assist with many conditions, she is regularly sought out for help. As well as the ginger root for settling stomachs, she has fenugreek for curbing appetite, liquorice for thirst, chamomile for anxiety, hyssop for head lice, mustard for chest infections, garlic for wounds, mint to repel fleas, feverfew for killing pain and inducing labour, and gingko for feelings of hopelessness and despair . . .

Kneeling on the deck, Meg looks up, pretending to stretch, to see if she can spot any of the other ships in their convoy. She likes the reassurance they're not alone on this great wide sea, far from everything and everyone they've ever known. An image of the people she's left behind instantly flashes up before she can wrench down the blinds on her memory. Her widowed mother, who would be so sick with worry about her eldest daughter. Her three little sisters and two brothers. She last saw them all when she appeared in court in Middlesex and, on that terrible last day, watched her mother's face drain of all colour when the judge read out the sentence: death. When it was commuted to transportation, it was little comfort. A living death instead, they said. What will become of her family without her wage to help support them?

She shakes her head as if to rid herself of her thoughts and focuses on the view. The weather is growing warmer every day now and the sea looks, and feels, a great deal calmer. Ah yes, there's the *Fortune* with its cargo of two hundred and sixty male convicts, that smudge on the horizon must be the *Porpoise* and close by is the *Lady Sinclair*, where she'd been taken just three days before. That was a strange episode. She wonders how Mary Putland is feeling now and hopes her trusted ginger root had its desired effect. To be honest, she didn't really want to spare any on a woman travelling in such comfort and style—her fellow convicts were much more in need of it—but she wasn't really in a position to refuse her. After all, it had earned her a trip off the *Alexander*, a ride in a small boat, and a look around another ship in the fleet. She'd also met Captain Bligh, the future governor of New South Wales, the man so many of the crew gossiped about endlessly. Surely, that couldn't hurt, either.

His daughter had been in a pretty bad way. Although she had her airs and graces, she was obviously suffering. Meg felt for her, despite the way Mary had looked her up and down, as if she were a creature from a zoo. And the way she'd said, 'She's a *convict*?' Yet she'd taken the precious ginger root tea and been told that Meg had left the cook with more for future doses. Perhaps Mary will be forced to come back to her again when more storms inevitably roll in, Meg muses. The thought pleases her. She's heard talk from the others that Mrs Putland has her husband on board, but she'd seen no sign of him. Maybe he'd run out of patience with his spoiled wife, she thinks with a smile.

Meg has nearly finished her part of the deck when the heavy steps of a mariner sound close behind her. She looks up.

'Hill?' he asks.

'Yes, sir,' she replies.

'There's someone here to see you. On the quarterdeck.'

Meg looks over past the main mast, but the sun's too strong to see who might be there. She scrambles to her feet. As they climb onto the raised deck, she looks up and sees the stout figure of Captain Bligh once more.

'Good afternoon, sir,' she says, trying to collect her wits. Then she stands with her head bowed. She worries something must be terribly wrong for her to be seeing him again so soon. Maybe his daughter . . . the possibilities don't bear thinking about.

Silence fills the air and suddenly she's unable to bear it. 'How is Mrs Putland?' she asks. If it is bad news, she might as well get it over and done with.

Captain Bligh coughs. 'She's quite well now, thank you,' he replies.

Immediately she feels a weight lift off her shoulders. Maybe someone else on the *Lady Sinclair* needs her attention?

'How old are you, Meg?' Captain Bligh asks, his voice soft.

'Seventeen, sir.'

'And tell me, what were you sentenced for? And I'm warning you, I can read the indent papers to check if you lie.'

'No, no, sir,' she protests. 'I would never do that.'

He stands waiting expectantly.

She wonders why he's picked her out but takes a deep breath. 'I was a foolish, foolish girl,' she says. 'I was employed as a servant at the house of Mr Daniel Wade and his wife in Old Town in the parish of Stepney, London. I was there for nine weeks until . . . until . . .'

Meg hesitates, but Captain Bligh remains silent.

'I was stopped while out shopping one day by a man called Thomas Carter. He took me for tea. And after that, I saw him each day. He was very well spoken and handsome, and he seemed to take a special interest in me. He worked for the East India Company.'

Captain Bligh nods, as if things are becoming clear to him.

'He told me that Mr Wade had borrowed a fob watch of his but was now refusing to give it back.'

'And you believed him?' Captain Bligh asks.

'Yes, sir,' Meg replies, hanging her head. 'He was very persuasive. He said he had previously been friends with the couple, and he described the inside of the house to me, and Mr Wade's habits and details of his wife's condition.'

'Her condition?' Captain Bligh echoes, raising an eyebrow.

'Yes, she was so sick, she sometimes had difficulties getting out of bed.' At that, Meg's eyes fill with tears. She swallows and tries hard to compose herself. 'I thought that he really did know them well, and he seemed to be kind and genuine, I didn't think he could possibly have been lying.'

'So, what did you do?'

'One night just before daybreak, when they were both asleep, I opened the back door to let Thomas in.'

'And?'

'Well, I thought he was coming in just to collect his fob watch,' Meg continues. 'But he went up to their bedroom and found the watch and then started putting so many other things into his bags. I couldn't believe it.'

'Did you help him?' Captain Bligh asks.

Meg looks shocked. 'No! Not at all,' she says. 'I was horrified. And I suddenly realised what I had done, and what he was doing. I pleaded with him to stop, but he just ignored me completely, and carried on filling his bags with everything he could lay his hands on.'

'You then just watched him?'

'No, I didn't,' Meg says. 'I didn't know what to do. I was too scared to wake Mr Wade in front of him, so instead I opened one of the other room's windows wide and screamed and screamed for help from the neighbours.'

Captain Bligh nodded.

Meg wonders if he's thinking her young and foolish, but he probably realises she has mettle, too.

'What happened then?' he asks.

'The next-door neighbour, Mr William Brown, heard me yelling. He leaned out of his window and asked me what the matter was, and I told him there was someone in the house. So, he put his clothes on and came round with his brother who lived with him. It was very dark, so I gave him a light, and then we heard more noise. I was terrified. But I think Thomas must have slipped out when we were talking.'

'Did Mr and Mrs Wade wake up?'

'Yes, they did, and then Mr Wade went to Shadwell police station to tell the constable what had happened.'

'Were many things missing?'

Meg looks pained. 'Yes,' she replies. 'The gold watch but many other things besides. Two rings. Six silver teaspoons, three and a half guineas in gold, a silver thimble. All manner of things. In court, Mr Wade said it would be worth a total of forty shillings.' A tear slips down her cheek.

'You were put on trial for theft?' he asks.

She nods. 'And breaking and entering.'

'And this Thomas?'

She nods again.

'What happened to him?'

She shakes her head. 'Nothing. They went to his house half a mile away and found all the property. But he said that I had put it there, and he had never been to Mr Wade's house. He said he knew nothing about it at all. He testified he knew me but said he'd believed I'd been an honest girl, and that he was shocked to discover the theft.'

'He was acquitted?'

'He was found not guilty,' Meg says. 'And I was found guilty. In truth, I am as much to blame as him. I know that. I am the one who let him into the house, so I must bear the responsibility.'

'But it seems unfair that he was let off, doesn't it?' Captain Bligh asks.

Meg shrugs. 'I don't know about that, sir,' she says. 'But I do think it was fair that I wasn't.'

8

A SCOUNDREL AND A THIEF

Mary Putland

15 FEBRUARY 1806, AT SEA

I fear Father is teetering on the edge of madness.

He has become absolutely obsessed with the idea that Captain Short is hell-bent on usurping his authority. I've tried to reason with him that the Admiralty has put Short in charge and therefore he has to make the major decisions about the convoy, good or bad. If Short chooses to ignore Father's advice, then that's his prerogative. And if any of his actions do turn out to have adverse consequences, then it's quite right and proper that the blame for his decisions fall squarely at his own feet.

But Father won't listen. Instead, he attacks every decree Short makes and disagrees with every suggestion, out of what I can only see as sheer pigheadedness. Short was rowed over to our ship in a longboat yesterday, in a gesture of reconciliation, and Father greeted him formally but I could sense the tension in the air. I immediately stepped forward and said, 'Good morning, Captain.' I wanted to smooth over the discord but also, I must admit, I was desperate for news of my husband. He bowed to me and said 'Good morning' back, but before I could ask how John was and whether his cough was still troubling him, Father gave me a harsh look and ushered the captain into his study.

They ordered tea but as soon as that formality was complete the volume of their voices rose immediately. Mr Griffin appeared and made to go in to join them, but then stopped suddenly, rubbed his hands together in that gesture I knew so well, and turned on his heel and went back to his quarters. When a crew member finally came up with the tea tray, I took it from her and delivered it myself, but Father made it clear I was not welcome to stay. I backed out hastily, nearly tripping over two eavesdroppers loitering outside the door. It was obvious that the crew of the *Lady Sinclair*, as well as the rest of the convoy, probably, were just as interested in the conversation as I was.

The two men spent half an hour in Father's study and their voices rose and dropped, rose and dropped. By the time they came out and shook hands again—purely for the sake of onlookers, I suspected— both men looked annoyed.

I took my chance and stepped forward. 'Captain Short,' I ventured, 'could you tell me, sir, how is Lieutenant Putland? How is his cough?'

He looked startled, but then his face softened. 'He is quite well,' he said. 'He has been very busy on the *Porpoise*, and I've appreciated his efforts. He's a fine seaman.'

'And do you think he might be able to visit me soon?' I asked.

Father was looking at me thunderously, and Short glanced up, caught his expression and then smiled, slowly and deliberately, obviously savouring the moment. 'I am sure we can arrange something,' he said. 'I expect you're both missing each other.'

'Oh yes,' I replied. 'I'm missing him terribly. It was our second wedding anniversary two weeks ago and—'

'Mary!' Father snapped, cutting me dead. 'Captain Short is a busy man and he has to be off.'

I could feel my face burning and I swallowed hard. 'Of course,' I said to Short. 'Please forgive me.'

Short shook his head. 'Nothing to forgive,' he said. 'I'm sorry to have taken Lieutenant Putland away from you. But he will be able to visit soon.'

At that, Father almost shouldered him towards the longboat waiting by the side of the ship.

'Thank you!' I called out after him, before hurrying down below to my cabin. At the thought of seeing John again, I could feel tears welling up and threatening to completely overwhelm me. Of course, Father hadn't given Short the chance to elaborate as to when 'soon' might be, but at least it was something. Just the thought of being in his arms again . . . I'd been trying not to think about my husband— it was painful to imagine him so close and yet so far—but now the tears flowed freely.

By the time Father returned to the cabin, I'd managed to compose myself. 'How did your meeting go?' I asked.

'Ha!' he replied. 'I left him in no doubt about who is in charge.'

'What do you mean?' I could feel my heart sinking at his look of triumph.

'He wanted the ships to make a stop in Madeira,' he said.

'That would be nice,' I said. 'A chance to pick up some fresh fruit and vegetables and maybe take on a maid for the voyage . . .' The lack of a decent ladies' maid was becoming most inconvenient, and I'd pinned my hopes on finding someone suitable at our next stop. And, of course, docking in Madeira would be an opportunity for me to see John and maybe even spend a few days with him in the port.

'No!' Father said in a tone that invited no argument. 'My orders were that we make as much haste as possible to New South Wales. That means no unnecessary stops.'

'So we're not stopping in Madeira?' I asked, knowing the answer.

'Of course not,' he said. 'What's more, I told the impertinent fellow we won't be landing in Rio de Janeiro, either.'

The crew had told me in Portsmouth that we should reach Rio in just under two months. But now that we weren't stopping in Madeira, everyone would be desperate for a spell on dry land. I knew I would be. 'But won't we need more water and provisions?' I asked. 'And the crew will surely want to go ashore.'

'Well, they won't be allowed to,' Father crowed. 'The ports we stop at are up to me, and Short has no option but to obey my orders.'

I hated him more in that moment than ever before. 'And what did Captain Short say to that?' I asked, my voice tight.

'What could he say?'

'Well, Rio is still such a long way away,' I said, plaintively.

'That's what Short said, too,' Father replied, smiling. 'He said we'd discuss it again, later in the voyage. I said of course we could, but that I wouldn't be changing my mind. You should have seen his face, Mary, the man was almost apoplectic!'

71

I turned away.

Father has been in a jaunty mood ever since, and today he says he has a pleasant surprise for me. It arrives on deck at lunchtime: the convict who gave me the ginger root. I do not see her as so pleasant. She is, Father declares, to be my new maid.

I try to argue with him. 'But she is a convict and a thief!' I exclaim. 'Should the daughter and the consort to the governor of one of Britain's newest colonies really have to put up with that? It's ridiculous.'

Father looks annoyed and the woman just stands there looking idiotic. 'Mary, I shouldn't need to remind you that Meg helped when you were seasick,' he says. 'I think you were very grateful then.'

'Yes, I was grateful . . . I *am* grateful,' I correct myself. 'But it's one thing helping me then; it's quite another inviting a convict to come and share one's quarters. How do I know that she won't steal my possessions or . . .' I take a good, hard look at her. She's only a slight thing, but appearances can deceive. 'Or murder me in my bed?'

Father guffaws and I can see a smile playing in the corners of Meg's lips.

It's my turn to anger. 'I don't see what's so funny about that,' I say sharply. I look at my father. 'We know nothing about her.'

'Well, ma'am—' Meg starts to answer, but I cut her off immediately.

'I am not talking to you,' I tell her. 'Pray, only speak when you are asked.'

'Sorry, ma'am,' she says, and I wonder if she is disobeying me on purpose. Insolent, too, no doubt.

'Mary, Mary,' Father says in a voice I know he intends to be soothing. 'Meg is just seventeen, and she is new to the ways of the convict world. I have talked to her about her offences and—'

'And how do you know she told you the truth?' I snap.

'I checked on the convict indents,' Father replies mildly. 'What's more, I also had a word to Captain Brookes of the *Alexander* and he said her behaviour has been exemplary on board. She is also something of a herbalist—she says she learned that from her mother—and brought a little store of medicinal plants on board with her. The captain allowed that as he knew some of the convicts were pregnant and would need her help.'

'Well, maybe they need her more than I do,' I say haughtily. 'Perhaps she'd be better off staying with her own kind.'

Meg's head is bowed, so I cannot see her expression.

'No,' Father says. 'It has been arranged. Meg is to be your new maid, and you'll be grateful for her services. I won't hear any more on the subject. I have selected a servant for myself, too, a convict called George Jubb who's been travelling on the *Fortune*.' He leads Meg down towards our quarters, with a crew member following carrying a bundle of rags that I assume contain her herbs.

I follow them. Maybe I have no choice in the matter, but I don't have to make it easy for her. She must think she has the most extraordinary good fortune, being chosen to serve me and live in comparative luxury on the *Lady Sinclair*, but she will have to work for the privilege.

Father shows Meg the little cabin where she will sleep off my rooms and then leaves us, he says, 'To become better acquainted.'

73

In the confines of the cabin, I can smell her, too. I wrinkle my nose and I know she sees me. So what? She must know she stinks of sweat and other putrid odours I don't want to think about.

'You need to wash,' I tell her. 'I think good hygiene is an important habit. And I will find you something half-decent to wear.'

I go into my cabin and pick out the blue linen dress that is caught and torn from when I was rolling around on the floor. I return to find her half-undressed, and she hastily tries to cover herself as I walk in. I toss the gown to her. 'I trust your mother also taught you to sew?' I say. 'This needs mending before you put it on.'

By the time she emerges again, she looks startlingly different. Her hair, which had been hanging in rat tails, looks clean and brushed and is much longer than I thought it was. Her face and arms are free of dirt streaks and the colour of the linen dress brings out the cornflower blue of her eyes. For a moment I regret giving her the gown. I look at her mending but can't find fault.

'I used to sew for my last mistress,' Meg says quietly.

'The one you stole from?' I retort sharply.

'Yes,' she replies and lowers her eyes.

I set her to work, airing and sponging my gowns, and mending them where needed. She's obviously never seen such fine clothes in her life. 'They are so beautiful, and there are so many of them!' she exclaims.

'And I have counted them all,' I warn her.

I go up to the deck when I hear the call that we're passing Madeira and look longingly towards the island. One of the sailors described it as the place where the mountains meet the sea, and among the most stunning of the world's sights. I discover that if I strain my eyes, I can see soft greenery stretching upwards into the sky and then cascading down to a strip of yellow sand on the edge of the ocean. Etched into the greenery are lines of white that I assume are houses. I sigh. Maybe I'll be able to visit on our way back to England in four or five or six years . . . Just thinking about spending such a long time away from home makes me miss it all over again.

I climb back down below and make my way to my little desk in the corner to continue the letter I had started to write home. I planned to post it from Madeira, but Father tells me that we will, from time to time, encounter other ships on their way to port, and they will take our letters for us. I send my dearest good wishes to our family and reassure them that we are both perfectly well. I inquire after Harriet's health, too; by rights she should have had her new baby now and I hope desperately that all went well.

I write that the weather is growing warmer all the time, and that I had been looking forward to a break from the ship in the fine climate of Madeira, but it is not to be. I say how much I am missing John, but that I hope to see him again soon if Captain Short allows it. In the meantime, I tell them that I spend my days walking around the decks, reading, sketching the sea and the skies, and practising my lute and piano. As I sit here writing, with all the cabin windows open in the hope of a cool breeze, I imagine my mother and sisters sitting around the fire in London, reading this letter with all the doors and windows closed against the cold and damp. What a strange world! Knowing they will be missing Father, too, I resolve to try to make them laugh. I recount the time I attempted to play backgammon with Father when the pieces kept sliding off the table with the lurching of the ship. And I describe the efforts of our ship's cook who, I say, is the worst I've ever had the misfortune to encounter. It doesn't help that he's so bad-tempered, either. I don't mention my new maid. I know my mother would be distressed to hear of it.

Father already has a sizeable bundle of letters to be sent ashore with the next ship we pass. One is for Mother and my sisters—his 'little angels', as he calls them—but the majority are for his superiors back in London: the Admiralty; Robert Stewart; Lord Castlereagh, the Secretary of State for War and the Colonies, who administers New South Wales among Britain's other colonies; and Uncle Joseph. When I ask him what on earth he has to tell them so early in our voyage, he shakes his head.

'A great deal, Mary,' he says. 'I have told them what a scoundrel Captain Short is, and how he undermines my authority at every opportunity. I have told them how I instructed him that he should consider me his superior and commanding officer, and obey my signals, but that he's refused. What's more, I've let them know that Short said he would only allow Lieutenant Putland to sail aboard the *Lady Sinclair* if I accepted his authority. The damned impertinence!'

I'm listening only vaguely until I hear John's name. I try to make sense of what he is telling me. 'Short said John would be allowed back if you agreed to his command?' I ask. 'John would be back to sail with me?'

'Yes, that's right, Mary,' Father says. 'Can you think of a more scurrilous ploy, a more unreasonable man?'

I'm silent, but yes, I honestly can.

9

FRIENDLY FIRE

Meg Hill
8 MARCH 1806, AT SEA

This father and daughter are the strangest pair Meg has ever met. Captain Bligh is obviously a man who likes everything his own way; that much was immediately apparent from their first meeting on the deck of the *Alexander*. He also seems to have little fellow feeling for anyone else on this voyage. Meg knows that two of the ships are running short of water, and that some of the convicts and a few of the crew are suffering from scurvy, but Captain Bligh refused to allow them to stop to refill the water barrels and bring on supplies of fresh fruit and vegetables. At the same time, however, he has treated her fairly and kindly for the three weeks that she has been in the service of his daughter.

Mary, on the other hand, Mary . . . Meg bows her head over the piece of ribbon she's sewing onto one of Mary's innumerable bonnets. She's simply never come across anyone quite like Mary before.

That first day was a shock. Mary behaved simply abominably. Absolutely no manners at all. She'd spoken to Meg as if she were dirt beneath her feet, worse even. A thief likely to steal everything she had and make off with them to where, exactly? A *murderer*? Meg smiles to herself. As well as being an indulged, spoiled brat, Mary was obviously a little simple. She might be twenty-two, five years older than Meg, but she certainly didn't act like it.

Meg replays that first conversation in her mind yet again. When Mary had suggested that Meg should stay on the *Alexander* with the other women, her heart leaped. She wouldn't have minded that at all. She was carving out a nice little space for herself there. Captain Brookes had called on her when one of his crew had a toothache and was in so much agony that he wouldn't let anyone so much as look into his mouth. Meg ground some cloves into powder and told the man to put it on his gums. By the end of the week, he was back on his feet again. She then brewed two lots of sage tea to help a fellow convict with a fever, and very soon the colour had flooded back into the woman's cheeks and she was kissing Meg's hands in thanks.

'Just tell me if there's anything I can ever do for you,' the woman told her. 'My name is Jane. Remember me. Anything, you hear!'

Of course, treating people's illnesses hadn't been a ticket of leave from the gruelling daily physical labour; Meg was still a prisoner, after all. But she didn't mind toiling away on the deck because she'd grown up working hard. After her beloved father had died in a fall from his horse, she'd had to earn as much money as she could. The survival of her mother and five younger siblings depended on it. But her father! She stops sewing for a moment to conjure up his image and realises, with a start, that the picture is growing blurrier with each year that passes. She sighs, but comforts herself that his character will always stay sharp in her mind—he was as different from Captain Bligh as night is from day.

As a Methodist minister, he'd always been a very humble, self-effacing man, and he'd taught his children to be the same. They must care for the poor, the sick and the lonely wherever they might find them, he told them, with as much kindness as they themselves would like to be treated. They should eschew fashion and fripperies and showiness as much as they were able. Meg chuckles as she recalls her astonishment at Mary's vast wardrobe of fine gowns and bonnets.

But while her father had done so much to prepare Meg for adulthood, teaching her his own strict code of ethics, as well as how to read, write and do basic arithmetic, he unfortunately had taught her little about the ways of the world outside theirs. When she'd met Thomas Carter, she'd behaved like a complete and utter fool. So she only had herself to blame for ending up as a prisoner of this self-important man and his arrogant daughter voyaging to the other side of the world.

A voice breaks into her thoughts. 'Meg! Where are you?'

She scrambles to her feet and puts aside the bonnet. 'Here, ma'am,' she calls back, heading straight for Mary's cabin. 'How can I help?'

Mary stands half-in and half-out of a magnificent deep forest green taffeta evening gown, trimmed with silver straps over the bodice and, as is the newest fashion, opening at the back. 'Fasten this for me, will you?' Mary demands impatiently.

Meg fiddles with the hooks and eyes but can't help noticing the piles of dresses and petticoats strewn all around the apartment. Mary sees her eyes taking in the dishevelled scene. 'I'm trying on a few of my dresses,' she says in a voice that sounds begrudgingly conspiratorial. 'I need to look my best for dinner with Lieutenant Putland tomorrow.'

Meg nods. Ever since Captain Short sent over a note saying the lieutenant would be given leave to dine with his wife, she's barely heard anything else. Mary had almost fainted with delight at the news but now she is obviously absorbed in the practicalities.

'Would you like me to do your hair?' Meg asks.

Mary looks uncertain. 'You can do it today and if it looks terrible, I will do it myself tomorrow.'

Meg nods as Mary parades with obvious satisfaction before the mirror. 'Now help me out of this, and then you can start on my hair before clearing up this mess,' she says.

The hairstyling takes two full hours before it meets with Mary's satisfaction. Meg is exhausted from the effort of holding her tongue for so long while her mistress complains about her father and how unreasonable he is, continually bemoaning the fact that if it weren't for him, her husband would be with her each day. Meg longs to tell Mary that she and her father have far more in common than she realises. Each of them is as stubborn and as high-and-mighty as the other. But she says nothing.

When Mary's husband arrives the next day, however, Meg is surprised. Despite his towering height, he's quiet and gentle and is so attentive to his wife, Meg is quite touched. He's also courteous and respectful towards everyone around them, in a way she had not expected. But she can't help noticing that he's also very pale, too pale, and has a nasty hacking cough.

After she serves dinner to the couple, she retires discreetly to sit in her room with her favourite book. It's an exceedingly well thumbed 1789 edition of *Culpeper's Complete Herbal*, the definitive guide to herbal remedies. She's been studying it intently for the past three years, ever since her mother first started giving her lessons in herbal medicine that had been passed down from her grandmother. The day before her trial, her mother had pressed the book into her hands, saying she felt sure it would stand her in good stead whatever happened. It's now Meg's most treasured possession.

As she looks at the familiar list of plants, their uses and the warnings that come with them, she wonders if the same plants will also grow in New South Wales, or whether she'll have to find alternatives. She falls asleep where she sits, dreaming of wandering through vast open plains and gathering herbs by the basketful.

She wakes with a start, stands up, stretches wearily, and tiptoes up to the deck to look at the silvery moon on the dark waters. As she passes Mary's quarters, she can hear Lieutenant Putland coughing. Meg doesn't like the sound of that at all.

The next morning, Mary says a tearful farewell to her husband, and ladens him with fresh eggs from the hens on board and two bottles of milk, then shuts herself in her cabin for the day. Meg is relieved as it means rare time off for her. But the lieutenant's visit has shown a different side to her mistress. She was genuinely moved by how softly Mary spoke to her husband, how she insisted on him being given the best pieces of meat, and how she fluttered around him, concerned by his cough. Meg takes note; maybe the way to establish a better relationship with Mary is through her husband.

After all the excitement of his visit, life at sea falls into an easy rhythm. Mary is a demanding mistress, but Meg is happy to be kept busy. There are always breaks in the tedium, too. Whenever a pod of dolphins appears, a shout goes up and everyone races to the deck to look. Sometimes there are rays and sharks following the ship. Always there are birds to watch and Mary often tries to sketch them . . . the petrels diving for fish, the black-tipped wings of the gannets, the huge ungainly albatross and the gulls that swirl through the air currents of the ship, ever hopeful of crumbs.

One day, two ships come into view with square-rigged masts. Sailing so close, a frisson of alarm spreads through the *Lady Sinclair* in case they are enemy vessels. They turn out to be Portuguese brigs, so Captain Bligh sends for the master of the closest one to come on board and present his papers. He does so, bringing a gift of oranges and a strange yellow fruit with him. Mary gives Meg a quarter of an orange, for which she is very grateful. Fresh fruit is a luxury she's rarely tasted. But the other fruit . . . Neither woman has ever seen such a thing before—long yellow fingers on a common stalk. Mary is just about to bite into one when the master stops her, laughing, then strips off the outside covering and hands it back to her. Mary takes one bite of the soft yellow fruit and spits it out, declaring it so unpleasant that it has made her feel faint. Meg ends up with a banana of her own, plus Mary's discarded one.

'It's delicious!' she says. 'Sweet, but with a hint of cloves.'

'It's disgusting,' Mary laughs. 'It will make you ill.'

Three days after Lieutenant Putland's visit, however, the strangest thing happens. Mary is walking on the deck with her father, and Meg is stretching her legs behind them. One of the crew shouts something to Captain Bligh and he goes straight to the quarterdeck, takes the telescope, and gazes, as far as Meg can tell, towards the *Porpoise*. When he drops it down from his eye, he has an animated conversation with the mariner. From a distance, it looks as if the man is pleading with Captain Bligh about something, but the captain is having none of it.

When he returns to Mary's side, Meg catches up with them so she can find out what is happening.

'Short is signalling for us to steer more to windward,' Captain Bligh is telling Mary. 'He doesn't understand that the breeze has picked up and that's not the way to go at all.'

'But he is in charge of the convoy, is he not?' Mary asks mildly. 'Shouldn't we do what he has asked?'

'No, damn him!' Captain Bligh replies. 'I have been put in charge of which course to follow, and this is the one I have chosen.'

'But Father—' Mary starts but her words are drowned out by an almighty roar and a loud smack on the water close by, that hits with such force that it rocks the boat. Mary stumbles, and Meg steps forward quickly to help her mistress stay upright.

'What was that?' Mary gasps.

Captain Bligh looks incensed. 'That dastardly villain. Short!' he yells. 'He's fired a shot across our bows from the *Porpoise*. How dare he!'

'He's firing at us?' asks Mary, stunned.

'Not directly at us,' her father responds. 'It was a warning shot, telling us to change our course.'

'So we must change it now?' Mary replies.

Captain Bligh shakes his head defiantly, and Meg thinks she can see a spark in his eyes she hasn't seen before. 'No, curse him. I refuse. This is the course that will speed our journey. Now, you women, get down below.'

Mary is standing stock still, as if frozen to the spot, so Meg seizes her arm and bundles her down to her quarters. 'Come, ma'am,' she tells her mistress. 'It's not safe up here. Let's do as your father says.'

Mary is plainly confused. 'How can our own convoy fire at us?' she asks Meg. 'It doesn't make sense. Here we are, in the middle of nowhere, looking out for enemy ships and now the enemy seems to be our own. And why doesn't Father just change course? This ridiculous vendetta against Short is going to get us all killed.'

'I don't know, ma'am,' Meg replies. 'Maybe he has his own reasons. But it does seem to me too that we should do as Captain Short asks.'

A bewildering thought seems to have struck Mary, and she brings a hand up to her face in an expression of alarm. 'John!' she says. 'He's on the *Porpoise*! What can be happening over there?'

Suddenly, there's another massive roar and a crash of water from somewhere behind them, towards the ship's stern, and the two women hold on to each other in terror as the ship lurches.

'He must have fired again,' Meg says. 'Surely your father has to change our course now?' She can see Mary is shaking, and she pours a drop of skullcap tonic into a glass of water and hands it to her. 'Take this,' Meg says. 'It will be good for your nerves.'

Mary drinks it obediently as they listen to the noises from above. They can hear shouting and footsteps pounding on the deck, and they sit quietly, wondering what is going on. Three minutes later, they feel it. The *Lady Sinclair* jolts and shudders, and they realise Captain Bligh has finally backed down and changed their course.

'Thank God for that,' Mary exclaims. 'He has seen sense at last.'

Meg can't agree more. She thought she'd had as much excitement as she could possibly stand these past few months, but she shakes her head. Now she realises that in the company of this man and his daughter, there will likely be many more, and far greater, dramas to come.

10

A CONFRONTATION

Mary Putland
15 MARCH 1806, AT SEA

Two days after Father nearly got us all killed with his lunatic obstinacy, I hear a familiar voice and race up onto the deck. It's John! I can't help myself and embrace him right there in front of Father, Mr Griffin and all the crew. My dear husband goes pink with embarrassment, but I think he is as pleased to see me as I am to see him. I can see Meg smiling to see him too as she follows me up into the sunlight.

'John, what are you doing here?' I ask. 'We had no warning. This is such a wonderful surprise.'

He laughs at my obvious delight but then composes his face again. My heart lurches when I notice how thin he's become and how ashen his skin looks. 'I've come with a letter from Captain Short for your father,' he replies. 'He has taken some of the convicts from the *Fortune* and put them in the *Porpoise*, and he wanted to let Captain Bligh know.'

I catch his hand in mine. 'Did Short tell you what he did the day before yesterday?' I ask. 'It was so terrible. He actually fired on us! We thought we were going to die.'

At that, I feel his hand stiffen in mine. I look up into his face. There's a strange expression in his eyes. 'It wasn't Captain Short who fired the shots across your bows,' he says slowly. 'It was I.'

'What?' I laugh, thinking I've either misheard him or he is telling me a joke I don't quite understand.

'I'm serious, Mary,' he says. 'I was the Officer of the Watch and Captain Short ordered me to fire.'

I let go of his hand as if it's burning hot and look over at my father. He's nodding. 'It's true, Mary,' Father says. 'That scoundrel forced him to fire on his own wife and father-in-law. What kind of a man does that?'

John looks stricken. 'It was across your bows and your stern,' he corrects Father. 'It wasn't aimed directly at you. But they were still two of the worst moments of my life. I didn't know what to do. I couldn't disobey him, but then again . . .' He trails off but then appears to collect himself. 'If, however, your father hadn't changed his course, Captain Short said I should fire straight at your ship. I can't tell you how relieved I was to see your crew trim your sails.'

I gasp. Poor John. No wonder he looks so drained. And poor us. What on earth had Father been thinking to put us through such torment? I look at him, and he's scowling.

'It's Short who's to blame,' he snarls. 'I shall write another letter to Lord Castlereagh tonight. And if it doesn't happen before, I shall make sure he's charged as soon as he sets foot on New South Wales soil. We shall see who's in charge then!'

I sigh and I can see John frowning. He's far too diplomatic to say anything to Father directly, but I'm sure he agrees with me that it's all Father's fault. 'How long can you stay?' I whisper to him.

'I'm sorry my love,' he replies. 'I have a little more business to talk over with your father, then I'm under orders to return to the *Porpoise* immediately.'

I hover while the pair converse then give him a quick embrace before he makes his way back down the side to the longboat that's waiting to steal him away again. I wave until I can see him no more.

It's hard being on this arduous journey without John. Our brief encounters, in some ways, make it even worse. They make me realise how much I'm missing him, especially at night when I'm alone in my berth feeling the vast sea heave beneath us and the ship groan in response and watching the shadows lunge eerily at me across the walls. A few times, I've woken in terror and reached out for him, only to find empty bedsheets beside me. Once, I actually screamed, and Meg came running.

I was pleased she woke me up and thanked her, but I reminded myself that I didn't want to become too reliant on her, and she must respect that. I still don't totally trust the girl. But she has been a help. Her ginger root has been a real blessing whenever the waves are rough and that terrible seasickness comes back.

Otherwise, the days drag on with almost total monotony. It's hard to keep track sometimes of how long we've been on this ship and how much further we have to go. I try to keep myself busy by writing home, drawing sketches of the birds and our life at sea, reading, studying music and singing to my lute-playing when I'm confident no one can hear me, but it's hard to distract myself from the tedium.

Occasionally, Father talks about what will be waiting for us in New South Wales. One morning he tells me that although the current governor, Philip Gidley King, is also from Cornish stock just like him, he is a weak man who likes his port too much and who has allowed the New South Wales Corps to run roughshod over the colony. Father, of course, is a much tougher character, and will show them who's in charge.

'They'll have quite the surprise coming if they make the mistake of thinking I'm cut from the same cloth!' he says.

I murmur my agreement, rolling my eyes under lowered lids so he won't be able to see.

Father is in full flight by now, anyway. 'Sir Joseph has told me that King has proved ineffectual in bringing the Corps under control and is now a sick man who needs to go home. He's also warned me to watch out for the Corps' main troublemaker, John Macarthur. He's become one of the greatest rabble-rousers in the colony. They say he's accumulated a fortune worth more than twenty thousand pounds, mostly at the public's expense, and will stop at nothing to make more. Well, if he thinks I'm going to be easy prey . . .' It's usually at around this point that I stop even pretending to listen.

He does tell me one fascinating story, though, about the first governor, Captain Phillip, who was under instructions from the king to learn more about the natives. So, unbelievably, he kidnapped some and brought them to town. And later, even more incredibly, he took two of them back to England with him. 'It was in all the newspapers at the time,' Father says. 'Unfortunately, one died in England with a chest infection, but the other, Bennelong, is now back in Sydney. Maybe we shall meet him, too, depending on what relations are currently like with the natives.'

'I would love to meet him,' I say. 'But how difficult must it have been for him, being captured and imprisoned and then taken to such a foreign land and brought back again.'

'Yes,' Father says, looking thoughtful. 'We'll see. Later on, there were reports of outright warfare with the natives led by a man called Pemulwuy, who they said couldn't be killed. But he was, and his head was cut off and sent to London to be part of Sir Joseph's scientific collection.'

My hand files up to my mouth. 'Oh my God!' I cry. 'That's horrible!'

Father frowns. 'Both sides can be just as bad as each other,' he says. 'There's a lot you're going to have to get used to.'

Meg sometimes takes a longboat over to the *Alexander* when someone is sick or giving birth, and on one of these visits I go with her. I swear I can smell the ship before I can see it, and the women are living in such dreadful conditions that I feel quite faint to see them. But then, as Father reminds me, they are being punished for their crimes and the alternative for many, were they to stay in England, was death. When he puts it like that, the conditions on the *Alexander* don't seem quite so bad.

Occasionally, Meg is called to the other convict ship, the *Fortune*, to treat the men's scurvy. A guard of soldiers always accompanies her in the longboat. She says there's little she can do for them, as the only proper cure is eating a diet that's richer in fresh fruit and vegetables. But she has some dried marsh trefoil flowers in her medicinal chest that she turns into a concoction so bitter that some of the men say suffering the weakness, aching limbs and bleeding gums of scurvy is preferable to drinking her 'witches' brew'. She laughed as she told me that, and then put a drop on my finger for me to taste. I think they are right.

One day, Meg suggests she could go over to the *Porpoise* to check on John and his lingering cough. I'm wholeheartedly in favour of that idea, but Father isn't so keen. He says he thinks it might be seen by Short as an admission of weakness. I tell him *not* going could be a concession of weakness. In the end, Meg boards a small boat armed with dried chestnut powder from her store. I spend the day in agitation, worried that John's condition may have worsened, but when Meg returns, she's all reassuring smiles.

'Lieutenant Putland is still coughing, but he looks much less pale than he did the last time we saw him,' she reports. 'The chestnut powder should help, too. And, of course, he sends his love over to you.'

'Thank you,' I say, and for the first time, I mean it.

We cross the Line on 28 March and the crew are given double rations of rum and the day off to celebrate, which is apparently a tradition when ships cross the Equator. Meg and I remain down below. It sounds pretty raucous on deck, and Father stays out of the crew's way, too. I imagine the rowdier the sailors get, the more likely they are to throw decorum and respect to the winds and start taunting him with that Bounty Bastard curse. He needs no reminders of that time.

Soon after, the *Fortune* peels off from our convoy to stop quickly at Rio de Janeiro to replenish supplies of water and to load up with more fresh fruit and vegetables, before the scurvy claims any lives. The merchant ship the *Justina* has already left us for St Helena, while the rest of the convoy continues as per Father's orders and he asks Captain Moore on the *Fortune* to buy some sapphires, emeralds and amethysts for Mother and my sisters while he's at port. He also hands over my letters and his ever-growing package of correspondence to the authorities in England for Captain Moore to post from Rio.

Father has now trumped up a total of nine charges against Short, from disobedience to drunkenness, from taking Lieutenant Putland away from the *Lady Sinclair* to the time Short fired on us, each incident painstakingly copied out by Mr Griffin several times to various officials. He's even enlisted me in his crusade, asking me to duplicate the letters still further. Every time I do as he bids, I wince at the ferocity and pettiness of his campaign against the captain. Surely he's a bigger man than this? But no, it doesn't appear so. He's not above using my presence on the *Lady Sinclair* against Short, too.

In one of the letters, he says the voyage '*has been made very unpleasant by Captain Short, who has behaved so extremely unlike a character I can ever admit into my society, that forever I shall keep him out of it. I have no alternative here but to bear his insults, or lose my Daughter, who I believe would not exist long if I left her to go to the* Porpoise.'

So . . . he's actually considered going to the *Porpoise* and forcibly taking charge, but only refrained because he has me to look after!

In other letters, he adds a formal demand that Short—whom he describes as a man with a '*brutal temper and bad heart*'—be court-martialled and returned to England immediately he sets foot on New South Wales, without receiving the six-hundred-acre land grant he was promised as payment for the voyage.

The first time I read this in his letter, I blanch. I sometimes think if I were a son to my father, I wouldn't hesitate to stand up to him, to point out the error of his ways, to moderate his pride, to make him a better person. If he had someone who could do this, he might not make such bitter enemies everywhere he goes. He might also welcome that from a son, and actually listen to him and pay heed. As it is, I find it so difficult not to be a dutiful daughter and simply agree with what he says. If I try to argue with him, I either whine and plead or, if things become heated, I overreact. I know I have inherited his temper.

'Father, do you really think it is worth ruining a family's life over this?' I venture tentatively one day after dinner when I think he might be in a more relaxed mood. Meg is sitting by the fire, sewing up a small tear in one of his shirts, and the cabin is cosy in the warm light. 'You'll have a lot of things to deal with when we arrive in New South Wales. Maybe it would be better to start with a clean slate?'

He looks confused. 'What are you talking about, Mary?' he asks. 'Whose family's life?'

'Short's. I know you have found a great deal of fault with him personally, but just think of his family. He has a wife and six children and two more on the way . . .'

His face darkens at the mention of the name, but I battle on. 'They've brought their entire household possessions with them, as well as everything they'll need to set up as settlers in the colony. John told me they have brought books on farming, seed, blades, hoes, sickles and flails to work their new land.'

Father harrumphs. 'Perhaps he should have considered that before he decided to be so insubordinate to his superiors.'

'But just think, if he is forced to return to England, what will his wife and children do in New South Wales without him? How will they survive?'

'Maybe they'll go back with him,' Father says. 'That's not my concern.'

'*Please*, Father,' I respond, 'he may have behaved badly, but is it really something that's worth ruining so many lives over? New South Wales is going to be a whole new life, and goodness knows, we'll need as many settlers as we can get to balance out all the convicts. Why don't we simply forget the unpleasantness that's passed between you and Short? Is it really necessary to report it all back to London?'

Father looks at me steadily and, for a moment, I think he might be weighing up this option. I smile encouragingly. Then I jump almost out of my skin as he smashes his fist down on the table between us. 'Don't be so ridiculous, girl!' he spits. 'Short must get his just deserts. He has continually defied me, and fired on me . . .'

'Fired *near us*,' I correct him.

At that, he narrows his eyes, then glares at me even more fiercely. 'Damn him! And damn his family! I won't be spoken to like this by anyone, especially not you!'

I stand up, summoning all my courage. 'But why *not* me?' I shout. 'Everyone else is too scared to tell you when you're wrong. And you're wrong on this.'

'Get to your own quarters, this instant, you silly girl!' he bellows. 'How dare you question me! I'd thank you to keep your mind on your own business—your ridiculous fashions and your pathetic little drawings. Don't interfere in things you know nothing about. I knew I would regret giving you this opportunity.'

I start walking towards the door, then feel something taut inside me snap. Ridiculous fashions? Silly drawings? *This opportunity*? I have been on this blasted ship for nearly two months now without my husband and have at least another four in front of me. This is not an opportunity. It is a sentence.

I am speechless with incandescent rage and a red veil descends over my eyes. Almost without thinking, I snatch a brass goblet off the mantle. Then I toss it at my father and dart out the door before I can see whether it's hit him or not. The stakes, I know, have suddenly climbed much, much higher.

11

AN UNCERTAIN FUTURE

Meg Hill
1 JULY 1806, AT SEA

Everyone on the *Lady Sinclair* is craning their necks towards the far distant horizon, waiting for their first sight of the colony at Van Diemen's Land. There's palpable excitement coupled with a heavy weariness. Captain Bligh had mustered everyone on the deck that morning to tell them the long voyage was nearly at an end and thanked them all for their service.

Meg is as relieved as everyone that their journey is almost over, but she's anxious about what might be waiting for her in New South Wales. Mary has given her no indication as to whether her services will be required at Government House, and that's not something she is in a position to directly ask about. If Mary doesn't take her, Meg knows her future is uncertain. From what the women on the *Alexander* told her, she could be given to another settler family to do whatever they might need, put into government service or—and this is her greatest fear—be assigned to a single master who'll no doubt use and abuse her like a common prostitute.

She'd tried to raise the subject delicately and indirectly with both Mary and her father, but neither seemed to appreciate the depths of her terror. Mary brushed her off, saying she would think about it later and, while she knows Captain Bligh thinks she's been a good influence on his daughter, he's too preoccupied with his imminent governorship and its challenges to pay much attention to a mere convict-servant. She feels her nervousness increasing as every day they inch closer to their destination.

Since the goblet incident, it's been an even stranger voyage than Meg could have imagined when she first boarded the *Lady Sinclair*. Meg had followed Mary to her quarters that evening and calmed her down, and then comforted her as her mistress lay sobbing on her berth. She tried to reason with her. 'Ma'am, I think it was a very brave stand to take,' she told her. 'I feel for Captain Short. I didn't tell you, but when I visited the *Porpoise* to see John, I also visited Mrs Short. She has been having a difficult pregnancy with the twins, and I wanted to help her. Captain Short gave me permission as I knew Captain Bligh never would.'

Mary quietened then and sat up. For a moment, Meg was nervous that Mary might reprimand her and report her to her father, but instead, she frowned and looked interested. 'That was kind,' she said. 'My father has no quarrel with Mrs Short, but doubtless he would have forbidden you from seeing her to punish her husband. And how was she?'

Meg shakes her head. 'I didn't like what I saw,' she said. 'She still has about a month to go by my reckoning, but she seemed so uncomfortable.'

'But she's having twins, isn't she?' asked Mary. 'Anyone would be uncomfortable. I remember my mother saying that her two pregnancies with twins were the worst.'

'Yes, but she looked so pale, and she said she's had some bad headaches and her vision has been blurred,' Meg replied. 'She's also had a lot of pain and some days she has been too weak to get out of her berth. And she's had some bleeding.'

Both women fell silent. Being pregnant with twins would always be a struggle but out here on the high seas, without a proper doctor and with regular bouts of seasickness, it would be intolerable. Not to mention the added stress Mrs Short must feel over her husband's fights with Captain Bligh.

Just a month later, their worst fears were realised. Captain Short sent a note requesting Meg's attendance at his wife's bedside. Mary authorised her visit without notifying her father. She didn't want to give him the chance to refuse. When Meg returned, everyone could see from her downcast face that it wasn't good news.

'Mrs Short has given birth to a healthy baby boy,' she announced on the deck of the *Lady Sinclair* to everyone who'd come up to hear the news. 'Just the one.'

Captain Bligh looked as if he were about to say something when he was silenced by a look from Mary. This wasn't the time.

When the convoy eventually arrived at the Cape of Good Hope in the middle of May, everyone was in dire need of time away from the ship. At Meg's urging, Mary had apologised to her father for the goblet incident, as the atmosphere between them had been proving unbearable for everyone else. But Meg could see that Mary was still harbouring a grudge and, quite frankly, she didn't blame her. Captain Bligh had behaved abominably yet they both knew he would never dream of apologising to his daughter. His pride wouldn't let him, even if he did think he was in the wrong. Instead, he accepted Mary's apology, told her she was a bad shot in any case, as the goblet had only hit him on the shoulder, and then seemed to deem the matter completely resolved. And Mary would be with her husband for the next two weeks on dry land, which would hopefully cool her lingering resentment.

Captain Bligh, Mary and John, and Mr Griffin were all invited to stay at the home of the acting governor, Lieutenant-General Sir David Baird, so they took Meg with them. Mary's father told them about Baird before they decamped there. He was a true war hero, Bligh said, who'd fought in India, been badly wounded and was captured by the forces of Hyder Ali and his famous son Tipu Sultan. Then he was held prisoner for four years in Seringapatam, the capital of the Kingdom of Mysore. Some years later, he returned—and successfully stormed the place where he'd been held captive. Much more recently, he'd led the expedition to capture the Cape against the Dutch.

John was impressed, but Mary and Meg were much more interested in the bathrooms of his mansion, the feather beds, the quality of the wine, the quantities of fresh meat, vegetables and fruit on his dining table each evening, and the ebony black skin of his servants.

'I wonder if Sydney is going to be like this,' Mary mused to Meg on their first walk around the town when John had been called away by Captain Bligh on an errand. They passed gleaming white villas on the side of a network of canals crossed by stone bridges, and wandered through the Company's Garden, which had been established by the Dutch East India Company to provide fresh vegetables for the settlement. 'It could be glorious. Maybe Sydney has beautiful mountains and sands and ocean, as well as this wonderful sunshine. For the past three and a half months I've just wanted the voyage to end. Now, at last, I'm beginning to look forward to our destination.'

Meg loved it when Mary was like this: relaxed and chatty and talking to her almost as an equal. But she still had no confirmation on her own future in Sydney. Meg tried again. 'You're going to be very busy there as the consort to the governor,' she said. 'You might not have much time to relax. You'll need a lot of help.'

'Oh nonsense!' Mary said. 'There'll be plenty of time.'

Only once in their whole sojourn on the Cape did the two women see Captain Short. He was walking briskly through the street, with his six children all hand-in-hand and skipping to keep up. Mrs Short followed behind holding her newborn, looking tired and as pale as their ships' sails. When Short saw Mary and Meg, he looked uncertain about what to do. Since Meg was more familiar with the couple, she took the lead and waved. He came forward and took off his cap.

'Good afternoon, Captain Short,' Mary said, following the initiative. 'It is so nice to see you. And how is your new son?'

'Very good, thank you, Mrs Putland,' he replied. He nodded to Meg and then moved quickly away, tailed by his little party.

'That was most odd,' Mary said.

'Yes, ma'am,' Meg replied. 'But understandable. I have heard he's been busy writing up charges against your father, in response to the charges your father has written up against him. He was obviously embarrassed to have encountered us, and eager to get away.'

Mary looked stricken, and then forced herself to laugh. 'Oh well, we've done our best,' she said. 'May the best man win.'

The convoy remained at anchor for three weeks at the Cape, waiting for the *Fortune* to catch up and undergoing repairs to ready the ships for the last part of the journey. This would be the most demanding leg, Captain Bligh told them, across the Southern Ocean to New South Wales. They could expect high winds and rough seas.

The day before they departed, however, a letter was delivered to Captain Bligh. When Meg saw it bore Captain Short's seal, she fetched Mary, hopeful the two men might be resolving their differences at last. It was indeed a plea for a reconciliation for this last part of the voyage. But Captain Bligh was having none of it.

'I won't reply,' he told the two women. 'This man's conduct has been so extremely improper that I shall ever spurn him and any overture he makes.'

Meg saw Mary biting her lip to stay silent.

As soon as the convoy casts off on 6 June, everyone can see the truth of Captain Bligh's ominous words about the route ahead. The sea is rough, the weather turns to violent squalls and the temperature plunges. The crew chatters about the risks posed by the mountains of floating ice they have heard they might encounter, the dangers of such high winds on the sails, their fears of striking whales.

Mary becomes immediately seasick again, and Meg makes more ginger root tea. She would have guided Mary up to the deck for fresh air, but it is so cold and gusty up there no one spends more time exposed to the elements than they have to. As soon as the seas quieten a little, Meg seeks Captain Bligh's permission to take a longboat to check on the women of the *Alexander*. There, she finds many of the women in pitiful condition. She walks among them, administering help where she can—fenugreek to promote the flow of breast milk for a young woman who's recently given birth, sage for a few women with fevers, chamomile for a woman about her own age who has terrible stomach cramps, and plenty of ginger root to help settle those who are suffering most from the ship's rocking.

She examines a woman whom the others say is constantly ill, and judges her to be three to four months pregnant.

'One of the sailors smuggled me away every week during the exercise period,' the woman confesses. 'He'd give me rum and anything was better than being here. But then he stopped coming one day. I don't know if he got found out or if perhaps he somehow knew about . . . about . . . my condition.'

Meg asks after another woman she'd befriended during her time on the *Alexander*, who no longer seems to be there.

'She's done all right for herself,' someone volunteers. 'She caught the eye of one of the officers and she's been hidden away in his cabin since the Cape.'

The rest of the women are inordinately grateful that Meg has come back to care for them and gather around to ask what life is like over on the *Lady Sinclair*.

'Much better than here, I'm afraid,' Meg says. 'But the Blighs aren't as good company as you, of course!'

'What are they like?' asks Jane, the woman she'd helped on a previous visit.

Meg pauses. 'Well, Captain Bligh is pretty much like his reputation,' she says. 'You remember the *Bounty* mutineers called him the Bounty Bastard and made all those charges against him? They weren't wrong. He's obviously a good seaman but he's such a proud man, and so self-important, that it frequently clouds his judgement. He also has a foul mouth, and a terrible temper when crossed.'

The women murmur. 'And his daughter?' another one asks.

'Mary,' Meg nods. 'She's a queer one, all right. She can be as nice as pie sometimes, and is all wrapped up in her drawings and her music and her fashion. You should see the number of dresses she has in her quarters!'

The women sigh collectively at the thought. Dresses! How wonderful. Their clothes are now little more than rags hanging off their bodies after wearing them each day on this voyage.

Meg smiles and continues, 'But other times, she's definitely her father's daughter. She has a temper on her, too, and can be pretty nasty when she wants to be. But at the same time . . . I don't know. She does have a strong sense of what's right and wrong. It must be hard for her, standing up to her father. I get the feeling she's rarely done it before. I don't know how they're going to go when we arrive in New South Wales . . .'

'And how about you?' interjects the same woman. 'What's going to become of you when we get there? Will you be staying with them or will you be back with us?'

'I have no idea,' Meg replies. 'They have given me no indication.'

'Well, God bless you,' says the woman. 'I only hope you won't be with us. Who knows what's waiting if you are?'

Today, standing on the deck of the *Lady Sinclair*, screwing up her eyes for the first sight of Van Diemen's Land, Meg reflects on the woman's words yet again. Who knows what would be in store for them in this new land? She can hardly bear to consider all the terrible possibilities.

Part Two

ARRIVING

12

WELCOME TO SYDNEY

Mary Putland
8 AUGUST 1806, SYDNEY

It's so wonderful to be on dry land again! I feel like dropping to my knees to kiss the ground after stepping ashore in Sydney a total of six months and nine days after leaving England. But, of course, I don't. That mud would make such a mess of the outfit I've chosen to wear for our arrival: a lovely new off-white gown that Mother sent over with John, with a fashionably high waistline just under the bust. And, besides, who knows what diseases I might catch from this new soil?

After being almost deafened by the blasting of the cannons, we walk along the government wharf through the middle of a New South Wales Corps guard of honour to the drumbeat of its band and, beyond the scarlet uniforms, I can see the locals staring at me open-mouthed. They've evidently not seen anything quite so, should I say, *à la mode*. Well, they'll soon have a lot more to feast their eyes on. I brought with me a selection of the latest gowns and bonnets and gloves, in all the styles, colours and materials now popular in English society. Looking at their drab, shapeless clothing, they'll have a thing or two to learn.

Beyond them, I can see what I suppose is the town—a motley assortment of scruffy little buildings that must be their cottages, shops and warehouses. On the ridgeline, I can see windmills squatting on the hillside, punctuated by tall pine trees. I take a deep breath. It's so much more backward than I'd pictured it. In the distance, there are wisps of dark smoke, which I suppose could be native fires. I look at the crowd and see a few black-skinned natives there, among the whites.

We're met by Governor Philip Gidley King, resplendent in his dress uniform, and his wife, Anna Josepha, tall and dark-haired but looking rather less impressive in a dark, old-fashioned gown with a waistline . . . oh goodness, no . . . at her waist. King bows to me, and his wife catches my hands in hers.

'Oh my dear,' she says in a surprisingly warm voice, 'welcome to Sydney. You don't know how excited we've been about your arrival.'

I smile graciously. 'You'll know how much we've been looking forward to it, too!' I reply.

At that, she laughs, and I see how pretty she is when you look past her frumpy clothing and those terrible ringlets in her hair. Mind you, she's been out here, in the middle of nowhere, for just shy of six years now, so perhaps it's little wonder she's so out of touch. I'm determined I shall not go down that same path, though. I have high standards, and I plan on keeping them.

'Yes, that journey is terrible,' she says. 'We intend to leave in a few days, as soon as you and your father are both settled in. I'm dreading the prospect, although I am keen to settle back in England again.'

I nod and glance around for John. The *Porpoise* docked before us, but I still haven't seen him. I want to see his face when he catches sight of me in such a glorious gown. I haven't set eyes on him now for nine whole weeks since Cape Town, and it feels a lifetime. I'm so excited it's almost like I'm a new bride all over again. Almost. But my eagerness for our reunion is tinged with anxiety about his health. I hope to God he's taken a turn for the better.

The governor is talking to Father just beside me, and I catch a mention of Captain Short so I tear my attention away from scanning the shoreline to focus on our present company. Apparently, Short beat us to Government House; he was off his ship early and came to see the governor immediately to plead his case. Good on him, I think to myself. The man has sense. He'll get a better hearing from King than from the next governor. But Father immediately begins a tirade of abuse against the poor man, and I switch off again. I do so wish Father would forgive and forget. I'm sure he's going to have plenty on his mind here, without brooding on past spats. But John, where is he?

'Mary, we should go inside and show you around,' a voice cuts into my thoughts. Anna has looped her arm through mine and is leading me towards a big old two-storey white house with a long verandah. It looks exceedingly ramshackle, and I realise, with a start, that this must be Government House. My new home. *Our* new home. It has nothing of the grandeur I so fondly imagined on the way here.

'Yes, yes, that would be lovely,' I say obediently.

We troop in through the front gates and, close up, the place looks even more derelict than it did from a distance.

Anna catches my expression. 'It's not exactly a palace, is it?' she says, laughing. 'I remember when we came, I was a little disappointed. But we've done some work on it.'

We walk in and it dawns on me how truly shabby everything is. It was built by the first governor, she tells me, so it must be less than twenty years old, but it looks like it's been put together extremely poorly. There's an overwhelming smell of damp and rotting wood and I can see that some of the plasterwork is coming away from the walls. That's what happens when you trust convicts to do the work for you without adequate supervision, I suppose. I wonder where Meg is. I haven't seen her since we left the ship, either.

'Just think, this was the first building in Sydney,' Anna tells me. 'It was mostly built with English bricks and timber brought over by the First Fleet, then finished off with some of the local sandstone. Before this, there was nothing.'

I hold my tongue. It's not as impressive as she seems to think; it really doesn't look like much now.

'When we arrived, it only had six rooms,' she continues. 'But we added another drawing room and a bedroom, and extended the verandah which the previous governor put on. We've now moved in to those rooms until we depart in seven days, following your father's investiture, so you'll have the rest of the house to yourselves.'

'Are you sure?' I ask her. 'We could camp in there until you go so we don't disturb you.'

'Thank you for the thought, but it's all already done,' Anna says. 'And our ship, the HMS *Buffalo*, leaves in a week anyway, so we'll probably spend a couple of nights aboard before our departure.'

I'm relieved. The place is poky enough without confining ourselves to only a small part of it. An image of our lovely town-house in London flashes into my mind, with my bedroom a vision in modern pastels and its views of the handsome streets outside. I push the thought firmly aside. It won't do me any good to make comparisons.

We walk up the wooden staircase to inspect the bedrooms upstairs and I make appreciative noises even though I'm anything but. Then we come back down and Anna shows me the little buildings behind the house. They're the kitchen, bakehouse, stables and offices, she tells me, while servants scurry around trying to look busy. 'I'll be sad to leave this place, but the governor isn't a well man,' Anna says. 'And our children need to be with their parents, being brought up by us in England.'

We have tea back in the drawing room and I get my first good look at Governor King. He does indeed look pale and tired and careworn, with the kind of bulbous red nose I always associate with an over-fondness for drink. He's telling Father about his successes here, and the problems he's faced. Father knows it all already, but he listens patiently, for once. King says he's cut the import of alcohol by about a third, but there are still those who make their own grog and sell it illegally, and the Corps continue to have something of a monopoly in the trade and are making huge profits. They often buy the goods brought from Europe and India from the ships that arrive in the harbour before anyone else has the chance to get a look in, and then sell them off with as much as a five hundred per cent mark-up.

The governor has also been helping the settlers with bigger land grants, and they'd been flourishing until the calamitous floods in the Hawkesbury in March. The water lay, in parts, eighteen feet deep and had swept away a huge amount of maize, wheat, barley and other crops, and drowned the livestock. Most of the farms had also been destroyed.

'People were starving and I commissioned two ships to bring rice from India and China,' King says. 'But both were lost.' He puts his head in his hands and Anna strokes his shoulder. When he looks up again, I'm sure I see a tear glint in his eye.

He recovers himself quickly, however, and goes on to say there have also been problems with the natives. In April, a group had tried to remove eleven sealers camped at Twofold Bay, three hundred miles south of Sydney, and had thrown a few spears. As a result, the sealers opened fire on the natives and killed nine, hanging their bodies from nearby trees as is the practice to strike terror into the natives to dissuade others from protesting against their presence. I can see Father frowning, and I'm secretly appalled. Spears versus muskets? And hanging their bodies from trees! How horrific!

King is still talking, saying there had also been a number of confrontations between natives and settlers along the Hawkesbury and in the Parramatta district. A stock keeper had been murdered and, although he'd said in his dying breath that it had been a white man who'd attacked him, most people thought it must have been a native. Some wheat fields had been set ablaze and a vessel on the Hawkesbury stoned. Other natives were living peaceably in the settlements, however, helping track down escaped convicts, working on settlers' farms and trapping native animals.

Father listens quietly and then abruptly switches to the subject I suspect he's been waiting to discuss. 'And what of this John Macarthur?' he asks. 'You've had trouble with him?'

At the mention of Macarthur's name, King's face changes completely. He scowls, and his eyes flash. I notice his complexion has suddenly flushed red, too, and his nose is almost glowing. 'That man!' he shouts. 'He's an absolute scoundrel! And London refuses to do anything about him! I sent him over to England after he wounded his commanding officer in a duel, but they didn't even court-martial him. What's worse, he then returned twice as rich with a new grant of some of our best land for sheep-breeding. I was surprised, in fact, that he didn't return as governor. One half of the colony already belongs to him, and it won't be long before he gets the other half. He's absolutely out of control. I warn you, watch out for him.'

Anna is now on her feet. 'Philip, dear, hush. Elizabeth . . .'

We all look over to where she's indicating—their little daughter has been ushered in by a maid and is standing by the door, waiting to be presented. Anna walks over to her, takes her hand and leads her over to us. 'Please meet our daughter, Elizabeth,' she says, and the little girl, who looks about eight, performs a careful curtsey. 'Our youngest, Mary, is asleep in the nursery,' Anna says. 'I hope her crying won't disturb you while we're still here.'

'I'm sure—' I begin, but the door opens again and we all turn around. Standing there is my John, looking so thin and gaunt that my heart leaps into my throat. His uniform looks at least two sizes too big for him. I jump to my feet and rush into his arms. I can feel his ribs through his jacket. 'John!' I gasp, looking up into his eyes. 'Are you all right?'

He smiles, and that old familiar light comes into his face. 'Yes, my dear, I'm fine,' he says. He holds me for a moment. 'Now perhaps you can introduce me to the governor and his wife?'

That night, I sleep fitfully in the unfamiliar bed but feel gloriously happy each time I wake to feel John by my side. His appearance worries me, though, and his cough sounds worse, if anything. I shall have to ask Meg to make something to cure that cough once and for all, and to build him back up. She'll know what to do.

Now that John and I are finally together again, nothing will be able to tear us apart. Just as he vowed to protect me, I won't let anything bad happen to him. Ever.

13

THE PICK OF US

Meg Hill
8 AUGUST 1806, SYDNEY

When the soldiers come, Meg is ready for them. She has her few meagre possessions tied up with her bundle of herbs and spices, she's washed and daubed a little ground hibiscus mixed with arrowroot onto her face as rouge and she's wearing the blue linen dress Mary gave her when she arrived on the *Lady Sinclair*. Meg hopes it will help distinguish her as the lady's maid to the governor's consort, and she'll be allowed to go on to Government House to join Mary and her father.

The men of the New South Wales Corps spread out across the deck, and one approaches her and looks her up and down. 'Name?' he demands.

'Meg Hill, sir,' she replies.

'And what are you doing on this ship?'

'I'm the lady's maid to the daughter of the new governor, William Bligh,' she says.

'Papers?'

She brings them out from a pocket in her gown. He looks at them and scowls. 'It says here you're a convict,' he says.

'Yes, I was ... I am ... but now I'm working for the governor and his consort.'

'So where do the papers say that?'

'Well, we've just arrived and they didn't have them ready,' she answers, hoping her words don't sound like she's been rehearsing them for the past two hours. 'They told me to meet them at Government House. They'll be waiting for me, sir.'

The soldier narrows his eyes. 'We saw them disembark hours ago,' he says. 'They didn't look like they were waiting around for your ladyship.'

Meg forces herself to smile as if amused by his words. It wouldn't do to antagonise this man who suddenly has so much power over her life.

'I was told to supervise their luggage coming off the ship, and then make my way there,' she says meekly.

'If they were so concerned, then why didn't they send a messenger with the papers?' the man snaps back. 'Nice try, girl. Now, it's a busy day. Get off and join the other convicts.'

At that, he picks up her precious bundle and tosses it over the side onto the wharf. Meg knows when she's defeated. She hurries off after it.

There's no mistaking her fellow pariahs. Blinking in the sunshine after so long in the bowels of their two ships, emaciated and dressed in what are now tattered grey rags, the two hundred and sixty men from the *Fortune* and forty-seven women from the *Alexander* are being herded separately onto the shore. Meg joins the women. Some recognise her and smile sympathetically; others look amused.

'Dumped you, did they?' asks one.

Meg bows her head, realising the cruel truth of the words. 'Yes,' she answers. 'They did.'

She didn't want to believe it would happen, but it has, and now she needs to face whatever comes next. Meg wonders if wearing the blue dress and making up her face was a mistake. At first, she had hoped to be easily singled out from the other convicts; now she wants desperately to blend in. She scans the crowd for the woman who'd been living in the officer's cabin during the voyage. She doesn't seem to be there. She's obviously fared better than Meg.

The military officers and privates are grouping the men together, and they yell at the women to stand in lines to wait. It seems they are selecting the biggest men to work for the government, doing the back-breaking work of rock-picking to clear land for agriculture, building roads, bridges and public buildings. The officers and settlers will then have their pick of the rest.

'Meg! Here!' hisses a female voice, and she looks up to see Jane, one of the women she'd treated on the *Alexander*, standing near the front in the second row. 'Come and stay by me. I'll try to look after you.'

Meg smiles gratefully and moves towards her. 'Thanks!' she whispers. 'Do you know what's happening here?'

'I'm afraid I do,' Jane replies. 'Those officers there are going to have the pick of us and, afterwards, it's the soldiers' turn.'

'What do you mean, the pick of us?' asks Meg, wide-eyed.

'Exactly that. They're going to choose the youngest, the prettiest and the strongest to work for them—either as domestics or on their farmlands—and do with us anything else they want besides.'

Meg feels sick at the thought, but Jane continues.

'And then—' she nods towards a group of men standing behind the soldiers '—it's their shot.'

'Who are they?' Meg asks.

'The settlers,' says Jane. 'They want farm workers and domestics and female company just the same. Next comes some of the ex-convicts and finally . . .'

'Finally?' Meg echoes dully.

'The ones who are left—the oldest, the crones, the ugliest, the feeblest, the lame, the pregnant—they're all sent to the work gangs or to the Female Factory.'

'How do you know all this?'

'My sister. She was transported over two years ago and managed to smuggle a letter back with one of the sailors. Mind you, I don't think she ever imagined I'd be here, too.'

Meg makes a sympathetic noise, thinks for a moment, then asks, 'And who picked her?'

'No one. She was older so she ended up at the factory,' Jane answers. 'She said it was hellish. Nothing more than a big empty room above the gaol where they had to live and work, so it was like a kind of gaol itself.'

'And what kind of work?'

'Spinning wool and flax and sewing clothes—they call them "slops"—for the convicts. But they were worked so hard, and were barely allowed out, so she managed one day to escape. She came to regret that, though.'

'Why?' Meg asks.

'She was caught and sent to one of the work gangs. That finished her. She started off rock-breaking as a punishment, then had to collect shells from the seashore to make lime for building works. When her body failed, she finally ended up on oakum duty, unpicking old ship ropes so the fibres could be used for caulking.'

'Where is she now?' Meg whispers, dreading the answer.

'I don't know,' says Jane dully. 'We didn't hear from her after that first letter. I'm hoping I might be able to find out. But, look, they've finished with the men. It's our turn. Now remember, you want to be picked by an officer. It's the least worst of all the evils.'

'But how do I do that?' Meg asks.

Jane sighs. 'You've got a good dress on so just smile and show those nice teeth of yours. Flutter your eyelashes. Do anything you can . . .'

The officers approach the lines of women. 'Step forward,' the man who looks as if he is in charge orders the first row. 'And hurry up about it. You girls stink to high heaven. What are we to do with you?' He smiles, but his eyes are cold.

He walks along the first line, prodding and poking at a few of the women with his cane. He grabs one and squeezes her breast until she yelps in pain, and he puts his cane under the hem of another's ragged dress to lift it almost to her waist. When she struggles and tries to push the cane away, he backhands her across the mouth. The woman whimpers. Her hand flies to her lips and is immediately covered in blood. Meg can sense the collective fear and hatred seeping from the assembled women, but nobody speaks.

'Now, how about you?' The officer singles out a young girl at the end of the line. The girl looks down at her feet. 'No, look at me,' he orders, grabbing her chin and lifting it roughly. 'How old are you?'

'Fifteen, sir,' she says softly.

'And tell me, can you read and write?'

'Yes, sir,' she replies.

'Right, then you're mine,' he announces. 'The rest of you, wait.'

He leads the girl off by the arm and indicates to his fellow officers that they can now take their turn. Meg notices that some hang back; maybe they already have enough help in their houses or on their land. Others jostle with each other in their haste; presumably to reach their first pick. She feels a sharp jab in her ribs and realises it's Jane. Two officers are standing in front of them, and Jane is smiling broadly at the man before her as if she's never seen anything quite so delightful. Meg looks at the officer standing too close to her and hates what she sees. He's hugely overweight and is breathing heavily, and his brow is slick with sweat. What's more, his eyes are greedy.

'What's your name?' he asks.

'Meg,' she replies, then adds, as she catches the warning look in Jane's eye, 'sir.'

'How old?' he asks.

'Eighteen, sir.'

He looks her up and down in a way that makes her blood run cold. 'You don't look too bad,' he says, and she tries not to recoil from the stench of rum on his breath.

She attempts to smile as if she doesn't feel like a lamb on its way to slaughter.

'What can you do?'

Meg hesitates. 'I can sew, sir, and I can do laundry and cook and clean and look after children and teach them to read and write and count.'

He looks pleased. 'Yes, you're coming with me,' he says as he pushes her forward by the shoulder. 'Come on, girl. We haven't got all day.'

Meg steals a look behind her to see that Jane has also been picked and is being similarly marched away. She's beaming as if she can't believe her luck. Meg, however, feels sick to her stomach with fear.

14

A HARD ACT TO FOLLOW

Mary Putland
9 AUGUST 1806, SYDNEY

The next day, Saturday, I have my first good look at Sydney town. Father, John and Mr Griffin have business to attend to, so Anna walks me through the streets, pointing out the landmarks. It doesn't take long. There's the site where the original St Philip's Church, a rudimentary wattle and daub building, once stood before it was burned down by convicts. Another stone replacement is planned for the same site, but in the meantime an old wheat store on High Street has been converted to serve as the church. Then there's the offices of the newspaper, the *Sydney Gazette*, behind Government House, a couple of mills, a bridge, a tannery, some shops, a house for the judge advocate, the site for a citadel to be named Fort Phillip on a hill overlooking the harbour, and a school for female orphans that Anna's husband set up when he first arrived. The girls live at the school and some are taught reading and writing, while others learn how to spin cotton and sew. It sounds as if Anna spends inordinate amounts of time there. I hope I won't be expected to.

'Oh, it's so rewarding,' she tells me, as if reading my mind. 'I love my time there. Without the school, I hate to think what would happen to girls here, all on their own . . .'

'Yes, of course,' I reply. 'They must love it when you visit, too.'

'I hope so. I certainly love going. I miss my eldest two children back in England so much, and I do hope they're being cared for well by the people around them. The school is my way of giving back to those who have no one.'

Anna is going to be a hard act to follow, I realise. All that work with orphans as well as looking after her children and supporting her port-soaked husband . . . I've heard she also took in his two bastards, born of a dalliance with a woman on Norfolk Island, before she married him. All in all, she seems quite saintly. I don't have a hope of competing.

Despite that, though, I do like her. In some ways, she's quite ordinary, but she has real spirit, and her dark eyes sparkle when she's amused. She seems to look at life with a readiness to be entertained and expectation to laugh, rather than simply preparing herself to be disappointed as I sometimes fear I do.

She's generous with her knowledge of the colony. Sydney town is still only one small part of it, she tells me. There's the growing settlement of Parramatta to the west, where there is a second Government House, albeit even smaller than this one; there's Hawkesbury about thirty miles to the northwest, by the river; and there's Newcastle further north up the coast. If only she had more time here, she'd love to show me around properly.

When we arrive back at Government House, John is waiting for me, his arms full of the most beautifully delicate pink flowers with blood-red centres.

'Hibiscus!' he says, presenting them to me. 'This place is apparently full of them.'

'They're gorgeous,' I say, taking them from him and breathing in deeply over the bouquet. I look up in surprise.

'Sorry, no scent,' he laughs. 'If only your Uncle Joseph were here to tell us why.' He winks at me at the shared horror of Sir Joseph ever being present to lecture us. 'But they are very pretty. They reminded me of you. I found them growing to the front of Government House.'

We all have dinner together that evening with a bewildering number of local dignitaries, although I wish I could be alone with John instead. Now he's back on dry land, his colour is gradually returning but that cough is as bad as it's ever been. Father dominates the conversation as usual, going on and on about Short again until Governor King agrees he should be stripped of the captainship of the *Porpoise*, with John put in his place. Father is not satisfied with merely that; he says Short should also be sent back to England immediately to face a court martial. I open my mouth to say something but am silenced by a look from my father. Perhaps we shouldn't go there again. King says he'll think about it. Anna just sits there, smiling. I wonder how she does it.

By Sunday, they have rushed out a special edition of the *Sydney Gazette* to announce our arrival to the general populace. I read the report to John and Father at the breakfast table. '*We are extremely happy to state that Governor King's successor is accompanied by his amiable daughter, Mrs Putland—*' I break off, mid-flight. '*Amiable*!' I repeat. 'Couldn't they have found a better description than that?'

'Get on with it, Mary,' Father scolds.

'*A circumstance*,' I continue, '*which conveys the greatest pleasure and cannot fail being attended with the most beneficial consequences.* Ha! They didn't even notice my gown!'

John laughs. 'I did, though,' he says. 'I thought you looked beautiful.'

I smile back. Father snatches the newspaper and buries his face in it. I think, frankly, we embarrass him.

We attend a church service presided over by the colony senior chaplain, the Rev Samuel Marsden, where I take a lot of satisfaction in the way people look admiringly at me and my outfit. This time, I've worn a white linen gown, tucked at the back rather than pleated, under a dark blue silk robe. My hair is caught in a modest blue bonnet, with a white ruffle around the edges. It's a dull old service, however. The Rev Marsden rants and raves and John has to nudge me when I look as if I'm dozing off. He chuckles at that but then starts coughing so hard I fear his lungs might collapse. He walks outside and I follow. It takes him a good two minutes before he can finally stop and catch his breath back again. I see the dark stain of blood on his handkerchief.

'Meg must be able to give you something,' I say to him. 'I'll ask her.' Then I stop dead in my tracks. Meg! I haven't seen her since we were preparing to disembark the *Lady Sinclair*. I'd assumed she'd been busy packing up our possessions and would catch up with us later; I'd made do with another maid from the Kings' staff in the interim. But I'd seen neither hide nor hair of her since.

'Where do you think Meg is?' I ask John.

He looks blank. 'Did you tell the officials who met the ships that she was with you?' he asks.

'No,' I reply. 'What difference would that have made?'

'All the difference in the world, probably,' he says ominously.

I'm puzzled. 'What do you mean by that? Do you think she's slunk off and escaped?'

'No, not at all, my dear,' John says, looking amused. 'There's no way that would have been allowed to happen. She was probably taken off with the other convicts and assigned to someone.'

'To someone else?' I ask indignantly.

'Yes.' John nods. 'Maybe to a soldier or a settler. She could be anywhere by now. We should head back into church. I'm fine now.'

I won't let it go so easily, however, and don't move. 'But surely they would have realised if she were aboard the *Lady Sinclair* that she was with us?'

He shakes his head. 'Not necessarily.'

'So what can we do to get her back?'

'That's going to be difficult. Surely you can pick a new lady's maid from those already at Government House?'

'No!' I say, realising at the same time how petulant I sound. 'I want Meg! She knows so much about medicine, and I think she'll be good for you . . . for us. Remember how she helped you on the voyage here?'

'But she might be happily settled in her new household,' John protests.

'I don't care,' I say. 'Please, John, *please* try to find her.' I catch hold of his arm and look up pleadingly. 'I'm sure she'd much rather live with us at Government House.'

He looks doubtful but smiles back down at me. 'All right, Mary,' he says. 'I'll do my best. I'll put the word out among the soldiers to find out where she went. I can't promise we'll find her but we can try.'

We spend the next two days preparing for Father's investiture as governor, which is due to happen on Wednesday. I don't see much of him, as he and Mr Griffin seem to always be out surveying various areas, checking on government projects or meeting some official or other. Governor King starts off escorting them everywhere but then his enthusiasm seems to peter out. I don't know whether his energy levels aren't up to it or he's just getting sick of his successor. It must be hard handing over to someone who acts as if they know better, even though they've only been here five minutes.

John often goes along as Father's soon-to-be-appointed official aide-de-camp, so I busy myself trying to get the household sorted out. My piano has survived the journey intact, thank goodness, and most of our other pieces of furniture, crockery and cutlery are gradually making their way into the house. I spend some time showing the maids how to handle my gowns, bonnets and shoes correctly so they won't get damaged. It's times like these I feel the absence of Meg even more. I suppose I didn't really appreciate how careful she was with my possessions back on board that awful ship, and I didn't recognise how much I enjoyed her company. She is a convict, of course—nothing changes that fact—but she was an ideal lady's maid. I only hope John can track her down for me.

As I wander Government House, I also think of my family back home. I hope Harriet and her child are both doing well and I wonder if Mother is missing her husband, and me. Possibly not. I write a long letter home and then enclose some feathers I collected from birds we saw during our voyage, and from the Cape. I plan to gather more from New South Wales. Already I've seen some very curious birds here—they seem to screech rather than sing. Sir Joseph would no doubt know what they are, but I find ignorance preferable to his company.

Father seems to be enjoying his time here so far. After he's installed as governor, he plans to visit the Hawkesbury where King has granted him a thousand acres of land on the river, which he's going to call Copenhagen after that damned battle. He's also been given two hundred and forty acres in the district of Petersham Hill to the west to build a house that he immediately declared will be called Camperdown, his other favourite battle, and another one hundred and five acres in Parramatta that he'll call Mount Betham after Mother's maiden name.

More excitingly, King has also given me and John a grant of six hundred acres of land at a place called St Marys near Parramatta. John immediately names it Frogmore after a town in County Kerry, Ireland. I don't know what we'll do with it yet. I suppose we could also start a farm, although I've never much liked getting my hands dirty. We'd have plenty of convicts to do the actual work, however. Or maybe, when we have children, we could actually go and live there. Who knows?

In appreciation of King's generosity with land, Father says he now plans to give Anna some land, too, after he takes over. It'll be interesting to see what she does with it since she is leaving with her husband on Friday, but I imagine she could rent it out or have it developed in her absence to provide them with an additional income they can have sent to England. The extra money will probably come in handy. I wonder if they know that Father is earning twice King's salary for the same job? I'd be outraged if I were them. But I suppose having land is a good back-up in case anyone does fall on harder times.

On Tuesday evening, while I'm getting ready for the investiture to appoint Father to the position of governor, John comes back to the house with news. He's found Meg!

'Where is she?' I ask excitedly. 'When is she coming here?'

He looks uncertain. 'Well, she's living at the house of a New South Wales Corps officer, a Henry Mackey,' John says. 'I was told of her whereabouts by one of his men, who has a friend of hers working in his household. But I don't think it's as simple as just asking her to leave and come here to us.'

'Why not?' I ask. 'She was with us first. He *stole* her from us.'

'Well, not really,' John says. 'As a convict, she's government property and he was quite within his rights to assign her to work for him.'

'Surely she'd rather work for us at Government House, for the governor's consort?' I ponder.

'I don't think her wishes come into it,' John replies.

'But *mine* should,' I insist. 'And I want her here.'

'No, Mary, no,' John says firmly. 'We can't go and take her. We're going to leave her be and you're going to find another lady's maid if you don't like any of those already at Government House. I am not going to the home of another man, especially an officer, and dragging away one of his servants.'

He pauses and looks into my eyes. He knows me too well. 'And don't think you're going to take this matter into your own hands, either,' he adds. 'I absolutely forbid you from going to that house. It's over, hear me? It's finished.'

15

SHOWING GRATITUDE

Meg Hill

13 AUGUST 1806, SYDNEY

Today is the day Captain Bligh is to be installed as the governor of New South Wales but Meg can find no cause for celebration. Every day in her new home is a torment. And every day is somehow worse than the last.

She's been living in Officer Henry Mackey's Sydney home for nearly a week now and she can't imagine how she's going to survive for much longer. Rock-breaking out in the fields on government rations of damper and mouldy salt pork would be better than this. Sewing slops in the Female Factory until her fingers bled would be preferable. She could never have expected that living in a house with an officer, his wife and two children would prove so intolerable.

It had started moderately well. Mackey took her home and introduced her to his wife, Sarah, and their sons, John, twelve, and James, ten. Meg had been instantly relieved to find he had a family. She'd been dreading that he might be a man who lived alone and had brought her home as his sex slave. A man with a family was a completely different proposition. Then he showed her the old wooden stable out the back where she could sleep. She'd heard that sometimes employers didn't provide accommodation—you'd be left to find something of your own, though God knows how you were meant to pay for it—so that was welcome, too, even though the stable was dark and damp and smelled of ripe manure.

That first evening, she'd kneeled down on the cold earth and straw and said her prayers, thanking God for small mercies. She refused to even think of what might have been, had Mary taken her off with her to Government House. She'd have to forget all about her, she reasoned. Mary had her own busy life now, in a prestigious position in the colony. Why on earth would she be bothered about a convict girl? She'd been ridiculous to have even considered it.

The next morning, Meg woke early to her first shock. She washed quickly in a pail of cold water she'd taken in with her the night before, then dressed and went to push open the door to go upstairs. It wouldn't budge. She pushed again. She bent down to look through the keyhole and saw it was blocked by a key in the other side. She'd been locked in.

It was a full hour before she heard heavy footsteps approach the door, and the clunk of a key turning. Mackey stood there in his nightshift.

'Ah, you're awake, pretty lady,' he said. 'But you're dressed. Couldn't you have waited for me?'

'What do you mean?' asked Meg, feeling a cold churning in her stomach.

'Ha! Don't play the innocent with me,' he said more sharply. 'You know what you're here for. I need you to show me how grateful you are to have a roof over your head.'

'Oh, I really am grateful, sir,' said Meg, ignoring the obvious intent of his words. 'It's very kind of you to put me up here.' She floundered for a moment, searching for anything else that might help her. 'And I do like your wife and your sons. It feels a privilege to be of help to them.'

Mackey looked confused. He advanced into the stable, and Meg saw her chance. She slipped neatly past him to the doorway and turned back. 'Thank you, sir, and I'll go and help Cook prepare the breakfasts now before I start on my duties.' Then she ran to the cook's outhouse as fast as her feet could carry her.

The cook was already there, stoking the fire, when Meg entered. She took one look at Meg's flushed face and asked, 'How did you go with big bad Henry? I think you're just his type.'

Meg shook her head. 'I left him out in the stable and it was as much as I could do not to lock the door behind me,' she said.

Cook roared with laughter. 'That would serve him right,' she replied. 'I think he may have found his match with you. The others weren't as spirited.'

'So he's done this before?' Meg asked.

'Oh yes,' Cook responded. 'Every time a ship of female convicts arrives, our Henry is down at the docks taking his pick and bringing one back. But most don't put up much of a fight.'

'But what about his wife, his children . . . ?'

'I think the mistress is used to him now and she puts up with it. Her sons are a handful so if Henry can get his rations, so to speak, elsewhere, then she's willing to turn a blind eye. I don't really blame her, do you? Being mauled by that fat hulk wouldn't be much fun.'

'No . . .' said Meg. 'But it wouldn't be much fun for me, either, especially as he locked me in.'

'That's true,' Cook nodded. 'He maintains the household is safer with convicts under lock and key to stop their thieving ways. But really, it's all about him wanting to be in control. You'll have to find a way to outwit him.'

'How did the other girls manage?'

'They didn't.'

Mackey left early that first morning for the barracks and for the rest of the day Meg tried to think of a plan. Sarah was distant but not unkind, while the boys were a joy to be around. Meg did some of the laundry and cleaned the rooms and took care of a big basket of mending that had been left out for her. As dusk drew in, she was sent to the shop to buy meat.

On her return, Sarah was waiting for her. 'Tomorrow it would be good to take the boys through their writing,' she said. 'I've been told you can read and write well.'

'Yes, ma'am,' Meg said. 'I will enjoy that.'

Mackey came home late that night, when Meg was already in the stable. She had taken the precaution of barricading herself in with some old broken furniture that she had dragged over to the door. She heard the key turn and then loud drunken swearing when Mackey discovered his way in was barred. The next morning she stayed still until she heard him trying again, pounding angrily on the door. When he walked away, defeated, she pulled away the furniture and raced off to the main house to the safety of company.

She knew she couldn't continue like that forever, though. It would become harder and harder to avoid her master, and Mackey would lose patience very soon. Who knew if he would turn violent and take her by force? She needed to come up with a cleverer ploy.

That afternoon, when the boys were taking a break from their lessons and playing ball outside, she crept over to the stable and took out her bundle of herbs and her Culpeper's almanac. Liquorice and chasteberry, she read, were both plants that could suppress sexual desire. Legend had it, she remembered being told by her mother, that monks in the Middle Ages used it to help them diminish their desires. And flicking through the pages, she recalled that chamomile could be potent in promoting sleep. She mixed careful proportions of the three powders, adding in a little more chasteberry for luck. Then she went to see Cook in the kitchen.

'When you're making soup this evening, could you drop a small spoonful of this into the master's bowl and mix it in?' Meg asked her.

Cook looked amused. 'And what will it do?' she asked.

'I think it might help to keep me safe,' Meg said.

'Will it hurt him?'

'Sadly, no,' Meg said. 'It should just make him a little sleepy.'

That night, there was no attempt to open her door and when Meg awoke the next morning, she was pleased to discover she hadn't even been locked in overnight. She dressed hastily and went up to the kitchen to find Cook smiling broadly.

'Well, aren't you a little miracle-maker?' she said. 'The master fell asleep over his mutton stew. Almost went face-first into it, I'd say. The mistress was most concerned and packed him off to bed, thinking he'd been taken ill.'

'Is he all right?' asked Meg.

'I'd say he'll be fine,' Cook replied. 'He's still in bed now, but he's snoring away. You'll have to make your potion a little weaker in future.'

Meg reduced the quantity of chamomile for the next two evenings' meals but she remained on edge. Every time Mackey passed her in the house when his children and wife weren't in the same room, he'd make a grab for her breasts or her buttocks and try to rub himself up against her. She increased the amount of chasteberry in the mixture, but it didn't seem to make any difference.

He saw her as his possession, she realised, and the more she resisted, the more he was enjoying the chase. But by the Tuesday, she could see his temper was fraying. He was becoming more daring, putting his big dinner plate of a hand down her front and squeezing painfully hard even when Sarah was in the same room with her back turned. 'I'll come to you tonight,' he hissed into her ear. 'So you'd better be ready—or else.'

Cook agreed to put the potion into his meal one last time but she was becoming nervous the master and his wife might start suspecting something was amiss and then she and Meg would both be at risk of being turfed out onto the streets.

'I couldn't cope with that life at my age,' Cook said. 'If you can't find work, there's precious little else you can do to earn money than go with men like Henry.'

Meg pulled a face. 'But surely there are lots of families who'd want a good cook? Or someone good with children and cleaning and laundry?'

'There are plenty,' Cook replied. 'But most of them can't afford it. And those who can . . . they'd always ask the people you were with before what you were like. It wouldn't help me to say my master took ill after my meals . . .'

'So there aren't any other ways to make money?' Meg asked.

'Well, apart from working, the only way people survive is through stealing and cheating, often both.'

Meg sighed. She really didn't want to take that route.

'I heard about one woman who made a good living on the streets with her husband. They'd do buttock and twang.'

'Buttock and *what*?' Meg repeated.

'Ha!' Cook snorted. 'The woman would lift her dress and lure a man into a dark side alley, then bend over to show him her arse . . .' She started laughing so hard she had a coughing fit. Meg handed her a cup of water. 'Thanks, love,' Cook said. 'So then, just as his trousers were around his ankles, her husband would come up behind him and hit him over the head and take all his money.'

Meg gasped. 'Goodness!' she said. 'I don't think I could do that.'

'No, me neither,' Cook replied. 'But you'll have to come up with something safer if you want to keep Henry out of your drawers. This is the last time for me.'

On Wednesday morning, the day of Captain Bligh's instalment, Meg is in a state of nervous agitation. She knows Mackey is putting on his dress uniform and the rest of the family are in their best outfits, so they should all be out of the house for a few hours. She wonders if she can take the chance to slip out. But it seems as though Mackey has read her mind.

'You. Get here!' he orders her, in front of his wife and children. 'Now out into the stable while we're away.' He frogmarches her outside, putting both hands on her breasts when he's out of sight of his family, and then knees her in the back as they reach the doorway, sending her flying through the air and landing heavily, flat on her face on the floor.

'I'll see to you later,' he says, his voice thick with menace, and he slams the door shut and turns the key.

Meg lies there quietly, feeling the cool of the earth on her skin, utterly drained of hope. She puts a hand to her forehead and flinches; she can feel a lump already forming. This time, she knows she's been beaten and is overwhelmed by a sense of dread. She will have to submit to whatever he's planning for her and learn to live with it—and him. Going to the gallows in London, surely, would have been far preferable to this.

Suddenly, from towards the front door of the house comes a loud, insistent knocking. She hears someone open the door and a soft rumble of voices drifts from the house to the stable, gradually growing louder. It sounds like someone is calling her name. She can make out Mackey's and Sarah's voices, and they sound angry, as if they're arguing about something. But two other voices are being raised to match them. The new voices are strangely familiar, but Meg can't place them.

And then, with a start, she realises: it's Mary and John.

16

THE COMMISSION

Mary Putland
13 AUGUST 1806, SYDNEY

When I marched out of Government House after telling John I couldn't stand by and not put up a fight for Meg, I didn't quite know how he'd react. He'd been adamant about me not going, but I think he knows me well enough by now to realise I have something of a wilful streak. I hate myself for saying it, but in some ways I'm more like my father than I care to admit. When someone tells me I can't do something, it's often like a red rag to a bull.

We only had two hours before Father's investiture and we were both dressed in our finery, but I sang out to him as I went through the door that I was going to call in on this man Henry Mackey to have a chat with him about Meg. If he could no longer imagine life without her help, and she was very happily settled, then I would leave them be. But I wanted to see Meg's new situation for myself.

As I strode down the street, I felt a rush of nerves. But I took a few deep breaths and pushed the flutter of worry firmly down. I would be civil to him and I was sure he would be civil back. After all, he'd know exactly who I was, and I reasoned it wouldn't make sense for him to upset someone of such standing in Sydney. As I knocked politely on the door that I'd asked Anna to point out for me the day before, I fought the desire to turn and run. And by the time it was opened by a big bear of a man, who was obviously part-way through dressing judging by his loose shirt sleeves and britches, I had steeled myself.

'Good morning, sir,' I said brightly.

He looked me up and down, plainly puzzled to see me on his stoop.

'Good morning, ma'am,' he said, and gave a little bow. 'What can I do for you?'

'I've come . . . I've come . . . to see Meg,' I said.

He looked mystified again.

'Your new maid,' I explained. Well, he obviously wasn't so attached to her if he didn't even remember her name.

'Ah, yes, the maid,' he repeated. 'What of her?'

'Well, you might not know this, but she was my maid on the ship over—for me and my father, the new governor, William Bligh,' I explained, realising he didn't recognise me and thinking it wouldn't do any harm to pull a little rank.

'And . . . ?' he asked.

'And . . .' For a moment I couldn't think of what to say. Then I shrugged. The truth is often simplest. 'I would very much like her back.'

At that, he smiled, but not in a friendly way. More in a 'I wonder what I can get out of this' way. 'Right, you would, would you?' he asked. 'And what about me? I've taken good care of her, I have. I've given her a place to stay, and food off my table and my wife and I have trained her and taught her how to look after us.'

'Yes, I don't doubt it,' I said, although, from his unkempt appearance, I honestly did. 'But I wonder if I could see her?'

A voice came from inside the house. 'Henry! Who is it?'

The man turned his head, 'It's that Bligh girl,' he called back, and a woman moved into view. She caught sight of me and stopped dead in her tracks.

'Good morning,' I said politely. 'I was just asking your husband here if I could see Meg.'

'Why?' she asked.

I tried to hide my irritation and turned back to Mackey. 'Where is she?' I then had an idea. 'Meg!' I called into the house. '*MEG!*'

Mackey folded his arms. 'She won't come,' he said with a smirk.

'Why not?'

'Because she can't,' he replied.

'*Can't?* Why? What's wrong with her?'

'Nothing,' he said. 'But she's locked in.'

'Locked in?' I repeated stupidly. 'Locked in what?'

'The stable,' he said.

I looked at him coolly. So, this is what he meant by looking after her? 'Can I see her now?' I asked.

Mackey gave a tight little half-smile. 'No, I don't think she'd like that,' he said, puffing up his chest and blocking the doorway. 'But thank you for your concern. I'll tell her you called.'

Another voice suddenly spoke up behind me. 'You'll do more than that,' it said. 'Now make way for the lady. She asked you nicely if she could see Meg. And I think it's best that you do as she asks.'

I turned round. John! He'd come after all! At that moment, I doubted I had ever loved anyone more. Although he was still far too thin, he looked so tall and regal in his full naval dress uniform, and also very determined. Mackey stared back at John and obviously came to the same conclusion. He shrugged his shoulders.

'All right, all right,' he mumbled, pulling out a ring of keys from his pocket. 'Come round here.'

He walked past us out of the front door and round the back of the house. There stood a rickety old stable that stank to high heaven. He put a key into the door, turned it and then swung it wide open. The smell made me feel faint, but I stepped forward. 'Meg?' I called into the darkness. 'Meg? Are you there?'

'Mistress?' a voice quavered back. 'Mistress Mary?' There was a rustling of straw and I could just make out a pale figure limping towards me. As she came into the light, I was shocked by her appearance. She had blood on her face and what looked like a lump on her forehead with the eye under it swollen almost shut. She looked muddy and bedraggled.

'Come along, Meg,' I said with a sharpness to my voice that I instantly regretted. 'You're coming back with us now. Get your things, and we'll be off.'

Meg looked at us open-mouthed. At me, then at John, then at Mackey. At that point, I saw something in her face I'd never seen before and couldn't think what it was. And then I realised: it was fear.

Then she swayed on the spot and John stepped forward and caught her just as she fell. I walked into the stable behind her and spotted the bundle of rags in which she kept her herbs. I grabbed that, but there seemed precious little else there.

'Now, let's be off,' I said, as John continued to hold a very confused-looking Meg upright.

'But you can't . . .' Mackey blustered.

'Just watch us,' I said.

The commission making Father the fourth official governor of New South Wales is read at noon in front of an assembly of dignitaries, with crowds of Sydney locals standing behind. You can see the hope in their eyes. They're currently on half rations because of the floods destroying their crops and animals and it's clear they're hoping a new governor will bring fresh luck—and perhaps a more generous attitude from Britain—to the colony. And, of course, they'll be praying Father demonstrates a tougher hand with the New South Wales Corps, whose officers have apparently been making the shortages worse by using their rum to buy any grain or stock that lands on the waterfront, then hoarding it to push up the price further still and only then selling it back to the poor settlers.

Meg had wanted to come to the ceremony, but John insisted she stay at Government House to rest. She does look very weak and has lost a fair few pounds in weight since we saw her last. That ghastly man probably never fed her either.

'You can start your duties tomorrow,' I told her.

'Or the next day,' John said quickly.

Anna stands alongside me as Father makes his speech, and then we listen to the fifteen-gun salutes from the ships in the harbour and the New South Wales Corps' marching band playing rousing tunes. John is now, officially, his aide-de-camp and also—which comes as a surprise to me—a magistrate. I wonder if John knew that was going to happen. Father then receives a formal welcome from three men. Representing the military is the commanding officer of the New South Wales Corps, Major George Johnston, a tall, slender man with ruddy cheeks and curly fair hair; for the civilian officers is florid-faced Judge Advocate Richard Atkins, dressed in too tight a shirt and with his trousers straining over a big belly; and, finally, John Macarthur welcomes Father on behalf of the settlers. There's a ripple of noise through the crowd when Macarthur stands to speak. I look at Anna quizzically.

'They're annoyed that he says he's representing the settlers,' she whispers. 'They think one of them should have been selected for the welcome. After all, he's only a settler by default, really. He came out as an army man . . .'

I nod and take my first curious look at this man I've heard so much about. He has a handsomely chiselled jawbone, a long aquiline nose and a high forehead that, together, make him look quite aristocratic, although I know he is most definitely not. His dark hair is swept off his face, and he carries himself with a very upright, haughty bearing. His whole appearance screams of unchecked arrogance.

'Mary, I have a favour to ask you,' Anna says softly as the speeches end, and I reluctantly tear my eyes away from Macarthur.

'Yes, Anna?' I wonder what's coming. I know Father bequested her a grant of land yesterday in return for all the land her husband

gave us, which she immediately called 'Thanks'—a very Anna honor-
ific!—and I wonder if she wants me to keep an eye on it. 'I'd be
happy to help,' I say. 'Anything!'

'That's wonderful!' she says, grasping her hands together. 'I worry
about all the orphans I'll be leaving, and I want you to take over as
patron in my place. I will feel so much better knowing that you'll
be involved in their welfare.'

I look at her, aghast, but I know I can't refuse. I was too quick
with that word *anything*. She's now looking at me with those wide
puppy dog eyes, so full of hope for all those mucky little orphans.
I do my best to smile. 'Of course,' I say through gritted teeth.

'Oh, thank you, Mary!' she exclaims. 'I was going to ask one
of the other officer's wives if you were to say no, but I'm so happy
you've agreed.'

I keep that smile glued to my face, too nervous of what it might
reveal to let it drop.

Later that afternoon, Governor King and Anna board the HMS
Buffalo where they will stay for a few days before they set sail back
to England. King is walking incredibly stiffly, leaning very heavily
on Anna with every step.

'Is he drunk?' I whisper to John.

'No,' he answers. 'Apparently it's gout. It's playing havoc with
his knees and making it hard for him to walk.'

Even if he can't get up and about, at least he'll have company
on board. Short was put on the ship yesterday, along with his wife,
their children and all their possessions. King had eventually given in
to Father's demand that Short have his six-hundred-acre land grant
cancelled, and that he be forced to return to England as soon as

possible to face a court martial. King is simply no match for Father when he's on his high horse about something, and there's nothing that excites his wrath and cruelty like that poor captain.

I feel for the Shorts, I really do. They have only just been through that terrible sea voyage and now they're facing it again. I wondered at first whether Mrs Short would rather stay here with the children and her new baby, but how would she earn a living? She probably had no choice. The last time I saw her in the Cape, she looked utterly worn out. I hope she has recovered her health a little in preparation for the trial-by-ocean to come.

By the time John and I return to Government House, it's getting late and the light is failing fast. It's so unlike England, where the twilight gradually darkens and deepens. Here, it seems one moment it is light; the next it is pitch black. I don't know if I will ever get used to it.

When we enter Government House, there's a warm glow about the place. Meg is up and about and has lit the lamps in preparation for our return. It looks as if she has been busy in other ways, too. The main room looks much cleaner and more orderly than when we left. There's no way the other servants have excelled in their duties. They seem perfectly content to do the absolute minimum—the Kings' legacy for us.

'Meg! You should still be in bed!' John says when he sees her bustling about. 'How are you feeling? Better, I hope.'

'Yes, much better, sir,' she replies, curtseying to us both, and I notice that the lump on her forehead has gone down to a graze haloed by a violet bruise. 'I wanted to say thank you for coming to fetch me. I'm very grateful.'

'We are very happy to have found you,' John says. 'Aren't we, Mary?'

'Yes,' I say, clearing my throat. Meg is still a convict and a servant, after all, and I wouldn't want her to think that she has any kind of hold over us that she could take advantage of. There's a short silence and I realise they're both waiting for me to say something more—presumably to effuse how glad I am that she is back with us, or to ask how she fared with that ghastly man and his family—but I resist.

'Now, I wonder if you have anything more you can give John for his cough?' I ask her. 'He is no better and, if anything, the cough is worse.'

'Of course,' she says, hurrying away towards the servants' quarters. 'I'll be back shortly.'

John looks at me. 'Mary, do you have to be quite so . . . harsh?' he asks. 'I know how soft you can be under that brittle exterior. Why not show it to others, besides me? After all, it was you who insisted on rescuing her and you were quite prepared to go alone to do so. I can't imagine any other woman having the courage to confront an army officer and demand he hand over his servant!'

'The hide, you mean,' I say, feeling pleased. Then I shrug. 'Father brought me up to never show weakness.'

John shakes his head with a wry smile as we walk towards our quarters. I take his hand in mine. 'Sorry,' I say, 'it's a hard habit to break. But I will try . . .'

Father is heading off to look around the Hawkesbury for the next two days. He wants to inspect his new land grant and see for himself the havoc that was wreaked when the river broke its banks. He says he doesn't need John to come, so we take the opportunity to spend time together at home. Meg has made John a warming potion and some foul-smelling herbal medicine for his chest, and already he seems to be coughing less. I'm thrilled.

We take the carriage out for a picnic on a grassy knoll by the water east of the town. On the way, we see some natives with skin so black they look almost blue, dressed in what look like settlers' old cast-offs and smoking clay pipes. We wave to them, but they don't wave back.

'They always look so fearful and resentful of us,' I remark to John. He says nothing.

There's another hibiscus bush by our picnic spot, with large yellow flowers this time. We gather some for Meg to decorate the dining room and our bedroom.

My father returns all too soon. The good news, however, is that he's in an excellent mood. He corners me in the dining room as soon as he walks across the threshold. The locals were tremendously welcoming of him, he says, and are keen for a good new governor to fix the colony's problems. It helped, I thought to myself, that he immediately announced he would be providing extra rations to help them overcome some of their difficulties. It's easy to win a man's heart if you first fill his stomach.

I listen to Father talk, wondering where John is and whether he'll soon turn up and rescue me. But when he does finally appear, his face is grim. King collapsed aboard the *Buffalo* and a doctor had to be called. He has been carried off the ship and into lodgings, and it seems he's too ill for the voyage to England just yet.

'Will he be all right?' Father asks John.

'Yes, I think so,' John replies. 'He had more colour in his cheeks later this afternoon, and Anna is tending to him carefully. He may, however, have to remain here for a few weeks yet . . .'

Father has already moved on. 'But what about Short?' he asks. 'If the ship doesn't leave, he won't be leaving either.'

'That's right,' John says evenly. 'He and his family have also taken lodgings until the picture becomes clearer.'

'I will be writing to London about that,' Father says, and John and I exchange a look. 'And I will take that opportunity to let them know my ideas about the colony. I plan to commission a series of comprehensive reports about everything happening here: the agriculture, the granting of land, the public buildings and the general state of the colony.'

John nods his head politely and I wonder if he is really interested or if he's merely showing good manners. But Father is only just warming up, it seems.

'And I want a report on the most pressing issue here,' he continues. 'The trade in rum. I want to know who in the New South Wales Corps is running it and how much profit they're making. I'd like to bring them into line once and for all. They may have broken King, and Governor Hunter before him, but they will have more than met their match in me.'

17

A VICTIM OF FASHION

Meg Hill
15 DECEMBER 1806, SYDNEY

When the parcel arrives, Meg is surprised it doesn't contain gold bars for all the excitement it's causing Mary. At first, she thinks it must be because it will bring news from home, and everyone wants that. But inside the brown paper package, fresh off the latest ship to arrive in the port, is a new dress that, according to Mary, is the very latest fashion in London. She is simply beside herself.

'Help me try it on!' she instructs Meg. 'It's beautiful!'

Mary holds up a silvery blue diaphanous gown that, below the waist, is almost transparent. It's made of a flimsy, gauzy material, yet it is completely unlined.

'They must have made a mistake with this one,' Meg says, shaking her head. 'No one could possibly wear a gown like this.'

Mary laughs delightedly. 'Yes, this is the newest fashion,' she says. 'And look—' she pulls out another little pile of the same fabric '—these are the pantaloons that go underneath it.'

'But . . . it's not decent, mistress,' Meg protests. 'No one could go out in public in this.'

'Don't be ridiculous, Meg,' Mary rebukes her sharply. 'Of course they can, and they do. In London, I imagine the streets are full of society women parading this new look, and isn't it exciting that I'm bringing such high fashion to the far outposts of the British empire?'

'Yes, mistress,' Meg replies obediently, but she is far from enthusiastic. Mary already has a wardrobe full of perfectly good gowns in her bedroom; dresses far more substantial, and indeed prettier, than this diaphanous one. But then, what does Meg know? She only has one good blue linen dress and a second that Mary gave her—in lieu of throwing it out, Meg suspects—and she feels that's more than enough for any sensible woman.

But Mary is thrilled by the dress her mother has sent over, along with three pairs of silk stockings, six pairs of gloves, four pairs of shoes and some new sheet music. She only stops examining her new trove of treasures for a moment to read the letter that accompanied them. Apparently, her sister Harriet has had a healthy baby girl, Elizabeth Catherine, and everyone is missing them and looking forward to receiving further letters about how everything is working out in New South Wales. Mary then hands the letter to another servant to give to her father and turns her attention back to the blue dress. She slips it over her head and pulls it down past her knees, asking Meg to fasten it at the back. Then she pulls up the pantaloons and stands in front of the mirror to admire herself.

'It's gorgeous!' she breathes, her cheeks pink. 'Look at the colour, it goes so well with my eyes.'

'Yes, it does,' Meg replies. 'But it's still a bit see-through.'

'Nonsense!' Mary snaps. 'I'm just standing in the light here. Outside, you won't be able to see anything. And if, by chance, you can glimpse anything, you'll only see the pantaloons. You're so unfashionable, Meg. You have no idea.'

That's something Meg is happy to concede. She has heard Mary's father rebuking his daughter for her 'obsession' with fashion and, secretly, she agrees with him. It seems bizarre to set so much store by a few pieces of material that are only there, really, to cover your body and keep you warm and decent. But when she voices that view, Mary only scoffs.

'No, no, Meg, you have no idea,' she scolds her. 'Fashion is . . . everything. It can define you, and you it. The right outfit can influence your mood and improve your posture and confidence. If I dress a certain way, it's a message to the outside world about who I am, my standing in society, and how I expect to be treated.'

Meg knows that's a well-rehearsed argument. She's seen Mary trying to persuade her father that her love of fashion doesn't make her any less intelligent or serious than those who pay no heed to clothing trends—men, in particular. Instead, Mary argued, it makes her a more well-rounded person, receptive to the many subtle clues about people, their personalities and their intentions that their clothing provides.

Her father, however, laughed in a derisory way. 'Come now, you are merely drawn to fripperies like ribbons and bows and pretty colours,' he mocked. 'Don't try to persuade me it's for any other reason.'

Of course, Meg knows that Mary is very much inclined towards ribbons and bows and pastel hues in particular, but she's sympathetic with her mistress's stand that this inclination should neither define her, nor brand her as shallow and superficial. 'So it's all right for you to strut around in a uniform decorated with gold braid and silver buttons?' Mary asked her father once when Meg was also in the room. 'What's the difference?'

She saw his brow furrow and she waited, knowing he hated feeling as if someone was making fun of him. 'There's a world of difference,' he replied, his voice sharp with irritation. 'A uniform shows others who I am, and my braids and buttons, as you put it, indicate my rank and my importance in relation to theirs, or their lack thereof.'

'Aha!' Mary exclaimed. 'And the cut of my gown, my hair, and my jewellery do exactly the same. Anyone who looks at me can instantly tell where I am in the order of things. They might not even realise at the time, but they're absorbing the signals.'

'So, they can tell how much money you're wasting on such trivial items?' her father asked disdainfully.

'If you want to put it that way,' she replied. 'They know I have money and that I can spend it as I wish. By the same token, if I wore old-fashioned gowns of inferior taste or quality, then they'd know I didn't have money to "waste" as you put it.'

He looked thoughtful.

Meg hoped that might be the end of it but Mary, encouraged by his silence, continued, 'It's also an expression of my individuality,' she said. 'People can see who I am by my choice of what to wear and when. And it's important, with you in such a pre-eminent position in the colony, that my appearance matches your status.'

'I think you should try harder to match my status in other ways, Mary,' he then barbed. 'Like by reading those reports on New South Wales, which I commissioned, to find out what's happening here, and spending more time at the orphanage. At least then you could offer me more intelligent, informed conversation, and you'd look far more serious about helping.'

Meg could see Mary's eyes burning with tears. Her father had a way of slighting her that never failed to cut her to the quick. She'd once confided to Meg that her mother was equally entranced by fashion and was just as concerned about her appearance, but her father never criticised her for that. Instead, he praised her sophistication and complimented her at every turn. Of course, as Mary commented sourly to Meg later, it didn't hurt that her elegance and position in society were key to making him the success he had become.

Whenever Meg sees Mary being criticised by the governor, she feels for her mistress. She can see how upset she gets, even though she tries hard not to show it, and, equally, she can see how frustrated Governor Bligh becomes, while it never seems to occur to him not to voice his views. He is a man after all, Meg concedes, and one who expects to be obeyed. She'd heard the talk about the *Bounty* mutineers and wonders if it led to any period of self-reflection and, perhaps, humility for Governor Bligh. But if it did, that has all but dissipated since he became the most powerful man this side of the oceans.

Both father and daughter are as stubborn as the other, and neither is prepared to give an inch. When Meg tries to thank Mary for saving her from Henry Mackey's grasp, for instance, her mistress simply waves her away and says she doesn't want to hear any more about it. But Meg knows she does care; John had told her how she marched out of Government House, determined to whisk her back. Some of that, of course, was because she wants Meg's help with her husband's health—especially as the doctor he went to see said not much could be done—but Meg also knows that Mary likes having her around.

Mary does treat her fairly, if curtly, and Governor Bligh is perfectly polite and respectful towards her. But, most of all, Meg likes John. Poor John. She's doing her very best to help him, but he doesn't seem to be improving, and she holds grave fears for his future. Sometimes, when she's presenting him with a new medication to try, or a fresh rub for his chest, she glimpses a fleeting look in his eye that tells her he knows it probably won't help. But that's a confidence she won't break.

She's getting to know Sydney town rather better, too. The streets are twisting and narrow and muddy but she finds it endlessly fascinating to see where they lead her each time. She loves wandering around the docks, where there are ships constantly arriving and departing for all kinds of exotic faraway places. Sometimes, the sight of them helps quell her homesickness, and one day she imagines getting on board and sailing back to her mother and family.

It's not far to walk to the green hills around the town and some of the fine houses on higher ground with the views down to the tangle of town and the blue of the harbour. She loves exploring but always does so cautiously, with her bonnet pulled down low over her forehead, so she won't be so easily recognised. She's constantly worried that she'll bump into Henry Mackey down some dark alley, where he'll pounce and she'll be unable to escape. He haunts her dreams at night, too, looming up out of the shadows to put one fat hand over her mouth to stop her screaming for help and using the other to wrench her dress up over her head. Frequently she wakes to find her cheeks wet with tears.

The Kings have gone to stay at Government House in Parramatta until the former governor is well enough to travel back to England, and Meg has accompanied Mary there a few times. She loves the barge trip down the river, watching the grime of Sydney gradually give way to the green hills of the west, and the tangles of bush and tall, stately gum trees, the sweet clouds of jasmine and colourful bursts of native hydrangea. Despite the eighteen-year age gap between them, Meg can tell Mary is fond of Anna, and Meg likes her, too. Mary always seems much kinder when Anna is around.

Christmas comes and goes, feeling little like the Christmases Meg knows from home. The weather here in Sydney is scorching hot and unbearably humid, and mosquitoes bother everyone incessantly. At Government House, they have a formal Christmas party and invite all the dignitaries from the colony, and Mary plays the perfect hostess, as she's undoubtedly seen her mother do so many times before.

Meg marvels at how well Mary fills this role. She smiles and greets everyone by name and makes them feel, for a moment, as if they have all her attention. If her mother is this skilful in social situations, Meg muses, then it's little wonder that her husband is in charge of such an important part of the world.

One day when she's out shopping, Meg hears a woman's voice call her name. She turns to see Jane, her fellow convict who'd been similarly assigned to another of the New South Wales Corps' officers. The two women are delighted to see each other and quickly exchange news. Jane tuts when she hears what Meg went through with her master and congratulates her on making it back to Mrs Putland's side. Jane has fallen on her feet with her own assignment, thankfully, and her new master and his wife turned out to be firm but fair.

'But he doesn't much care for our new governor,' Jane tells Meg. 'He says he's arrogant and short-sighted and just doesn't understand how life works here.'

Meg nods. 'Yes, that's all true,' she says. 'But he is trying his best to change things for the better.'

'He should be careful, though,' Jane warns. 'He's making a lot of enemies.'

Jane's warning isn't new information. Meg has made some good friends among the other staff at Government House and, whenever anyone of any importance in the colony comes visiting, she'll often talk to their maid, manservant or coachman. In this way, she picks up various titbits of gossip and news from around town. Sometimes, she'll share them with Mary. Other times, she keeps her own counsel.

From all her conversations, she's quickly learning how adept Governor Bligh is at making enemies, and not even his daughter's charm during dinner parties can dissipate their rancour. He has now had a few meetings with John Macarthur, and Mary had been hopeful they might find some common ground, since they both grew up in Plymouth. But towards the end of one appointment, as Meg was about to enter the study to replenish their port, she was shocked to hear raised voices. She hesitated for a few seconds, during which time their heated conversation quickly developed into a fully-fledged shouting match over the rum provisions and the governor's plans to limit the trade.

Two days later, Meg was told by someone in his household that Mr Macarthur's wife, Elizabeth, had written a letter describing the two men's clash from her husband's point of view, saying that Governor Bligh had *already shown the inhabitants of Sydney that he is violent, rash, tyrannical. No pleasing prospect at the beginning of his reign.* It doesn't augur well.

The governor does seem to be much more popular in the Hawkesbury region, however. He likes the way they farm their small plots and sees that as the future of the colony, rather than those, like Macarthur, running huge tracts of land for their sheep. He's promised the ruined farmers supplies from the government stores, as well as a donation of one bushel of wheat from every ten produced elsewhere, in return for the government paying a fixed price and grinding the grain free of charge. Meg hears talk in the town that, in opposition to the murmurs of criticism from some Sydney locals, those from the Hawkesbury won't hear a word against him. For the moment, anyway.

It appears Governor Bligh has bought more land in the Hawkesbury area and installed the former convict Andrew Thompson as his overseer, saying he plans to create an experimental farm there to demonstrate how good farming practices can prove profitable in the colony. That's all very well, but Meg has been told Thompson has already annoyed a lot of the real farmers by employing between twenty and thirty of the Crown's convicts to construct one thousand pounds' worth of buildings, taking items from the public stores to do so, and borrowing animals just about to give birth to stock the place, and then returning only the mothers afterwards.

'My master asks how on earth he can present such a farm as a proper experiment?' Meg was told by one of the farmer's servants who was visiting the town. 'We can't obtain equipment or haven't nearly so much access to free labour! And yet Governor Bligh, already on a fine salary from the British Government, can take everything for himself without paying for it.'

Meg can understand the farmers' frustrations. She mentions it to Mary, but Mary says she's sure her father will more than pay the money back to the Crown out of the farm's returns. She doesn't seem to think it's a matter of much concern and, on one visit, plants an oak tree by the farmhouse.

Back in town, Governor Bligh is always keen to keep up appearances and, that Sunday, he insists they all attend St Philip's Church together in a show of family unity. He wears his full dress uniform and asks John to do the same, while Mary sees it as the perfect opportunity to debut her gauzy blue gown. Meg dresses in her newer second-hand frock.

They arrive early in their carriage and take seats in the front pew. They keep their heads bowed over their prayer books as the soldiers and the locals file in behind them. When the reverend tells them to stand to sing a hymn, however, a titter runs through the congregation which quickly grows into loud guffaws. Meg is the first to turn to see what is causing so much mirth. To her horror, she realises it's Mary's dress. In the harsh Sydney sunlight shafting in through the high windows, the material is completely transparent and everyone behind them in the church has a wonderful view of her lacy pantaloons.

For a split second, Meg doesn't know what to do. She whispers hastily to Mary that she should sit down.

'What?' asks Mary, bewildered. 'Why?'

'Please, mistress, *please*,' Meg hisses. 'Just sit down.'

Mary stares back at her, mystified, then glances around at the people behind them. She sees them laughing into their hands, their eyes all fixed on her legs. She looks down and suddenly sees what they see.

At that, all colour drains from her face. 'Mary! Are you all right?' Meg asks, alarmed, putting an arm around her shoulders.

'No . . .' Mary mumbles back. 'No . . . no . . .'

And at that, she faints clean away.

18

FRIENDS AND ENEMIES

Mary Putland

6 FEBRUARY 1807, SYDNEY

I have never been so embarrassed in my life. I'm mortified. I don't remember much after listening to all those fools in the church laughing—and then realising they were laughing at me. Apparently, I fainted from the shock and horror of it all and had to be carried back to the carriage by John and Father.

In the privacy of our vehicle, John does his best to mollify me, as I weep hot tears from the shame of it all. Father fumes. Then he leaps back out, saying he's going to teach those damned mongrels a lesson they won't forget.

'No, Father,' I call after him. 'Let it be. You'll only make it worse.'

I don't know if he even hears me. It makes absolutely no difference.

Meg has the presence of mind to follow him but, from the safety of the carriage, I can hear him calling together the Corps officers outside the church, berating them soundly and demanding an explanation. One of them denies the soldiers were laughing at me; he insists a soldier found a feather on the floor and stuck it playfully into someone else's cap. Their denials only serve to rile Father even more. He says the feather would have had to be stuck somewhere a great deal more inappropriate to cause such mirth. Further, he says that behaviour like that, coupled with such a ridiculous explanation, is an insult to the office of governor and he will be taking the matter further.

As he continues to rant outside, I turn to John. 'Please, can we go?' I beg him, my face burning. 'Father and Meg can make their own way back. I just want to get out of here.'

John nods sympathetically and orders the coachman to make haste back to Government House. As soon as we arrive, I take to my bed. I decide to remain there forever so I don't have to face any of those idiots again.

The next morning, when Meg comes to rouse me, I bury my face in the pillow and tell her to get out. I can still hear her moving around my room, however, and so finally I sit up.

'Come on, mistress. You can't stay here all day,' she says. 'I think you have to get up and put what happened behind you.'

'How can I?' I moan. 'Those men . . . those animals . . .'

'You must forget it,' she insists. 'I'll put a lining in the dress so that the next time you wear it, it will be perfectly respectable.'

I can't help smiling. Sometimes Meg really can be wise beyond her years.

But I still spend the next few days at home, licking my wounds. I pass away the hours practising my piano and playing on my lute, which always reminds me of home, and, when I'm sure there's no one around I sing in accompaniment. I've been told I have a good singing voice, but I've always been shy of singing in public. I write another letter back to my family in England. I thank Mother for the dress—'*It is very elegant . . . altogether different and superior to anything of this kind that had been seen in this country*'—but say nothing of the embarrassment it has caused me. I've been collecting shells down at the sandy shores of Woolloomooloo to send to her, adding to her extensive collection, and I write that I hope some of them will be new to her. I then parcel them up to send with the next ship, along with a couple of my sketches of the colony and of Government House, so they'll have a better idea of how we're living.

I wander the gardens of the Domain around the house, drawing more sketches of how I would like to see it look as a more fitting setting for our seat of government. I think it could be made bigger with a path all the way around. Father glances at my blueprints to humour me, I think, but he's not really interested. He has far greater concerns on his mind and now, because of me, his enmity towards the New South Wales Corps has only deepened. If I mention the pantaloon incident to Father he scowls and becomes angry all over again. He's still trying to find out which soldiers laughed the hardest, so he can punish them.

I have managed to make a few friends, and during my cloistered weeks after the church mishap I spend a bit more time with them, too. Anna King is probably the woman I'm closest to. Although she is so much older than me, she has been in the equivalent position and knows exactly what its challenges are. I've visited the Kings in Parramatta a few times during their sojourn there, and she drops in on me from time to time at Government House. She happens to visit three days after the church misadventure and, when I tell her all about it, to my surprise she breaks into peals of laughter.

'It really wasn't at all funny,' I rebuke her. 'It was horrible.'

She struggles to bring herself back under control. 'Oh, I'm so sorry, dear,' she says. 'But pantaloons! Those soldiers must have thought themselves in heaven to have had their prayers interrupted so.'

At that, I can't help smiling. 'Well, I suppose it would have been one of the last things they were expecting to see in church,' I muse. 'But I was terribly embarrassed when I realised what was happening.'

'Mark my words, you'll be very popular with those soldiers when you next encounter them,' Anna says mischievously. 'I think you'll be surprised by how gallantly they treat you.'

'They certainly won't be getting another look,' I say, 'however gallantly they behave.'

Anna laughs again, and I feel a warmth towards her that I could never have expected when we first arrived off the *Lady Sinclair*.

But Anna's not going to be here for much longer, I remember with a jolt. She says her husband is much better now, so they've been making fresh plans to depart for England on the *Buffalo* on 10 February. Her departure, I know, will be a great loss to me.

One fellow *Buffalo* passenger who won't be any kind of loss, however, is the Rev Samuel Marsden, who's returning home to see his family. I'm not overly fond of him. In the pulpit, he's all bluster and swagger, and out of it, he's . . . much the same. His wife, Elizabeth, is as quiet as a church mouse, but I think she has little choice, being married to him. Father has a different view—King told him that Marsden, who seems to be far more enthusiastic about rearing his sheep than saving souls, is the best practical farmer in the colony, and Father is keen to learn more from him. Personally, I think the chaplain should be more concerned about his human flocks than his woolly ones. But in Marsden's absence, we will be making do with a new chaplain, the Rev Henry Fulton. He has been stationed on Norfolk Island where he was transported, apparently, for being sympathetic to the Irish rebellion, but has since been pardoned by King. I've met him once already, and he has a completely different style of preaching to Marsden. Although he's a couple of years older, he seems twenty years younger in both his bearing and his attitudes, so he seems almost the same age as me, in fact. With a shock of floppy black hair that he's always pushing off his face, he has startling blue eyes that you feel can see right into your soul and a beautiful Irish lilt to his voice, like John's. Yet he seems completely unaware of his powerful physical presence; he's quiet with a mild, kindly manner, and I liked him from the moment we were introduced.

My father and I have other friends around the colony now, too. I like the judge advocate's wife, Elizabeth Atkins, who's also originally from Ireland, and is sweet and considerate towards me. In fact, she's sweet and considerate to everyone, really, which I think may well be her downfall. Her husband, Richard Atkins, is ghastly, and I am sure the only reason a lot of people put up with him is because of her. He is a terrible drunk and wafts around in a stink of rum, and he is a shocking braggart. He's always going on about his 'connections', who usually turn out to be his three brothers, who are all wildly more successful than him, and his alleged 'great friend', the judge advocate of London, Samuel Thornton. I would wager that Mr Thornton hasn't even heard of him. It's said that Atkins isn't even his real name; he took it on in recognition of an English baronet who left him some money in his will. Meg tells me that he's held in contempt by many of the servants in his household for being a womaniser and someone who does everything he can to wriggle out of paying his debts. And apparently he has little clue about the workings of the law, even though he's our chief legal officer. If he were to behave like this in England, he'd be out on his ear. But it seems he can get away with anything here. Or perhaps there's simply no one to replace him?

John Macarthur's wife seems like a very interesting woman and one I'd like to get to know a little better. That's tricky, however. With Father and her husband crossing swords so often, it might not be so wise to try to cultivate a friendship. I've decided I'd better steer clear of that.

Father is becoming increasingly fond of Andrew Thompson, the manager of his model farm in the Hawkesbury, whom he views as the model pardoned convict. Indeed, Thompson is impressive. He's been the Chief Constable of the area for some time now and, during the floods, he won the undying devotion of the Hawkesbury populace for his many daring rescues. He's now become the grower of a huge amount of grain and, some say, one of the wealthiest people in the colony.

We spend some evenings in the company of Robert Campbell, his brother-in-law, John Palmer, and their wives. Mr Campbell is a well-built Scot with distinguished silver streaks in his red hair, who lived for a period in India as an agent for the East India Company and who now runs one of the biggest companies in New South Wales, importing goods and livestock through Calcutta. Father sees him as something of an ally in his mission to smash the Corps' monopoly on incoming cargoes, someone who can help him establish alternative shipping links.

'Aye, that's critical,' Mr Campbell tells Father the first time he comes to Government House for dinner. 'Free trade is most important for this colony to be able to take care of itself. You don't want characters like Macarthur controlling the supply of livestock and drink. That way lies disaster.'

Father smiles. 'But I hear you yourself got into trouble once with Governor King, accused of bringing in an excessive quantity of spirits,' he says good-naturedly. There's a moment of silence and I fear that could be another potential friend lost. But then Mr Campbell throws his head back and roars with laughter.

'Ye cannae separate a Scotsman from his drink, true enough,' he guffaws.

Father looks pleased to have amused him so. Later, he tells me that Mr Campbell will be a valuable asset. 'He's a very successful merchant who has become very wealthy from his enterprises but, at the same time, he has a reputation for being very fair and honest in all his dealings,' he says. 'We need more men like him.'

Father also likes Mr Campbell's brother-in-law, John Palmer, even though you couldn't find two men more physically different. Mr Palmer is a dapper Englishman, as pale as wheat and almost as slim, but always astonishingly neat and tidy. He is probably about ten years older, and came over with Captain Phillip on the First Fleet as its purser, and now lives on his land grant, Woolloomooloo Farm. He is the Commissary General, responsible for the colony's supplies, as well as a magistrate. I've met him a few times as he's on the committee of the orphanage, and Father has lots in common with him, having both served at sea. 'Little Jack', as he's known, is good company and a kind man—he apparently sold bread from his bakery very cheaply to those affected by the floods in 1806— and over time he's becoming a trusted friend to us. His American wife, Susan, tends to mother me a little, which I can't say I don't enjoy. With Anna leaving Sydney, I hope Susan will take her place as a confidante.

We all turn out to wave the former governor and Anna off, with the customary salutes and volleys of gunfire. King looks tired and sick of all the fuss. He shakes hands solemnly with Father, hands him an envelope which he tells him contains a letter of information about the natives, wishes him luck, then limps onto the boat with as much haste, it seems, as he can muster. Anna and I embrace one final time.

'Look after yourself, my dear,' she says, 'and that precious husband of yours. I will think of you often and maybe one day I will be back to visit.'

'I do hope so,' I reply, and am surprised to feel tears streaming down my face. 'Please do write with news of the voyage and your safe arrival. And I will make sure to visit you when Father's term finishes.'

'I will both write and look forward enormously to the next time we meet.' She smiles. 'In the meantime . . .'

'Yes?'

'Please do take care of my orphans.'

'Yes, I will,' I pledge as graciously as I can.

I see her glance over my shoulder with a pained expression and I turn around to see what has attracted her attention. Captain Short and his wife and their six children are trudging together towards the ship, their heads bowed. I'd hoped Father's attitude towards him might have softened in the interim, but to no avail. My father could hold a grudge for England. He is still insisting that Short leave, and it appears his wife and children are determined not to stay on in New South Wales without him. Short boards the ship and ushers on his family, studiously avoiding meeting our eyes. I'm not sure I can ever forgive Father for such stubborn inhumanity.

Back at Government House, Father tears open King's letter. 'What does it say?' I ask him.

'It's King's thoughts on the natives,' he replies. He reads silently, then looks up again. 'It's very interesting. He sent a couple of very well-known natives to Norfolk Island in 1804 after some trouble and says that quietened all the natives here down.'

'Why would that be?' I ask, genuinely curious.

'Well, he says here that a lot of people in the colony have talked about making the natives slaves, but he's never had any time for that way of thinking. Listen to this line: *As I have ever considered them the real proprietors of the soil, I have never suffered any restraint whatever on these lines, or suffered any injury to be done to their persons or property. And I should apprehend the best mode of punishment that could be inflicted on them would be expatriating them to some of the other settlements . . .'*

'So he doesn't agree with hindering their movements or countenance any attacks on them?' I ask slowly. 'And he thinks sending those two away was the worst punishment possible.'

'Yes, it sounds as if he thinks so,' Father replies. 'Fascinating, though, that he sees them as the real proprietors of the soil. That isn't a view shared by many of the settlers.'

I nod. It was a thought that put the colony in a completely different light. Even during our short time here, I was all too aware of how fiercely the settlers defended what they felt was their land, protecting their farms and businesses against native raids. Settler farmers would often react with violence out of all proportion, and I could never forget the story about those sealers at Twofold Bay. To think of that land as really belonging to the natives . . .

But Father has already moved on. He puts the letter to one side, switching his focus to what he sees as New South Wales' major problem: the Corps' liquor business. He wants to make a move against it as soon as possible. I urge him to introduce any reform slowly, to talk to Major Johnston and Mr Macarthur first, and somehow try to get them on board with his ideas. But, of course, he never listens to me.

When Mr Macarthur makes an appointment with Mr Griffin to see Father, I'm hopeful they can talk out their differences. But Father immediately goes on the offensive. Instead of calmly explaining what he's trying to achieve, he instead raises Mr Macarthur's latest application for more land for his livestock. Father leaves him in little doubt about what he thinks of its merits.

'What have I to do with your sheep, sir?' Father asks in a voice loud enough that we ladies can hear him in the drawing room. 'What have I to do with your cattle? No, I have heard of your concerns, sir, you have five thousand acres of land in the finest situation in the country but, by God, you shan't keep it.'

'But what about your land grants?' Mr Macarthur thunders back. 'What have you done to deserve those? What are you contributing to the colony?'

I gasp. Meg had told me there was already some anger in town about the grants given to us by King, and Father's grant to Anna, as it was known that all large land grants made by governors had to be approved by England first. That hadn't been done by either man. What's more, I knew they hadn't been recorded, either. That knowledge could be dangerous in someone like Mr Macarthur's hands.

Meg is sitting beside me in the drawing room, and I see her turn pale to hear such fierce words. 'Don't worry,' I tell her, although I know I'm trembling. 'They're just men. It's just words. They'll come to an agreement, I'm sure.'

Two days later on 14 February, Father announces, with much pomp and ceremony, his first major reform. He makes an order which prohibits absolutely the exchange of spirits or other liquors as payment for grain, animal food, labour, clothes or any other commodity whatsoever. What's more, there will be severe penalties for anyone breaking this regulation. A settler can be fined fifty pounds, a former convict can be imprisoned for three months and fined twenty pounds, and a convict will receive one hundred lashes and hard labour for a year.

I'm shocked at both the harshness of the punishments and the fact that Father is introducing the new orders so soon after his argument with Mr Macarthur. Meg tells me both men's words are being repeated everywhere in the colony, with much hilarity. Mr Macarthur has never been terribly popular, but suddenly he seems to be held in higher regard by both officers and settlers alike for standing up to the 'Bounty Bastard'. Meg says she's heard the New South Wales Corps officers make up to two hundred per cent profit on all imported spirits, while some of the wealthiest settlers are also taking a handsome share of the spoils, and neither group wants to be deprived of such a substantial source of income.

I suggest to Father that perhaps he should signal that these changes will be implemented in due course, so everyone has a little time to adjust to them first.

'When I want your advice, Mary, I'll ask for it,' he replies curtly. 'Until then, I suggest you pay more attention to the things that should concern you, like entertaining our guests at Government House, playing your music and making sure your dress is halfway bloody decent.'

19

A WORD THAT CANNOT BE SPOKEN

Meg Hill
12 JUNE 1807, SYDNEY

Meg is dressing Mary in preparation for a dinner party at Government House that evening and, as she is tugging a soft white kid glove up to Mary's elbow, her mistress grabs her hand.

'Meg, I need to ask you something,' Mary says, with real urgency in her voice. She sits down on a cushioned seat, finishes pulling up the glove herself, and pats the space next to her.

'What is it, mistress?'

'I . . . I need to talk to you about John.'

'Yes?' Meg replies, sitting down, although she suspects she knows full well what is coming.

'Are you honestly seeing any improvement in his condition?' Mary asks, with an almost pleading note in her voice. 'I know you have been giving him various potions to help with that dreadful cough, but every time I think he's getting better, he seems to relapse again. He's coughing up so much blood now and has terrible night sweats.'

'The surgeon Dr John Harris has been treating him, too,' Meg says. 'Have you spoken to him?'

Mary shakes her head. 'He only tells me what he thinks I want to hear,' she replies. 'He says we have to be patient. John has had this bad chest for a good while now, so it will take just as long for him to get over it. But I don't see any progress . . .' She pulls out a handkerchief and now Meg can see how red her eyes are.

'Oh, mistress,' Meg says, 'Dr Harris is right. We have to wait a while to see how John responds to our medications.'

'But it's been so long already,' Mary says, 'that I'm beginning to lose hope.'

Meg wonders if she should put an arm around her, then decides she'd better not; she doesn't know how Mary might react. Her mistress, she's well aware, doesn't like to show vulnerability and can be awfully prickly at the best of times.

'Don't lose hope,' Meg says instead. 'I haven't, and Dr Harris hasn't, and John hasn't, so neither should you. Have you talked to John?'

'Yes, I have,' Mary replies, tears now beginning to course down her face. 'But he also tells me not to worry, and that he'll be fine. But I can't help . . .'

Meg throws caution to the wind and puts her arm around her mistress. 'Come on,' she says. 'We have to stay brave for his sake. And we're all praying for him.'

She can feel Mary's shoulders shaking as she gives into her fear, and neither woman pulls away. They sit like that for a good few minutes, drawing comfort from each other.

Then Mary rises to her feet. 'Goodness, this will never do!' she exclaims. 'We have a motley collection of people for dinner tonight, including that awful Mr Macarthur who's causing so much trouble for Father. It will never do to let him see I've been crying, in case— God forbid!—he thinks he's been the cause of it.' She picks up her shawl from the back of a chair, puts it lightly around her shoulders and then turns back to Meg. 'Thank you,' she says. 'And please don't tell anyone of this.'

Meg watches her leave the room, then starts tidying the mess Mary has left behind. When she told Mary not to worry, she'd meant it, but she didn't necessarily mean that there was nothing to worry about. John has just been on a voyage to Norfolk Island after being made captain of the *Porpoise* in Short's absence, and everyone had hoped that being back at sea might help to revive him. Instead, he returned home even paler and sicker than when he'd left.

Usually, when Meg was administering anything she could find that she thought might help, as well as some liniment she'd prepared specially to be rubbed on his back and chest, John fell quiet. On one occasion after his return from Norfolk Island, however, he'd started talking to Meg about Mary.

'If anything happens to me, I'd love it if you could continue to look after Mary,' he said.

Meg tried to hush him. 'Nothing's going to happen to you,' she replied.

John smiled. 'I appreciate the sentiment but I think we both know that's probably not true. I think it's fairly obvious what I have. And there's no coming back from it.'

'But, sir—' Meg started.

'There's no buts about it,' John continued. 'Everyone's tiptoeing around me, but I'm no fool.'

'No, sir, you're definitely not that.' Meg smiled. She'd always had a soft spot for John. She'd never forget the respect he invariably showed her, from the moment she was a lowly convict plucked from the awful conditions on the *Alexander*.

'Tell me, Meg, do you think Mary knows?'

'I think she may suspect, but she doesn't want to say the word,' she replied. 'No one does.'

'I can understand that,' John said with a shrug. 'Even Dr Harris has never mentioned the possibility of consumption to me. But, of course, in my heart of hearts I know that it's a distinct possibility. And if the worst comes, I do worry about how Mary will cope here. She can't confide in her father, and with Anna King now gone, she doesn't really have many women friends here. She's much softer than she seems to be on the surface, Meg.'

'Yes, I know,' Meg said. 'Hopefully, you won't be going anywhere but, if anything does happen, you have my word that I will look after her.'

The night of the dinner party, Mary has been gone for a good few minutes before Meg slowly makes her way down towards the dining room. All the servants have been aflutter with the news that Mr and Mrs Macarthur are coming to dinner, along with the Atkins and the Campbells.

Tensions with Mr Macarthur have hit a new high. Two stills for making alcohol were seized off one of his ships coming from England, and Governor Bligh confiscated them and ordered their return. Mr Macarthur had also been in court over the value of a promissory note for wheat he'd been given by the governor's Hawkesbury farm manager Andrew Thompson. Mr Macarthur argued that the note was for a fixed quantity of wheat, but the court ruled it was for the value of the wheat instead and, with the price of wheat soaring due to the floods, he was therefore entitled to far fewer bushels than he claimed. He has already signalled his intention to appeal the decision, but the governor will be the one sitting in the court of appeal.

Meg knows Mary persuaded her father to invite the Macarthurs to dinner in the hope of dispelling some of the friction, but Governor Bligh also asked the loathsome judge advocate Atkins to be there to add some gravitas, as well as the Campbells to provide their support. Sometimes Meg doubts the governor's political acumen. She likes Mr Campbell and his hearty Scottish humour, but is he really the appropriate choice of dinner guest with the Macarthurs? While Mr Campbell is now a magistrate and, effectively, Colonial Treasurer, Bligh has also recently appointed him Naval Officer . . . so he will be the one to retrieve any spirit stills that are illegally imported by Mr Macarthur.

When Meg goes in to help serve the potato soup, boiled chicken, roast mutton with stewed celery, and the saffron rice pudding for dessert—wheat is far too expensive for cake—she notices Mr Macarthur sitting in his seat sullenly, saying little. Mr Campbell is doing his best to jolly along conversation, recounting the time two years prior when he and his family had sailed to England with a cargo of seal oil and fur skins, and his ship was seized in London for illegal entry. Mrs Macarthur laughs and compliments him on his enterprise, but she receives no help at all from her husband.

In the kitchen, their coachman tells Meg that Mr Macarthur had been complaining all the way from Parramatta about having to come to dinner. 'Mark my words,' he says, 'there's trouble ahead.'

It doesn't take long to arrive, either. A few weeks later, Governor Bligh dismisses Mr Macarthur's appeal about the wheat without even giving him the chance to state his case, then announces he has started looking into the legalities of some of the leases of land around Government House. He tells six people to vacate their homes and pull them down as he's satisfied they're not entitled to be there. All too predictably, Mr Macarthur is one of those who has a lease challenged, this time on Church Hill where he'd just been erecting a fence. Bligh orders him to tear it down.

Mary tells Meg she fears Mr Macarthur may be intent on causing trouble for her father, and Meg can't help but agree. Of late, difficulties seem to have been coming at them from a number of other directions, too.

At the orphanage, the lovely master and matron Anna had liked so much had decided to move closer to their daughter and her new husband to the west, and it was proving difficult to find a married couple to replace them. The governor suggested the Rev Thomas Newsham and his wife, who'd been on the *Alexander* in our convoy from Britain. He'd been sentenced to seven years' transportation but no one seemed to know what for, and his wife had been one of the few to accompany their convict husbands to New South Wales.

Meg had never liked Newsham, but she could never quite put her finger on why. It was something to do with the way he had looked at the younger female convicts on board, and she felt uneasy whenever she was in his company. She mentioned it to Mary, but her mistress needed a couple to put in the orphanage and they were the only candidates. Besides, her father had given them his blessing. The pair were duly installed and were there for seven months until, in October, rumours started circulating about Newsham's scandalous behaviour with the girls. It came as a terrible shock to everyone to hear the report from one of the orphanage's committee members, John Harris. 'Master of the school, preached in the afternoon on Sundays and took unwarranted liberties with the girls on Mondays,' he said.

The couple were immediately dismissed and Newsham was sentenced to two hundred lashes and then to stand in the pillory three times in the town centre where, tied to a wooden frame, he could be insulted, kicked, spat on and pelted with vegetables, rotten eggs or even excrement by the local populace. After that, he was sent to Newcastle for a punishment of hard labour, while Governor Bligh wrote to England to ask for a suitable couple to be sent over to take charge of the orphanage.

Meg finds herself comforting Mary again, who is distraught that such a thing took place on her watch. She vows to take a closer interest in the running of the orphanage.

'I just can't believe what that awful man did,' Mary says to Meg, her voice breaking with emotion. 'I'm so sorry, Meg. You did warn me, but I didn't listen. And to think of those poor girls . . . everyone in their lives had let them down, and now we've failed them too—the people who should have been protecting them.'

'Don't take it so hard, mistress,' Meg replies, although she did feel aggrieved at the time that she hadn't been listened to. 'I didn't know for sure. No one did. How could we?'

'But we owed it to those girls,' Mary says, shaking her head so vigorously Meg can feel some of the tears dripping from her mistress's eyes landing on her own skin. 'It would never have happened if Anna were still here. But now I'm going to make it my mission to visit much more often and talk to the girls about their lives here and listen to see if they have any complaints. Something like this must never be allowed to happen again.'

Mary also works hard at being a good hostess at Government House. In August, she comes up with the idea of illuminating the building to celebrate the birthday of the Prince of Wales. The glow is so bright, it can be seen for miles around. But while visitors congratulate Mary on the brilliance of her vision, Meg hears from their servants that they are privately questioning the cost, wondering if it's seemly to put on such a lavish spectacle.

It's at that point, though, that both women suddenly have a major distraction: a sharp decline in John's health. He takes to his bed and spends most of his time sleeping. When he's awake, he has just enough strength to talk, or to listen to Mary reading to him.

Mary again pleads with Meg for her prognosis. This time, Meg doesn't hold back. 'I'm so sorry, mistress,' Meg starts as she watches the colour bleed from Mary's face. 'Yes, I think now it is bad news.'

Mary's hand flies to her mouth. 'Is it . . . is it . . . ?' she whispers.

'Yes, I think he has consumption,' Meg finally utters the word. It hangs there in the space between them, sucking all the air from the room, just as it's been stealing the air from poor John's lungs.

Eventually, Mary rouses herself, and Meg can see her eyes are wet. 'I appreciate you telling me,' she says. 'You are the only one who has told me the truth. Every time I've brought up the subject with John or Dr Harris or even Father, they've said there is nothing seriously wrong. I will forever be in your debt.'

Meg hangs her head. She can't stop the tears, either. 'Mistress, it's also true that we have no idea how long this may take. It may take weeks, it may take months, so I think we need to make him as comfortable as possible in the time he has left.'

'Yes.' Mary breathes out and nods. 'We'll do everything we can for him.'

It feels as if a dark cloud has descended on the household. Everyone speaks in hushed voices and is careful to walk around without making a sound. One day, Meg brings a letter from Anna King to Mary, hopeful it may contain good news.

Mary reads it aloud to John and Meg but halts a few paragraphs in and takes a deep breath. She's started, so she can't stop now. On 10 April, she reads in a much shakier voice, Mrs Short died on board their ship, near the Cape.

Apparently, Mrs Short had previously requested that, if she were to die, her body be preserved—and the only way the sailors were able to accede to her wishes was to take out her entrails, put them in a small case and toss them overboard, and then place her body in a cask of pickles. '*It was dreadful,*' wrote Anna. '*Had she reflected before her death what was necessary to be done for the safety of all our healths, I am sure, poor soul, she would much rather have consented to a watery grave. Should it please God to take my life on the sea, I shall not care what becomes of my body provided it all goes together—but to be mangled (as poor soul she was done) is enough to frighten any Christian from consenting to be served so. Poor Captain Short is left with six children to bemoan the loss of his dear wife, and their youngest is only twelve months old.'*

'Oh no, that poor man,' says Mary.

'And that poor woman,' adds Meg.

They fall into silence, broken only by John's laboured breathing.

'I'm sorry I brought you this letter at this time,' Meg whispers. 'I was hoping it would be good news that might cheer us all up.'

'How could you possibly have known?' Mary replies. 'How could any of us have known? Although . . . I did wonder about her health, but Father refused to see reason. I would imagine Short, at his court martial hearing in England, will have even more reason to blacken Father's name, and I can't say I will blame him.'

There is much less entertaining and far fewer guests visiting Government House since Mr Macarthur publicly announced he wouldn't visit again. He reasons that he doesn't believe the governor is treating him fairly, and the head of the Corps, Major Johnston, is also refusing to have any dealings with Governor Bligh, saying he's been interfering in the Corps and swearing at his soldiers.

Mary decides to write to her mother to tell her of everything that has been going wrong in New South Wales, and to inform her about John's ill health. She writes that her father is *'dreadfully harassed by business and the troublesome set of people he has to deal with'*, while John *'has been constantly ailing and has had every symptom of consumption'*. She looks at the words on the page, and then adds a line. She can't help it. *'But is now, I trust in God, gradually recovering.'* Somehow, it makes John's state feel much less real. She adds the letter to the governor's dispatches for the next ship to leave for England.

Her father also pens his own letter to his mentor, Sir Joseph Banks. He is much more matter-of-fact. '*My daughter and her husband have been a most inestimable treasure to me but alas we are now in great distress,*' he writes, '*expecting his dissolution each day from consumption.*'

20

AN ORDER

Mary Putland
15 NOVEMBER 1807, SYDNEY

My dear sweet darling John. What a cruel, cruel world we live in. As I sit here each day, watching his beautiful sleeping face, I reflect on what might have been.

We were so happy on our wedding day, full of plans for our future, dreams of our happy home in Ireland, echoing with the laughter of children and warmed by our love for each other. Later, we talked of setting up on our new estate here, at Frogmore, to start our family. Now none of that is to be. None of it.

Instead, I can only sit here, unable to do anything to help him I simply watch him, helplessly, as he slowly wastes away. I haven't slept in my own bed for weeks now, preferring to sleep in a chair at his bedside, where I can wake if he stirs. Do I blame New South Wales for his terrible illness? Do I blame my father? I'm trying not to, but some days I can't avoid it. If John had stayed in Britain, without that terrible six-month voyage, would he ever have grown so sick?

I wrest my mind back to the present, away from those pointless if-onlys. I sit here most of the day now, dabbing a cool cloth on his burning forehead and hoping against hope for a sign, a stirring, a murmur, a little colour in his cheeks that might indicate a miracle—that he is to be saved. Meg sits with me when she can, and I find her quiet presence soothing. Dr Harris also comes some days, but I quickly become impatient with him. I still resent the fact he would not tell me it was consumption; I could have made the most of the time John had left before he took to his bed. Mr Griffin calls in briefly and, despite what Harriet once said about his affection for me, he seems so genuinely distressed that I can't help warming to him. Other days, our delightful deputy chaplain the Rev Henry Fulton comes and is quiet and respectful. We often pray together over John.

'You're very fortunate to have known such a great love,' the Rev Fulton says when he drops by late one afternoon and can clearly see I've been weeping. 'And John is equally fortunate to have found that with you. Obviously we're all very much hoping John can be saved, but if the Lord in His infinite wisdom chooses to take him from us, you must always remember John as you once knew him, and bask in the warmth of that love you both shared. No one can ever take that from you.'

I nod through my tears. Strangely, I find that enormously comforting.

Father comes up, from time to time, to check on the patient. His mind is on other things, though, I can tell. Usually, he spends only a few minutes inquiring about John before he brings up the subject he really wants to talk about. And that's mostly Mr Macarthur.

I try to look interested.

'We've discovered that the convict we've been looking for, John Hoare, managed to escape from Sydney by hiding aboard the schooner *Parramatta*, which was bound for the Pacific,' he says. 'And guess who owns the *Parramatta*?'

I look at the flush on his face and I know there's only one possible answer. 'Macarthur?'

'Exactly!' Father exclaims. 'And who is one of its two bondsmen?'

'Macarthur?' I recite, tiredly.

'Yes!' he says in triumph. 'So the bond is forfeited, and he's appealing against that, of course. But you'll never guess what the blighter did next?'

I say nothing, but he carries on regardless. 'He told the crew he'd abandoned the ship and wasn't going to pay them, so they came onshore and filed an affidavit against him. So now I've told Atkins to summon Macarthur to answer their accusations against him.'

His words somehow get through to me. 'Do you think that's wise?' I ask. 'Do you really want to antagonise him further?'

'Blast him!' Father replies, and I glance nervously at John to make sure he hasn't been woken. Father looks from me to John and then leaves. I think it's just as well.

But the next day, when I'm sitting in companionable silence with Meg, Father comes again to John's bedside, and he looks as if he's bursting with excitement. My heart sinks.

'What's happened now?' I ask, knowing that's exactly what he wants to hear.

'Macarthur refused to answer the summons.' There's a note of victory in his voice that makes me feel distinctly uneasy. 'So now Atkins has issued an arrest warrant.'

'For Macarthur?' I ask, alarmed. This is elevating their enmity to a whole new level.

Father grins, almost maniacally. 'Yes, for Macarthur. What do you think he'll do now?'

I look at him icily. I am sitting with my dying twenty-six-year-old husband, set to be a widow at just twenty-four, and he's asking me what I think about a petty squabble he has fabricated with an equally over-bearing, blustering bully?

'Father,' I say, 'please leave me be. Can't you see this is a difficult time?'

He looks confused, but Meg, bless her, springs to her feet, takes his arm and steers him out of the room. I can hear her apologising on my behalf, telling him that I'm overwrought and really shouldn't be troubled with such matters. I'm inordinately grateful.

But it seems I simply can't avoid fuss and nonsense. I hear from Meg that Macarthur was finally brought before a bench of magistrates, including both Atkins and Johnston, and has been committed for trial, to be heard on 25 January 1808. He has been released on bail, but I have a terrible feeling about it all. Macarthur seems intent on causing as much mischief as he can and is now saying he cannot be tried by Atkins because the judge advocate has owed him money for the past fourteen years. Until that debt is discharged, he says Atkins has no right to be on the bench for his trial. Meg tells me she is not surprised by his allegation; Atkins' servants once told her he has many debts that he fails, routinely, to honour. I've always found him such a drunk that I have some sympathy for Macarthur. I wouldn't like to be tried by him for anything, either.

Our second Christmas in New South Wales is a dour affair. John is visibly fading away and surely can't go on for much longer. His breath is raspy and uneven, and his bouts of consciousness are now shorter and shorter. One afternoon, he opens his eyes and looks as if he's struggling to sit up. Meg races over and we each hold him under an arm and manoeuvre him upright. It's horrifying how insubstantial he is now, and how his bones protrude from his pale skin.

'What is it, my darling?' I ask him. 'What do you want?'

He takes a breath and then looks from me to Meg and back again.

Meg immediately says, 'I should leave you both now,' and she moves to withdraw from the room.

But John becomes agitated. 'No, stay,' he wheezes in a voice so soft I have to bend in close to hear him. 'I want to say something.'

We sit back down on either side of his bed, and I hold both his hands in mine. 'Mary, Mary,' he whispers, 'you are so precious to me.'

I feel tears burning my eyes already. 'And you to me,' I say.

'But you have to promise me something. When I die—'

'No, no,' I begin, and he puts a finger to my lips.

'When I die . . . I want you to remarry.'

My tears are flowing fast now. I shake my head. 'I could never . . .' I murmur.

'Yes, you could,' John says. 'And you will. I want you to be happy, dear Mary.'

'But . . . but . . .'

With what looks like a huge effort, he shakes his head. 'That's not a request, my love.' He smiles. 'It's an order. And Meg . . . I want you to make sure it's carried out.'

At that, we both laugh, although mine quickly turns into a sob. 'Oh John, please don't go,' I beg him. 'Don't leave me.' I feel him squeeze my hand, and then he lies back on the pillow as though exhausted. I lay my head in his lap and weep at the misery and unfairness of it all.

That evening, I tell Father about John's words, but he seems to be only half-listening.

'I've always liked John,' he says distractedly. 'A very smart fellow. And why shouldn't you remarry? You're still young.'

At that point, I have to leave the room.

We receive a letter back from Mother in England. It's not good news from there, either. Short has been facing his court martial and has taken the opportunity to make plenty of accusations against Father, including that he is unreasonable, temperamental, foul-mouthed and corrupt. The fact that his poor wife died on the way back to England has won him a great deal of sympathy. It's all playing straight into the hands of the friends of the *Bounty* mutineers who are all still doing their best, even in Father's absence, to vilify him. Apparently, they're now agitating for Father to be recalled and replaced by a military man, General Francis Grose, instead of a naval one.

'That'd be the friends of Macarthur in London scheming!' rages Father as we read the letter together. 'That damned long pelt of a bitch! I'll show him who's in charge.'

I let him rant on.

Macarthur has been busy while I've been preoccupied with John. He's now written to Father twice to ask him about Atkins' debt and to say it cancels out the judge advocate's right to try him. He also had some of his soldier friends construct a fence around the piece of land by the church that Father says he has no right to. Father has ordered that the fence be taken down again.

On the afternoon of 4 January 1808, all that shrinks into insignificance. Our world, for a moment, stands still. As Meg and I sit by John's side, he takes one long wheezing breath, shudders and then lies still. I scream and fling myself onto his bed. Meg puts one hand on my back and, with the other, closes his eyes.

We were just three and a half weeks shy of our third wedding anniversary, and I know I will never be happy again.

21

SUMMONS FOR TREASON

Meg Hill
5 JANUARY 1808, SYDNEY

It's hard for Meg to console Mary over the loss of John given she herself feels so distressed by his passing, but she tries. She sits with the sobbing widow for hours at a time, wondering how one body can generate so many tears, and occasionally she cries with her. But she knows her place and realises there's work to be done, and Meg is the person on whom that responsibility falls.

She finds Mary's black gown in her trunk and hangs it up to air. Mary had refused to take it out, even when John looked to be on the verge of death, so as not to jinx his chances of God smiling down and granting him a reprieve. Meg could understand that completely. But now she talks to her mistress gently about the need to hold the service and burial as quickly as possible. In this climate, and in the middle of summer, it's an absolute necessity.

That seems to rouse Mary, and the pair go to talk to her father. He says a full military funeral should be held at St Philip's, and then John's body could be laid to rest in the mausoleum he has been building near the church. Together with the appropriately named Nicholas Divine, the Superintendent of Convicts, Governor Bligh has designed the mausoleum for the families of all governors, now and in the future. Mary says it looks very much like their family mausoleum back in Lambeth but, while it's not yet finished, it is close enough to completion to accommodate John.

Mary shakes her head. She doesn't want John left behind when her father's term as governor finishes in 1811—or later if the British Government asks him to stay on—but suggests his body could be laid temporarily in the vault until it is time for them all to return to Britain. At that point, he could be taken out and brought back with them on their ship to be buried in his beloved Ireland, with his family present.

She has already discussed this with Meg, and the two women agreed that it is what John would have wanted, although they still shuddered to recall the state in which poor Mrs Short's body was sent back to England.

'No, Father,' Mary says firmly. 'John will be coming home with us. But he can stay there while we're still in Sydney. I need him to be in a spot where I can visit him whenever I want to and bring him flowers and sit by him. We pledged to look after each other in New South Wales and, although I can now do that only in death, it's still very important to me.'

The governor nods his head solemnly. He can hear the note of strident determination in his daughter's voice and, for once, has absolutely no inclination to argue.

So, three days after John's death, on 7 January 1808, his grieving widow, his father-in-law and Meg find themselves back in the church where Mary had experienced such embarrassment, by John's side, less than a year before. Meg glances at Mary, wondering if she's remembering that day, and comparing it now to today's solemn occasion. In her heavy dark formal gown, there's absolutely no chance of sunlight piercing her modesty this time.

John's coffin sits at the front of the church beneath a naval flag, while Major Johnston and all the officers of the New South Wales Corps, along with every naval officer in Sydney, stand in their dress uniforms with their heads bowed. The Rev Fulton talks of John's valour in the battles he fought, and his selfless service to the office of governor in New South Wales. There are hymns, there are prayers, and then finally his coffin is carried from the church to the sound of a sombre drumbeat and taken to the hastily finished mausoleum, with the men of the Corps lining the route. They stand frozen in a mass salute to a fellow serviceman who had died while doing his duty for his country on the other side of the world.

The coffin is placed carefully in the vault, and the Rev Fulton leads more prayers for John's soul. At the end, Meg hands Mary a slim wreath she's made with the couple's favourite pink hibiscuses. Mary takes it, steps forward and pulls from it a handful of petals. These, she scatters around the entrance, then kneels and places the garland lightly onto the lid of the coffin.

'Goodbye, my love,' she whispers, as everyone falls silent. 'Goodbye.' Meg turns away, blinded by tears, as Mary's father helps his daughter back to her feet.

The governor nods to Major Johnston and the crowd and everyone takes his signal to depart, leaving only Meg, Mary and her father by John's coffin. Meg puts an arm around Mary's shoulders again, but this time, Mary steps away.

'Thank you, but I'm fine,' she says in a croaky voice. 'I just want to stay here for a while, on my own, with John.'

While life in the colony goes on, Meg and Mary sometimes feel quite removed from it. The two women carefully pack most of John's possessions to send to his family, along with a letter from Mary offering her deepest condolences, and her gratitude for what she calls the greatest gift she's ever been given. Mary visits John's grave daily. At other times, Meg brings her a chair, and she sits on the lawn in front of Government House by the bush of pink hibiscuses. The best of them have wilted, mostly shrivelled by the hot summer sun, but Mary tells Meg they remind her of John, and she loves to see them, and think of him, whenever she walks the grounds.

True to her word to Anna, Mary has been spending more time at the orphanage, and Meg often accompanies her. She's genuinely impressed by Mary's newfound zeal and the softness with which she talks to the girls and encourages them with their reading and writing. Mary even takes an interest in a new venture the orphanage is embarking on—the making of straw hats. A new couple, Mr and Mrs Marchant, had been appointed to run the institution, but they have only just taken charge when Mr Marchant suddenly dies. No one seems to know what happened. Mrs Marchant is so grief-stricken that no one can get any sense from her and rumours are swirling that he was perhaps murdered. Mary takes his death particularly hard, too. Thankfully, it isn't long before another couple, who applied for the post from England, arrives on a ship. Their names are Mr and Mrs Perfect.

'And let's hope they are,' Meg says to Mary. Certainly, on first impression, they seem to be.

Governor Bligh, meanwhile, seems to be trying to respect his daughter's time in mourning and is making a herculean effort not to drag her into his arguments with Macarthur. But it is becoming increasingly difficult to avoid them. On 20 January, thirteen days after the funeral, one of Macarthur's servants calls at Government House to ask for a copy of his master's indictment. He's told to wait in the kitchen while the governor considers. Twenty minutes later, the servant is sent packing—the governor has simply refused the request.

Two days later, a letter from Macarthur is delivered to the governor. Mr Griffin confides in Meg that he's protesting about having to appear in court in front of his debtor, Atkins. 'But Governor Bligh has told Macarthur he doesn't have the power to intercede in the running of the court,' Mr Griffin says. 'A governor just can't do that.'

That night, there's a dinner at the New South Wales Corps officers' mess, and the governor donates a large quantity of wine for the occasion. Meg and Mary imagine the officers talking and laughing and shouting well into the night. The thought makes Meg shudder as she remembers the evenings Henry Mackey would get drunker and drunker before making for her shed.

Two evenings later, on 24 January, there's another dinner in the mess attended by one of Macarthur's sons and his nephew, as well as Macarthur's two bailsmen, the head of the Corps, Major Johnston, and the six officers who are due, along with Atkins, to hear Macarthur's case in court the following day. On this occasion, the conversation sounds much more subdued, and Macarthur's voice is absent. A servant tells Meg he was seen walking outside the mess room, deep in thought and in full view of the diners.

The next morning, on 25 January, Meg goes for an early morning walk in town, and feels a strange tension in the air. There aren't many people about and those who are on the streets seem to be avoiding everyone else's gaze. People who would usually greet her warmly scurry off with their eyes cast down. When she returns to Government House, she mentions it to Mary.

'What do you think is happening?' she asks.

Mary looks blank. 'I wonder if there are ships leaving today, or any special ones due in. I can't think of anything else. Apart from . . . it's Macarthur's trial today, isn't it? But I wouldn't have thought the people would be particularly interested in that.'

'No, I don't suppose so,' Meg replies. 'The governor is in his office and he hasn't said anything either. I shall keep an ear open for anything unusual.'

A few hours later, there's a hammering on the front door of Government House. It's the governor's messenger—he has run all the way from the courthouse and looks flushed and agitated. He enters the drawing room where Meg, Mary and the governor are having tea.

'Mr Macarthur . . . He put in a protest at the court against Mr Atkins,' the messenger gasps. 'So the court didn't sit.'

'It didn't sit?' the governor echoes. 'How dare he! He knows full well that I don't have the power to interfere, so why on earth has he done this?'

He disappears into his office while Meg and Mary sit and wait. He bursts out an hour later and hands the messenger a letter to deliver to Major Johnston. 'I've asked him to come immediately,' Governor Bligh says. 'I need to talk to him about what to do about this villain's act of insubordination.'

The next time there's a knock on the front door, everyone is waiting. But it's not Major Johnston: it's the same messenger again, looking exhausted and now also frightened. 'Sir, Major Johnston says he is not well enough to come to you,' he tells Governor Bligh. 'He was at the mess dinner last night and had an accident on the way home in his carriage. He says he is too sick to leave home.'

Meg watches the governor's face turn pink with indignation. 'Oh, for God's sake,' he blusters. 'What on earth is happening? Go and get me Mr Atkins instead.'

The next morning, the colony is abuzz with the news that Atkins had issued a warrant for Macarthur's arrest, and Macarthur is now being held in gaol.

The atmosphere at Government House is strained. The governor is pleased that his greatest enemy is now behind bars, but Meg and Mary are both nervous that this isn't the end of the matter. At eleven a.m. a letter arrives for the governor, and he reads it aloud in their presence. It's another of Macarthur's protests against Atkins, but it is accompanied, this time, by a complaint from the six officers due to have sat in court, who claim to object to the gaoling of Macarthur.

'The damned hide of them!' splutters the governor.

'What are you going to reply?' Mary asks him.

'I've a good mind not to,' he says. 'The bloody impertinence. I've half a mind to charge the six of them, too.'

'With what?'

'Treason!'

'But, Father, can you really do that?'

'Atkins told me I could. Now just watch me!'

He goes back into his office, and Mary and Meg exchange worried glances. 'I don't like this,' Meg says.

'No, me neither,' replies Mary. 'I do so wish John was here.'

The two women fall silent, each wondering what John might have said, or done, in these circumstances. Would he have been able to calm the governor down? They would never know.

An hour later, the governor reappears, brandishing an envelope triumphantly. Mr Griffin is by his side. 'Here we are, summonses for the six officers to answer the charges of treason and usurpation of the government,' he declares. 'I'll send a note to Major Johnston, too, to let him know.'

Meg looks around at the faces in the room. Mr Griffin's features are impassive, as usual, giving nothing away. Governor Bligh's cheeks are flushed red with excitement at the thought of his impending triumph over those who would disobey him.

And though Meg scarcely believed it possible, Mary's face has become even paler above her black mourning clothes.

Part Three

REBELLION

22

ARMED ONLY WITH A PARASOL

Mary Putland
26 JANUARY 1808, SYDNEY

It's the twentieth anniversary of the day our first governor, Sir Arthur Phillip, raised the British flag at Port Jackson as the commander of the First Fleet, claiming the land as a British colony. As a result, we have a big celebration dinner planned at Government House. I can't say I feel very much like celebrating anything, but I realise that, despite my grief over the loss of John, and my worry about Father having gaoled Macarthur and charged six officers of the court with treason, I still have to abide by my duty.

Meg lays out my black gown, edged with white lace around the collar and cuffs, together with a matching bonnet, and pulls my hair into a smooth bun. I look at myself in the mirror while she tinkers with my hair. These past eighteen months in New South Wales have definitely aged me, and I say as much to Meg.

'No, no, mistress,' she lies. 'Let me put a little rouge on your cheeks and your lips and you'll be back to the full bloom of youth.'

We both laugh, despite our low moods. 'You're clever, but I don't think even you can perform miracles,' I say. 'I'm getting to be an old lady now. I'll be twenty-five at my next birthday in April.'

'And I'll be twenty on my birthday in May,' Meg replies. 'I'm not far behind.'

I'm thoughtful. 'It's about time we found a husband for you,' I say with a smile. 'What do you think of that?'

Meg blushes. 'No, thank you,' she says quickly. 'I met a man who I thought loved me once and look how that turned out.'

I'd heard from Father about Meg's background, and the young man who had tricked her into letting him into her employers' home, so I shrug my shoulders. 'Not every man is like that; you mustn't let that experience put you off them all. No, we shall find someone for you, a good man like John.'

Meg shakes her head. 'But remember the promise you made to John to remarry one day?' she replies. 'Maybe we should look for a good man for you first.'

At that, we both fall silent.

When I finish dressing, I go downstairs to greet our guests. Among them are Mr Griffin, fidgeting even more nervously than usual; a grim-faced judge advocate Mr Atkins; our commissary Mr Palmer, looking as pale as a ghost alongside his wife, Susan; the bulky Scots merchant Mr Campbell; and the dear Rev Fulton, whose smile is no less warm for the tension in the air over the troubles with Macarthur and the officers of the New South Wales Corps.

Everyone except Father seems on edge over recent events as we take our drinks and sit down at the long dining table. The staff serve the first course, and Father launches into a lecture about how he's taken a firm hand with those soldiers trying to make life difficult for him in the colony.

Mr Atkins says, 'Hear, hear!' at various junctures, although I can already make out a slur to his words. Mr Campbell also encourages Father with gruff murmurs of assent. But I can see the Rev Fulton looking anxious and the rest of us eat in strained silence. When we've finished, Father stands to make the loyal toast to the King.

'To the King,' we all chime in response, raising our glasses. *And to us*, I think to myself.

Mr Atkins shifts his bulk uneasily in his chair, then says he needs to check something in town and asks to take leave of us for a few minutes. I wonder what on earth he's doing but there's no point in asking. He returns after about ten minutes, saying that something is going on, and it looks like trouble. There are a lot of soldiers milling around by the barracks in their uniforms, laughing and shouting at each other with high spirits. There have also been a few bonfires lit in town. 'And on one, I thought I could see—' Mr Atkins pauses for dramatic effect '—I'm sorry to say, an effigy of the governor.'

Father's face darkens but he tells us to continue our meal. Everyone is unsettled and no one has much of an appetite. I wave at the servants to clear the plates away and we then sit around, talking and drinking wine. When a messenger arrives, it's almost a welcome break in the tension. We all rise to our feet.

'Sir, Major Johnston has assumed the position of lieutenant-governor,' the messenger tells Father. 'He has also signed a warrant for the release of Macarthur from gaol. In addition, the major has now assembled around three hundred armed soldiers from the New South Wales Corps and they are, at this very moment, marching from the barracks through the town to Government House, intent on overthrowing you.'

Mrs Palmer lets out a scream of terror while I stand horrified, frozen to the spot. The men around me are open-mouthed. Father, however, a much quicker thinker than us all, calls to his servant George Jubb to make his horse ready and races upstairs.

I'm confused, but the seemingly unflappable Mr Palmer, who has placed one hand on his wife's shoulder to calm her down, explains that he's likely gone to dress in his uniform and perhaps gather together his most important papers. 'Then I imagine your father will ride to the Hawkesbury to gather a troop of farmers loyal to the government,' he says. 'He will need all the support he can muster.'

There's shouting outside, and suddenly we can all hear the piercing fife and the thundering drums of the New South Wales Corps' band, growing louder and louder.

'They're not far away now,' exclaims Mr Atkins unhelpfully.

Everyone is now standing around the table, and no one seems to know quite what to do. Meg enters the room, looking frightened. I probably look exactly the same beneath this rouge.

I feel suddenly exhausted by it all. This damned place and its politics! And the trouble that seems to follow Father wherever he goes. Is this going to be yet another mutiny on his long list? Will he never learn? Does he not realise how ruinous his ill temper and poor judgement of men can be?

I glance out of the window. It's early evening but still light, and there's a faint glow of fires from the town. I can hear the barking of dogs, the yelling of men's voices and the notes of 'The British Grenadiers' coming ever closer. From here, I can also see my dear John's hibiscus bush, the petals of the last few dying flowers scattered like tears on the grass.

I think of John. We dragged him all the way to the ends of the earth, even though he was probably sick before he even left. But he came, willingly, in the hope of helping to create a better life, a stronger order, and a more civilised society in this colony. And he died for this place. Sacrificed everything for it. For us: for me and my father. Is all his suffering now to be for nothing?

My eyes are stinging with tears but this time the tears are of rage. I can feel my fury mounting. It floods through my body and I see the red veil descend. My darling husband is dead, but I'll be damned if I let his death be in vain.

I snatch my parasol from the corner of the room and stride out of the house towards the cast-iron gates of Government House. I don't know what I'm going to do; I only know I can't do nothing. I see hundreds of redcoats with their white cross belts marching up the hill towards me and I can hear their accursed anthem, their battle cries and the steady pounding of their feet. I stand behind the gates, push them closed and wait.

As the men grow closer, I can make out the flushed face of Major Johnston at the front. Now Lieutenant-Governor Johnston, I presume. He reaches the gates and signals to the men behind him to halt. For a moment, we lock eyes. I don't look away. He will have to make the first move. I will not give him any help.

'Madam,' he says finally, 'move aside! We have not come for you. We have come for your father.'

I bristle with indignation. 'Well, you shall not have him,' I say. 'Go back to your own homes and your families. Leave this instant!'

I'm pleased to see he looks startled. He obviously hadn't expected this kind of reception. He clearly doesn't know what to do. I survey the scene behind him for any sign of that brute Macarthur. He's obviously the one running this show. When is he going to slink out from the crowd and give his puppet Johnston his orders?

For a moment, I wonder if I've won. We have reached an impasse. He wants to get in the gates, but I'm going nowhere. He could so easily order his men back, and then tomorrow Father could sort out all this mess. Perhaps he could withdraw those charges of treason and sit and talk to Macarthur; they could come to a compromise like two reasonable men. No one will win from a mutiny like this. Ask Father and Fletcher Christian.

Then Johnston reaches forward to the bars of the gate between us and rattles them, trying to push them open. I resist the urge to step backwards and instead hold my body stiffly erect and continue to stare at him imperiously. Johnston nods his head almost imperceptibly and a thunderous clatter ripples through the amassed crowd of three hundred men as they raise their muskets. At that, Johnston and the men at the front quickly push open the gates.

I lift my furled parasol above my head and then bring it down on the chests of Johnston and his craven compatriots. 'You traitors!' I yell. 'You rebels! Get back!'

I get in a good few blows before they seem to comprehend what's happening and push past me. I run after them, still shouting my insults and wielding my weapon. I notice some walk straight through the hibiscus bush, crushing it into the ground with their heavy boots. I can't contain my rage. 'You rogues!' I scream, still trying to lash out with my parasol. 'You've trampled over my husband's grave and now you've come to kill my father! You'll have to kill me first.'

The men keep on coming, however, and simply jostle me aside. A parasol, I realise, is no match for so many soldiers wielding loaded muskets and bayonets. I try to make my jibes sharper. 'My father will hang you for this,' I screech. 'Get back, while you still can.'

One of the men grabs me and yells to the others, 'That Bligh girl, I've got her!', but I wriggle out of his grip and then run after the rest of them towards the house. If this costs me my life, then so be it. Without John, and perhaps soon without my father, I don't have much to live for anyway.

23

LIKE A HEROINE OF A FORMER AGE

Meg Hill
26 JANUARY 1808, SYDNEY

Meg and the other guests at Government House stand transfixed at the window and watch the scene at the gates unfold with differing degrees of horror, fascination and admiration for Mary. At first, Meg is terrified for her mistress and makes for the door until she is stopped by the ever-sensible Mr Palmer.

'Don't go out there,' he says, barring her way. 'It's better if we stay here together. I don't know what Mary is thinking, confronting the troops like that, but it won't do to see anyone else risk their life out there.'

'Maybe I can help her,' Meg protests.

Mr Palmer shakes his head. 'Have you seen how many muskets those men have?' he asks. 'Only God can help her now.'

The huddle of people around the window watches as the troops push back the gates and a sea of red and white surges through them, pushing past Mary towards the house. They see Mary disappear for a moment and then re-appear with her arms being held by one of the soldiers.

Meg tries again for the door, and Mr Palmer halts her once more. 'But they have her!' Meg cries. 'We have to do something.'

'No, no,' the servant George Jubb calls over. 'She has shaken him off and she is now free again. She is like a heroine of a former age!'

They gather back at the window. 'Here they come now!' Mr Atkins calls feebly in another of his statements of the obvious.

Surprisingly, it's the mild-mannered deputy chaplain, the Rev Fulton, who steps up to offer the only other opposition. He moves determinedly to the front door and stands there ready to bar the way of any of the insurgents who might break in. He's holding something with both hands in front of him, and Meg wonders if he has a weapon. As she advances towards him, she sees it is his Bible.

They can all hear the heavy tread of the men reaching the front door, but none of the others goes to join the reverend. To Meg, he looks a little like Jesus Christ after the Last Supper, waiting to be slain by the Romans.

There's a crash, and shards of glass explode into the Rev Fulton's body. Mr Palmer darts over and tries to pull him away. The chaplain resists. 'No, no,' he says, those blue eyes of his flashing. 'I need to defend the door.'

'You can't,' Mr Palmer tells him. 'You can't stop them entering. They are coming through the verandah doors at the back, too. They'll just smash this one down. You'll be killed if you don't get out of the way.'

'No,' the Rev Fulton insists. 'Maybe I can slow them down to give the governor more time to get away.'

Meg looks towards the stairs. In all the fuss, she'd forgotten about the governor. She wonders if he's still upstairs or whether he's already been able to make his way out undetected, and escape with his horse to the Hawkesbury.

The front door reverberates with another crash and splinters of wood fly into the room. Mrs Palmer screams again, and the burly Scotsman Mr Campbell joins Mr Palmer in dragging the Rev Fulton away from the door, despite his protestations. They then slide the heavy bolts to one side and step back, and immediately a tide of soldiers flows through the doorway.

'Where's the governor?' one of the officers in his tasselled silver epaulettes asks their small party. 'Where's Governor Bligh?' No one says a word and, frustrated, he turns away. 'Search the house!' he commands the troops. 'He has to be here somewhere.'

Another group surges in and among them is a small figure in black. 'Mary!' screams Meg. 'Oh thank God, you're safe!'

Mary doesn't stop, however. She makes straight for the bottom of the stairs and lifts her trusty parasol once more. The officer sees her and walks towards her. She obviously recognises him. 'How dare you come in here uninvited, Lieutenant Minchin,' she yells. 'You have been our guest at our dinner table so many times. Is this how you repay our hospitality?'

'Mrs Putland, move aside,' he says. 'We have no quarrel with you. We are here for your father.'

'Well, you'll have to kill me first,' she says, looking at his bayonet. 'Stab me or shoot me in the heart and spare the life of my father. Or are you too much of a coward to do that?'

The Rev Fulton rushes over to Mary and takes her arm. 'Please, Mrs Putland,' he begs. 'Come away now. We have done our best. There is nothing we can do to stop them now. Please, let them pass.'

She looks at him with glazed eyes, and suddenly it seems that all the fight leaves her. She allows herself to be led away, and Meg takes over and sits her on a chair. Six soldiers are assigned to guard their little group. They watch and wait to see what will happen next.

The soldiers are traipsing throughout the house, pulling open doors, searching the rooms, kicking furniture aside, entering cupboards and clearing shelves with their bayonets. Meg realises she's keeping a wary eye out for Mackey but so far she hasn't seen him. Will she ever be free of that fear? A fresh contingent of men mount the stairs and Meg can hear them rushing around, hunting for their prey. The house is full of the sounds of doors opening and slamming, drawers being jerked out and dropping onto the floors, and the angry murmur of voices. They obviously haven't yet found him.

'Maybe your father managed to get away before they came,' Meg whispers to Mary. 'You delayed them at the gates. That gave him more time.'

'I'd love to think so,' Mary replies, now trembling with nerves. 'He could be on his way to tell his supporters about this terrible evening and the Corps' disgraceful behaviour.'

'Let's hope so, mistress,' Meg says.

'Silence!' one of their guards shouts. 'Stop whispering.'

Mary purses her lips in defiance. 'These men will receive their just deserts for this scandalous act of treachery,' she says in a loud, clear voice that she knows they will all hear. 'Mark my words, they will pay for it.'

The same guard walks over. 'Be quiet, madam,' he commands her. 'For your own safety, if nothing else.'

Mary nods to him, but then whispers to Meg, 'Have you seen Macarthur yet? And where is Johnston?'

'The major is in the drawing room, waiting,' Meg replies. 'And no, I haven't seen Macarthur yet, but I imagine he must be around somewhere.'

'Absolutely!' Mary says. 'None of this would be happening without his say-so.'

The pair fall silent, pondering the part he must have played in this insurgency, until a cry of triumph rings out from somewhere upstairs, and everyone in the group, as well as their guards and the rest of the search party downstairs, look upwards expectantly.

'We've got him!' a deep voice shouts. 'We've got Bligh. The tyrant is ours. The Bounty Bastard is here.'

A few minutes later, three soldiers appear, followed by the governor with Minchin clasping one of his arms. Mary's father is wearing his uniform and his medals but the material looks dusty, as if he's been crawling around on the floor. There's a look of such confusion and bewilderment in his eyes that it makes Meg's heart go out to him. She glances at Mary and sees her face soften too at the sight. Yes, he may have brought this latest disaster on himself, but both women knew he thought he was always doing his best for King and country. It's just that his best mightn't have been good enough.

'Father!' Mary calls. 'Are you all right? Have they hurt you?'

He looks over at her with an expression so hangdog and beaten, her voice catches in her throat.

It seems to take him a huge effort to reply. 'No, no, my dear,' he says. 'I'm fine. Well, I would be if these blighters . . .' He trails off. There's no need to say anything more.

Johnston emerges from the drawing room and Minchin pushes Bligh forward.

'We found him hiding under a servant's bed in the attic,' he says roughly. 'Hiding like a coward and sending his daughter out to face us.'

There's a flash of the old anger in Governor Bligh's face. 'That is not true,' he says. 'I was trying to gather my papers. Until this traitor here came along . . .' He stares daggers at Minchin.

'And my father didn't send me,' Mary chimes in, her voice heavy with indignation. 'He had no idea. He was obviously otherwise engaged when I tried to stop you doing such a foolish thing.'

Johnston, who has remained silent during the exchange, hands the governor a document. 'What is this?' Bligh asks.

'It's the papers for your arrest, sir,' Johnston replies.

'Well, they won't be worth the paper they're written on, then, will they?' replies Bligh, tossing them to the floor.

Johnston patiently picks them up and hands them back again. 'I think you'll find they are. As well as being the warrant for your arrest, they say you're no longer governor.'

Mary rises to her feet and walks over to Johnston. She looks him squarely in the eye again, and this time her gaze burns with undisguised hatred. 'And to think you were a chief mourner at my husband's funeral,' she says bitterly. 'How could you have done this to us, with his body hardly cold?'

Then she turns and takes the papers from her father and starts to read in a voice as strong and as clear as a bell. '*The alarming state of this colony, in which every man's property, liberty and life is endangered . . .*' She pauses and arches her eyebrows. 'I'm assuming John Macarthur wrote this?' She glances at Johnston, who colours slightly. She nods. 'I thought as much. Well, this paper goes on to say that this so-called "alarming"—' she repeats the word with clear ridicule '—state induces us to instantly place Governor Bligh under arrest and to assume the command of the colony. *We pledge ourselves, at a moment of less agitation, to come forward to support the measure with our fortunes and our lives.* And it's been signed by nine civilians.'

She waves the paper in Johnston's face. 'Nine civilians!' she reiterates. '*Nine!* Is that the best you could do? The most you could muster to authorise this uprising against His Majesty's Government?'

Mary stops and peruses the nine names. At the top of the list is Macarthur's signature, as expected, and below that is one she immediately recognises: Mr Divine, the man who'd worked with her father on the vault where her beautiful dead husband is now lying. She narrows her eyes. 'I hope you know what you're doing. No good can possibly come of this. You will be sent to England and tried for treason.'

Meg, watching from the corner of the room, is amazed by Mary. While she had once dismissed her mistress as the spoiled daughter of a controlling father, she now watches her emerge as the stronger, the more determined and perhaps even the eminently more human of the two Blighs.

'Hear, hear, Mary,' she says under her breath. She thinks of George Jubb's admiring words from only moments ago. 'A heroine of a former age.'

24

PRISONERS IN THEIR OWN HOME

Mary Putland
26 JANUARY 1808, SYDNEY

The abominable George Johnston has had all our male guests, as well as poor Mr Griffin, taken away for questioning, leaving me, Father, Meg, Mrs Palmer and the rest of our servants at Government House. Oh, and he's left us our own armed guard—a group of six soldiers of the Corps who are under strict instructions to stay, at all times, only six paces away from Father and me.

I suppose I should be flattered. He obviously thinks me quite capable of fleeing at any moment from six burly men with bayonets and muskets. I'd like to think I would be more than a match but, in truth, I know I wouldn't stand a chance.

That night, I don't think any of us sleep. We can smell the bonfires and hear riotous singing and shouting and swearing and fighting drifting in from the town, and it doesn't hush until daybreak.

'Let them have their celebrations,' Father says at breakfast. 'They won't be celebrating for long. I have already started writing my account of last night's events and what led up to them to send to Lord Castlereagh, the Secretary of State for War and the Colonies. I know he will be appalled at what's transpired and he'll punish them accordingly.'

'But how will you get a letter to him?' I ask, glancing past him out the window where my beloved hibiscus bush has been utterly destroyed. Father doesn't seem to have grasped that we're prisoners here, being watched night and day, and that the colony is now under martial law. If we have any friends left, their movements will be closely monitored, too. It's no longer as simple as sending out a messenger with a letter for the next ship leaving Sydney. Anyone caught doing that kind of favour for us would likely end up in gaol.

Father looks nonplussed. 'I'm sure there will be a way,' he says stubbornly. 'We must let Britain know that disaster has been visited on the colony.'

After breakfast, I ask the guards if Mrs Palmer can be freed to go home. She's silent and withdrawn, obviously anxious about her husband. Surely there's nothing to be gained by keeping her at Government House with us? The guards confer and then one lopes off to the barracks to ask for instructions. Susan looks at me gratefully.

An hour later, much to our astonishment, the guard walks back in accompanied by none other than John Macarthur. 'Good morning one and all,' he says in such a hale and hearty manner that I'm completely taken aback. But then, thinking about it, why wouldn't he be in fine fettle? He's finally achieved what he's wanted all along:

to topple a governor and snatch power for himself. Now he can grant himself all the land he desires for his blasted sheep, build whatever fences he wishes around public areas, import all the stills he likes and charge whatever he wants for rum and any foodstuffs he can pick up at the wharves.

Father glowers at him. 'What are you doing here?' he growls. 'Come to gloat, have you?' Macarthur takes a seat and Father immediately snaps, 'I didn't give you permission to sit.'

I sigh. Here we go again. Why can't Father wait to see what he has to say before riling him so? What's done is done, and now we are his prisoners. We're hardly in a position to order him around.

'I'm sorry, sir, but you no longer have any authority over me,' Macarthur says evenly. 'I've come here to do you the courtesy of letting you know what's going to happen.'

I sit up straight in my chair, and I see Meg silently join us.

'First of all, Mrs Palmer is now permitted to leave,' he says.

Susan gives a little gasp. 'But . . . what about my husband?' she asks.

'He will be released shortly, when we've finished questioning him,' Macarthur replies. 'Along with your other guests.'

I nod. It would seem odd, in the circumstances, to thank him.

'And us?' I ask, as it doesn't look as though Father can lower himself to speak to Macarthur.

He swivels round in the chair. 'Ah, Mrs Putland, my sympathies to you for the loss of your husband. I understand you had quite a day yesterday. I do trust you were treated well by the men?'

I ignore that. If being treated well means having three hundred muskets pointed at you and then being jostled out of the way as soldiers trample your heart's dearest memories, then perhaps I was. I am still alive to remember it, at least. 'So what is to happen to us in your grand scheme?' I ask.

He sits back in his chair. 'We will be sending your father back to England, and I imagine you will want to go with him. But it is up to you what you choose to do. If you would like to stay in Sydney, that will be permitted. But you may prefer to leave with him.'

'Until then?'

'You will stay here in Government House. Your father will remain inside, but you will be allowed to leave if accompanied by two guards.'

'And what of you? You're free now?'

'Yes,' he says with a smile. 'As you know, your father ordered me to be imprisoned in much less comfort than you are here.' He spreads his arms and glances around the dining room to emphasise his point. 'My life was in danger in that gaol. There were prisoners in there who I had helped put behind bars for theft. One of the attendants told me he had hidden a cutlass in my cell and said I might need it before the night was out.'

'But you didn't,' I say sourly.

'No, but only because Major Johnston rode into town and ordered that I be released.'

'And then you instigated the coup against my father?'

'I didn't. We were instructed to arrest the governor by the will of the people.'

'Ah yes,' I say. 'I'd forgotten that. All nine of them.'

Macarthur looks as if he might be on the verge of losing his temper, and I glance over at Father. He's looking into the distance

219

as if he's refusing to listen. Meg, though, is paying close attention. She lowers her eyes and I realise she's warning me not to go further. This man has complete power over us, and it wouldn't do to goad him too much.

I stand up as if dismissing him from our presence, although, of course, I have no authority to do so. 'Well, I am sure you have many important things to do running the colony,' I say. 'Don't stay on our account.'

Macarthur stands, too, and looks at Father, but there's not a flicker of interest in his eyes. He's obviously determined not to give him the satisfaction of any attention. So, Macarthur instead gives Meg and me a little bow, and then strides out the front door.

Time passes agonisingly slowly. I spend most of my days at home, playing my piano or my lute, while Father occupies most of his time at the dining room table, since his study has been locked up and he's been barred from entering it. He has been busy writing out a detailed list of his grievances against Macarthur and an account of the events that led to the coup. I can only hope that one day we will find a way of getting all his pages to the government in London.

Early every morning, so I won't be seen, I slip into town trailed by my two armed guards to visit John and put a flower at his vault. Father had been designing a headstone to be installed there but he's in such a black mood, I don't like to ask him about his progress. On my way to the mausoleum, I take note of the previous night's drunken carousing to celebrate what's now being called The Great Rebellion, and the 'heroism' of Macarthur, whom Johnston has appointed Colonial Secretary to run New South Wales. There are often still glowing embers from bonfires—a few, no doubt, with effigies of my father—and rum seems to be flowing freely. Some of our supporters are still being harassed and questioned. I share the details with Meg but think better of telling my father.

Six days into our incarceration, however, he brings up the subject of John's tombstone himself. He's received a letter from Johnston's secretary asking him if he plans to finish the mausoleum. If he does, then the bill for its completion will be sent to London for the British Government to decide if Father should pay it himself, or if it should come from the public purse.

'This is absolutely ridiculous!' Father says. 'That vault was intended for the remains of governors, or their families, who might die in this colony. How could they expect me, personally, to pay for it?'

I don't say anything. I'm afraid if I do, I might start weeping, and then I mightn't be able to stop. To see people bickering over the body of my dear husband is too much for me.

Meg sees the look on my face and comes over. 'Sir,' she says, 'I know the plan was for John to join us for the voyage back to Britain. In the current circumstances, that may be sooner rather than later. So why don't we suggest the vault be covered over and a flat stone put on it until we have the opportunity to take John back?'

Father looks at me for my reaction, and I nod. 'Yes, that is a good idea,' he says. 'Thank you, Meg. I'll write to Johnston later and tell him what we've decided.'

I notice Father takes twelve days before he pens the letter, however. Obviously, John isn't high on his list of priorities.

We have a few visitors. Mr Griffin comes back to us after being grilled by the Corps about our activities and he diligently joins Father at the dining table, helping him prepare his documents and saying characteristically little about his own ordeal. Mr Campbell and Mr Palmer both call in to see how we are faring. In truth, we are probably faring better than they are. Mr Palmer has lost his position as commissary as a result of his loyalty to us, replaced by his deputy, who has pledged allegiance to the rebels. It looks as though he's now going to be charged with sedition, something that might once have been absolutely unthinkable for such a proper and respectable Englishman. Similarly, Mr Campbell has been stripped of his rank of naval officer and has been dismissed as treasurer and collector of taxes. Both men look bound for a period in gaol.

The pair are searched on their way into the house and searched on their way out again, presumably in case we have passed them any documents or letters. Mrs Palmer is conspicuous in her absence. I imagine she's not so keen anymore to pay the price of being my friend. Mr Atkins also fails to appear, but we learn he's been replaced as judge advocate by the Surveyor-General Charles Grimes and assume he's taken even more solace in the bottle.

Happily, the Rev Fulton also visits. He was, like us, confined to his own house after the insurgency, and was then suspended from duty, banned from holding church services in both Sydney and Parramatta.

As soon as he walks into Government House, Father clasps both his hands around his. 'I have been told of your bravery on that terrible night,' Father tells him. 'Thank you, thank you.'

'I tried to stop them coming in, but in the end I couldn't,' the Rev Fulton says miserably. 'And my heroism was nothing compared to your daughter's.'

'Yes, I've been told about that. She could have been killed.'

I make a face at the Rev Fulton behind Father's back. My father just doesn't seem to have it in him to offer me any praise. Perhaps if I'd have been killed standing by him, he might then have commended me? I guess I will never know. The chaplain smiles at me. He knows exactly what I am thinking.

Father hasn't noticed our exchange. 'I am sorry you are now suffering so much for your loyalty,' he continues. 'But I wonder if you would do us the favour of being our family's chaplain?'

'It would be my honour,' the Rev Fulton says graciously. 'I have written to Lord Castlereagh to inform him of all your fine work trying to break the monopoly the Corps operate with rum and imported provisions, and to tell him the rebel administration are building a Babel. They have been taking their petition, which they said justified their coup, around to all the townsfolk to add more signatures. Apparently, many are too fearful to refuse to sign. They now have one hundred and fifty-one signatures to shore up their case.'

My father looks alarmed, then his shoulders droop. This whole episode has definitely affected him deeply; I think it's shattered his confidence. A period of self-reflection might once have been healthy for him—he could have been a better person for it—but now I see how beaten, aged and exhausted he looks, and I can't help feeling for him.

The Rev Fulton obviously notices, too. 'Some of us are now writing an address of loyalty to you and signing that,' he says. 'We even have some signatures from those who signed the petition against you—which shows how ridiculous their position is.'

The reverend comes by often after that. He often brings books, for which we're very grateful. The Corps confiscated not only all of Father's paperwork, but also, unfathomably, his books.

I sometimes take one with me as I wander in the garden, again always with my two armed shadows. I wonder if anything will happen to our plans to extend and beautify the Domain. I can't imagine Macarthur and his military administration having any interest in that endeavour. It will, presumably, have to wait until the British Government reinstates us or appoints a new governor or sanctions, God forbid, Macarthur and his military government. Father is adamant he will once again be in charge of the colony but, secretly, I have my doubts.

Meg is able to come and go as she wishes, although she is also searched to ensure she does not carry any letters for us. She is a source of much valuable information. Her old friend Jane from the *Alexander*, who was assigned to a Corps officer, tells her that the officers have all been given special privileges, particularly with extra rations of meat and rum, and have paraded Macarthur around the town on their shoulders. Drunkenness, as a result, is now so rife that the crime rate is rising fast, too.

Jane also passes on the fascinating news that Johnston had informed his superior officer, Colonel William Paterson, of the rebellion, expecting him to take charge. The colonel, however, is down in Van Diemen's Land establishing a new settlement and has refused to return to Sydney. He's no friend of Macarthur, who wounded him in a duel seven years ago, and seems eager to stay out of it. He says he'll wait to receive orders from England, a stance that's proving enormously frustrating for both Johnston and Macarthur.

Father is amused by that, but is less entertained by the next piece of news Meg brings us. There's an art exhibition in town and in pride of place is a watercolour of Father, Lieutenant Minchin and two other soldiers. It shows the former governor being dragged out from under a servant's bed in Government House, as if he'd been hiding to evade capture in the most cowardly position possible.

Of course, no one really knows what he was doing upstairs before he was seized by the soldiers, but the caricature is apparently proving so popular among audiences that many copies are being ordered and bought. With so many now changing hands, I fear this image will soon become the universally accepted truth. While I will never know what really happened upstairs during the coup, I know Father would have been beside himself with panic at the thought of yet another mutiny besmirching his reputation, and he would have been desperate to escape. So is there any truth to the portrait of him cowering beneath a servant's bedclothes?

It's heartbreaking to admit, but I really couldn't say one way or the other.

25

THE LONGEST DAY

Meg Hill
4 JULY 1808, SYDNEY

The weeks of house arrest continue to drag on, and uncertainty about what is going to happen is wearing everyone down.

Governor Bligh has suggested he be allowed to return to England on his flagship the HMS *Porpoise*, of which he's still the commandant. But that, he's told, won't be possible. The ship is required to evacuate people from Norfolk Island—which will no longer be maintained as a colony because of its inaccessibility in rough seas— to the new settlements on Van Diemen's Land. Instead, Father is offered passage on another ship, the twenty-nine-year-old frigate HMS *Pegasus*, which has been fitted out as a transport ship with a reduced armament. But Father deems the frigate not sea-worthy enough for his passage. He wants his four-year-old, twelve-gunner *Porpoise*.

Meanwhile, the rebels send Lieutenant Minchin and the new judge advocate, Mr Grimes, over to England with what Jane describes to Meg as an extremely colourful document justifying the overthrow of Governor Bligh, describing him as tyrannical, corrupt and greedy, determined to terrorise the courts and loathed by the vast majority of the good people of New South Wales. Colonel Paterson, technically Father's deputy, is still refusing to leave Van Diemen's Land, and Macarthur and Johnston seem unable to decide what else to do.

'I have no idea what's going to become of us,' Mary says to Meg as they walk through the gardens one cold winter's day. 'Sometimes I think it'd be easier if they just took us out and shot us!'

'Oh, mistress, don't talk like that,' Meg implores her. 'I'm sure something will happen soon and we'll either be freed or on our way back home. They can't keep us here forever.'

'I guess not,' Mary replies morosely. 'It's just Father's health I worry about.'

Meg smiles to herself. Once, Mary wouldn't have given two hoots about Governor Bligh's health but, with the pair of them stuck in this impossible situation, she seems to have made the major leap from being her father's tormentor to his protector. As his grip on power loosens, Mary seems to be picking up the slack.

'He was talking again this morning about wanting to leave on the *Porpoise*, and trying to press them harder,' Meg says. 'But then he has also been talking about whether the Hawkesbury farmers will stage a revolt on his behalf. Or whether Paterson will eventually come and free him. Or David Collins, the lieutenant-governor of Van Diemen's Land. Then he said maybe the news has now reached the British Government, and they will send an armada.'

'I fear he's deluded,' Mary says. 'I don't know where a reprieve will possibly come from.' She looks out at the water lapping the lush grasses of the Domain, and then up at the dark green branches of the tall pines that dot the parklands. 'I wager we'll still be here at Christmas . . .'

When they return to the house, there's a letter waiting from Mary's mother—which happily their armed sentries agree they can read—but the news isn't terribly good. Mary reads it out loud to her father and Meg. Mrs Bligh sends all her love, and that of the children, to them both, thanks Mary for those wonderful shells, and inquires gently about John Putland's health. Mary's words catch in her throat at this point. 'She does so hope he is recovering well from his ailment,' she says.

Meg takes over. '*Captain Short has been acquitted at his court martial in London, and Governor Bligh's enemies are circling,*' she reads. 'But Mrs Bligh says she's doing her best to appease some and outwit others with the gifts you've both sent over from New South Wales.' Then it's Meg's turn to pause. 'But she warns you to be careful,' she continues. '*Enemies can be everywhere. Even where you least expect them.*'

Life continues in its tedium with only faint glimmers of hope. News filters in of Bligh loyalists being tried in court on trumped up charges; being convicted and receiving one hundred lashes; being imprisoned or sent in chains to dig in the coal mines in the hellhole of the north, Newcastle. Rumours abound of illegal hangings of Bligh supporters. Letters are now routinely allowed to be brought into Government House, and one eventually arrives from

Lieutenant-Governor Collins in Van Diemen's Land, pledging his loyalty to Bligh.

The next day, 29 July, Meg and Mary return from yet another circuit of the gardens to find the house in a state of commotion. Mary's father looks wild-eyed, and he's put on his full dress uniform, his medals pinned to his breast. 'Have you heard the news?' he asks. 'Wonderful news!'

'What's happened?' Mary asks him as he seizes her arms and swings her around in a strange kind of madcap dance. 'What's going on?'

Bligh takes a moment to catch his breath after so much unfamiliar exertion. 'Major Joseph Foveaux has just arrived from London on the *Lady Sinclair*—our old ship!' he says. 'He's now going to be lieutenant-governor. So, I would think he'll be along shortly to see me and restore me to my rightful position.'

'That's wonderful . . .' Mary says, as Meg pulls over a chair for her father to sit on. 'Hopefully, we'll be his first call.'

By nightfall, Foveaux still hasn't come to Government House, and Bligh is still sitting in his uniform waiting, his eyes fixed firmly on the door. At midnight, Meg has to persuade him to go to bed, promising she'll wake him the moment she hears anyone come. The next morning, he's up at daybreak, this time pacing the drawing room. It's the longest day anyone in the house can ever remember.

When, two nights later, there is still no sign of Foveaux, Meg slips out unnoticed to Jane's house and knocks softly on her bedroom window to wake her. Jane gestures that she'll meet her outside. They hunch down together behind an old well in the garden so they won't be seen.

'Do you know what's happening with Foveaux?' Meg asks. 'We've been expecting him to come to Government House to see the governor, but there's been no sign.'

Jane sighs. 'He's been with Macarthur and Johnston,' she says. 'I'm sorry, but it looks as if he's thrown his lot in with them. He and Macarthur go back a long way. When Foveaux first went to Norfolk Island as acting lieutenant-governor eight years ago, he had to get rid of his livestock, and Macarthur was the one who paid a pretty price for them all.'

'But shouldn't he be loyal to Governor Bligh?' Meg asks. 'After all, he is the rightful authority.'

Jane pulls a face. 'From what they say, he doesn't sound that keen on Bligh,' she answers. 'He was in London when they were court-martialling Captain Short and he wasn't impressed with Bligh's treatment of him. And, of course, he'd heard about Short's poor wife dying on the way home . . .'

Meg shakes her head. If only Bligh could have kept a rein on his temper during the voyage over! He's now paying the kind of price he could never have foreseen. 'Thank you, Jane,' she says. 'I'm very grateful again!'

As she makes her way back to Government House, Meg can't help thinking that Bligh made his bed, and now he must lie in it. She does feel sorry for him but, at the same time, can he really expect Foveaux to face down the all-powerful Corps and simply reverse everything they've done?

She tells Mary what she's found out, and the two women decide not to pass it on to Bligh. He's gloomy enough already and, besides, they can't really be sure Jane knows the truth; she might have only heard the version her officer master had been told.

Later that day, however, Foveaux finally turns up at Government House. Bligh looks delighted, but Foveaux is grim-faced. The pair disappear into the drawing room, and there's the sound of raised voices. When both men emerge, neither looks happy. As Foveaux departs, Bligh turns to Mary and Meg.

'Well, Foveaux has stood down both Macarthur and Johnston,' he announces.

Mary goes to hug him in delight, but her father pulls away. 'He will not, however, be reinstating me as governor,' he says, sitting down heavily in a chair. 'Instead, he will be assuming power himself.'

'The turncoat!' Mary cries. 'The traitor!'

Her father shrugs. So much of the fight seems to have been drained from him.

Meg steps forward. 'But what does this mean for you?' she asks softly. It was all very well to be passing judgement on his stand, she felt, but surely the practicalities of their incarceration were more important.

Bligh nods. 'I will ask Foveaux again for the *Porpoise* so we can return to England and present our case to Lord Castlereagh.' He looks over to the doorway where his secretary has been hovering. 'Mr Griffin? Can you bring me paper?'

Foveaux doesn't reply to the letter, nor does he answer Bligh's next flurry of requests and commands. Instead, he offers him passage on the convict transport ship the *Admiral Gambier*, which Bligh declines. Then Foveaux decrees that if Mary and her father aren't leaving, they must move out of Government House in Sydney. He tells them they can move into the second Government House in Parramatta instead. He's obviously becoming more and more irritated by Bligh's intransigence and wants Government House for himself. Meg considers that an infinitely reasonable request, but, again, Bligh refuses.

Finally, running out of options, Foveaux informs them that he is waiting for instructions from either the British Government or Paterson when he arrives back in Sydney. Whichever comes first.

Bligh tells Meg and Mary that he has high hopes of Paterson but, when he finally sails into Port Jackson in the New Year, on 10 January 1809, he seems to have no intention of restoring Bligh's rule, either. Instead, it seems to Meg that he's ready, like Foveaux before him, to take command of the colony himself as the acting governor.

Paterson appears to have little patience for neither Bligh nor the rebels. While Bligh is testy and unyielding, Macarthur is . . . much the same. However, the rebel leader seems to be causing more trouble, by all accounts.

Meg feels exhausted by all the tension in the colony but knows something will soon have to give. Right enough, Foveaux is the first to snap. He accuses Macarthur, during his time as self-proclaimed Colonial Secretary, of appropriating some five hundred pounds worth of goods for his own use. Enraged by the allegation, Macarthur does what he always does—as Paterson well knows from his own painful experience—and challenges Foveaux to a duel. Meg visits her friend Jane on the afternoon of 19 January, the day of the duel, to find out what happened so she can report back to Mary and her father. It's a strange result. Both men tossed a coin for the right to fire first, meaning the loser would face the shot completely defence-lessly. Macarthur won the toss and shot . . . but missed. Foveaux then had the right to shoot Macarthur but, instead, declined to fire his weapon and handed it back to his second. Meg was bewildered. 'No,' Jane explains to her, 'that is the ultimate insult.'

There is so much trouble, and so many arguments, that Meg knows Paterson will be forced to make a decision. And he eventu-ally does: former Governor William Bligh, Mr John Macarthur and Major George Johnston should all be sent back to Britain on the *Admiral Gambier* to face the courts and the government, so the authorities can decide on the merits of the revolt or otherwise. Meg finds that quite reasonable, but Bligh refuses point blank to travel on such a ship, especially in the company of his two greatest enemies, and Mary stands by him. He wants the *Porpoise*. Furthermore, he forbids the use of the *Porpoise* for voyages between Norfolk Island and Van Diemen's Land. He is still, technically, in control of the ship, and writes to its captain John Porteous, who has always remained loyal to him, to say he's refused to sign the order allowing the *Porpoise* to be so redeployed, vehemently declining to relinquish his naval authority.

Meg immediately expects trouble, and it doesn't take long to arrive. Johnston turns up at Government House on 13 January with another officer, and they bundle Bligh into a one-horse chaise.

'Stop!' Mary screams. 'What are you doing? Where are you taking my father?' She lunges at Johnston.

Meg tries to grab her to hold her back. 'Mistress!' she says. 'Please. Let's wait to see where they take him.'

'No, no!' Mary cries. 'I don't trust them. They might be taking him off to be shot.'

Johnston jumps lightly into the chaise beside Bligh and picks up the whip. 'No, Mrs Putland, we have orders to take your father to the barracks,' he says evenly. 'Don't concern yourself.'

'Oh, but I do,' Mary replies. 'You've betrayed us once, who's to say you won't do it again?'

Johnston turns away and cracks the whip above the horse's head, and it charges up the hill towards town, rattling the chaise behind it.

And just as Meg is watching them depart, out of the corner of her eye, she sees Mary lift her skirts and bolt off behind the chaise.

26

THE WIND AT MY FEET

Mary Putland
13 JANUARY 1809, SYDNEY

I do it out of sheer instinct. One minute, Johnston has my father; the next I am running—yes, running—after the chaise, feeling my whole body powered by panic. My bonnet flies off and my hair comes unpinned, flying in the breeze behind me, but I just can't stop.

Somehow, this is exhilarating after nearly a year of inaction. To be running full pelt like this, not caring a jot what anyone thinks, trying to catch up to Father's chaise, feels so real. They called me a heroine for trying to repel those rebels marching upon us in Government House; well, perhaps this is my second attempt at martyrdom.

If anyone had suggested to me in the past that I would have put myself on the line for my father, I would have laughed at them. The man who always belittled me, whatever I did. The man who always praised my sister Harriet while talking me down. The man who sometimes, I felt, absolutely despised me. But, since the revolt, he has changed. Seeing his power wrested from him at gunpoint and watching the way he was left so helpless and bewildered and suddenly unsure of himself, has made me re-evaluate our relationship. Now I am the stronger one. I am the one he needs to look after him. John always tried to tell me that Father thought far more of me than he ever let on. Well, today I think that John might have been proud of me.

At the thought of my poor dead husband, I feel an extra wind beneath my feet and I draw level with the chaise. I can see Father staring at me in alarm, and Johnston, driving the horse, looks utterly shocked. There are people on the street, open-mouthed at the sight of me. I hear them point me out—'That Bligh girl!' they shout—but I keep running. I don't care what anyone thinks. My father brought me to this Godforsaken land, my husband died here, and I'll be damned if I'm going to let this place beat me. My father is the only person I have left here. I refuse to lose him, too.

'Mrs Putland, stop!' I hear someone shout, and I think it's probably Johnston. 'Mrs Putland!'

I ignore it. I can see we're nearing the barracks, although the sun is starting to blind me. It's about midday and the sun is hot, burning right above us. I can feel the warmth on my bare head, and the heat in my cheeks. Still, I power on. It's a steep hill but I don't slacken my pace. I need to keep going. There are a few soldiers standing around and they step back to give me room to pass and then watch me as I tear on.

Finally, we reach the gates and I see the chaise slowing and Johnston pulling at the horse. 'Mrs Putland! Mrs Putland!' he's still shouting. And now there's another voice joining him, 'Mary! My dear Mary!'

At the sound of my father's voice, I slow down and approach the chaise. I don't think I have any breath left in my body and I have no idea what I'm going to do. I only know that I need to rescue my father.

'Father!' I shout back to him. And then the whole world swirls, and everything goes black.

I come to lying on the ground in my father's arms. He's fanning my face and, as I open my eyes, I see a number of faces atop scarlet jackets looking down on me. I close them again. It takes me a moment to remember what happened.

'My darling girl,' I hear my father saying. 'My dear, dear Mary.'

For a moment, I wonder if the sun has got to him, too. I have never heard him speak to me so tenderly. I half-open my eyes again. Yes, I'm lying here in the street outside the barracks, my dress in disarray, my hair wild and untethered by my bonnet, feeling quite queasy. I suppose, in retrospect, it might not have been such a clever thing to do, running in such hot sun after my father.

I hear another familiar voice, and when I open my eyes again I see it's Meg, who must have run up here after me.

'Mistress, are you all right?' she asks, kneeling down beside my father and me. 'I was so worried.'

I take a deep breath and try to sit up. My head doesn't feel as if it belongs to my body. 'Yes, yes, I am fine,' I reply. 'Now what is happening here?'

Meg and Father both help me stagger to my feet, and Meg brushes me down with the palm of her hand.

Johnston steps forward. 'That was quite a feat,' he says, and I detect a note of admiration in his voice. 'I never thought you'd catch us and, even when you did, that you'd be able to keep pace.'

'Well, sometimes people have a way of surprising you,' I say to him icily, hoping he'll understand my intonation.

'That they do.' He nods agreeably, completely oblivious to my barb. 'That they do.'

'So what is it you are going to do with us now?' I ask as haughtily as I can manage while looking like someone who has left her wits far behind her.

'We don't plan on doing anything with you, madam,' Johnston replies. 'But we have instructions to bring your father to the barracks and hold him here.'

'For what exactly?'

'I'm just following orders, madam.'

He then takes Father by the arm and steers him towards the entryway of the barracks. I follow close behind, with Meg at my heels. Two soldiers step forward to try to stop us, but Johnston gestures for them to let us pass. Eventually, he leads Father into a small room, and Meg and I enter after him.

'Mrs Putland,' Johnston says, 'your father will be staying in this officer's quarters, and I am not sure for how long. I think it would be unwise for you to be here, too; one of very few women among so many men in the barracks. If anything were to happen . . .'

'I am staying with my father,' I announce imperiously.

'But you will have to share his close confinement.'

'I don't care. He needs me here.' I can see Father looking at me sideways, almost gratefully, and I feel a little more of the ice I have always reserved for him in my heart begin to melt.

'You will be much more comfortable back at Government House,' Johnston protests. 'Really, Mrs Putland, that might suit everyone better.'

'Suit you better, you mean?' I ask.

He smiles; he looks as if he can't help it.

Meg steps forward. 'Mistress, if you are determined to stay here, I shall go back to the house and fetch you some things. And for your father.'

'Thank you, Meg,' Father says, making us all jump. Even though this is all about him, in the heat of the moment we'd almost forgotten he was here.

'I can send a couple of soldiers to help you,' Johnston says to Meg, and I'm surprised by the kindly note in his voice.

It's at that point I remember the talk that he had taken a convict woman as his concubine. A woman named Esther, whom he met coming over on the First Fleet. So during the time he was acting governor, after usurping Father, we had a convict as First Lady! I wonder what Lord Castlereagh thought of that, when the news eventually reached him.

Johnston ushers Meg out with her helpers and Father and I look around the room. Happily, it's not as bad as I thought from first sight. It's obviously a lower officer's quarters but, while the room is small and hot, with just a couch and a table, there's a second room just off it, and this one has a bed.

'You have the bed, Mary,' Father tells me. 'I'll sleep here.'

'No, no, you take the bed!' I say.

But then I see the look on his face. 'Yes, thank you, the bed will be comfortable,' I add. Father looks as if he doesn't have much pride left; it would be wrong of me to strip him of his last vestiges.

The first two days in those barracks are the worst. The hardest thing is being in such a small place with so little to do. At home I could play my music, walk in the garden and slip out to town. Here I am barely able to do anything. Father sits quietly most of the time, sometimes with a book in front of him, but not, I suspect, reading. He says he isn't in the mood for conversation. He is, apparently, thinking.

We have three armed sentries guarding us at all times, and the use of a man servant. Some of the soldiers' wives bring us food, for which we're grateful. Of course, they're all on the rebels' side and so may not feel so well disposed to us, but they bring it, nonetheless. The meals aren't particularly palatable, and Father grows annoyed that the women and the soldiers aren't as courteous towards us as he thinks they should be. I try to mollify him, but I recognise the testiness as a glimpse of my father of old, and feel heartened that he's perhaps recovering his strength just a little.

After two days, Meg is allowed to visit us and I am glad of her company. She informs us we are occupying the quarters of Foveaux's secretary, the New South Wales Corps' Lieutenant James Finucane. He's the one who has given us his man servant, but we should be careful, she warns us, in case he is spying for the rebels. Foveaux seems to be growing in power in the colony, too. Paterson is not a well man, she says, and seems to want to solve the problem of the governor, dispatch Father, Johnston and Macarthur off to England to face trial, and then leave everything else to Foveaux.

When Meg and I are alone, we speak in hushed voices in the bedroom so as not to disturb Father and his mental machinations.

'When do you think this will end?' I ask her. 'They can't keep us here forever.'

'The talk from the officers in town is that they're waiting for your father to break,' she says. 'They still want him to take the *Admiral Gambier* to England so they can use the *Porpoise* for Norfolk Island.'

'I don't think Father will give in. In eleven days it will be the first anniversary of the revolt and, look, we're still here.'

'Yes, I think they're running out of patience, but they don't really know what to do.'

Every day, Johnston visits us and talks with Father. It seems he's the emissary chosen by Paterson to conduct negotiations. He says Father can have the *Admiral Gambier* fitted out just as he'd like for the voyage; Father says he has no interest in that. He says Macarthur and himself will be billeted as far from his quarters as possible; Father says that's still plainly unacceptable. Their talks go back and forward, round and round, and all end up at the same place: on the *Porpoise*.

I take my turn to plead with Father. 'This is a ridiculous state of affairs,' I tell him. 'We can't go on like this. It's been almost a year that we've been imprisoned now, and I think I'd like to go home. What is so wrong with the *Admiral Gambier*? It will only be six months and then, just think, you'll be back with Mother and my sisters and all the family. And we'll be able to see Harriet's little ones . . .'

His face softens momentarily at that. 'But Mary,' he then says, seizing my hand, 'we can't let these scoundrels win. They need to know that I am not a man who gives in. I am the rightful governor of this place, and they'll have to eventually accept that.'

'But I don't think they ever will.'

'Mary, we must stay strong. I remember when I was at the Battle of Camperdown—'

I interrupt him. 'No, Father, this is a very different situation. Please, it's time for us to go home, I beseech you.'

On our sixth day at the barracks, however, the conversation between Johnston and Father takes on a more subdued tone, and Meg and I crane our necks—in vain—to hear what they are saying. When Johnston leaves, Father looks triumphant.

'I think at last they are coming around to my way of thinking,' he says. 'You see, Mary, you just have to be determined.'

I raise my eyebrows at Meg, who smiles with amusement. I know we're both thinking the same thing. We are getting back something of the old Captain Bligh, but perhaps we don't want too much.

The next day, Johnston arrives looking ebullient. 'Good morning, ladies,' he greets us. 'I think you're soon going to be on your way.'

Father harrumphs in the background.

'And good morning to you too, Governor. I have the response to what we discussed yesterday.'

The pair disappear into one of the barrack's rooms and Meg and I sit impatiently, waiting to find out what is being agreed. When they reappear not long afterwards, Johnston is smiling. 'You're now free to return to Government House whenever you'd like,' Johnston says with a small bow. 'I'll have the soldiers help you with your things and arrange for a carriage. Unless, Mrs Putland, you'd rather run . . .'

I can't help smiling at that. 'No, a carriage would be most suitable,' I reply.

As soon as he's gone, we ask Father what is happening.

'They've agreed to give me back the *Porpoise*!' he says, beaming. 'I knew they would.'

'And did you have to agree to anything in return?' I ask.

'Yes, that we would immediately embark and set sail for England.'

I'm delighted, and I embrace him warmly, something I've rarely ever done in my life. 'That's wonderful, Father! Well done, indeed. I didn't think you could do it, but you did!'

Then, much to Meg's surprise, I hug her, too. I feel so happy at the prospect of an end to this terrible situation, I'd probably hug Johnston, too, if he were there. It's probably just as well he isn't.

We return to Government House for fourteen days, which are spent in a fever of packing, farewells to our friends and a last visit to the female orphanage to say goodbye to the girls, before Johnston and Paterson arrive with the paperwork on 4 February. Father takes them into the drawing room and peruses it carefully. It apparently states that he has been permitted to embark on the *Porpoise* and take with him anyone he wants, providing he sails direct for England, without touching at any ports in the territory or interfering with the government in any way. Apparently, they fear he might try to set up some kind of blockade in the harbour. But, to me, it seems to be a fair way of settling this stalemate once and for all. Finally, with a flourish, Father signs. Everyone looks relieved, but I am overjoyed. We're finally to be free of this place, and I'll be back with my family.

Johnston and Macarthur are due to sail to England on the *Admiral Gambier* on 28 March, so hopefully we'll beat them to have our petitions heard by the British Government, too. It's all now, finally, working out well.

I suggest to Father that we collect John from the mausoleum by St Philip's and take him back to England with us on the *Porpoise*. From there, I will travel with him to Ireland, to return him to his family. Father is strangely reticent about that, however.

'No, Mary, I think it's best if we leave him there for a little while longer,' he says. 'We need to make all the proper arrangements, and we can always send for him later.'

'But Father, I don't want to leave him here alone,' I protest.

'He won't be alone. I'm sure the Rev Fulton will be happy to visit him and lay flowers on your behalf.'

'But . . .'

'No buts, Mary. That's my decision.'

He also seems to be dragging his feet about packing everything. Some of his furniture he is oddly happy to leave in Government House. I think that's unnaturally generous of him in the circumstances, but I say nothing.

There's only one fly in the ointment. Father draws up a list of the people he wants to accompany us on our voyage and present evidence on our behalf when we reach England, including the long-suffering Mr Griffin, of course, and the Rev Fulton, Mr Campbell and Mr Palmer. The Rev Fulton apologises, saying he's now allowed to minister to the people of the Hawkesbury so he feels he needs to stay in New South Wales to do so, while Mr Campbell also tells us, in his gruff Scots accent, that the timing doesn't quite suit him, but he will follow by a later ship. The painstakingly proper Mr Palmer, however, dearly wants to come but Paterson has forbidden it, arguing that Mr Palmer, a stickler for the rules to the point of pedantry, is still refusing to let Johnston see his ledgers without the British Treasury's express permission—which is causing no end of problems for the new regime. Father insists that, according to the signed agreement, he can take anyone he wants, but Paterson stands firm, arguing that Mr Palmer has not settled his accounts. The debate rages on.

Eventually, on 20 February, Father, Meg, Mr Griffin, the servant Mr Jubb and I leave Government House for the last time and board the *Porpoise* for our long voyage home. We're in the company of its loyal Captain Porteous, and a full crew of sixty-five. I look for the lean pale figure of Mr Palmer, but he's nowhere to be seen.

A few people from town turn out to watch our departure, and we think we can make out the figures of Paterson and Foveaux in the distance, but there is none of the ceremony of our arrival in Sydney two and a half years earlier. Such a relatively short period of time, and yet so much change. We arrived here to a huge fanfare with hope in our hearts, and me looking forward to a future with a husband I adored, but now we're leaving quietly in ignominy, thoroughly cowed and beaten, and me as a widow.

As we cast off, I push those thoughts aside. We're on our way home, and soon I shall be back in our gorgeous house in Lambeth, talking to Mother, gossiping with my sisters, and playing with my nephew and niece and any other family members who may have arrived in our absence. I look over at Meg, and she's smiling, too, no doubt also looking forward to being back home with her mother and her three sisters and two brothers. Maybe Father could have her pardoned, and she could join me as my lady's maid in London. What fun we would have!

I feel the warm summer's breeze on my face, and breathe in the salty air. I see the tall, majestic heads of the harbour looming up in front of us, the smoke of a native's fire on the clifftop. This has been an astonishing adventure, but now it is time to go home. I'm excited and happy to be free.

I can hear some shouting nearby but take little notice of it. 'Man the topgallant clewlines! Haul taut, furl topgallants, helm a-lee, haul taut, down jib, settle away the topsail!'

And then, suddenly, we stop and drop anchor. I look around, confused, and see my father standing on the deck. He's grinning like a madman.

27

BROKEN WORDS

Meg Hill
20 FEBRUARY 1809, SYDNEY

It's like a moment frozen in time. The three of them are motionless: Mary staring at her father, Bligh looking enormously pleased with himself as he peers up at the furled sails, and Meg looking from one to the other, then one to the other again. Neither woman has any clue what's going on.

Meg breaks the spell. 'Sir,' she shouts over the noise of the waves thudding against the hull, 'what's wrong? Why have we stopped? Is there a problem?'

He looks her full in the face. 'No, not at all, Meg,' he replies. 'Quite the opposite. The problem is that of the vile wretches who put us in this position. Now we will see how they like it!'

Meg turns to Mary to see if she can make any sense of what he's saying. But Mary is looking at him dumbfounded.

'Father!' she cries. 'Father! What on earth are you doing? You made a solemn pledge that we would sail straight to England. We've only been away for ten minutes and you are breaking it already?'

'Ah, they broke it first,' Bligh replies. 'They said I could have whoever I wanted with me, so when they denied me Mr Palmer, the agreement was effectively broken. Thus I am not tied to my part.'

'But Father . . .' Mary beseeches him. 'We're on our way home. We *were* on our way home. Can we not just continue and leave this accursed place behind us?'

'No. I am the rightful governor of New South Wales,' says Bligh. 'And I shall now show them who is really in charge.'

Meg can see tears of anger and, she imagines, crushing disappointment in Mary's eyes. She feels for her. Mary has done so much for her father in recent times and she must see this now as a complete betrayal.

'Father, was this what you intended all along?' Mary suddenly asks. 'Is this why you wouldn't let me bring John? Were you planning this?'

'Yes,' Bligh says triumphantly. 'It's brilliant, isn't it?'

'No,' says Mary coldly. 'And I don't know if I can ever forgive you.'

The *Porpoise* stays in the harbour and Bligh writes out a proclamation that New South Wales is in a state of mutiny. Mr Griffin dutifully copies it out a number of times, then a longboat is dispatched to deliver the notes to every ship in the harbour, forbidding each one from helping any of the rebels to leave. This is exactly the situation, Meg realises, that Paterson had hoped to avoid.

Mary has retreated to her cabin below deck and refuses to have anything to do with her father. She's outraged that he is behaving this way and devastated that they will not be going home after all. What's more, she's immediately engulfed by wave after wave of seasickness. Meg gives her mistress all the ginger root tea she can possibly drink, but it doesn't seem to make much difference.

Meg slips up to the deck on the second day and, spying Bligh standing alone, tells him how ill his daughter is, and how she can do so little for her while the water is so rough on this section of the harbour. He listens to her in silence and she has no idea whether or not he's heeding her words. But the next day, Bligh orders anchors away; the sails are unfurled and the ship jolts back into action.

'He must have seen sense at last,' Mary tells Meg as they feel the *Porpoise* come to a halt, then surge forward with such force that Mary drops the book she's been reading and they nearly fall from their chairs. 'Thank God!'

The two women climb up to the deck and Mary looks out again as their ship passes deftly between the heads. She smiles, until the ship suddenly lurches starboard, heading down the coast. 'What the hell . . . ?' she splutters.

Mr Griffin is standing nearby and she turns to him. 'Do you have any idea what's going on?' she asks.

He looks embarrassed. 'Maybe you'd better ask your father,' he says timidly.

'No, Mr Griffin. I'm asking you.'

He looks around as if trying to spy an escape route.

'Mr Griffin, please . . .' Mary says, more gently this time.

He sighs. 'Well, your father now has a plan to sail to Van Diemen's Land,' he says. 'The lieutenant-governor there, Mr Collins, wrote to him a short while ago.'

'Yes, I remember,' Mary says sharply. 'Pledging his loyalty.'

Mr Griffin hesitates. 'So we're now on our way there as Governor Bligh hopes he may prove . . . a valuable ally.'

'An ally in what?' Meg pipes up, confused.

'An ally in bringing New South Wales back into line,' he says.

Mary pales. 'So he wants to mount a rear-guard action?' she asks. 'He wants to stage a rebellion against the rebels?'

'It would seem that way, madam,' Mr Griffin says. 'Now if you'll excuse me, I have a lot of paperwork to catch up on.'

When he's gone, Meg turns to Mary. 'It would seem this is only the start of a fresh battle,' she says.

Mary frowns. 'And it will probably end like many of Father's personal battles,' she says. 'In utter humiliation. For him and everyone around him.'

The *Porpoise* reaches Van Diemen's Land and then sails up the Derwent River to anchor, on 30 March, off the territory's second settlement of Hobart Town.

Mary has been ill for almost the whole journey, so she doesn't have the strength to argue when her father comes to take her ashore. He and Meg almost carry her to the longboat to be rowed to the wharf, where Collins greets them—not without some surprise.

He hurriedly arranges a rudimentary guard of honour to welcome them, but Meg can clearly see he doesn't really know what to do.

He's well aware of everything that happened in Sydney but, while he was happy to privately express his support for Bligh, he looks in an absolute quandary at actually having the toppled governor as his guest.

The two men greet each other warmly, but Meg suspects it's purely good manners on Collins' part. The lieutenant-governor leads them into Government House, and seats them while he leaves to organise dinner for them all. As soon as he's out of the room, Meg looks at Mary and her father and sees they're also shocked by the conditions in which Collins lives. It's a small, mean, three-roomed building that the cold wind whistles through.

'I knew he would be overjoyed to see us,' Bligh says.

Mary rolls her eyes but she still looks too weak to argue. Meg is just about to say something when Collins returns with the promise of a good meal to welcome the weary travellers.

'Well, I wasn't expecting this,' he says, taking a seat with them. 'I'd believed you'd left Sydney for England.'

'As did the rebel government,' Bligh says jovially. 'But William Bligh doesn't always do what others expect or demand—especially when they have no right to do so.'

Collins looks uneasy. 'So does Lieutenant-Governor Paterson know you're here?' he asks.

'No, but he probably will very soon,' Bligh says. 'And he won't be pleased at all.'

From the look on Collins' face, Meg thinks to herself that Paterson isn't the only one.

Bligh explains that he's hoping Collins will help him retake Sydney, and the lieutenant-governor of Van Diemen's Land listens politely. He's obviously a man of impeccable manners and invites Bligh and Mary to stay with him. Bligh thanks him and leaves Mary and Meg there, with Mary overcome with relief that she is back on terra firma. Bligh stays on the *Porpoise*; Meg suspects he realises his ship is much more comfortable than this Government House.

The town itself is in a pretty poor state, too, and having recently received a further five hundred people from Norfolk Island, it is evidently having trouble providing enough food and shelter for everyone. Yet what's even more appalling to Mary and her father is the way Collins openly flaunts his relationship with his sixteen-year-old convict mistress. He left his wife behind in England, he had two children with another woman in Sydney, and yet he wasted no time finding another 'wife' here. This one is now clearly pregnant, and Collins makes absolutely no attempt to hide such a scandalous state of affairs.

But why should he? Meg thinks privately to herself. He obviously treats her well, and she's happy enough in his company. His only major problem is his new visitors. He's obviously waiting on instructions to arrive from Sydney and is working hard to be as hospitable as he can in the interim.

A few weeks later, at the end of April, the pleasantries grind to a halt. The news has reached Paterson that Bligh made for Hobart instead of heading straight to England, and he's apparently furious. As a result, one of Collins' maids confides in Meg that the lieutenant-governor has been sent orders that no one in Van Diemen's Land should have anything to do with Bligh and his daughter, nor should they supply their ship with fresh provisions. Collins then has the proclamation read out in church in an act that makes it immediately obvious to everyone that Collins won't be supporting Bligh in his quest to reclaim Sydney.

Later that day, Meg and Mary are visited by Bligh at Government House, and he tells them that the usual sentry is no longer posted at their door. He fears the worst, he says: they are all about to be arrested and sent back to Sydney.

As a result, he has the three of them hurriedly rowed back to the *Porpoise*, and then repositions the ship out of range of any shots that might be fired from land. But with the ship's store of food running so low, Meg knows that Bligh will have to rely on local sympathisers rowing over to them under the cover of night. One settler is caught red-handed bringing over a stash of mutton and laying hens and is sentenced to receive five hundred lashes, a punishment so severe that it almost kills him. At the same time, as was probably intended, it effectively dissuades anyone else from trying to help Meg, Mary, Bligh and his crew.

Then Meg hears that Bligh has discovered a midshipman on the *Porpoise*, who has been found drunk while on duty, happens to be one of Collins' illegitimate sons. To her horror, Bligh rules that the fifteen-year-old should receive two dozen lashes. It marks the end of all semblance of civility between Bligh and the lieutenant-governor.

The *Porpoise* moves further down the Derwent to its mouth, and Bligh tries to blockade Hobart Town. He resorts to demanding food, and spirits, newspapers and news from every ship attempting to enter the harbour. That's how they hear about the death of the former governor King. It was expected in some ways—he'd looked so ill when last they'd seen him boarding the ship home in February 1807—but it was still a shock to hear he'd died in September 1808, less than a year after he'd reached Britain. They say a prayer for him on deck, and another, at Mary's insistence, for his widow, Anna.

As the months at sea drag on, Meg can see Mary becoming more and more disheartened. Bligh navigates the *Porpoise* up and down the Van Diemen's Land coast, anchoring a few times off Adventure Bay south of Hobart, where, Mary says, he once talked fondly of first meeting natives. He often tries to reminisce to Mary but Meg can see she doesn't want to hear. She's still suffering terribly from seasickness and, in the moments when she's at her lowest, she has hallucinations that her husband John Putland is still the captain of the *Porpoise*, as appointed by Bligh after Captain Short left for England, and he is coming to rescue her. Meg tends her with a syrup she makes from the bitter bugleweed to try to calm her down, and gradually Mary starts to regain her lucidity and her strength.

Meg begs Bligh to give up and order the crew to sail on to England, but he flatly refuses. 'I'm waiting for the British Government to reinstate me to the governorship,' he tells her. 'I need to stay here and wait for that to happen. There's more at stake here than you appreciate.'

Meg is running out of patience. 'Your daughter's life?' she retorts.

He falls quiet at that. But still he does nothing. The weeks continue on in all their monotony. A few of the crew desert, the manservant Jubb is caught stealing spirits from Bligh's cabin, and morale on board hits rock bottom.

But finally, one day, the captain of a passing ship tells Bligh that an eight-vessel convoy is enroute from England, with a Colonel Lachlan Macquarie in charge, bringing over his own 73rd Regiment to replace the New South Wales Corps. Bligh is jubilant. This is the news he has been waiting for. It can now only be a matter of weeks before he's recalled.

And sure enough, on 2 January 1810, a mind-numbing nine months after he first arrived in Van Diemen's Land, an oarsman sent by Collins approaches the *Porpoise* with official orders from London.

Bligh is delighted and can't stop smiling in anticipation as he takes the envelope with its official seal from the messenger, with both Mary and Meg watching on excitedly. But when he breaks the seal, takes the letter from its envelope and starts to read, his face falls.

Colonel Lachlan Macquarie will be arriving in Sydney shortly, it says, where he is to be appointed the new governor of New South Wales.

28

ANCHORS AWEIGH!

Mary Putland
2 JANUARY 1810, VAN DIEMEN'S LAND

In an instant, all the fight seems to ebb out of my father. While the rest of us, even gloomy Mr Griffin, are pleased that our pointless period of exile might soon be over, Father takes to his bunk in his cabin. I can understand why he needs a moment alone to lick his wounds. His dreams of a triumphant return to Sydney have been dashed. He feels he's been betrayed by the British Government. He suspects that Macarthur and Johnston have won after all.

I give him a few hours to wallow and, later that afternoon, I knock softly on his door.

'Who's there?' he calls gruffly.

'It's me, Mary.'

I push open the door and he swings his legs over from the bunk to sit on the edge. 'Yes? What do you want?' he asks.

His face appears grey and haggard in the shadows, and I realise my father has aged even more since reading that letter this morning. Although I'm still innately furious at him for his deception at not sailing for England, I still can't help feeling sorry for him. He's always been such a proud man, so convinced of his own rectitude about everything, and so sure of his decency and integrity, that it's hard to see Father so broken. But every time I soften towards him he seems to take advantage of my trust, lashing out in unexpected ways.

'Father, everyone's waiting to see what we're going to do,' I say. 'We've been here so long now, and we're all impatient to get moving. It's not fair to keep us in suspense.'

He grunts, but I press on.

'So, shall we set sail for England now? There is nothing left for us here. And surely Mr Collins will be glad to see us on our way and out of his waters? Think: we could be on our way home to Mother and the girls . . .' I suddenly have another brilliant thought. 'And you could press your case to Lord Castlereagh as soon as we get there. Minchin with his despicable petition would have seen him a long time ago, and Macarthur and Johnston will surely have already arrived and will be chewing his ear off.'

Father says nothing and I wonder if he's been listening.

I kneel on the floor at his feet. '*Please*, Father,' I say. 'Let's leave this place now.'

He gazes at me as if from a long way away. 'I'm sorry to have put you through all this, Mary.'

He looks so crushed and genuinely contrite that I reach out and touch his hand. 'None of this is your fault,' I reply, knowing full well that is a lie. 'But let's now move on. I want to go home. Everyone wants to go home.'

Father heaves himself up from his bunk and I scramble to my feet. 'All right, dear girl,' he says, patting me on the shoulder. 'We will leave at daybreak tomorrow.'

'Thank you, Father,' I say. And I mean it. 'Thank you.'

Wreathed in smiles, I report the news to Meg and Mr Griffin. They're both delighted, too. I sleep soundly that night for the first time in months, knowing we'll soon be on our way home. Of course, I'll spend so many of the next months curled in a ball, wretched with seasickness, but at least it will be for the last time. I vow to myself that, once I'm home, I'll never set foot on another ship again.

The next morning everyone is up and about before first light. There's an air of busyness, of excitement, of purpose. Father orders the anchor aweigh and we set off. I'm surprised, though, after the first two hours, that we seem to be heading due north, tracking within sight of the coast.

I ask Mr Griffin about it and he stoops even lower than usual, looking sheepish. 'I'm sorry, Mary, but your father says he needs to talk to Macquarie. He feels he has unfinished business. We are returning to Sydney.'

We reach the heads on 17 January and anchor a little way into Port Jackson. Father has been in a good mood all the way here, despite the horrendous seas, but he suddenly appears to lose confidence. It seems, now that we've arrived, that he can't be sure whether we'll actually be welcome. Macquarie might have taken the side of the rebels and be ready to arrest Father. And I know it's uncharitable of me, but I can't help feeling that it would serve him right. I don't know where that would leave me, of course. Maybe back in those terrible barracks with him? But I'm not sure now if I would be quite so keen to defend my father and endure imprisonment by his side. I think he has near exhausted my goodwill.

We pace the deck waiting for some sign from Sydney about whether we're in favour or not. It feels horribly like Hobart Town all over again. The *Porpoise* is a warship, so we would be able to defend ourselves, but I doubt we would stand much chance against Macquarie's might.

We wait and we wait until finally we spy a small boat coming towards us. Everyone holds their breath until the soldier on board gives us a friendly wave. You can almost hear the simultaneous expulsion of air from many relieved mouths. The soldier clambers on board, all smiles, formally salutes Father and introduces himself as Captain Henry Antill, Governor Macquarie's aide-de-camp. He then hands him an official-looking letter.

Father tears it open: it's a message of welcome back to Sydney and an invitation to dinner this evening at Government House. I'm thrilled but Father is the picture of icy control.

'Could you thank the governor,' he tells Antill. 'But I am afraid we can't make dinner tonight.'

I'm horrified. What on earth is he thinking? What do we have to do that's more important than meeting the new governor? I'm speechless, but not a single muscle in Father's face moves.

'Maybe tomorrow will be more suitable for you?' Antill asks politely, although he looks a little taken aback, too.

Father says nothing and the ensuing pause feels as though it goes on forever.

Antill eventually regroups. 'The governor will look forward to seeing you another time,' he says finally.

Damn Father and his pride! All Meg and I want now is to get off this stinking ship and visit Government House in all its battered splendour and sit down and eat some decent food. I glance over at her; she looks as crestfallen as me. We lock eyes and she shakes her head almost imperceptibly. I nod. My father, we're both agreeing, can be an absolute idiot at times. He might be the globe's best navigator, he might even have been a fine governor had he been given more of a chance, but an able politician he is most certainly not.

That evening, another small boat arrives with some letters for Father, and two more for us from Mother. I can't help crying as I read all the news from home, although my tears are perhaps more because we could have been there ourselves in person by now. So much has happened; we've missed so much. And what do we have to show for it?

Harriet has had more than her fair share of both happiness and heartbreak. She's had two more little boys join her family—a son she named William Bligh after her first who died, and then another called Robert. Tragically, Robert lived only two weeks. Oh, how terrible! I can't imagine how Harriet has been able to endure such agony. But she says Henry and Elizabeth are growing up fast and I do a quick calculation. Henry will be nearly six by now, and Elizabeth will be four in a few days' time. How much I've lost of their childhoods already!

Mother is faring well, and my sisters are all missing us, but she says she's been very distressed to hear what has befallen us in New South Wales. She's been busy meeting with Sir Joseph and all of Father's friends and allies, encouraging them to petition the government on his behalf. Johnston is facing a court martial and Macarthur a possible trial for what they did to Father, and she's determined to win him justice.

She has also by now received my letter about John's death and passes on everyone's condolences. What a fine young man he was, she writes, and what a great match for me. She had so much been looking forward to us having a long and happy marriage and had hoped we'd be blessed with children. But she tells me to be strong. I am young, she says—although I feel an old lady now at almost twenty-seven—and she's sure I will find love again, if I make sure I'm open to the possibility. I smile. Dear Mother, echoing my darling John's words.

Father listens as I tell him everything she's said, and his face softens to hear all she's doing for him back in London. 'Your mother is a saint,' he says when I have finished reading.

'Yes,' I respond, with real feeling.

He doesn't seem to notice.

Afterwards, he goes through his other letters. One has the seal of the British Government, and he attacks that first. 'At last!' he says, skimming over the words. 'Justice at last!'

'What's happened?' I ask, still basking in the warmth from home.

'The British Colonial Office has declared that the rebellion was illegal, and the action was a mutiny!' he replies. 'I knew they would! Those treacherous buggers Macarthur and Johnston will get what's coming to them now. Huzzah! But they're also letting me know that Macquarie has been appointed to replace me. I really don't understand why. If I am innocent, why wouldn't they simply reinstate me?'

'I don't know Father,' I say, although I secretly suspect I do. It was all simply too hard, and they would know my father wouldn't make it any easier for anyone.

That evening, a thirteen-gun salute is fired from the shore in our honour and Father looks pleased; Macquarie obviously has manners. As we eat yet another dinner of old salt pork and weevilly rice, I do wonder what he must be thinking, and saying, about us. And what he might be eating himself.

The next morning, I dress carefully in a formal midnight blue gown with a thick petticoat underneath in order to make the best impression on our hosts. Father wears his dress uniform, Mr Griffin dons his best suit, which isn't really much of a suit at all, and I give Meg a daffodil yellow dress of mine that I think will suit her better than me. Then we sail right into the harbour, receive another thirteen-gun salute, and are welcomed directly onto Government Wharf. Governor Macquarie has outdone himself. He has a guard of honour ready from his 73rd Regiment to mark our arrival and I walk between them, keeping my eyes trained on their faces. I'm fearful of catching the eyes of any of the soldiers of the New South Wales Corps who might be standing watching beyond them, because we understand they haven't yet been sent back to Britain. I'm even more nervous that Father might see someone he knows from his imprisonment in the barracks and become involved in a shouting match. That would never do on our first day back in Sydney.

We're met at the end of the guard of honour by a very tall, hand-some, distinguished-looking man in a perfectly pressed uniform with a staggering display of medals. He salutes us, then introduces himself as the lieutenant-governor, Colonel Maurice O'Connell.

'Welcome back to Sydney, sir,' he says to Father in a soft Irish brogue that instantly reminds me of John. He turns and bows to me. 'And welcome, Mrs Putland. We've all been looking forward to your return.'

I don't believe him for a minute, but I think it's nice of him to say so.

He escorts us to Government House and chats amiably about the weather, the gardens and the state of the town. He towers over both me and Father. I guess he must be at least six feet tall, a good foot above my height, and he's broad-shouldered and well built to boot. I also admire his good humour, especially when Father snaps at him that the weather, the gardens and the state of the town look as if they've changed little since his reign.

'Yes, of course, sir,' he says evenly.

I smile at him, and he winks back. I feel myself colour immedi-ately. Meg notices—she misses little—and raises an eyebrow.

We come to a halt in front of the doors of Government House and I look up at the old place with a mix of pleasure and pain. It's had a fresh coat of paint since we were last here, and I can see some work has been done on the garden. I glance out of the corner of my eye towards the old hibiscus plant and see, with a pang, that it's now regrowing.

'Governor Lachlan Macquarie and Mrs Elizabeth Macquarie!' O'Connell announces, as the governor and his wife come out of the front door to greet us. 'Please meet . . . Commodore William Bligh and Mrs Mary Putland.'

His hesitation before saying my father's new title is lost on no one. I can see Father frowning. He would have liked, I can see, to have been called governor. But he has to face facts: that time has well and truly passed.

The men salute each other and bow to me and Mrs Macquarie. I estimate Elizabeth to be about five years older than me, but her husband appears much older, maybe only six or seven years younger than Father. The difference in their ages surprises me.

'I'm very glad you were able to come today,' Governor Macquarie says to Father in a lilting Scottish accent, and I wonder if that's a jibe about us not coming to dinner the previous evening. 'It is very nice to make your acquaintance.' He gestures for us to follow them inside, and Mrs Macquarie immediately puts her arm through mine.

'Come inside, Mary,' she says, with a similar lilt to her voice. 'I have been so looking forward to meeting you. I understand you have the most *fabulous* wardrobe. I can't wait to see some of your outfits!'

29

MAKING MORE ENEMIES

Meg Hill
18 JANUARY 1810, SYDNEY

The governor and his wife seem to be doing everything they can to make Bligh and Mary feel at home. That afternoon, after receiving them at Government House, they take them out in their carriage to visit the camp of the 73rd Regiment just outside town, which fires another formal salute for the benefit of the former governor. Bligh seems totally unimpressed, however, and when Macquarie invites him and Mary to dinner that evening, he again refuses.

'Well, how about tomorrow?' Macquarie asks jovially. 'I don't think you can turn me down three times!'

Meg can see Mary is looking mortified. Bligh catches sight of her face, too. 'Yes, that would be fine,' he finally says.

'Splendid!' Macquarie exclaims. 'We will see you then. Take the carriage back to the wharf for your ship.'

When they board the *Porpoise* again, Mary explodes. 'Why on earth did you refuse dinner again?' she asks. 'They are being so nice to us, yet you are treating them with such disdain. Are you trying to make more enemies?'

'Nonsense!' Bligh shoots back. 'I've been told his orders from Britain were to reinstate me as governor for one day to demonstrate the illegality of mutiny. But instead, he had himself proclaimed as governor with undue haste.'

'That's ridiculous!' Mary says, her voice rising. 'He arrived on 31 December and you were nowhere to be seen. What was he supposed to do? Hang around in a non-official capacity until you might perhaps deign to turn up?'

'He could have waited,' Bligh says sulkily.

'No, he could not. He had to get on with it and clear the place up. Wouldn't you be complaining if you'd arrived and found the New South Wales Corps still in charge?'

'That's enough, Mary. I have a headache, and I'm going to bed.'

Mary and Meg eat together in Mary's cabin that evening. Meg tries to reason with her mistress. 'You must remember how much he's hurting,' she says. 'He's a proud man and this situation is very difficult.'

'I know that,' Mary replies. 'But he doesn't make it easy for himself—or for anyone else.'

The next day, the group go ashore again. Mary and Meg visit John at the vault near the church and leave fresh flowers there. Walking back to the wharf, Meg is surprised to find she's nervous. Knowing the men of the New South Wales Corps are still in Sydney, she's anxious all over again about the possibility of bumping into

Henry Mackey. She thought she'd be over her fear of him with the passage of so much time, but her dread had only been put on hold for all the months they were away from Sydney. Now, with the Corps still around, and its soldiers having nothing left to lose . . . She finds herself constantly on the lookout for the tell-tale dark mustard facings of the Corps' uniforms among the forest green lapels of the 73rd Regiment's.

Meg accompanies Mary, Bligh and Mr Griffin to Government House, and slips off to the kitchen while the others dine with the Macquaries and O'Connell. The governor and his wife have obviously gone to a great deal of trouble, serving a magnificent meal of shrimp pâté, hashed calf's head, pheasant, braised pie of rabbit fricassee, stewed beef steak, plover's eggs, gooseberry fool and orange jelly. Mary, her father and Mr Griffin haven't eaten so well since the mutiny, the second anniversary of which is coming up in a matter of days. Meg, sitting in the kitchen, is also fed handsomely.

'Are the master and mistress always this generous?' Meg asks the cook.

'Not always,' the woman responds. 'But I think Commodore Bligh is a very special guest, and they want him to feel at home. The governor obviously feels it was a terrible thing that happened.'

The serving staff from the dining room report from time to time on the progress of the dinner. They say Macquarie is making little headway with his guest; Bligh seems determined to pour scorn on all the new governor's ideas about improving the colony, saying it's a hopeless task as New South Wales is so integrally corrupt with a population made up overwhelmingly of amoral drunks. The only hope for it, he insists, lay with the small farmers of the Hawkesbury. Everyone else could go to hell.

Meg blanches as she listens to their account. The governor tries to appease Bligh, telling him that the New South Wales Corps will be leaving Sydney on a convoy soon, to answer to possible charges arising from the mutiny. And under orders from London, he'd cancelled all the grants of land made by Macarthur, Johnston and then Paterson after them. Paterson would be returning home on the same convoy, probably at the start of April, while Foveaux would be leaving earlier, in March.

But, by all accounts, Bligh seems unmoved. Meg slips into the dining room just in time to hear him declare, 'They all need to be prosecuted as traitors. It's no more than they deserve. And Paterson and Foveaux siding with the rebels . . . The courts need to come down hard on those buggers.'

O'Connell stands at that point and suggests the ladies repair to the drawing room.

'I would like that,' Mrs Macquarie says pleasantly.

Meg sees Mary shoot O'Connell a look of profound gratitude. She no doubt feels that her father's foul mouth jars horribly with the present company.

When all the women are in the drawing room, Meg sees Mrs Macquarie approach Mary and ask if her father is always so . . . difficult.

'I'm afraid he is, Mrs Macquarie,' Mary replies. 'This has all taken a huge toll on him.'

'Please call me Betsey,' the governor's wife says. 'And may I call you Mary?'

Mary nods and smiles, and Meg feels a sense of relief. At least one of the Blighs is ready to make friends. Mary certainly seems keen. 'It's very kind of you to make us so welcome here,' she says.

'No, not at all,' Betsey replies. 'You have been through a ghastly time; I can't imagine what it must have been like. And I was so sorry to hear about your husband.'

'Thank you.' Meg can see Mary swallowing hard. She knows that when her mistress isn't expecting John to be brought up, the rush of emotion still takes her by surprise. Then Mary tries to change the subject. 'Have you been married long?'

'No, not long at all,' Betsey says, looking suddenly quite girlish. 'We've only been married a little over two years.'

'Goodness, so new!' Mary laughs. 'I imagine a posting like this will prove a tough test of any relationship.'

Betsey laughs as well. 'I think it well might,' she says. 'Now, tell me about the latest fashions in London.' Meg smiles to herself. This will be a subject Mary will love but she's surprised to see her shaking her head.

'You left far more recently than I,' she protests. 'You would be much more in touch.'

'Oh, I don't think so,' Betsey says. 'In the Scottish Highlands we don't stay up to date much with the trends, and I understand from what people say that you're way ahead of them.'

Meg holds her breath. How will Mary deal with this? But she's pleased to see Mary suddenly smile. 'Oh, you heard about my misadventure in the church, did you?' Mary asks pleasantly.

'Yes, I'm afraid I did, my dear,' Betsey chuckles. 'And do you still wear the same outfit? I'd love to see it.'

The two women fall into easy conversation and only look up when O'Connell comes back into the room. 'Sorry to interrupt, ladies,' he says, 'but Commodore Bligh says it's time for you to return to the ship.'

Bligh, Governor Macquarie and Griffin follow him into the room. 'You know, you'd both be most welcome to stay at Government House for the rest of your time here,' Governor Macquarie says. 'We would be happy to host you.'

'Thank you, but no,' Bligh says quickly. 'Mary and I are most happy to stay on the *Porpoise* until it is time to leave.'

The next few weeks pass quickly. Meg is relieved to see Bligh being given back the armaments that were taken from him by the New South Wales Corps and some of his paperwork, but still he protests that a number of important documents are missing. He's spending most of his time with Griffin, gathering evidence against the mutineers, and filing witness statements for the legal actions in London.

Meg, meanwhile, accompanies Mary to visit John's grave again and then escorts her to Government House where she spends time with Betsey, discovering that they share a love of music. They both play the piano and, while Mary plays the lute, Betsey has her own cello. They agree they must both play at a soiree before Mary leaves. They also enjoy walking together through the gardens that Mary once planned to extend and Mary confides in Meg that she is pleased to discover that Betsey is now drawing up similar plans.

The governor's wife is also, gratifyingly for Mary, taking a keen interest in the female orphanage. Mary confesses to Meg that she still feels guilty she didn't pay it as much attention as she should have at first, and so she is delighted that Betsey is picking up the slack. 'I would like to move it away from the town, though,' she tells Mary once in Meg's hearing. 'I don't like those vulnerable girls being so close to the men's lumber works opposite. Maybe Parramatta would be a nicer, safer place for the institution, what do you think?'

Mary is supportive. 'I think that'd be an excellent idea,' she says. 'Those girls have had a difficult time and anything we can do to make life easier for them . . .'

Meg also takes the opportunity to spend time with her old friend, Jane, who had finally managed to track down her missing sister but, tragically, it was too late. Her sister had died just three weeks before Jane found out where she'd been living. More happily, Jane has been courting an emancipist, a freed convict turned merchant, and they have plans to marry. The officer for whom she works has applied for a ticket of leave for her.

'And how about you?' Jane asks Meg. 'You should be thinking about your own future, too. You won't be a convict forever, and you won't want to spend all your life serving Mrs Putland. Maybe you should ask her for a conditional pardon when she sails for Britain so you'll at least have some kind of freedom, even though you still won't be able to leave the colony.'

'She has become almost a friend to me now,' Meg replies. 'She treats me well.'

'That's good, but she's not your friend; she's your mistress. You must never forget that. You can't trust these people. They use you and when they are finished with you . . . That's it.'

'I might have thought that once, but not now,' Meg protests. 'She takes me into her confidence and she relies on me. We are part of each other's lives.'

Jane looks unconvinced. 'You are a part of *her* life,' she says. 'You don't have your own life, and she probably rarely thinks of you as someone who is entitled to one. You deserve more than that. You need to think of what will happen when she's ready to leave. Have you decided whether to go back with her when she returns to England with that awful father of hers, or will you ask to stay?'

'I haven't actually considered it,' Meg says.

'You'd better hurry up,' Jane replies. 'I hear they're planning to leave in a couple of weeks.'

Mary, her father, Meg and Mr Griffin take the time to call on many of their old friends. Some have suffered badly on account of their loyalty to the old regime.

When they visit John Palmer—who stopped Meg from rushing out to help Mary on the fateful evening of the coup, and was prevented from joining the *Porpoise* on its intended trip to England—they discover he was committed for trial by the rebels on charges of sedition just four weeks after their departure. True to form, his fearsome fastidiousness meant he refused to plead, as he held the court had no real authority. He was found guilty nevertheless and sentenced to three months' gaol. He was cleared when Macquarie arrived, but was only given the role of assistant commissary, on half-pay. When Bligh asks him if he'd be willing to go to England to be a witness to the mutiny, he agrees immediately.

The Rev Fulton, who has also been exonerated by Macquarie, is similarly keen to make the voyage to London for the court case.

Robert Campbell has also been dismissed from his roles, and was tried, and then gaoled, on spurious charges that he was trying to set up a trading monopoly with Bligh. This is patently ridiculous given his dedication to smashing monopolies with his various enterprises. He's since been reinstated fully by Macquarie. When Bligh asks him to return to England, however, he's less enthusiastic; he has his businesses to run in New South Wales.

Mary and Meg feel genuinely sorry for him. The big Scotsman has his family in New South Wales to look after, too, and while they know he wants to be loyal to Bligh, they can see his dilemma.

Yet Bligh doesn't. 'I am sorry,' he says. 'But I have to insist. You will be needed as a witness in court. British justice demands it.'

Mr Campbell's broad shoulders visibly slump. 'But won't you already have enough witnesses?' he asks. 'Mr Atkins is apparently going to London on the same convoy.'

'Mr Atkins!' Bligh pronounces the name with real disgust. 'That drunken lout. It was on his advice that I first charged Macarthur and the officers of the New South Wales Corps with treason. And what a traitor he turned out to be himself! He changed sides the moment I was imprisoned and became the judge advocate under Foveaux.'

'Lord Castlereagh has ordered his recall, so he'll be travelling back with you anyway,' Mr Campbell says mildly. 'Have you seen him? He looks a very broken old man now. I'm not even sure he'll survive the voyage.'

'He won't be any use to me in London,' Bligh says. 'I'm afraid I'll need you to come.'

'And Dr Harris is over there already,' says Mr Campbell, trying one last tack.

Meg sits up, suddenly more interested. 'How is the surgeon?' she asks. 'You'll remember Mary, he was very kind to us when John was so sick.'

Bligh is silent. He isn't an admirer of the doctor and had dismissed him as a magistrate during his term as governor. As a result, when the rebels came to power, Johnston had reappointed him.

Mr Campbell glances at Bligh before answering Meg. 'Although he was given a position, Dr Harris never liked Macarthur,' he says. 'His criticism turned him into something of an embarrassment for the rebel cause. He ended up sailing for England last year, so he'll be there, too.'

That afternoon, Meg decides to leave the carriage and walk back to the wharf for a breath of fresh air and some thinking time on her own. She's been mulling over Jane's words about how she needs to work out what she wants from life, rather than waiting to see what crumbs Mary will toss her.

She doesn't agree with Jane's blunt assessment that her mistress really doesn't care about her, but then again, how can she be sure? And it had never really occurred to her that she might have a choice about whether to leave with Mary and her father for England or to stay behind in New South Wales. If she did want to stay, she feels sure she'd be able to persuade her mistress, but does she want that? Could there perhaps be more opportunities here than back in London?

Meg is so deep in thought that she doesn't notice the two boys on the street. But they notice her. 'Meg!' they yell in unison. She looks up in time to see John and James Mackey charging at her and hugging her around the waist.

For a moment, she's stunned. She hasn't seen these boys for three and a half years, but they had recognised her instantly. They look so grown up now. 'Hello!' she laughs, delighted to see them again. 'It's good to see you, too!'

Then a sudden thought strikes her, and she looks up from their faces. Standing just behind them is a familiar rotund figure dressed in a New South Wales Corps uniform. It's Henry Mackey.

'Well, hello, Meg,' he says in a sneering voice. 'So lovely to see you again. Now boys, will you please excuse us. Go and play. We have some unfinished business to discuss.'

He reaches out and grabs Meg's wrist, digging his nails into her flesh. She feels as though she's fixed to the spot. She's frozen in terror and her legs refuse to move. Her breath has been knocked out of her.

'Bye, Meg,' the boys call as they move off.

Meg tries to scream but nothing comes out.

'I've been looking for you,' Mackey says, taking a firmer hold of her arm and starting to drag her towards an alleyway. 'Thought you'd got away from me, did you? Too good for the likes of me? Too busy with your precious governor and his whore of a daughter, were you? Ha! They can't save you now.'

He continues pulling at Meg and she stumbles on the path and falls over, cracking her knee on the ground. He pulls her back to her feet and the shooting pain jars her into at last recovering her wits.

'Get away from me!' she shouts, trying to shake him off. 'Leave me alone!'

'No, no, my beauty, you're mine now,' he snarls. 'All mine.'

Meg is fighting for her life, but he's a strong and solid man, and his grip is vice-like. He's hauling her closer and closer to the entrance of a dark alley, and she knows if he gets her in there, anything could happen. She might not get out alive. But just as she's giving up hope, she hears a crunch of boots on the gravel of the path and hears another man's voice.

'Meg!' he says. 'Do you know this man? Can I be of assistance?'

She looks up in her panic and terror and sees the dark green facings and cuffs of a 73rd Regiment uniform. And then O'Connell's kindly, concerned face.

30

MOVING ON

Mary Putland
17 MARCH 1810, SYDNEY

The gardens around Government House have been finished and Betsey has invited everyone who worked so hard on them to a big St Patrick's Day Feast. It's a bold move. There are lots of people who disapprove of convicts being invited to dine at Government House, even in a marquee in the grounds, and there are some murmurings that it's a step too far.

But Betsey and Lachlan—yes, we're all on first name terms now—are resolute. They believe that even though the British courts are punishing them for their crimes, the colony's convicts all deserve a second chance. And I must say, I'm coming round to agreeing with them. Sometimes, I feel terrible about how disdainful I was to Meg on the *Lady Sinclair*. She has shown herself to be an upright, respectful and thoroughly good person, and I constantly feel lucky to have her here, helping me.

There are plenty of others who disagree with the Macquaries' stand, though. My father, although he has always been firm but fair with convicts, is not quite on board with their emancipist views. He's absent today, choosing instead to visit his old friends on the Hawkesbury and inspect his farms with his overseer Andrew Thompson. I don't think the timing is a coincidence. But I'm pleased he's not here, scowling at anyone he considers an old enemy and continually trying to bring up the subject of the mutiny and how badly he has been treated. While Lachlan says he considers him wronged, Father feels very strongly that the governor is more concerned with trying to establish peace than seeing justice, and he would rather sweep the whole affair under the carpet and move on. Of course, I sympathise with both sides. We went through a terrifying ordeal and then endured a loss of liberty for so long, yet there is a point where you must decide not necessarily to forgive, but to try to forget. Father hasn't reached that point yet, and I wonder if he ever will. He's still busy gathering evidence and depositions and documents that will support his case in England, and also keeps delaying his departure.

I know it is driving the Macquaries mad, although they try hard not to show it. Every time he disembarks from the *Porpoise*, he insists on being formally saluted with gunfire and receptions—as if he were still the governor—which is exhausting for everyone. He's about to be appointed the commodore of the ship the HMS *Hindostan*, and doubtless we'll go through the same rigmarole with that. In the meantime, we're renting a small house by the Tank Stream. I thought that remaining on dry land would cut down on some of the palaver . . . until Father insisted on being provided with a protective guard from the 73rd Regiment at all times.

Meg has volunteered to help serve the convicts at the feast today, and she's plainly enjoying the role. Everyone is in such a good mood, and spirits are high. I can see Meg chatting to all the guests, including one who seems to be particularly smitten with her. I can see her laughing at something he's just said. He looks nice: a warm smile, soft hazel eyes and a cap sitting at a jaunty angle on tousled brown hair. I shall ask her about him later.

I'm relieved she seems to have got over the shock of being accosted by her old master in town a couple of weeks ago. I thought it was simply lucky that O'Connell happened to be there, until Betsey told me later that he'd confessed to the governor that he'd actually set out to keep an eye on Meg, worried about her walking alone through a part of the town that can be lawless. He never mentioned that to Meg, and I was impressed by his thoughtfulness and discretion. He has also made sure that Mackey remains under guard until he's shipped back to England with the rest of the Corps, which I know has been an enormous comfort to Meg.

'The lieutenant-governor seems like such a nice man,' Meg said to me the evening he escorted her back to the ship. 'I think if he hadn't turned up, I would have been . . . I don't know . . . but I might not be still here.'

'That Mackey is a thoroughly despicable creature,' I replied. 'I didn't like him when I first met him, and I dislike him even more now. I'm so sorry, Meg. It's my fault you went through that torture with him the first time.'

'No, I'm just very grateful you came back for me,' Meg said. 'But now he won't be able to get his hands on any more women. I feel sorry for his wife, but she must have known what was going on.'

'Mr O'Connell says Mackey's wife has decided to stay here while he returns to England. So I think she must agree with you.'

'On another subject entirely,' Meg said, 'have you noticed the way Lieutenant-Governor O'Connell looks at you?'

'I don't know what you mean,' I lied.

Lieutenant-Governor O'Connell—Maurice—seems to have been at nearly every dinner party and soiree we've attended at Government House. He is always the most charming company and, Meg is right, he does seem to pay me particular attention. It's flattering, of course, but it has only been a little over two years since John died, and I'm not ready for any new romantic attachments. It was so painful losing John; I couldn't bear the thought of going through anything like that again. And I do need to look after my father. I am kept busy cleaning up his diplomatic messes wherever we go.

Indeed, Betsey has no time for Father. 'I can understand that you want to protect your father,' she said to me on the morning of the St Patrick's Day feast, as she directed the setting up of the tables and the laying out of the food. 'But you're still young, and you have your whole life ahead of you. What are you now? Twenty-six?'

'Twenty-seven in a couple of weeks,' I say.

'That's far too young to devote yourself to your father . . . especially one so crabbit as him . . .'

I can't help but laugh. She's so direct and guileless. I find it refreshing.

'I was twenty-nine when I married Lachlan,' she continued. 'Lachlan had been married before, but lost his wife to consumption, the same fate as befell your husband. But don't leave marrying as long as me. I think you get set in your ways as you get older. And surely your late husband would want you to be happy?'

I suddenly found myself blinking back involuntary tears. 'Yes, he would,' I whispered. 'In fact, he told me on his deathbed that I should be sure to remarry.'

'A good man,' Betsey said.

'Yes, very,' I agreed.

That afternoon, the unusual guests at Government House, all dressed in their Sunday bests, seem to have the time of their lives and make a touching speech thanking the governor and his wife. They're obviously both delighted the event has gone so well, and vow it shall be the first of many. Both Meg and I love being in the warm glow of this vivacious couple's company.

With Father away at the Hawkesbury, I'm invited frequently to Government House, and I can't help noticing that Maurice seems to be seated closer to me at the dining table each time. When I ask Betsey about it, she smiles.

'He's a lovely man, isn't he?' she asks. 'Do you enjoy his company?'

'Yes, I do, but he's so much older than me.'

'Only sixteen years,' Betsey says immediately. She's obviously been thinking about it. 'Exactly the same age difference as Lachlan and me. And it works for us. Even better, Maurice has never been married before. It's harder being someone's second wife, especially when the first is much younger and more beautiful.'

I look at her quizzically.

'As I mentioned, Lachlan's first wife died at just twenty-four years of age,' she says. 'It's harder to live in someone's shadow. But for you, Maurice could be the perfect match.'

'And do he and I have any say in this?' I laugh.

She tilts her head on an angle. 'Maybe,' she says. 'But I think you should both hurry up before your father gets back.'

Not everyone at the Macquaries' table seems to be so well inclined towards me, however. The new judge advocate who replaced Atkins, Ellis Bent, seems to almost disapprove of me. I try hard to engage him in conversation, but he's such a dour, serious young man, I can feel myself getting sillier and sillier to try to coax him out of his shell. I like the look of his wife, Eliza, and wonder if she might be a friend for me, but she is such a quiet thing that I struggle to find anything even half-sensible to say to her.

Whenever I enter a room and the Bents are already there, I see them examining whatever gown I happen to be wearing and curling their lips. They look so nondescript themselves, I would never take their views on fashion seriously, but their opprobrium does encourage me to go further than I might normally. Betsey cheers me on silently from the sidelines in this endeavour, and I think even Maurice finds it amusing.

'Mrs Putland, what glorious ensemble are you wearing tonight?' he exclaimed once, when I wore a clinging, unlined muslin dress with draped filmy panels that twisted around me to accentuate my figure. 'Is this truly what they're wearing in London these days, or are you mocking us?'

'Yes, this is the latest fashion,' I replied, holding my shawl open so my audience could take in the full effect, and twirling to send the layers floating in the air around me. 'What do you think?'

'Gorgeous!' Betsey said. 'And are those pantaloons you're wearing underneath?'

'Yes, everyone is wearing them now,' I said, noticing Mr Bent whispering something to his wife. 'Everyone who has taste, anyway . . . and maybe even those who have none.'

I watched Maurice joining in the general laughter and smiled with satisfaction.

I like it that while he often talks to me about serious subjects, he doesn't seem to mind if I'm silly at times. It feels wonderful to be so suddenly carefree; able to show both sides of my character and not have my father hovering disapprovingly nearby.

When Betsey asks me if I'd like to come and stay at Government House for a while with Meg, I readily agree. The only difficulty with my friendship with Betsey is that she seems to be good friends with John Macarthur's wife, Elizabeth, who also comes to visit from time to time. It strikes me as odd that they should have such a warm relationship given Lachlan is the governor and Macarthur was responsible for unseating the previous incumbent. But Mrs Macarthur seems to hold a special place in the colony. She was the first officer's wife to settle here and is a formidable woman, looking after a growing sheep empire at Elizabeth Farm in Parramatta, as well as at Cowpastures in the remote southwest, in the absence of her husband. I'm civil enough towards her when we meet, but I prefer to avoid her. I think that best in the circumstances.

I find it hard to believe a wife wouldn't know that her husband was plotting a military coup. Thus I always consider her more of an enemy than an impartial bystander.

I enjoy staying at Government House this second time around, however, especially without the politics and worries that seemed to cloud our first time here. We have a few musical evenings, and I play the piano to a mostly appreciative audience. Betsey says she's far too rusty to play in public and, as she puts it, she has 'a certain dignity to maintain'. I chuckle at that. Maurice, I notice, is always the first to start the applause and the last to finish it.

He calls by so often that I accuse Betsey of match-making.

'And what if I am?' she asks. 'Do you object?'

'But we're meant to be leaving for London in April,' I say.

She looks amused. 'And are you sure that's what you want?'

'Of course, it is.' Yet suddenly I'm not so certain.

To be truthful, I am becoming more and more fond of Maurice. I find him excellent company; funny and smart and attentive. He's an interesting man with real depth. He's from County Kerry in Ireland, and I ask him if he knows of Frogmore, the place after which John named our land grant in Parramatta.

'*Everyone* knows Frogmore,' he says, in the same tone I used when talking about how everyone wears pantaloons, and I have a sudden giggling fit.

But Maurice also has a more serious side. He's apparently the cousin of the renowned social reformer Daniel O'Connell, known as 'The Liberator', who successfully led the campaign for Catholic emancipation in England. Maurice studied for the priesthood in France at one stage, before deciding it wasn't for him. He left and signed up to the French army before transferring across to fight for Britain. He became a captain in the 1st West India Regiment and served with great distinction in the Caribbean, being thanked by the House of Assembly after repelling an attack by a much larger number of men than he had. He then transferred to Lachlan's 73rd Regiment and became lieutenant-colonel last year.

'You've had such an exciting life,' I say to him one day over an afternoon tea that Betsey arranged and then suddenly became too busy—or so she said—to attend. 'What do you think is next for you?'

He pauses and then a smile slowly spreads across his face. 'I think I'm looking at her,' he says.

31

AUTUMNAL ROMANCE

Meg Hill
1 APRIL 1810, SYDNEY

Meg is starting to view the upcoming voyage back to England with dread.

She's picturing another six months at sea in the company of Mary and her father and the inevitable friction and arguments, as well as the strain of being part of a convoy that's, politically, so dramatically divided. While they'll be travelling on the *Hindostan*, she knows that the presence of Colonel Paterson and the former judge advocate Atkins on other ships in their convoy, along with the entire body of the New South Wales Corps, will be a constant irritant to Bligh. And it isn't as if he needs much stirring to rouse his bad temper.

Bligh has repeatedly put off the date for their departure, telling them that the *Hindostan* isn't ready, but now the final date has been set for 27 April. As it grows ever nearer, Meg starts to wonder

286

whether she might truly be better off staying in New South Wales—if, of course, Mary would allow her.

It was a surprise for Meg to realise she's actually quite happy here. With Bligh in the Hawkesbury, life is a great deal more relaxed, and Mary seems to be in such a cheerful mood these days, she's a pleasure to be around. Meg has enjoyed staying at Government House, too, with the staff she knew from when they were last there, and she's loved rekindling some old friendships.

But, most of all . . . most of all . . . she is taking great pleasure in the company of a man she met at the St Patrick's Day feast. Mary had spotted it immediately.

'So, Meg,' she'd asked her the next morning, 'aren't you going to tell me who that man was you spent so much time chatting to at the party?'

Meg laughed. 'I can't keep any secrets from you, Mary, then?'

'No!' Mary said. 'Tell me, what's his name, and what is he doing here?'

'His name is Daniel Panton,' Meg said, smiling. 'And he's a stone-mason. A very busy one, I believe. He did some of the stonework around the garden of Government House.'

'And what's he like?'

'He's very funny and he makes me laugh.'

Mary nods. 'I could see that,' she said.

'I'd heard of him before I met him. Jane had mentioned him and his name is quite legendary around town.'

'Why's that?' Mary asked.

'Well, you may have heard of the *Barwell*, the ship he came over on?'

Mary shook her head.

'It came out eight years before us, and it was quite notorious. Twenty-five of the convicts on board were plotting to take over the ship but they were discovered before they reached the Cape. The ship stayed there for eight weeks and then the officers uncovered a second plot, this time between another group of convicts and some of the crew members.'

'Oh my goodness!' Mary exclaimed, horrified. 'And was Daniel involved in those?'

'He swears not,' Meg replied. 'He says most of the convicts on board heard about the scheming, but wanted nothing to do with it. They were keen to get to Sydney to start their new lives.'

'So why is his name so legendary?' Mary asked, fascinated.

'Well, do you know the word "pommy"?'

'No? Should I?'

'In London rhyming slang, it means an English immigrant, which changed to Jimmy Grant and then to "pomegranate". And Daniel was the man, so they say, who was so impatient to be rowed to the shore from the *Barwell* so he could start his life afresh, that he shouted, "C'mon you pommy bastards! Row harder!"'

Mary burst into laughter, and Meg joined her.

'I wonder what the pommy bastards thought about that!' Mary said when she caught her breath back.

'I don't know,' Meg answered, 'but it made him an instant hero among his fellow convicts. Apparently, for months afterwards, everyone went around calling each other pommy bastards.'

Since the afternoon of their first meeting, Meg and Daniel have been on a few walks together, and she finds herself charmed, and occasionally horrified, by his irrepressible good humour and high spirits. When they strolled through the Domain one afternoon, he leaped on top of a small wall—the one he built, he pointed out—and then repeated, word-for-word, Governor Macquarie's speech from the day of the feast, mimicking every mannerism. Meg looked around nervously in case anyone could see or hear him, but they were, thankfully, alone.

Then he jumped down and snapped off a bunch of grey-white flannel flowers from one of the newly planted beds, went down on one knee and presented it to Meg.

'M'lady, take this as a symbol of my affection,' he said with exaggerated courtesy. 'And don't worry, there's no one here to see.' Then he kissed her hand.

This is all terribly new to Meg and she's grateful that Daniel seems to realise that, and is taking the courtship slowly. He's a good bit older than her twenty-one years and doubtless far more experienced in the ways of the world. While she's always amused by his antics, she likes his serious side, too. He confesses he misses home terribly: his father, who is also a stonemason, his long-suffering mother, and his six brothers and sisters back in London's Bishopsgate, two miles west of where she'd been living in Stepney. He doesn't imagine he'll ever be able to return, though. Even after he serves out his term, it will be hard for him to save enough for the fare for the voyage back.

Meg is honest with him, telling him that since she's still a convict with a life sentence, she must do what her mistress orders, and she is due to return to England in a matter of weeks. At that prospect, he always grows quieter, before quickly recovering.

'I'll just have to persuade you to stay, then,' he says.

'I may not have the choice,' she answers him.

'I think you will,' he insists. 'From what you say of your mistress, she will be very fair to you.'

Meg is relieved that Mary knows about Daniel now, and wonders how her mistress feels about their imminent return home. She and Maurice seem to be getting on so well, and Meg doesn't think she's ever seen Mary this happy. She loved her first husband, of course, but Meg had only ever known them both weighed down by his illness. This relationship seems different: much simpler and more carefree. That would be a lot to do with Maurice himself, Meg suspects. So much older and wiser than Mary, he's more than a match for her, and is a good foil for her quick temper and moodiness. While she can be feisty and outspoken at times, he always seems unflappable and kind and generous to a fault.

Still, Meg hears all the gossip about the unlikely pairing. The staff, who all loved John but had often suffered Mary's sharp tongue when she first came to the colony, speculate about whether Mary has deliberately set out to woo one of the most eligible bachelors in the colony in order to place herself in a position of power again. Maybe she wants to take revenge on behalf of her father, they conjecture, and settle scores with his old enemies. Her bravery the day of The Great Rebellion, when she faced the troops alone, is renowned, but no one can quite believe she could emerge from the whole ordeal without harbouring deep grudges. Maurice—someone also extremely popular at Government House—could be little more than a pawn in her plan.

Meg speaks out against such chatter whenever she hears it, but it's impossible to completely quell. There are others higher up who seem to have taken a dislike to her mistress, too. Mr and Mrs Bent are in an influential position in New South Wales, and they clearly don't approve of her. Meg's friend Jane's new husband is a friend of Mr Bent's, and he was amused to hear the judge advocate's summation of her character. He couldn't help telling Jane, who duly passes it on to Meg.

'Mr Bent describes Mary as rather pretty but proud and conceited and affected to a greater degree than any woman he's ever seen before,' Jane says with obvious amusement. 'He says everything is studied about her—her walk, the way she talks, everything—and you only have to see the way she sits down to realise she's practised it!'

Meg is shocked. 'Well, I suppose she is conceited, but then aren't most of the women in her position? She was the colony's First Lady, too, so imagine what the criticism would have been if she wasn't at all elegant.'

'But here's the best bit,' Jane goes on. 'Mr Bent swears he's been told that she is extremely violent and passionate; so much so that she would fling a plate or a candlestick at her father's head.'

At that, Meg can't help smiling. 'Yes, that part's certainly true,' she admits.

'He doesn't much like her father, either. He says he is extremely revengeful and would be delighted to hang, draw and quarter all those who deprived him of his government.'

'True again,' Meg laughs. 'This Mr Bent is quite astute in some ways, isn't he?'

'He also thinks Mary's very clever and accomplished and plays very well on the pianoforte, but he doesn't like her clothes. He very much disapproves of those. While he says she has a nice figure, and a rather sensible face, he feels she dresses with some taste but "very thinly". And to compensate for the want of petticoats, she wears breeches, or rather, trousers.'

At that, both women fall about with laughter. Meg knows Mary is aware that Mr Bent isn't keen on her but decides to keep his reasons to herself. It wouldn't do for Mary to know she has any more enemies than she already believes she has.

On the morning of Mary's birthday, Meg is surprised when her mistress asks her to visit John with her again at the vault. She often prefers to go alone, but it seems this time she has something she wants to discuss within John's presence.

They walk there in companionable silence and Mary puts a posy of pink and yellow hibiscuses on the flat stone covering the vault. The two women kneel down together and say the Lord's Prayer, then Mary manoeuvres herself into a sitting position. Meg can't help but notice the deliberately careful way she does so, and silently damns Mr Bent for making her aware of it.

'Meg, I've been thinking,' Mary says. 'You know Maurice and I are becoming . . . good friends?'

Meg smiles. '*Just* good friends?' she asks. 'I'd say it's rather more than that from the way he looks at you.'

Mary reddens. 'Yes, we have become fond of each other,' she continues. 'Very fond. And so I wanted to talk to you about that.

Nothing's been said yet, and nothing's been decided, but I was wondering what it might be like if I ended up staying in New South Wales. I have been looking forward to going home—of course I have—and seeing my mother and sisters again but . . .'

'You maybe have a better reason to stay here than to leave?' Meg finishes for her.

Mary looks relieved that Meg seems to know what she's thinking, even before she almost does herself. 'So, my dear friend,' Mary resumes, 'how would you feel if I stayed behind in the colony? Would you be happy to return to England with my father? It is only fair to you that you are taken home. That was always the intention.'

Meg is silent. 'I suppose this isn't too much of a surprise to me,' she says finally. 'I've seen your relationship with Maurice developing, and I can see how happy you make each other.'

'Thank you, Meg.'

'But I might actually want to stay here, too.'

'Really?' Mary claps her hands in delight. 'Is that anything to do with Daniel?'

'Maybe,' Meg replies. 'We haven't progressed as far in our relationship as you have in yours, obviously. But I do like him very much.'

'That's wonderful!' Mary says. 'From what you say about him, he sounds like a good man and it would be excellent to see you married off.'

'Hold on, hold on,' Meg protests. 'We haven't even spoken about that as a possibility. Have you? Has Maurice proposed?'

'No, not yet, but I think he may very soon. At least, I hope he will.'

'I'm so happy for you,' Meg says.

'And I you, my friend,' Mary adds, covering Meg's hands with her own. 'Who knew that so much happiness could come out of such misery?'

At the mention of misery, a thought strikes Meg. 'What about your father? What will he say? He surely will be bereft not to have you returning to England with him?'

Mary's face clouds over. 'One thing at a time,' she says. 'We must see if Maurice asks me to marry him first. He might simply be enjoying an amusing dalliance with me that means nothing.'

'I don't believe that's Maurice's style at all, and neither do you,' Meg says. 'He's as solid as a rock, and wouldn't have a manipulative or duplicitous bone in his body, I'd wager.'

'Yes, I think you're right,' Mary says. 'But we only have four weeks before we're scheduled to depart. If he's going to ask, he needs to hurry up . . .'

BLESSINGS

Mary Putland
13 APRIL 1810, SYDNEY

Every time I see Maurice these days, I'm on tenterhooks. Will he propose or won't he? I have only two weeks left until I'm supposed to be sailing off on the *Hindostan*, and yet still he's said nothing. In the end, I take matters into my own hands. Patience has never been my strongest suit.

'There's something I need to ask you,' I say to him when we're sitting together after a dinner of roasted partridge and an oyster ragout at Government House. The Macquaries have left the room to see off their other guests, but Maurice seems to be eking out the evening as long as he can.

'What's that, my dear?' he asks softly.

Oh my goodness, that gentle Irish brogue does it for me every time. 'Maurice, can't you guess?'

He looks flummoxed. 'I'm sorry . . . ?' he replies. 'Have I done something?'

'No, it's what you *haven't* done that's worrying me,' I answer.

His face is blank. He has absolutely no idea what I'm talking about.

'Maurice!' I finally say in exasperation. 'Are you thinking of asking me to marry you?' I suddenly become overwhelmed by nerves, and quickly add, 'Or . . . maybe not?'

He laughs and gathers me in his arms. 'Of course I want to marry you, Mary,' he says. 'There's nothing that would make me happier. But I have to wait for your father to return from the Hawkesbury to ask his permission.'

'No, you don't,' I tell him. 'Not at all. It's me you have to ask.'

He moves back so he can look me directly in the eye. 'Oh. Well, all right, then, Mary, will you—'

'No.' I break into his sentence before he has the chance to finish it. 'No, you have to do it properly,' I say.

He nods, stands up to his full six-foot-something height and then bends down onto one knee. 'Mary, my darling—' he begins.

I realise, at that point, that I just cannot wait. 'Yes, of course I will!' I say in a rush. 'I'd love to!'

He is so tall that even from one knee, he's still able to lean over and encompass me in his arms before kissing me, hard, on the mouth. As I kiss him back, and feel my body respond to his embrace, I can't remember a time when I've been happier.

By the time the Macquaries return to the dining room, Maurice has gone. I've told him that he shouldn't ask my father for permission as there's a real danger he might say no. Instead, I've suggested we arrange a meeting with Lachlan and Betsey, and ask for their blessing instead. Once we've obtained that, perhaps everything else will fall into place.

That evening, I stop off at Meg's room on my way to bed and tell her that it's happening: I'm to remarry. She's thrilled for me. I know she is Maurice's second biggest admirer and believes us to be as near perfect a match as we can be in the circumstances.

'What do you think your father will say?' she asks me.

'I honestly have no idea,' I reply. 'I hope he will be happy for me, but he may well be more unhappy for himself. I know for sure that the possibility I won't be sailing home with him will not have occurred to him. I suppose we will have to deal with that when he returns.'

The next morning, I write Betsey a formal note asking if Maurice and I can have an audience with her and Lachlan the next day, Sunday. Betsey sends an affirmative message straight back, and I imagine she may have already guessed what it is about.

The next afternoon, Maurice arrives in his uniform and I dress in a very modest ice-blue frock. Betsey welcomes us both warmly, while Lachlan looks absolutely mystified.

I ask them to sit, while we stand in front of them and I take a deep breath. 'The past two years haven't been easy for me,' I say. 'Since my husband passed, I've often thought I would never find happiness again. I believed it was my duty in life to look after my father in his time of need. But then I met Lieutenant O'Connell . . .' I hesitate and look up at him. He smiles back encouragingly.

'We wanted to see you,' I continue, 'as both our head of state and dear friends, to ask for your permission to marry . . .'

There's a moment of silence. Lachlan looks dumbfounded, but Betsey rises to her feet and takes my hands.

'That is wonderful news!' she says, beaming at us. 'Many congratulations!'

She looks at Lachlan and raises one eyebrow. It seems to jolt him into action. 'Yes . . . What a surprise!' he says finally. 'I join my wife in offering our congratulations and wishing you both every happiness.' He stands to shake Maurice's hand and then kisses me on the cheek. 'And what does your father say?'

I look down at my shoes. 'As you know, Father is in the Hawkesbury seeing friends so I haven't had the chance to share our news. I am not sure he will be pleased.'

'So will you both be leaving for England with your father later this month?' Betsey asks me.

I shake my head. 'No, we plan to stay here. This feels like my home now, and I know I will be happy here with Maurice. I will miss my mother and my sisters back in London, and my father won't like it, but he has his life and I have mine. He will just have to accept it.'

Lachlan nods. 'Yes, I very much hope you're right and he will accept your engagement,' he says. But I can see doubt lingering behind his smile.

When I tell Meg how the Macquaries reacted, she nods as if it played out exactly as she'd expected. Then she sympathises with me. It is going to be hard to break the news to my father. I realise I'm dreading it. Throughout the past two years of difficulties, I've always been there by his side, fighting for him and consoling him through his darkest days. I simply don't know how he will react to this news. He might be happy for me to have found love again with such a suitable, high-ranking match—or he might feel it's the ultimate betrayal. His own flesh and blood, deserting him in his hour of need as he prepares to make the interminable voyage back to meet who knows what kind of reception in England.

Father is due to return to Sydney on Tuesday, 17 April, and when he arrives from the Hawkesbury to yet another formal welcome, he seems as happy and relaxed as I've ever seen him. It doesn't seem like the right time to spoil his good mood. He tells me how pleased the Hawkesbury farmers were to see him, and how some of them, still so loyal to his reign and grateful for the help he gave them as governor, have given their sons the middle name 'Bligh'.

'Such good men,' he muses. 'The salt of the earth. They are the future of this colony, mark my words. Small farms are what will work in this place, not the vast land parcels that grasping men like Macarthur insist they need to be given for their sheep.'

I try to change the subject. 'Did you see Andrew Thompson while you were there?'

'Yes, I did,' Father says. 'He was dismissed from his position as chief constable under the rebel regime, but Foveaux gave him a grant in town where he built a house. That's where the new judge advocate Mr Bent has been staying. You've probably seen it. And Paterson gave him another grant at Minto in the southwest, near Macarthur's Cowpastures, and Macquarie allowed him to keep them both. It sounds as if Macquarie favours him as much as I did, and is about to make him a magistrate.'

'A magistrate?' I echo. 'A former convict?'

'Yes,' says Father, nodding. 'It's quite a step up, isn't it? But he's a very fine fellow, and he deserves it. His health isn't too robust at the moment, though. There were terrible floods in the Hawkesbury again last year, and apparently he performed a number of heroic feats, swimming through the waters to save locals in trouble. He hasn't quite recovered from that yet, but I hope he will. Now, what's been happening with you in my absence?'

'Ah, not much,' I lie. 'I stayed with the Macquaries in Government House for a while, which was nice. I really do like them, Father. They've very good people.'

He rolls his eyes. 'Not good enough to support me, though, eh?'

'They have!' I protest. 'They've been very kind to us both.'

'Being kind is different from acting honourably,' he snaps. 'They should have cleared out the New South Wales Corps immediately, and reinstated me.'

I say nothing. It's impossible to reason with him when he's in this kind of mood.

'Oh well, only a few days left in this hellhole,' he says. 'And then we're finally on our way home.'

When I see Betsey the next day, she asks me how Father had taken the news. 'I didn't tell him,' I say. 'I'm waiting for the right moment.'

Maurice comes over to see me, too, and I report my inaction to him. 'Would you like me to ask him?' Maurice suggests. 'It might be better coming from me.'

'Thank you so much,' I say. 'But I promise you, it won't. This is something I need to tell my father myself.'

Meg commiserates with me once again and so I pretend she is Father and practise telling her. It goes horribly each time and, after bursting into tears on my last attempt, I abandon the exercise.

'You are going to have to tell him soon,' Meg says gently. 'The Macquaries have their official event to mark our departure on Monday, 23 April. Then we're supposed to be setting off on the Friday. You're running out of time.'

The farewell fete is an extraordinary occasion; the Macquaries are obviously doing their best to show Father that he's still a very important person in the colony. Government House is brilliantly lit up and beautifully decorated with festoons of flowers encircling both our initials. I blanch to see it. The day turns into an evening ball, attended by the colony's leading military and naval officers, and other citizens. The celebration continues late into the night, culminating in a fireworks display. By the end of the reception, however, I still haven't told him. Betsey corners me and asks me what I'm going to do.

I tell her I'm still waiting for the right moment.

'Do you think there will ever really be a "right moment" for something like this?' she asks. Then she hugs me and wishes me good luck, and tells me that she and the governor have agreed Maurice and I can use Government House for our wedding if we'd like to. I think she hopes it will cheer me in my hour of need.

As the days pass and Father grows ever more bad-tempered, I start to think she's absolutely right. Every time I approach Father, something distracts him or I judge him not to be in the right frame of mind, or I feel wholly unprepared for the conversation myself. The men of the New South Wales Corps board their ship, along with their wives and children, amid speeches and salutes and cheering crowds. Our luggage is loaded on, including my precious wardrobe of dresses. I'm given one of the best berths on the ship—it has been prepared just for me.

Somehow, when the day of our embarkation onto the *Hindostan* arrives, I still haven't told Father. Meg is horror-struck when she hears of the elaborate ceremony being prepared to see us off.

'Oh, this is terrible,' she groans. 'What will happen when we have to come back onshore after all these farewells? How can we face everyone again?'

'I'm very sorry,' I say. 'I'm so foolish to have left it to the last minute. But I think there's a part of me that wants to tell him, then see him sail straight away, so I don't have to face his reaction.'

I feel sick to my stomach all morning, and cannot eat a thing at breakfast. Father chides me, reminding me that the food on the ship is never up to much. I don't answer him; I think if I try to swallow anything I will suffocate. When Mr Griffin comes in, he kindly inquires if I'm feeling well, and I mumble that I am but avoid his eyes. If it's true that he's sweet on me, then my news will be distressing for him, too. At eleven a.m., we approach the port to see a vast line of 73rd Regiment troops extending from the wharf around by Government Gate and down the avenue to Government House. It's like a strange kind of waking nightmare. At eleven thirty a.m., Father and I enter the ranks at the end of the bridge and walk to Government House, where a group of military officers and civilians are waiting to farewell us. Then at midday, Father and I, along with Governor Macquarie and a company of his officers, walk towards the wharf with the military presenting arms and the 73rd band at the front of the procession playing 'God Save the King'. I feel, in some surreal way, that I'm walking to my death. We move onto the barge and then pass around all the ships in the harbour as they salute us. And then finally we arrive at the *Hindostan* and embark.

I immediately tell Father I need to see him in his quarters. He suggests we wait till morning. I tell him no, what I need to tell him cannot wait.

And when I finally tell him, it's so much worse than I could ever have imagined.

Father reasons with me, telling me I have my whole life ahead of me in London, and that Mother and the girls will be distraught. He says he realises what a difficult time I've had over here, and how badly John's death affected me. He insists there will be dozens of eligible young men queuing up for my favours at home, and he will see to it that I make an extremely good match.

When I stay my course, he grows angry and shouts at me that I'm a silly young girl to have my head turned by the first man to pay me any attention since my husband. Maurice, he says, is a man ridiculously covered with Spanish stars and orders and must be extremely vain to persist in wearing them all. He rants that Maurice has only his salary to live on, whereas I have Frogmore and all its cattle and my pension from John Putland. Further, Maurice should have asked him properly for my hand in marriage; to not have done so is simply the latest slight Father has had to endure. I tell him that it was me who wouldn't allow Maurice to ask him, but I don't think it registers.

Finally, in what is the hardest thing to bear, Father starts to beg me not to leave him. He's come to depend on me, he says. He can't imagine how he could have survived the torment in New South Wales without me remaining faithfully by his side. For God's sake, we'd just gone through the biggest farewell in all Christendom, too. How on earth would it look if I were to go back on shore after all that pomp and ceremony? If I were to leave him now, it would be the most terrible betrayal he's ever had to face. And he doesn't think he would ever recover.

I argue, I weep, I stay silent. But all the time, I keep picturing Maurice's smiling face and the future I think I will have with him here. In between, I look at Father, one moment the martinet, the next the despondent victim, then the man pleading for his life. When at one point he starts to cry, I think my heart will truly break.

'Please Father, *please*,' I beseech him. 'I don't want to leave you but I need to live my own life. Your home is with Mother and the girls. My home is here now, with Maurice. Please be happy for me. I came over to this distant corner of the world with you when you wanted me to. I've done everything I could to make you happy. And now it's my turn. It's my time.'

By morning, Father looks broken, and my eyes are red and sore. But he finally says the words I've been longing to hear. 'Mary, Mary, I can see I won't sway you,' he says. 'So, yes, you have my blessing.'

33

SO MUCH TO LIVE FOR

Meg Hill
8 MAY 1810, SYDNEY

Mary makes the most stunning bride. She says the wedding is a lot smaller than her first one, but Meg finds that hard to believe.

Nearly everyone who is anyone in New South Wales is invited, and they all attend. Those who've never met her are curious to see the woman they've all heard so much about, and those who have are equally intrigued to see what kind of a match she makes with Maurice.

Meg is thrilled when Mary asks her to be her maid of honour, and she arranges for her to have a gown made of peach silk with puffed sleeves, trimmed with bands of a deeper russet velvet as it becomes wider towards the hem. It's the first new dress Meg has ever had, and she loves it. But Mary's gown is absolutely magical. A heavy silver lamé over a slim silver slip, it's embroidered with tiny shells as a gesture to her mother, and pink hibiscuses as a nod to John. The sleeves are trimmed with French lace that Mary has had stored in her portmanteau, which she and Meg painstakingly sewed onto the dress themselves.

To everyone's shock, Mary's father again delays his departure from the colony so he can give his daughter away. Mary is both overjoyed and embarrassed, knowing that the Macquaries can't be pleased to have to endure his company for even longer. They are gracious about it, however, very gracious. True to Betsey's word, they allow the wedding to take place at Government House and have the place decorated just as magnificently as it had been for Bligh's rather premature farewell two weeks ago. This time, however, it is Maurice's initials entwined with Mary's within the garlands of flowers.

The Rev Samuel Marsden, recently returned from England, conducts the ceremony, much to Mary's annoyance. She'd wanted the dear Rev Fulton to do it, but Marsden insisted. Sydney is his parish after all and, since the wedding was taking place at Government House, he was eager to prevail.

As Mary kisses her father on the cheek then walks towards Maurice, who stands waiting in his magnificent dress uniform with all those medals gleaming, Meg notices Bligh's lip curl, ever so slightly. And then the moment passes. She thinks he still doesn't really approve of the match, but there was nothing he could do or say in the end to deter Mary. *'Mary, Mary, quite contrary,'* Meg heard him reciting to himself the other day when he didn't realise anyone could hear. But she thinks he's wrong. She believes Mary is following her heart.

Mary and Maurice announced their nuptials at a formal dinner of wallaby tail soup, boiled snapper with oyster sauce and roast venison, hosted by Maurice at his house on 3 May, with the governor and Betsey and some of the officers with whom he's most friendly. Most of them were delighted for the couple. Mary had been so nervous when Meg was helping her dress. She was worried his friends wouldn't approve of him marrying a widow, and the daughter of a man so many reviled—but perhaps not in that order.

'Who cares if they don't approve?' Meg reassured her. 'It's Maurice you're marrying, not them. They'll come around to it in the end when they see how happy you make him. Mark my words.'

'But Maurice could have the pick of the women in the colony . . . or beyond,' Mary says. 'Surely they'll feel he could have done so much better for himself?'

'Better for himself than a woman who once faced up to three hundred armed men on her own?' Meg reminded her. 'Your fame spreads far and wide.'

Mary laughed at that. 'It's astonishing what you can do when you don't think you have much to live for,' she said. 'They were very dark days. John had just died, and Father was teetering on the precipice. It's different now. With Maurice, I suddenly feel I have so much to live for. So if the New South Wales Corps storm Government House tonight, you'll find me hiding under my bed.'

'And I'll see you there,' Meg giggled.

There are always the snipers, though. There's still the gossip that Mary is only marrying Maurice so she'll be perfectly placed to take revenge on her father's enemies. Jane told Meg that Mr Bent is one of those gossipmongers. He wrote to his brother calling it 'an accursed match', and saying that he extremely regrets the marriage, firstly because he dislikes Mary, and secondly because he feels the longer she stays in the colony, the more the acrimonious split in the colony between Bligh loyalists and rebels will widen. He's adamant that Maurice and Mary's union marks an end to all hope of a more unified society going forward.

On the other side are those who accuse Maurice of nefarious motives. They say perhaps he has half an eye on her dowry—including the land grant of Frogmore, given to her and John Putland by Governor King—though the happy couple were also given another land grant as a wedding present from the Macquaries. It's two and a half thousand acres of rich farmland between Parramatta and Richmond, possibly equal to the worth of Mary's land, and Maurice immediately names it Riverston after his Irish birthplace. But no, Meg is convinced that Maurice, like Mary, has the purest of intents.

The wedding goes off without a hitch, followed by a splendid dinner of lark pie, roast goose, loin of veal, and claret jelly and then, just like Bligh's farewell, fireworks to top off the evening. Betsey had insisted Mary and Maurice invite Elizabeth Macarthur, and Mary had reluctantly agreed. Meg notices both Mary and her father studiously ignoring Mrs Macarthur's presence, although the other woman doesn't seem at all fazed. She beams at everyone and talks and chatters and laughs almost as if she owns the place which, had her husband been just a little more successful, she would have.

Mary's father looks pleased that there are plenty of his friends there, although Mr Griffin turned down his invitation, saying too much rich food wouldn't agree with him. Meg tried to persuade him, but he wouldn't budge, and she felt she understood why. Still, Mr Palmer is there along with the Rev Fulton and the Campbells, although Mr Campbell looks the most miserable anyone has ever seen him. He clearly still resents Bligh's order for him to travel over to England on the new date set for the voyage, in just four days' time on 12 May. Happily, Colonel Paterson already boarded his ship on the convoy, the *Dromedary*, a week ago, with everyone presenting arms and saluting as the band played, so he's been staying out on the harbour, waiting. Accordingly, an invitation to the wedding wasn't considered appropriate. It's quite enough that one man returned after being so thoroughly farewelled.

Bligh is quite jaunty for other reasons, too. He seems to enjoy being the father of the bride, but Meg knows he also received a letter from his wife a few days ago that seemed to cheer him no end. It said that Mrs Bligh was still being kept busy making representations about her wronged husband to everyone in power in London who would listen, but she wanted him to know he has lost one adversary. Poor Captain Short, who remarried shortly after his return to England, presumably to help him cope with all those motherless mites, had just died. Mary's father relayed his death to Meg and Mary with much relish.

There's one enemy less this side of the world, too. The Van Diemen's Land lieutenant-governor, David Collins, the man who refused to support Bligh in perhaps his greatest hour of need on the Derwent, has apparently died suddenly at the age of just fifty-three.

'I suppose it saves us the trouble of prosecuting him,' Bligh grumbles. 'But I would have liked to have seen him behind bars for his treachery.'

The wedding feels like a bright spot on the horizon and the excitement grows among everyone else. Happily, Mary suggests Meg bring

Daniel along to the wedding as her guest, and when he appears in his Sunday best, looking nervous and out of place, Meg has to smile.

'This is the first time I've ever seen you look unsure of yourself,' she tells him.

'Well, who'd blame me?' he answers back. 'Look at what a fine lady I'm escorting here.' He bows to her, and she can see the admiration in his eyes when he rises back up. 'You look . . . very beautiful.'

'Why thank you, sir,' Meg replies, giving him a little curtsey. 'You don't look too rough yourself.'

He glances around at the glittering ballroom of Government House, with its candles and flowers and everyone dressed in their finest attire.

'So this is the kind of company you keep when you're not with me,' he says. 'I imagine this is why you made the decision to stay here; nothing to do with me at all.'

'I think you might be right,' she replies mischievously.

He puts an arm around her. 'It's a beautiful day and it will be a wonderful evening,' he says, looking deep into her eyes.

She catches her breath. The scent of romance is in the air. Is this her moment?

'Now, let's have a drink. What can I get you?'

Four days later, it's time finally for Bligh and his retinue to depart. Mr Griffin says a very formal goodbye to both Mary and Meg, with no sign of the distress Meg believes he might well be feeling. Mary hugs him, but Mr Griffin holds himself quite rigid in her embrace. 'I hope you will be very happy,' he says softly. 'I'm sure you will.'

When it comes time for Bligh to leave, Meg is quite surprised by how emotional she feels to be saying goodbye to someone who once seemed all-powerful and now looks more like an old, sad man with much of the stuffing beaten out of him. He first lost his ship, then he lost his colony and his pride, and now he's losing his once-greatest ally, his daughter.

Much as Meg can see his faults, however, he was always very fair and kind to her. If it hadn't been for him, she would have spent that whole voyage to Sydney on the *Alexander* and could well have ended up with a brute like Mackey as her master for life. He had shown faith in her, given her a chance, and bestowed on her, as a result, a much richer, happier life.

When she curtseys before him, and hands him a little package for the journey ahead, with thyme for a sore throat or cough, sage tea for fevers and dandelion root for bile, he reaches out for her hands, and she holds his tight. 'Thank you, Commodore,' she says. 'Thank you for everything. It has been an honour to serve you.'

'No, thank *you*, Meg,' he responds. 'You've been a wonderful companion to my daughter and a faithful servant to us both. I'm very grateful for everything you've done for us.'

Meg is surprised to realise she's weeping.

'Don't cry,' he says kindly. 'I am sure we will meet again. I will probably be back all too soon to visit Mary and her children, or you will accompany her to England one day.'

'Yes, sir,' she says, feeling at the same time quite sure she will never see him again. 'I would like that very much.'

His farewell to Mary is even more heart-wrenching. As much as father and daughter fought, as much as he derided her, and as much as she, at times, loathed him, it is very hard for each of them to say goodbye. They cling to each other until her father gently prises her hands away and gives them to Maurice, who stands by watching them solemnly.

'Take good care of my daughter,' Bligh tells him. 'She represents the very best of me, and always has done. I have just never told her.'

And then he marches off past his very last line of soldiers in Sydney presenting arms, to his very last fanfare on New South Wales soil of 'God Save the King'.

Mary and Meg stand arm-in-arm and wave until he boards the *Hindostan*, then watch as it raises its anchor and slips between the heads. The governor and Betsey, meanwhile, take their carriage to South Head to watch the flotilla slowly disappear over the horizon.

As sad as many are, there's also a palpable air of relief that Bligh, the man who ruled and divided a community, has finally gone home.

Two and a half weeks later, the colony's newspaper, the *Sydney Gazette*, makes the decision not to write a full report of Mary's wedding, which many are calling the society event of the year. It's a difficult time. Bligh's name still conjures up a lot of fractious feeling, and Mary has inherited, rightly or wrongly, the same discord. Instead, the editor publishes a poem about the couple's nuptials and, in order to avoid any criticism at all, omits their actual names.

Meg reads it to Mary as she's getting dressed that morning.

> Strike! Loudly strike the lyric string;
> To Bridal Love devote the song;
> Let every muse a garland bring,
> And joy the festive note prolong!

To P . . . d, amiable as fair

Soft as her manners pour the warbled lay;—

Another—bolder strain prepare

For brave O'C . . . . l on his Nuptial day!

In Australia's genial clime proclaim,

Their love and valour blend their spotless flame.

And wreaths of sweetest flow'rs prepare

For lovely P . . . d's flowing hair.

For some reason, they both find it very funny.

That evening, Meg reads it again to Daniel as they sit entwined on the sofa of his house. 'Hmm, it's not really to my taste, m'love,' he says. 'I've never quite understood poetry.'

'I know what you mean,' she replies, toying with a curl in his hair that won't sit flat however much he tries to tame it. 'But it is kind of romantic. They had such a lovely wedding.'

'They did indeed.'

Meg seizes the moment. 'Do you think there's ever a day when you might want to marry?' she asks, feigning nonchalance.

Daniel reaches for her face and turns it towards him. He looks deep into her eyes, then he kisses her lightly on her forehead, on her closed eyelids, on her nose and on her lips.

'Of course I would,' he says huskily. 'I would love nothing more than to marry you.'

Her eyes fly open at the words, but she sees he is looking solemn.

'But Meg, I'm afraid I'm already married.'

Part Four

HOMECOMING

34

ANOTHER KIND OF SICKNESS

Mary O'Connell
30 MAY 1810, SYDNEY

It's strange to be living in New South Wales without my father, having spent nearly every day of the last four years here by his side. But, at the same time, it feels like a fresh beginning. As the new wife of the second most powerful man in the colony, my future looks bright. Maurice is a good, kind, thoughtful man—quite different from my father—and hopefully we'll soon be blessed with children. Once, I might have regarded the prospect with dread. Today, I'd love nothing more.

While I try to concentrate on everything that's ahead of us, I sometimes can't help being struck by memories of the past. It's a little better now that I'm not seeing men of the New South Wales Corps on the streets wherever I go, since they're now safely on their way back to England in Father's convoy, to see back in England if any of them have charges to answer to in relation to the mutiny.

Yet I know many of those who won't be directly implicated will soon be returning to supplement the 73rd Regiment. I view that prospect with dismay.

One day, I would like to confront John Macarthur in person to talk to him about what he did. I realise that may be a long time away, depending on the length of the gaol term he's given in England for his treason. But one day, one day . . .

I can see that Meg is far more relaxed with Henry Mackey having been sent off with the Corps, too. One afternoon, as she's braiding my hair before supper, I remark casually that perhaps it's now time she also thought about marriage.

'I found a good man for myself, and it seems you've found one, too, in Daniel,' I tell her. 'Shouldn't he now make an honest woman out of you?'

To my horror, her face crumples and tears begin to roll down her cheeks. I stand up and put an arm around her shoulders. At that, she breaks into sobs.

'Meg, what's wrong?' I ask. 'I'm so sorry. Sit down here,' I pat the stool in front of the dresser, 'and talk to me.'

She sits obediently, and I give her a handkerchief to dry her tears.

'Have you had an argument? Has he said or done something?'

She looks up at me, a picture of absolute misery. 'No, well, yes . . .' she starts. Then she smiles, despite herself, through the tears. 'What I mean to say is . . .'

'Yes?' I encourage her.

'Well, after I read him the poem about your wedding we did actually start talking about marriage,' Meg says. 'And it turns out he's not against the idea at all.'

'That's good,' I say. 'So, what's the problem?'

'The problem is that . . .' She hesitates. 'The problem is that he's . . . married to someone else.'

'What?!' I can't help myself. 'He's *what*?!'

'Yes,' Meg says, her voice thick with sadness. 'It turns out he has a wife back in England.'

'Oh hell,' I say.

'Hell indeed,' she repeats. 'Her name is Elizabeth and they have a daughter, also called Elizabeth.'

'And where are they now?'

Meg shrugs. 'He doesn't know.'

'She chose not to come out here with him?' I ask. I now knew that a lot of wives, particularly if they had children, decided not to accompany their menfolk when they were transported to New South Wales. And who could really blame them? Better the devil they knew.

'No, they split up and lost touch even before he was convicted and sent out here,' Meg replies. 'But they're still married. So, it means he's not free to marry me.'

'Ah!' I say. Many of the convicts simply cohabited without marriage and didn't seem to worry about it. It is a major irritant for the Rev Marsden and I know Lachlan Macquarie has promised that he will try to encourage more convicts to marry. But for Meg, I realise that could be a problem. The daughter of a minister can't so easily turn her back on the morals she was brought up with.

'I understand,' I say to her. 'And normally, none of us like the idea of a woman living with a man who belongs to another. But these are very different circumstances. We are a long, long way from home. And it sounds as if his wife no longer wants him, does she?'

'No, I suppose not,' Meg says warily. 'He says he hasn't seen her for years.'

'Then I can't believe there would be anything wrong with the two of you being together,' I say firmly. 'Tell me, do you love him?'

'Yes,' Meg says without hesitation.

'And does he love you?'

'Yes.'

'Then who will it hurt if you're together? And won't it make you both very happy?'

Meg suddenly gives me a brilliant smile. 'When you put it like that,' she says, 'it suddenly sounds very simple.'

'That's because it is,' I say. 'The only person who will mind will be the Rev Marsden—and do any of us really care what that old dullard thinks?'

We're now living in the military barracks in Sydney, and life has gradually settled down to a very pleasant rhythm. We spend a lot of time with the Macquaries, both because Maurice has to deputise for the governor from time to time, and the fact that the four of us like to socialise together. Shortly after our wedding, Lachlan gave me another land grant adjoining Frogmore, a further one thousand and fifty-five acres. Although we haven't built a house there yet, or on Riverston, it's a real possibility for the future. For the moment, we just keep seven thousand head of stock there, which earns us an income of four hundred pounds a year. It's a good living.

The new grant is generous of the governor, and I think he hopes it's a way of smoothing over past problems. He keenly wants to heal the rift in New South Wales between those who remained loyal to my father and me, and those who supported the rebellion, and I believe he sees my continued presence here as key. If I can be accommodating to those I view as my enemies, then maybe they will, in turn, take their lead from me. Similarly, if he is open-handed towards me, then I will not dwell on the fact that he really should have reinstated Father. I understand what he's trying to do, but I don't know if I have it in me to either forgive or forget. We shall see.

I like spending time with Betsey, though, and have only grown closer to her in the time since Father left. She seems to have lost some of her reserve with me. I suppose I can understand why she might have found it more difficult to open up with him around. She's still very good friends with Mrs Macarthur, and whenever we come across each other we're perfectly polite but terribly formal. I can't really blame her for her husband's actions, but she appears so devoted to him, I could never completely trust her.

Betsey, though, confides in me freely. She says that she's most anxious to give Lachlan the one thing his first wife couldn't: a child, and preferably a son and heir. She had a daughter two years ago, in England, but she died at just two and a half months. Then last year, in 1809, she suffered a miscarriage, and then another this August. She found it heartbreaking. Now Lachlan is in mourning over the death of Andrew Thompson, who never recovered his health after saving so many from drowning in the Hawkesbury floods. He was just thirty-seven. I write to Father immediately to tell him the grim news. I know he'll be sorry, too.

Despite the sadness, Betsey still manages to be very good company and we visit the female orphanage together—where I'm careful to wear the straw hat I was given as a wedding gift from some of the girls—and we make a number of enjoyable excursions throughout the colony. In January 1811, the four of us and a group of officers travel in a cluster of rowboats to South Head, where we have a picnic on the high cliffs overlooking the harbour. We eat pork pies and fresh plums and I can almost believe we're revelling in a summer's day back in England, especially when it starts to rain. Two weeks later, we attend a parade of the 73rd Regiment and then go along to the officers' ball in the evening. While the weather is still fine in April, we travel by boat again, this time to Camp Cove on the southern side of Port Jackson, for another picnic in the shade of a magnificent fig tree. Then we all go to Parramatta together, staying at the second Government House, where Betsey plans to reorganise the gardens and build the new female orphanage, of which Maurice is the trustee, near the river. Later, we take a ride further out to Castle Hill.

I try to make friends with Eliza Bent, the judge advocate Ellis Bent's wife, but somehow we never quite get along. I don't know why. I get the distinct impression she still doesn't like me but, apart from my clothes, I don't know what I can have done to offend her. I know my father wasn't pleased when Mr Bent gave him his legal opinion that the miscreants Johnston and Macarthur couldn't be tried in England for treason, but I can't see why she would hold that against me. It's a mystery.

On the public holiday of 4 June 1811, the morning of the grand ball the Macquaries are holding to mark the King's seventy-third birthday, I start to feel not quite myself. I'm queasy over breakfast, then feel so faint I go and lie down in my bedroom. Meg comes in to see how I am.

'I haven't been feeling well for a couple of days,' I tell her. 'I don't know what's wrong with me. I really don't want to miss the dinner and ball tonight. It's the first event the Macquaries have held in their new saloon.'

Meg smiles at me, which for some reason irritates me. 'What's so amusing?' I ask her tetchily. 'I don't feel well, and I don't want to be sick.'

'Well, mistress,' she says slowly, 'do you think it's a possibility that you're with child?'

I spend the next few months in a trance of happiness. Maurice is thrilled. He is so thoughtful and tries to do so much for me that I end up telling him that our child and I will both die of boredom if he doesn't let me get on with my normal life. At that, he finally backs off.

He writes to my family and sends them gifts, though, as if he somehow has to express his gratitude to them for having to manage without me. He sends two cages of parrots to Father, more shells to Mother to add to her collection, and lots of gifts to my sisters and Harriet's children. I find it very sweet of him, and tell him so.

'Mary, men—especially military men—don't find it terribly flattering to be called "sweet",' he chides me. 'Chivalrous, perhaps. Gallant, possibly. Magnanimous, even. But *sweet*? No, not at all.'

I giggle. 'No, my love,' I reply. 'You are the sweetest man I've ever met and I'm sorry if you don't like it, but it's true.'

He rolls his eyes in despair. 'Just don't ever let anyone hear you calling me that, then!'

There is news from home, too. Macarthur, after spending time in Rio trying to do deals over sandalwood, eventually reached England on 9 October 1810, just sixteen days before Father arrived in Spithead. In his letter, Father said he was hopeful that Macarthur would be put to trial very soon. More disappointingly, he wrote that Johnston had only been court-martialled and cashiered, losing his rank of major and being dismissed from the army as a result. Father was incensed that he received such a comparatively minor punishment and even more outraged that Johnston was now setting out on an appeal.

At the same time, Father also said I was so much in his thoughts. My sister Harriet had just had her second daughter, the fourth of her living children, and she has called her Mary. And, in even more good news, Father has been elevated to Rear Admiral of the Blue Squadron in a reassuring indication of the continuing high regard in which he is still held by the Admiralty and the British Government alike. I'm happy for him. I know how important that would be for him.

I have an exceedingly uncomfortable Christmas in 1811, due to my size and the heat of summer, which I suddenly find excruciating. Betsey is a regular visitor, regaling me with marvellous stories about trips she and Lachlan have made south of Sydney to Jervis Bay and north to Port Stephens, where they met a number of natives. I'm envious, still having met none in my time here.

'You should have seen them!' Betsey says. 'They came alongside us in their canoes and talked to us, although we couldn't understand a word they said. Then they tried to repeat our names and other English words, and one was brave enough to come on board and got himself shaved.'

I laughed. '*Shaved*?'

'Yes,' Betsey says. 'He seemed pleased with his new look. Then when we went to Port Stephens, I was sitting in the boat when a native came running up and, although he seemed very nervous of us, he handed me a fish! In return, I gave him some tobacco and he was very pleased with that. But he was still too uneasy to shake our hands. He just darted off to a safe distance and then did a little dance.'

'I wish I could have been there to see that,' I said. 'When I'm in a fit state again, we must go there together . . .'

Meg is marvellous, giving me a tincture she says will cool me, and a magical mixture of herbs for the pain, as she holds my hand and urges me on through the long hours. But then, just as I think I can't bear it a moment more, I go into labour. On 13 January 1812, at nine-thirty at night, I'm delivered of a fine baby boy that we immediately decide to name Maurice Charles, after his father.

'He's so beautiful,' Maurice says, with tears in his eyes as Meg hands him his son to hold for the first time. 'Just like his mother.'

I smile at him. 'Let's just hope he has as sweet a nature as his father, though,' I reply.

This time, he doesn't object.

I write home to England immediately to tell everyone about the addition to our family. I know they will all be delighted, Mother especially. I hope it's not too long before I see them all again, and Mother will be able to meet Maurice Junior in person, as well as my husband. I know she will love them both as much as I do. With Maurice in such a distinguished position in the military, it's always conceivable that we will be transferred to another country at a moment's notice and Britain is a very likely posting. It's so different from the life Mother had with Father in the navy, when she was always left behind as he struck out to the rest of the world. With the army, the wife travels with her husband and, I must say, it's a lifestyle I much prefer.

The governor offers to be our boy's godfather and we accept, so the christening is performed on 27 February by the Rev Marsden at St Philip's Church. It's a wonderful, happy occasion, and even Eliza Bent looks pleased for me. Lachlan says in his speech that a child always represents a new beginning, and I know he's actually addressing me.

Little Maurice is a healthy child and very active. We move out of the barracks and lease a single-storey stone cottage called Vaucluse House for twenty-five pounds a year, surrounded by woodland and cleared coastal scrub overlooking a beach at the harbour's edge. It's owned by the Irish convict adventurer Sir Henry Browne Hayes, who was banished here after he kidnapped a rich heiress and forced her to marry him. He's a very odd man, but it's a beautiful place to live for a boisterous little boy, especially since Sir Henry swears he dug a trench around the cottage and filled it with Irish peat to repel snakes. Maurice says that's probably nonsense, but I loathe snakes so much that I'm willing to believe anything.

By nine months old, our son is already almost walking. But the day he takes those first steps, we receive another letter from home. It is the one I have always dreaded.

Father writes that he has terrible news: my adored mother has died. She passed away in April at the age of fifty-nine. I read the news in shock. That would have been before my letter about the arrival of her newest grandson reached England. So she would never have known of little Maurice's existence. How cruel is this distance between family members! I don't think I will ever get used to it.

And I keep wondering if the strain of all the legal action and disputes over the mutiny contributed to Mother's death. The more I think about it, the more certain I am that it did.

35

THE RUPTURES OF THE PAST

Meg Hill

25 OCTOBER 1812, SYDNEY

Whenever Mary makes an overture of friendship to Eliza Bent, Meg holds her breath. She's aware that the Bents secretly dislike Mary so much that they'll only truly respond in kind if they know she's leaving New South Wales, or is perhaps on her deathbed. From what Jane tells her, she knows the couple are trying to stir up ill feeling against her and that quite possibly whatever Mary does won't be good enough to stop them. She could crawl on her knees to Mrs Macarthur, asking for forgiveness for having a father who wouldn't give in to her husband's constant demands for land and more livestock and power, and still she'd be damned in the Bents' eyes.

For a lawyer, someone you'd expect would be committed to being fair and even-handed, Meg finds Mr Bent's venom disturbing. Even Mary's pregnancy was a target. She hears he joked to his brother that Mary had been in a family way for fifteen months before she had her son, and for twelve of those she had her cot, linen and caps all ready, but 'the Mountain will not bring forth even a mouse yet'.

'Why is he so nasty?' she asks Jane when she hears the latest round of abuse.

'I think he disliked Bligh so much that he is taking some of that out on his daughter,' Jane replies. 'But, to be fair, he's also very, very loyal to Governor Macquarie, and he sees Mary could cause trouble for him.'

'But how could she cause trouble?' Meg asks.

'She can't help herself. It's so obvious every time she comes across someone who was a supporter of The Great Rebellion, or she chances on one of the New South Wales Corps officers who returned as civilians, or she catches sight of any of the New South Wales Corps rank and file who are now serving in the 73rd Regiment. She holds a real grudge against them, and she's snippy and nasty and tries to stir up ill feeling against them. I've seen it with my own eyes.'

Meg has to admit she's seen it, too. Although Mary is as happy as Meg has ever seen her with her son and her husband, she knows Mary carries around a deep store of resentment against those who helped topple her father and who, she's now begun to say, helped cause her mother's death. And in Mary's loyal mind, if they weren't actively *for* Bligh, then they must have been against him.

Although Meg knows Betsey Macquarie is personally very fond of Mary, she's seen Governor Macquarie being much more wary. He's known to be very keen to reconcile the ruptures of the past and having his lieutenant-governor married to the one woman who personifies that division can't be easy.

Meg tries to warn Mary against showing her feelings too readily, but her mistress won't take the hint. 'My father is over in London telling everyone of those terrible events,' Mary responds. 'So how can I sit here, pretending they didn't happen?'

'I'm not saying you have to pretend,' Meg tries to explain. 'But maybe you shouldn't make your antipathy to your father's enemies so obvious?'

'Do you really think they deserve to be treated as though they didn't behave abominably?' Mary rails.

'Well, perhaps not, but I'm thinking of you,' says Meg.

'Oh, don't worry about me,' Mary replies haughtily. 'They might want to silence me, but they can't. Maurice is in such a powerful position here, he will always protect me.'

Meg fears, however, that there are some forces against which Maurice is powerless to protect his wife. The British Government, for one. In early 1813 she hears from Jane that Mr Bent is talking about the governor asking London to replace the 73rd Regiment— and Maurice along with them.

'He thinks if Maurice and Mary go, then this country will be perfectly free from all factions,' she tells Meg.

'But that would be terrible, sending them off God knows where,' Meg says, dismayed.

'Yes, although even worse, what would happen to you?' Jane asks. 'That's what you should be thinking about. Would you go with them and have to start another life elsewhere without Daniel? Or would you be assigned to another master or mistress here?'

Meg suddenly looks horror-struck. 'Oh, surely the British Government can't do something like that!'

'Just you watch them,' Jane says. 'They can do anything they want.'

With Meg's cautions to Mary falling on deaf ears, she resolves to get on with her life and hope that Mary can do the same without censure. She spends more time with Daniel and often stays at his lodgings in town when she knows Mary won't miss her. He works long hours but in his time off they go walking through the town, drink with friends or just enjoy each other's company.

In March 1813, they travel to Parramatta to attend the first fair ever held in New South Wales. People gather together from all walks of life, from the governor and his wife, and Maurice and Mary, to farmers selling their cattle, sheep, horses, pigs and produce, those buying it and others, like Meg and Daniel, who are just there for the spectacle. It goes so well, it's decided it will become an annual event.

Two months later, a rumour spreads around the colony that Johnston has arrived back. Mary can hardly believe her ears and visits Betsey in Government House to ask her if it's true. Betsey confirms it. Apparently, in addition to being merely cashiered for his role in the mutiny, Johnston's appeal received a sympathetic hearing. Because he had served for so long in the army, and previously so faithfully, the Colonial Office had agreed to provide him with his passage back to New South Wales.

'I can't believe it!' Mary tells Betsey. 'Surely it isn't true?'

Betsey puts her hand on Mary's arm. 'I'm afraid it is,' she says. 'And I think we just have to accept it. Lachlan is determined that bygones be bygones and what's done is done. The British Government has instructed Lachlan to treat him as he would any ordinary settler.'

'That's just not fair!' Mary says, knowing, even as she says it, that fairness doesn't come into it. 'He isn't an ordinary settler. That man could have killed me and my father!'

'But he didn't,' Betsey replies quietly. 'And now we all have to move on.'

When Mary repeats the conversation back to Meg as she plays with Maurice Junior in the nursery, Meg nods sagely. 'I'm afraid if you don't move on, then they will find a way to make you,' she says.

Mary plunges deep into thought, until Meg throws a ball to Maurice and unexpectedly, he catches it. She immediately claps with delight.

'He's a very smart boy!' Meg says, changing the subject.

'Yes, he is,' Mary laughs.

'I only hope my child will be half as smart.'

Mary smiles, then does a double-take. 'Your child?' she exclaims. 'You're having a baby? Oh my dear, congratulations!'

Meg looks relieved. 'You don't mind?' she asks.

'Why on earth should I mind?' Mary says. 'I'm very happy for you and Daniel. When are you due?'

'January next year,' Meg replies. 'Around Maurice's second birthday.'

'A double celebration, then,' declares Mary. 'We shall have so much fun!'

Mary seems to be seeing the Macquaries a little less nowadays, but in July 1813, Betsey sends Mary a note asking her to come and visit at Government House. Meg walks with her and then goes to the servants' quarters out the back, while Mary enters by the front door.

The head housekeeper is sitting in the kitchen and greets Meg warmly. 'Lovely to see you again,' she says. 'What's brought you here today?'

'Mrs Macquarie wanted to see my mistress,' Meg replies. 'Do you know why?'

'Ah yes,' the housekeeper says. 'We are all so excited. The mistress is with child, and we think this time all will be well. She's obviously now ready to share the news.'

'That's wonderful!' says Meg. 'She's lost children before, hasn't she?'

'Yes, she's miscarried no fewer than five times after losing her first child so young. But this time . . . this time . . . Things look very promising.'

'When is she due?' asks Meg.

'March. And when are you due?'

Meg blushes. 'Is it that obvious?'

'You can't hide that bloom in your cheeks.' The housekeeper smiles.

'January,' Meg replies.

The two women sit and chat until the bell rings and the house-keeper has to rush off. Meg wanders back out towards the front of the house, just in time to see Mary and Betsey warmly embracing.

'Many, many congratulations!' Mary is saying. 'We shall be praying for you.'

Meg's son has an easy entry into the world on 18 January 1814, just a few days after Mary's son's birthday. Meg and Daniel name him Nathaniel, after Daniel's father.

'We shall watch our sons grow up together,' Mary announces, 'just as we have grown up together.'

That pleasant thought doesn't last for long, however. A few days later, Mary tells Meg that Maurice returned from a meeting with the governor to report that his 73rd Regiment is being withdrawn from New South Wales by the British Government, to be replaced by the 46th Regiment. He is being redeployed to Ceylon.

'Ceylon?' asks Meg, shocked.

'I said exactly the same thing,' Mary tells her. 'But when I asked him why, he said an officer's place in the armed services is never to ask why; just when. And this is going to happen soon, in March or April. So, we have just a few months to pack up.'

'But what if you want to stay here?' Meg asks.

'Oh, I do,' Mary replies. 'But Maurice said what we want doesn't enter into it. When he signed up to the military, this is what he signed up to: to serve his country in whatever way the government deems best.'

'But what about little Maurice?' Meg asks.

Mary sighs. 'He's young and children are adaptable. Maurice says the climate in Ceylon is good, too, and that we will probably all enjoy the change.'

Meg feels sad for her friend, but she was fearful something like this might happen. She'd warned Mary to forget all her old enmities, but she just hadn't found that possible.

'I wonder what Father will think of it,' Mary continues. 'I recently received a letter from him, letting me know he had been promoted to Rear Admiral of the White Squadron, up from the Blue, and is expecting, by the end of the year, to be promoted to the Rear Admiral of the Red Squadron.'

'He's retired now, hasn't he?' asks Meg.

'Yes, he's now on his naval pension and has moved out of Lambeth to the countryside in Kent with my unmarried sisters, Elizabeth, Jane, Frances and Anne. I wonder how they're all faring without Mother? I imagine my father, especially, will be struggling.'

Meg knows how much Mary would love to see her family again and how hard it will be not knowing how long the posting to Ceylon will be. Perhaps it will be short, followed by a period of home leave. Meg smiles to herself thinking how strange it was to think how much Mary would enjoy seeing her father again after loathing him for so many years.

There's so much packing and organising to do that Meg finds herself extremely busy coordinating it all, sometimes leaving Nathaniel with young Maurice and his nursemaid to free up her time. Mary stops her one day as she is in the middle of wrapping up some of the household crockery.

'Meg, would you consider coming to Ceylon with us?' Mary asks. 'Obviously, with Nathaniel.'

Meg is surprised by the offer but gratified at the same time. 'Mary, I'd love to,' she says. 'It would be such an adventure. But I'm sorry, our lives are now here with Daniel. I wouldn't dream of leaving him, and I imagine it would be hard for him to find work there.'

'Of course, of course,' Mary says. 'That's exactly what I thought you'd say. But I just wanted to ask . . .' And then she drifts off back into the drawing room.

It does make Meg wonder what she will do when Mary and Maurice leave. She'll probably be assigned to another mistress or master, but she is loath to imagine it and pushes the thought to the back of her mind. That can wait for another day, another week, another month.

A few days later, Mary asks Meg what she thinks she should do about John. Should she take his body to Ceylon with them, or leave him in the vault by St Philip's?

'I think we should let him rest in peace,' Meg says.

'Thank you,' Mary replies. 'I do want that, but I feel a little guilty for leaving him behind.'

'Don't worry, mistress,' Meg says. 'I shall keep an eye on the vault and leave fresh flowers there every week. He will not be forgotten.'

At that, Mary's eyes fill with tears. 'I am more grateful than you can ever imagine,' she says. 'But I'm sorry, I'm getting very sentimental.'

'That's understandable in your condition,' Meg says.

Mary stares at her. 'Oh my God, how did you know?' she asks. 'There's no hiding anything from you!'

Meg laughs. 'Many congratulations,' she says. 'I've been waiting for the right moment to say it.'

She wonders if Mary will mention anything now about Meg's future without her. But, again, she says nothing. Meg wonders if, after all this time together, and having been through so much, Mary will simply forget her. She left her behind once; she could well do so again. Meg hates to even think about it.

A grand farewell dinner is thrown at Government House for Mary and Maurice, along with the officers of the 73rd Regiment, their wives and the leading members of the colony. There are fifty-eight guests all in all. Ten days later, on 26 March 1814, Mary and Maurice walk with Lachlan and Betsey from Government House to the Government Wharf, with the street lined by the two flank companies of the 46th Regiment, to a salute of thirteen guns. Then, with all the assembled spectators cheering, they move onto the governor's barge to board the *General Hewett*. The date for sailing is set for 6 April, so later they return to shore for their last days before departure.

On 28 March, Mary and Maurice have dinner with another large party at Government House with only one person missing—Betsey. She's upstairs in labour while everyone else is enjoying the evening downstairs. When the party eventually breaks up, Lachlan stands in the corridor outside the bedroom, listening to his wife's agony. Mary and Maurice are staying the night at Government House and can hear him pacing the landing outside their room. But half an hour later, just before midnight, there's silence, then a sudden cry.

'He burst into the bedroom to see Betsey holding their son, Lachlan,' Mary says when she recounts the scene to Meg later. 'We also rushed in to see them, to congratulate them. Lachlan was holding both the baby and Betsey as if he never wanted to let either go. It was such a beautiful sight.'

'It sounds wonderful,' Meg says. 'How happy Mrs Macquarie must be now, after so many years of waiting.'

Eight days later, Mary and Maurice prepare to set out from the house at Vaucluse for the last time to travel to the wharf, ready to board their ship to Ceylon. Mary is now three months pregnant, and admits to Meg that she's dreading the voyage, but she is determined to put on a brave face.

Meg sympathises and has already prepared plenty of ginger root to help her mistress. She feels anxious herself, however: Mary has still said nothing about her future.

But in the drawing room, after Mary has said goodbye to the other servants, she calls Meg over.

'My dear Meg,' she says, holding both her hands, 'I did so want our children to grow up together. But will you promise me you will write?'

'Of course, Mary,' Meg says, feeling a lump in her throat. She may well be homeless from this moment on, but she will certainly try.

'And I've been waiting to tell you,' Mary adds, smiling, 'from now on, you will be free. I have secured an absolute pardon for you from the governor.'

Meg gapes at her, speechless.

'But if you would like work, Betsey needs a new lady's maid and I suggested you. Her head housekeeper agrees you would be perfect for the role. Of course, you don't have to take it, but if you want the post, it's yours.'

36

CEYLONESE CONFLICT

Mary O'Connell
6 APRIL 1814, AT SEA

So here I am again, on another long voyage to a different part of the world, this time to Ceylon. I am, of course, dreading it. I know I'll suffer the usual seasickness, which is likely to be even worse with my pregnancy. And I feel sad to be leaving my friends behind in Sydney—particularly Meg and Betsey—and not to be on my way back to England to see my father and sisters. But I need to be brave for my two-year-old son and for his father. I'm pretending this is going to be such an exciting adventure for us all. I only wish I could believe it.

I don't know much about Ceylon beyond what Maurice has told me. He says that the Dutch, who conquered a part of the island, were easily supplanted by the British back in 1796. Now we run most of the country, apart from the Kingdom of Kandy in the central part of the land.

Along with our ten officers, three hundred and sixty-two soldiers from the three companies of the 73rd, and their two hundred and fifty-nine wives and children, we sail via New Guinea, New Britain and the Moluccas Islands. After an extremely tedious four months, we stop on 26 June at the spice island Ambon, with its beautiful beaches and crystal-clear waters, its breeze scented with the heady aroma of nutmeg. We stay for a few days, but I wish it could be a few weeks. After so long confined on the ship, Maurice Junior adores running around outside. But his father tells us that the coastline of Ceylon is supposed to be absolutely enchanting, too. It won't be long now.

We set off again, but quickly run into gales and monstrous seas. I spend most of my time ill in my cabin and have to ask one of the other officer's wives to watch my son. Seeing the island of Ceylon finally appear on the horizon is one of the best days of my life. Our first landfall is Galle, with its imposing fortress overlooking the harbour anchorage, and we stop there to await better weather.

Maurice is anxious to get started, though, and at Galle he dis-embarks and makes his way overland north to Colombo with a few of his troops, while the rest of us sit and bide our time. I would have liked to have travelled with him but in my state, now eight and a half months pregnant, he won't hear of such a thing. The seas quickly settle, however, and the winds turn more favourably for us, and we soon sail on to Colombo, arriving on 17 August. And maybe it's just as well I waited. We're only in Colombo for two weeks before I give birth to my second son. He has spent so much of his existence so far at sea, I can think of no other name that's more fitting than William Bligh O'Connell.

I write home to Father to tell him, and also to Sydney to let Meg know. I think they will both be amused.

In Colombo, we are stationed inside the ramparts of the magnificent Dutch-built Fort Colombo that is now the centre of the British administration of the island. It's huge—nearly half a mile wide, and the same in length—and on its western side is the old harbour and the sea. To its east is Beira Lake, with just two causeways over to the mainland, which makes it perfect for protecting the city against attacks both from the ocean and from the interior. The streets inside the fort are straight and shaded by double rows of trees and, I notice with a little leap of my heart, boast tangles of hibiscus shrubs, mostly with big yellow flowers. Maurice has selected a large two-storey house for us, built, he believes, by the Portuguese before they were vanquished by the Dutch, and now owned by the British. It's very grand, with high ceilings, columns and a massive dark teak staircase, which little Maurice, now a very active two-and-a-half-year-old, insists on trying to clamber up and down all the time, as I watch with my heart in my mouth. And it is so big that even when we move in all our possessions, it still looks empty. Depending on the direction of the breeze, some days all you can smell is the sea on the warm air; other days the house is heavily perfumed with the sweet smell of cinnamon from the plantations of the interior.

Maurice tells me he may be working long hours. There have been problems with alcohol among some of the British troops stationed here, discipline issues and even cases of mutiny. I turn pale at the thought. I've had enough military mutiny to last me a lifetime.

He introduces me to the governor of Ceylon, Robert Brownrigg, who seems a thoroughly decent man. I warm to him immediately. He was appointed to his position only last year and arrived with his second wife, Sophia. I find her utterly charming, too. She introduces me to the other officers' wives and I soon fall into their routine of going out at the crack of dawn, before the day grows too hot, for a ride of three to eight miles in our carriages around the town, sometimes accompanied by our husbands, and sometimes just the women. There are three main gates to the fort and we leave from one and come back in by another, passing the massive rampart walls, the gun batteries, the garrison church, the Dutch hospital with its courtyards, open verandahs and the armies of fruit trees planted by the natives, and beyond them the stretches of thick, impenetrable forest. Sometimes we arrange a rendezvous halfway under the spreading branches of a tamarind tree, where the servants prepare cool drinks of coconut juice.

In the late mornings, we make our social calls, either in curricles or palanquins, which I discover are little more than chairs with a covering so they look like large boxes carried by four to six bearers. Maurice Junior loves them, but I much prefer the open carriage and its two horses. It feels so much more civilised, somehow.

I'd assumed Maurice would be spending most of his time in the capital with me and his two sons, but early in 1815 he is sent to the interior. It turns out it will now be one of Maurice's tasks during his seven-year tour of duty to lead a campaign by the 73rd Regiment against the King of Kandy, whom Maurice says is widely hated for his barbarism. One of the king's ministers was discovered to be secretly communicating with the British in the capital Colombo, leaving messages on palm leaves. He escaped, but the king had his children publicly beheaded and his wife, who was threatened with rape before an audience, was forced to pound their severed heads with a pestle before being drowned in a lake.

'Oh my God, Maurice!' I exclaim. 'Did you really need to tell me that? That's an horrific image I will never be able to forget and now I shall be terrified every time you leave home.'

He looks contrite. 'I'm sorry, Mary,' he says. 'I'm repeating what I was told, and you're right, I should never have mentioned it. But can you see how important it is that we gain control of Kandy? We can't have such lawlessness and brutality going on unchecked.'

I fret every day he is away, and seek company among the other officers' wives who are all in a similar state of unease. When Maurice finally returns, victorious, he's full of stories of the great mountains he and his men had to traverse, along narrow, winding paths with dizzying views over misty blue fields and magnificent forts that stand on many of the hilltops. Every time they came across one, Maurice says he and his men steeled themselves for a volley of gunfire, but only two or three wild shots ever came, and then the locals would simply run away.

'They preferred to fight us in the thickest parts of the jungle,' Maurice says. 'They'd fire on us when we couldn't see them, then they'd drop down holes that they'd dug close to the road to a depth of about four feet, so we couldn't find them. But their king is said to be one of the most rapacious, predatory men in the world and, as a result, many of his troops came over to us.'

'Did that make it a lot easier?' I ask.

'I wouldn't say *easier*,' Maurice replies. 'One of the major problems for us was always the threat of disease in such an inhospitable climate. And it's such a remote quarter, there are many wild animals. One lieutenant and a sergeant from the 73rd attacked an elephant and then the animal turned on them and ripped the sergeant apart. The lieutenant spent hours hiding in a tree until the elephant finally gave up and ambled off.'

'Oh my goodness!' I say. 'How awful!'

'But eventually the Kandy nobles welcomed us in and were as keen as us to get rid of the king. So, we went in and then searched for him, as he'd gone into hiding. When we found him, he agreed to be exiled to India with his harem and the Kandyan Convention was signed, basically annexing the territory to the British Crown. Now, for the first time in history, the whole island is ruled by one power.'

'I am so proud of you,' I tell him. 'And hopefully now you'll be home much more often.'

In May the following year, 1816, I receive a letter from Meg full of gossip about New South Wales, telling me how much we're missed. She took the post at Government House and says Betsey is proving a good and kind employer. Young Lachlan Macquarie is growing big and tall, she says, although his mother mollycoddles him terribly. Betsey had a terrible stroke of bad luck when her carriage ran over a small child in the streets of Sydney, and she took to her bed for weeks trying to come to terms with it. Meg treated her with chamomile for anxiety and gingko for feelings of hopelessness and despair. As a result, she soon emerged and demonstrated how strong she could be, by recently becoming the first white woman to cross the Blue Mountains.

I read the letter and then re-read it several more times. Meg also says the detestable Johnston has settled back in Sydney and he has at last married his convict mistress, Esther—the woman who so briefly became the colony's First Lady when he snatched power. I still find it hard to wish him well. More excitingly, Meg says she's pregnant again and her baby is due to arrive before the end of the year. I do a quick calculation: my next child is due about then, too. Oh, how I wish we could bring them up together!

Two days after Christmas that year, my third son is born, a wriggling, squealing baby boy we call Robert Brownrigg O'Connell after the governor of Ceylon. We all dote on him, especially his older brothers.

A year later, the 73rd are ordered to replace the 19th at Trincomalee, one of our most important naval bases on the other side of Ceylon, so we pack up again and set off in another ship to sail around the island to the north-eastern seaboard. I'm by now pregnant for the fourth time and it's an horrendous voyage. The gales rage night and day, the ship rocks violently and so many of us are ill. My littlest son, Robert, suffers particularly badly, but I'm so sick myself it's hard to nurse him as well as I want to. Miserably, the only doctor travelling with the convoy is on another ship and can't help us. Then, nine days after disembarking our ship, on 3 February 1818, Robert, aged only thirteen months, breathes his last. Maurice and I are devastated, and his brothers are horribly confused, and keep asking for him. We bury him along the foreshore at Trincomalee. It's said to be one of the most beautiful ports in the world, but I can only see it now as an ugly place of misery and death.

In Trincomalee, we live in another mansion inside Fort Fredrick, overlooking the sea to the east and the esplanade to the west. In my grief, it's hard for me to appreciate anything. But I know I have to keep going for the sake of my sons.

It's also difficult to keep track of the news from both England and Sydney. Father is sick with an internal complaint, I hear from my sister Harriet. It's believed to be cancer and he's not expected to live. My sister Elizabeth has married our third cousin Richard Bligh and she's deliriously happy. And in Sydney, Meg has just had her second baby, a daughter called Sarah. But the grimmest news of all is that Macarthur, after everything that happened, isn't being tried for treason. Instead, after months and months of lobbying, he has been given permission to go back to Sydney to live as a free man—as long as he agrees to stay out of politics.

This appalling injustice, I'm sure, is very likely to have caused Father's dramatic decline in health. And when I hear later that Father had collapsed and then died while visiting a cousin in December 1817, I curse Macarthur through my tears. One day, I vow, I'll confront him and I will, somehow, get even.

ROAMING WITH THE REGIMENT

Mary O'Connell
26 JULY 1818, TRINCOMALEE

We're set to be here for three years and already I'm getting used to it. I've formed firm friendships with some of the other officers' wives and we socialise here as much as we did in Colombo. I'm still grief-stricken by the loss of Robert, but six months after his death, on 26 July 1818, I give birth to a daughter and name her Elizabeth Alice, after my mother. The boys are delighted and it's as much as I can do to stop them grabbing her and trying to carry her around all the time. It's touching, though. I love that they're so besotted.

Maurice is still busy with his soldiers trying to quell a fresh wave of rebellion in Kandy against the British Government, stoked by Kandyan chiefs unhappy with the colonial administration. A leading British official is killed, and dissatisfaction quickly spreads, with the chiefs joining the rebel movement until it threatens to completely disrupt British rule over the island. Troop losses are enormous, not only from the wounds of battle but also from disease and dysentery in the jungle areas, and reinforcements have to be brought in from India.

Horrifically, the only officer from the 73rd Regiment to be directly killed by the rebels is Lachlan and Betsey's nephew John Maclaine, the son of Betsey's sister Jane, who came over to New South Wales with the pair. A heavy drinker and exasperatingly hot-headed, the twenty-six-year-old John had ridden into a jungle area, ignoring warnings about the dangers of hidden marksmen. He'd been shot dead with a single bullet—a victim of his own folly, Maurice says. On his return that week, he writes a sombre letter to the Macquaries to tell them and offer his deepest condolences. He continues to acquit himself so well, however, that the major-general hands over command of the Trincomalee district to him in November that year.

One of the most amazing experiences of our time in Ceylon turns out to be a grand commemorative dinner in June 1819 celebrating the fourth anniversary of the Battle of Waterloo, the final showdown between Napoleon and the troops led by the Duke of Wellington. All the civil, naval and military members come along, and Maurice gives a rousing speech about how Britain will never be cowed by its neighbours. Shortly afterwards, he's promoted to colonel.

Among the hardest moments, however, is sending our eldest son, now seven years old, back to Britain on board the ship *Dauntless*. I realise he needs to go to school and get a good education, but it's a difficult decision. We're all haunted by the memory of one of our major's four young sons, who were sent home to Britain from Galle three years ago on board the East Indiaman *Arniston*. The ship was wrecked at Cape Agulhas, South Africa, and his four sons, along with three hundred and sixty-eight other passengers and crew, all perished, with only six surviving.

Of course, we tell Maurice Junior nothing of that and instead say it's going to be a fabulous adventure. But I don't think he really believes us. He wants to stay with his mother and father and brother and sister. It's one of the real trials of army life. As I watch him step aboard, trying to be brave for all of us, my heart feels like it is being wrung out. I can't help thinking of my own father, who went to sea at the same age as a ship's boy or servant to the captain. I sometimes wonder how his mother felt.

But if I thought that was hard, I was unprepared for the heart-rending trial ahead. It wasn't long before reports came back that the ship had been struck by cholera, and at least thirty of her crew had fallen victim. Those excruciating months waiting to hear if Maurice had survived, or been struck down, were perhaps the most horrendous of my life. Thankfully, he made it ashore untouched.

In December that year, I receive another letter from Meg. She's had a second daughter, Ann, and her brother and sister are thrilled by the new arrival. But she sends bad news, too. The land grants we were given by Governor King have been deemed by the courts in New South Wales to have been unlawful, she reports. Father, they ruled, was the rightful governor from the moment we stepped onshore, so King hadn't been entitled to give us the lands he did. As a result, Macquarie has now declared them to have been illegal. Just like that! I imagine my father turning in his grave. The only reward from that terrible time, gone.

When I tell Maurice he looks outraged. 'We'll see about that,' he tells me. 'I still know attorneys of influence in New South Wales.'

'I think you should write to them and ask if we have grounds to fight this,' I say. 'Those grants were given to us in good faith, and we accepted them in good faith. It's not right to go back on them afterwards.'

We might actually be the least of Macquarie's problems, however. Meg writes that things aren't going too well for the couple. Although Macarthur had given the British Government his word that he would no longer dabble in politics, he still most definitely is. He seems to be causing trouble constantly, though I am not in the least surprised. The governor is now desperate to leave and take his wife and son back to his estate in Scotland. He wants Lachlan Junior to know what it's like to grow up in his birthplace and receive a decent education. He's been in the colony ten years, even though he was appointed for only eight.

And then, to make the situation even worse, the British Government has announced it is sending over a commissioner to conduct an inquiry into the affairs of the state. The governor, Meg says, is sure the report will reflect well on him. But Mrs Macquarie has confided that she isn't so sure. The British Government is in trouble and the easiest way to deflect that politically is to point to other issues elsewhere.

Mary immediately pens a letter to Betsey. 'Stay strong,' she writes. 'That evil man Macarthur will receive his just deserts in due course. And the commissioner is bound to find that you have done wonders for the colony, restoring it to a place of calm and order after the mutiny, constructing many fine buildings and giving so many of the convicts hope for the future by giving them responsibility and the chance to prove themselves.'

At the beginning of August 1820, I hear back from Betsey, and I don't think I've ever heard her sound so glum. The commissioner, John Bigge, is becoming firm friends with Macarthur, she says, and is taking evidence from anyone with anything negative to say about the Macquaries. The first question he always asks is: 'Have you any complaints to make against Governor Macquarie?' Reading her letter, I realise I've screwed up my hands into fists, so deep is my hatred for Macarthur. Doubtless he is behind all this.

A few days later, on 17 August 1820, I give birth to another son, Charles Philip. It feels something of a luxury to have spent this whole pregnancy on dry land. But not long afterwards we're told the 73rd Regiment are being posted back to Britain on 25 June 1821. Some of the fittest men are permitted to stay in Ceylon if they want to, or they may volunteer to serve in India, while the rest of us go home. In another case of terrible timing, I fall pregnant just four months before our departure. We travel on board the transport *Elizabeth* and I'm sick nearly all the way home. We finally land at Gravesend, Kent, on 10 November 1821 and I give birth to my sixth child, Richard, two and a half weeks later.

It's wonderful to be reunited with Maurice Junior and I'm shocked by how tall he's grown in the eighteen months since we waved that anguish-filled goodbye. I suppose he's had to grow up, being on his own, but his delight in seeing his brothers and his sister again, and meeting his newest siblings, Charles and Richard, brings tears to my eyes.

I enjoy being in England again, spending time with my sisters, Harriet's four children and Elizabeth's two, Richard and Frances. We talk fondly about Father and they tell me how he tragically died within days of Elizabeth's wedding. And we take a family trip to the churchyard at St Mary's where he is buried alongside our mother. I kneel down at his tombstone and read:

TO THE MEMORY OF
WILLIAM BLIGH ESQ., F.R.S,
VICE-ADMIRAL OF THE BLUE
THE CELEBRATED NAVIGATOR
WHO FIRST TRANSPLANTED THE BREAD-FRUIT TREE
FROM OTAHEITE TO THE WEST INDIES.
BRAVELY FOUGHT THE BATTLE OF HIS COUNTRY,
AND DIED BELOVED, RESPECTED AND LAMENTED,
ON THE 7TH DAY OF DECEMBER 1817
AGED 64

I suddenly look up at Harriet. 'That's not right!' I say. 'He was just sixty-three when he died.'

She colours. 'Yes, we made a mistake,' she says. 'And we didn't have the heart to fix it afterwards. But don't you think that might amuse him? His reach spread far and wide . . .'

I grin. 'Yes, you're right,' I say.

We spend a delightful two years in London, where my children get to know their aunts and cousins, and I reacquaint myself with all the latest fashions of the moment. Skirts are now bell-shaped, flat at the front and gathered or pleated into the side and back. Hems are stiffened to make them keep their shape, while the bodices often have piping or decoration in the same material as the gown itself. I think they're glorious!

Yet Maurice is still very ambitious, so it's not long before we're given our next posting. This time, we don't have so far to travel—just up to Scotland in June 1823, where the 73rd is garrisoned in the new barracks at Edinburgh Castle.

The children are thrilled with their new home, the grand Governor's House in a real live castle! It's a huge building with two main floors, two wings and attic rooms, and I tell them, when we climb Castle Rock, that we're treading in the footsteps of kings, queens and even pirates, along with people who lived here long, long ago. I describe this as the most besieged place in the whole of Britain, and we play vigorous games of attacking a castle made up of blankets in the drawing room until Elizabeth, not yet five, wakes up screaming in terror from nightmares. After that, I'm a little more cautious.

The impenetrable castle is a splendid sanctuary, not from invading armies these days, but from the teeming denizens of the buildings that line the cobbled High Street that stretches at least a mile down past the grand St Giles' Cathedral to the King's Edinburgh residence of Holyrood Palace. These 'closes', as they call them hereabouts, are tenements built atop each other and burrowed into the rock beneath so that some of them are ten storeys tall from roof to cellar. They are warrens inhabited by cut-purses, prostitutes and, it is rumoured, body-snatchers and grave-robbers who sell their grisly ill-gotten gains to the university's medical schools. I say nothing to the children about that.

I'm happy to ride past with a small escort as I venture to the fine buildings and surprisingly fashionable salons of the New Town on the other side of the marsh. At least I don't have to run for shelter when a cry of 'Gardie-Loo' rings out, either, warning pedestrians that someone's night soil and wastewater is about to be hurled from a window into the open drains below. Edinburgh is a city of contrasts, indeed. Literature, fashion, art and music flourish in abundance only a few furlongs from a seething mass of humanity in its lowest form.

Meg still writes to keep me up to date with everything happening in New South Wales and she's never short of news. She had her fourth child last year, whom she named William after my father. I was extremely touched.

'If my son grows up half as strong and clever and brave as your father, I shall be very happy,' Meg wrote. 'But I won't be pleased if he swears anything like as much!'

She tells me the Macquaries finally left the colony last year after a miserable final period to their reign. Bigge had halted some of their building programs, like the new Government House Betsey had been designing with the convict architect Francis Greenway, and then he presented a damning report on everything they had done to the British Parliament. They'd travelled home and Lachlan had gone to London to try to persuade the King to allow his rebuttal of all the claims against him to be publicly read, but so far his pleas have fallen on deaf ears. I wonder if I could visit Betsey on the Isle of Mull but it's a long journey, and very difficult with five children and now pregnant with another. I write to Betsey and promise to visit her as soon as I am able. Even more disturbingly, Meg says the new governor Major-General Sir Thomas Brisbane, has, with great enthusiasm, adopted Bigge's recommendations for reform and, even worse, very much favours Macarthur. Indeed, he's now even considering making him a magistrate.

When I read that, I see red. 'How could Brisbane possibly ever countenance that?' I rage to Maurice. 'Macarthur is a vile wretch, a wicked, wicked miscreant, an oaf destitute of all moral scruples. He brought down the King's duly appointed representative and could easily have seen us all killed. How on earth can this be right?'

'Hush,' Maurice says, rocking me in his arms and stroking my hair.

I leap up and away from him. 'Don't tell me to hush!' I shout. 'This is a scandal. It's the most evil thing I've ever heard. I can't believe our government could ever behave like this—'

Richard starts screaming in his crib at the sound of my raised voice and I go over to him immediately. 'I'm sorry, my darling,' I whisper in what I hope is a soothing voice. 'Mama's just very upset at something that's happened and now she shall calm down.'

My second daughter, Mary Honora, arrives on 20 November 1823, and then in the December we're posted to Ireland, living in Athlone, at the medieval Athlone Castle in the centre of the country.

Meg writes again and although Maurice warns me against reading the letter, I can't resist. It makes me even angrier. For years, Macarthur had been trying to set up an Australian Agricultural Co on a one-million-acre grant at Port Stephens. And in 1824, he succeeded. Yet that was only the start of his rapid return to respectability. The next year, Meg tells me, he is to be appointed as one of the three unofficial nominated members of the newly created Legislative Council. In the meantime, the man over whom he held such terrible sway, George Johnston, who lost his commission and then all his money trying to defend his actions, has died.

It's the start of a flood of bad news. A letter from Betsey arrives shortly afterwards, letting us know that Lachlan has died in London, his rebuttal to Bigge's charges, aided and abetted by Macarthur, still unread in Parliament. Brave Betsey says she is now refusing his widow's pension until his report in answer to those allegations is tabled. I write straight back with my condolences, and my unstinting admiration for her stand.

But if I find those events terribly distressing, they're nothing compared to the next tragedy. My little girl Mary suddenly dies at the age of just fifteen months—almost the same age as her brother Robert. It happens without warning on 19 February 1825 and, even though we've been through this before, it doesn't make it any easier. Maurice holds me in his arms in bed, as I weep so hard I fear I will never be able to stop. Of course, eventually, I do. I have my other children to think of.

We're moved around Ireland, and then Maurice is sent to England with some of his regiment to suppress riots in Yorkshire and Lancashire by rioting hand-weavers, smashing power looms in protest against the economic hardship they say they're causing.

In mid-1827, I'm given the honour of being asked to present the new regimental colours to the 73rd in a ceremony in Waterford in the south-east of Ireland, and then we're immediately up and off again, this time to Gibraltar. Macarthur's ghost follows me even there, although I take great pleasure in the news this time that he's fallen out with the new governor, Ralph Darling. Meg says in one of her letters that Darling has been heard to cast aspersions on his 'soundness' and has publicly likened Macarthur to 'a wayward child'. That's some small comfort, but I still can't believe it's taken this long for the authorities to see him for what he is. I look forward, one day, to having my say, too. I know Betsey will be relieved at his downfall and I'm thrilled to learn that she's at last succeeded in her mission to have Lachlan's response to Bigge's report tabled in Parliament, and she's now, finally, living on her widow's pension.

Our son Maurice, at the age of sixteen, also becomes a commissioned officer in the army, serving in Gibraltar under his father, and it's with enormous pride that we both watch his first participation in a military parade. In 1830, when the 73rd are transferred to Malta, he's promoted to lieutenant, while his father becomes major-general.

We return to London two years later, where Maurice is knighted, and I become Lady O'Connell—fancy that! We then move to Brussels and it's there that I receive a letter from Meg bearing the most devastating news: Macarthur is dead.

Maurice is perplexed as he thought I'd be pleased. But I'm not. I'm distraught. For I realise that now I will never have the chance to confront him for the terrible wrongs he did to me, my father, my mother, and the memory of my first husband.

38

A RETURN TO THE PAST

Mary O'Connell
31 JULY 1838, PLYMOUTH

I've never been so shocked in my life as when Maurice returned home from a meeting to tell me he had received his latest appointment: as lieutenant-governor and commander of the forces in New South Wales. New South Wales! I could barely believe it.

'But why are they sending us back there?' I asked him, puzzled. 'You're now seventy. Surely, it's time you started thinking about retirement?'

He smiles. 'Yes, but it is a great honour to be appointed lieutenant-governor again, all these years on,' he replies. 'And you are only fifty-five, plenty young enough for both of us. I thought you might like to revisit the place that was your home for so many years, and we could show it to our children.'

'Oh, I'm not sure . . . That terrible, terrible voyage . . .'

'But you've done it twice before, so you know what it'll entail,' Maurice says. 'Besides, surely by now you've got your sea legs? They're going to outfit the *Fairlie* especially for our voyage, so it should also be a great deal more comfortable than when you travelled before.'

I thought back to that time. Hard to believe that it was now thirty-two years since I first travelled to New South Wales with my father, so proud and unbending, and me a little ball of resentment and rage. So much has changed in the interim. Father's position was taken from him and then all that anger I'd harboured, finally, as I saw him so broken, ebbed away to leave in its place something a lot closer to acceptance, sympathy and, yes, respect. I suppose I'd grown up. And, of course, John was gone and Maurice was now in his place, and we had our beautiful children . . .

'The Admiralty have said I can have Maurice Junior as my military secretary,' Maurice continues. 'I think they like it that I have sons with military experience and it will be a great opportunity for advancement for them, too. And I'll be appointed to the Executive and Legislative Councils when we arrive. It'll all be very, very different from when we left.'

'It certainly will,' I say. Lachlan Macquarie will have been dead fourteen years by the time we arrive, and Betsey, sadly, just three years.

'But there will still be people there who we know,' Maurice ploughs on gamely. 'Your friend Meg, maybe?'

'Oh yes, it would be wonderful to see her again, and meet her children,' I concede. 'I would like that very much. And you're right, there will still be others: the Rev Fulton . . . Mr Campbell . . . Mrs Macarthur . . .'

Maurice looks surprised. 'Mrs Macarthur?' he replies. 'I wouldn't have thought you'd be keen to see her again.'

'Well, maybe I would,' I say, and then move quickly on. 'There's also our lands and livestock at Frogmore and Riverston to check up on. And then there are also Father's land grants at Camperdown and Parramatta . . . We need to spur those lawyers into action to make sure we can keep them.'

'Excellent!' Maurice says, as if the decision has been made. 'We're set to depart in July.'

And so it is that today we're all aboard the *Fairlie*—Maurice and me, our eldest son, now Captain Maurice O'Connell, aged twenty-six, together with his lovely Jersey wife, Eliza; William, now twenty-three and a lieutenant; Elizabeth, twenty; Charles, seventeen; Richard, sixteen; and my sister Elizabeth's eldest son, Richard Bligh, nineteen—along with two hundred and seventy-seven other passengers, among them churchmen, a shipbuilder, mechanics, tradesmen and agriculturalists, and tons of merchandise. And Maurice is right. I don't feel seasick at all.

We arrive in Sydney on 6 December 1838 and, on passing the battery, we're saluted with those oh-so-familiar honours. It makes me smile to remember how Father used to insist on them constantly, much to everyone's irritation. Maurice goes directly to Government House to meet the new governor, Sir George Gipps, who started in February this year, while Elizabeth, Eliza and I are whisked off in a carriage to the Postmaster General's house in, fittingly, O'Connell Street. How amazed the other children will be to see that!

The next day, Meg and her youngest, sixteen-year-old William, visit me there, and we fall into each other's arms. As we sit and chat, the years melt away. It's astonishing to realise how much time has passed in the interim; almost a lifetime, really. Daniel, at fifty-eight, is still working as a stonemason, and their three sons have all followed him into the profession. Even though Meg only turned fifty this year, she already has five grandchildren, and plans on having many more.

'It's wonderful being a grandmother,' she tells me. 'So much more fun than being a mother! You get all the pleasure without the hard work.'

'I have big hopes for my eldest, Maurice,' I laugh. 'He's just got married and I'm hoping that soon . . .'

Meg beams. 'I'm looking forward to meeting your children, Mary. Do they look like you?'

'Fortunately, not so much. They all have Maurice's height. How about yours? Do they take after you? This young man here does, I think.'

'Yes, he's a chip off the old block, but the others look more like Daniel,' Meg says.

'And William,' I say to the young man sitting beside us, looking bored as we catch up, 'tell me, do you swear much?'

He looks bewildered, as if I've caught him out unexpectedly.

Then Meg and I both break into peals of laughter. 'Your mother will explain later,' I reassure him.

We talk about the state of politics in New South Wales: the Bigge report that did so much damage to the Macquaries; Macarthur's constant terrible stirring to try to unseat everyone in power and seize it for himself; the ruin of Johnston but then the kindness shown to him by Macquarie, before their very sad deaths. But today it seems, from what Meg tells me, that New South Wales is no more peaceful than in its past. It's back in a state of drought and the politics are turbulent.

Six months before we arrived, an horrific massacre of natives had taken place at Myall Creek on the Liverpool Plains, where more than twenty-eight unarmed women, children and elderly male Aborigines had been slaughtered by a number of white colonists. Unusually, the men suspected of conducting the killings had been charged with murder, and seven out of the eleven were found guilty and hanged the day after our arrival.

Maurice and I had discussed it at length when we found out about it. No one could talk of anything else. My heart had lurched at the news. Of course, the men deserved to be hanged for committing such heinous crimes against their fellow human beings, but I felt sick at the thought of all the senseless killings that had gone on in the colony for so many years, and the fact that so many more had doubtless happened unreported.

'The rule of law must be upheld,' Maurice said solemnly. 'And it must apply to everyone equally.'

'I agree wholeheartedly,' I replied. 'But I do hope this will mark the final bloody full-stop on it all.'

He looked surprised at my language—after all, he never knew Father at his worst, I reflected.

But sitting in my new home now with Meg, I wonder how the new Governor Gipps is managing everything.

She shakes her head. 'These are difficult times,' she says. 'The decision to charge the men with murder was very controversial and then the verdict and the executions . . . Many settlers are also very angry that The Aborigines' Protection Society has been formed in London. The British Government has instructed Gipps to establish The Protectorate to appoint protectors or guardians of Aborigines, especially in the frontier districts. As well as encouraging the natives to settle, educate their children and become Christians, it's also aiming for equality before the law.'

I raise my eyebrows. 'I can only imagine the fuss that will be causing,' I say, remembering Governor King's words about the natives being the real proprietors of the soil. Maybe that sentiment was en route to being recognised at last.

'Yes, there are a lot of very angry people around,' Meg replies.

'But I don't see many Aborigines in the streets of Sydney,' I say. 'Where are they all?'

Meg looks pensive. 'There are still some fishing camps around the harbour, but most of them have been driven out of town and have moved away from Sydney to the Hawkesbury, Parramatta and the Georges River.'

'That's sad,' I say, and Meg nods in agreement. 'And how do you find Gipps otherwise?' I ask.

'It's very early days, probably too soon to tell,' Meg says. 'He seems to have similar views towards the convicts as Governor Macquarie— about treating them fairly and so on—but we've heard the British Government is now considering stopping transportation.'

'Yes, they've got a Select Committee looking into that in London,' I say.

Meg bites her lip. 'But if they do stop it, there's going to be a lot of farmers who are very angry at not having a cheap source of labour anymore,' she says. 'And Gipps has already annoyed the graziers. There's so much squatting on the land and he's insisting they stay within their own boundaries. They're mostly defying him.'

'Ah, echoes of Macarthur,' I say.

'Indeed,' Meg agrees.

'And how is Mrs Macarthur?' I ask.

Meg looks startled. 'She seems fine,' she says. 'It's said her sons have fallen out over the terms of their Father's will, which is hard for her . . . But why do you ask?'

'I was thinking of seeing her to talk to her about her husband and his actions,' I say, with as much nonchalance as I can muster.

'Really?' Meg replies. 'Is that wise?'

'I don't know,' I say. 'But I think it's something I have to do.'

While the family gets settled into the Postmaster General's house, I slip out to the old graveyard to visit John in his vault. I see flowers there that are obviously only a few days old and realise Meg has stayed true to her word, even after all this time. I stay there for a few hours, telling John about everything that's happened since I was last at his resting place, and sharing my plan around Mrs Macarthur. I feel so much calmer having told someone.

Maurice has also been busy in our first few days. He buys five acres of land up on a ridge in what used to be called Woolloomooloo Hill but has been renamed Potts Point, and hires the noted English-born architect John Verge to design us a stately villa. He calls it Tarmons, after the Gaelic word for 'sanctuary', which was also the name of his family's home in County Kerry.

It ends up a magnificent two-storey sandstone mansion down a long tree-lined carriageway from the entrance on Macleay Street, with its own massive ballroom, a reception room, a grand staircase, and fabulous views over the harbour and across to the shore on the other side. It's only later that I find out Verge was the same man Macarthur used to plan his Camden Park House.

'Do we really need all this grandeur?' I ask Maurice, examining the Australian cedar panelling on the walls.

'Of course, we do,' he replies. 'In our position, we'll need to do lots of entertaining, so why not do it in style?'

When Meg comes for tea, she's obviously taken aback by its opulence. 'This could be a house in one of the grandest streets of London!' she exclaims.

'Perhaps,' I reply. 'But I don't think we'd be able to afford its equivalent there.'

Maurice also visits our lawyers and lodges our land claims, asserting our right to the land given to Father by Governor King at Parramatta, Camperdown and the Hawkesbury. They seem to think we have a good case as to the validity of the grants and we're keen to press them. We instruct an attorney to send out eviction notices to all the people who appear to be squatting on Father's one hundred and five acres of land in Parramatta, which he'd named after Mother. There's been a great deal of building that has taken place since we were last here and now the buildings on that grant include the Female Factory, Parramatta Gaol, the Catholic St Patrick's Church and chapel, the King's School and a number of houses. Our attorney estimates that, these days, the land will be worth around forty thousand pounds—a small fortune for anyone.

As such, we can see it's going to be a difficult dispute to resolve, but we dig our heels in, hard. Father had enough taken from him during his lifetime, without being robbed after his death, too.

Maurice tells me that Governor Gipps has to inform the Colonial Office in England about the issues. Of course, it's tricky for him, since Maurice is technically his second-in-command and the first in line to replace him as viceroy were anything to happen to him. But at the end of the day, perhaps it will be up to London to decide.

In the meantime, Maurice gets to work. He employs our sons and nephew as his staff in his HQ, where he administers control of the three thousand soldiers scattered across the colony, from Sydney to Hobart Town in the far south, and from the fourteen-year-old town of Brisbane in the north to the nine-year-old town of Perth on the west coast, as well as the newly established towns of Melbourne and Adelaide south of New South Wales. At the same time, he sits on the Executive Council with the Anglican bishop, the colonial secretary and the treasurer, to give opinions to the governor on the running of the colony. Separately, he sits on the Legislative Council to advise the governor on the making of laws. He also looks after Frogmore and keeps an eye on our livestock, and runs horses in the Hawkesbury, becoming one of the founders of horse-racing in the colony and a steward of the Sydney races.

My time becomes steadily busier, supporting Maurice and making all the necessary social connections after so long away. I renew old acquaintances, tidy John's vault, make morning calls all across Sydney and Parramatta, and visit the new girls in the female orphans' school that's now in Parramatta, in the building Betsey designed in the image of her childhood home in the Scottish Highlands. I also spend time with the governor's wife, Lady Elizabeth. She's fourteen years younger than me, with just one son, seven-year-old Reginald, whom she dreads having to send over to England for his schooling when he's old enough. I sympathise, having had to do the same myself. She confides she's unhappy being so far from the rest of her family and tried to persuade her husband not to take the position when he was offered it, but he felt it was too good an opportunity to turn down. She's trying to make the best of it, however.

She frequently visits the Female Factory in Parramatta where along with her housekeeper she helps teach needlework to unassigned convict women. She tends to stay at Government House in Parramatta more often than the one in Sydney, which these days is very decrepit. As a result, a new Government House is now being built in the Domain, close to the stables and servants' quarters that Betsey designed with Greenway when they were originally planning a new house, before it was halted by Bigge.

The rest of my time I spend with my family, making calls or hosting dinners and balls. I do enjoy entertaining, although I find it hard work. The best part about it is having the opportunity to wear my whole new wardrobe of gowns I brought over with me from London and Brussels. Meg chides me for saying so, but the years that have passed since I was last in Sydney have, sadly, seen no improvement in the standards of dress of the womenfolk.

And then, finally, just as I feel I have become newly established in Sydney, I pick up my pen and write a letter to Mrs Macarthur to ask if I may visit her, or if she will consent to visit me. I notice, with some surprise, that my hand is shaking.

39

THE END OF AN ERA

Meg Hill
18 NOVEMBER 1840, SYDNEY

Meg and Daniel walk down towards the harbour's edge just before
dawn breaks on the morning of Wednesday, 18 November, and join
a slow-moving mass of people with the same idea. When they reach
the shoreline, they all stand and wait, with their eyes firmly fixed
on the horizon. Gradually, a ship emerges from the early morning
mist and everyone watches in silence as it approaches the wharf. As
it draws near, they can make out the faces of some of the people on
the crowded deck, blinking as the watery sun fills the sky.

Meg has tears in her eyes, and Daniel notices and puts his arm
around her shoulders. 'Don't be sad,' he says. 'Be happy! It's over
now, thank God.'

She shivers; she can't help it. 'Yes, thank God,' she repeats. 'But
I can hardly believe it. After all this time. All those poor souls.'

'And us,' he says.

'Yes, and us.'

The pair have risen early to be part of the crowd witnessing what they all realise is a pivotal moment in the colony's history. This ship, the *Eden*, with its cargo of two hundred and sixty-nine men on board, has been sent from England as the last convict transport ever to arrive in New South Wales. The British Government made the decision, and Governor Gipps relayed it to everyone in Sydney: after she has docked, there will be no more transportation. From now on, the ships will bring only free migrants who are either paying their own passage or coming under a bounty system that gives, as an inducement, thirty pounds to couples under the age of thirty, ten pounds to single men and fifteen pounds to 'respectable' spinsters under thirty years of age.

For the throng of settlers, convicts, ex-convicts and convicts on tickets of leave who have come to watch the last moments of the system play out on the harbour, it's an emotional time. Meg can see many of the women around her also in tears, and a number of the men surreptitiously wipe their eyes. Most of them would be from convict stock, she assumes. The settlers are still divided on whether the end of transportation is a good thing.

'I suppose a lot of people here would say transportation has built the colony,' Meg says to Daniel. 'And in some ways it did. But how many lives did it also destroy? I can't help remembering my first days here . . . that man Mackey. I know I wouldn't have survived if I'd been forced to stay there. How many other women were put in situations like that?'

Daniel knew all about Meg's first assignment and how much it had scarred her. 'Yes, you were very lucky,' he says. 'We both were.

I was fortunate that I had a skill so much in demand that I didn't have to join a road gang where so many men were worked to an early death. You were lucky to have had Mary.'

Meg shivers. 'The trouble is, it was all such a random lottery,' she says. 'Who knew who you were going to get? You could get a good master or a bad one. But there was never anyone overseeing the system and making sure you were protected.'

'Because we were all expendable,' Daniel says.

They watch as the last group of convicts clamber off the ship and onto the wharf, looking tired, dirty, hungry and afraid. They're quickly surrounded by soldiers, who divide them into groups to send them off to the next part of their journey.

Meg turns away. 'Let's go home,' she says. 'I've seen enough. Let this be the end of a wretched system that even the vilest politicians in London can no longer justify. It's gone and good riddance.'

The next day, she calls on Mary at Tarmons and tells her of the relief she feels knowing that others won't be sent to New South Wales and assigned so arbitrarily. Mary had followed the machinations of the British Parliament's Molesworth Committee, which had been looking into transportation while she was in Europe, and she nods her head.

'Before I left, they were already saying that the assignment system had become open to abuse,' she says. 'Convicts were treated so differently depending purely on their masters' kindness—or lack thereof—and it had nothing to do with the seriousness of their crimes.'

'That's right,' Meg says. 'I know Governor Gipps very much supported the end of the system. And if my children are any indication, we won't ever run short of labour in the colony in the future. I have two more grandchildren now on the way . . .'

Mary laughs. 'Singlehandedly, you'll be responsible for repopulating New South Wales,' she says. 'Congratulations, my dear.'

The two women spend a pleasant afternoon chatting and walking in the great expanse of garden in front of the Potts Point mansion. A section of the house has now been divided off for Mary and Maurice's daughter, Elizabeth, who married one of Maurice's officers, Lieutenant Henry Somerset, two months ago.

'You never know, maybe they will start having grandchildren for me before too long,' Mary says wistfully. 'Mine seem to be terribly late starters.'

It's not long, however, before the subject of the disputed grants made by King to Mary's father comes up. Maurice's attorney took the matter to the New South Wales Supreme Court and the case was heard in 1839. It was a messy matter. Maurice was pressing that ownership be re-established for the sake of the late Governor Bligh's heirs—Mary and her sisters—but the court ruled that Maurice had taken little interest in the grants during his time away from the colony, while the people who'd built on the land had invested heavily in its future. On the other hand, Maurice's current standing and importance in New South Wales was lost on no one, and Mary's position at the epicentre of Sydney society also carried enormous sway. The whole affair was considered a potentially major embarrassment both for the governor and the Colonial Office back in Britain.

Meg sees how much negative publicity Mary and her family are attracting with their stand and gently tries to advise her. 'Is it really worth all this torment?' she asks. 'The newspaper keeps reporting on it and suddenly everyone seems to have an opinion about you.'

'But then why doesn't the British Government just step in and finish it?' Mary protests. 'I don't see why we have to give up our inheritance just to make it more convenient for those who've had the temerity to build on our land.'

'It's not just any old buildings, though, Mary,' Meg pushes on. 'Think: the school, the church, the gaol, all those houses. People have got used to seeing those there over the years, and they feel a real ownership of them.'

'Then maybe they should be willing to pay us compensation,' Mary sniffs.

'But it's not just about the money,' Meg implores her. 'Children are being educated at that school, the locals worship in that church. They are assets that are part of the community. I fear you're making yourself unpopular by pressing your claims. Don't you have enough land and wealth anyway?'

Mary shakes her head. 'It's not a question of money,' she says. 'It's a question of *principle*. Father was given that land. How can anyone now try to take it away from him? It's like what Macarthur did to him all over again.'

At the mention of that name, Meg abruptly changes tack. She's making no headway there; she might as well move on.

'What happened when you wrote to Mrs Macarthur?' she asks. 'Has she come back to you? Have you seen her yet?'

40

A FULL CIRCLE

Mary O'Connell
1 DECEMBER 1840, SYDNEY

Just the mention of the Macarthur name sends emotions sweeping through me. After all this time, you'd think I'd have come to terms with what John Macarthur did to my father and to me. But I haven't. I can't. However hard I try, it doesn't seem in me to forgive and move on.

Over the years, everyone has tried to reason with me: Meg, Betsey, Maurice. 'If you seek revenge, you should dig two graves,' Maurice told me once, quoting an old Chinese proverb. I understood what he meant. Staying angry for so long isn't good for anyone. But how do you shake it off?

For years, I imagined one day coming back to New South Wales and confronting Macarthur. I'd ask him why he did what he did, and whether it was all worth it in the end. I pictured him hanging his head in shame, and saying it wasn't. Because while it ruined our lives for a long time—and I don't think Father ever really recovered—he didn't fare well afterwards, either. He was forced to spend many years in exile in Britain, trading favours and fighting for his life, unable to return to his wife, his home and his children. He missed out on so much, too.

When Meg broke the news of his death to me in Brussels six years ago, I was devastated. In an instant, I'd been robbed forever of the chance to challenge him, to stare him down, to talk to him about what he'd done, to make him realise the depravity of his actions. But gradually I started thinking about an alternative. At least I could meet up with Mrs Macarthur and ask her why she had stood by and allowed this to happen, and why she had done nothing to stop her husband. It's a thought that, once planted and watered, roots and grows and blossoms. It's now beginning to feel so urgent, it's almost suffocating.

I've written to Mrs Macarthur twice now, asking to see her. Each time, she's written a perfectly polite note back, saying she's sorry, but she leads a quiet life, and likes to restrict socialising to a minimum. I know that's true. She's an old lady now, seventy-four years of age, and tends to leave home only when it's absolutely necessary, such as when she is occasionally summoned by Governor Gipps. The rest of the time, she stays close to her family.

'Perhaps you should forget this notion of meeting up with her, Mary,' Maurice counsels me. 'It's not as if you had anything to do with her in the old days. She doesn't really know you, nor you her. What's to be gained?'

'Maybe nothing,' I tell him. 'But I know I just can't leave it like this.'

'But you can't *force* her to see you,' Maurice says.

'Yes, I know.'

Then, the day before Christmas, I determine that I have to do something, so I take a carriage out to Elizabeth Farm in Parramatta. The maid who opens the door is clearly startled to see me.

'Mrs O'Connell?'

'Lady O'Connell,' I reply.

'I'm so sorry,' she says, blushing. 'Er . . . I don't think Mrs Macarthur is expecting you . . .'

I seize the initiative. 'Then maybe you should show me in and let her know I'm here.'

When Mrs Macarthur walks into the drawing room and sees me sitting there, she looks completely taken aback. I leap to my feet.

'Mrs Macarthur, forgive me,' I say. 'I didn't mean to startle you by showing up unannounced. I just needed to see you . . .'

She recovers her composure quickly. 'Miss Bligh . . . Mrs Putland . . . Lady O'Connell . . .' she says, running through my names. 'I am sorry I haven't seen you earlier. It's very rude of me not to have welcomed you back.' She rings a bell for a servant to bring tea and takes the chair opposite mine. 'Now, what may I do for you?'

I pause and collect my thoughts. I've been waiting for this moment for so long, and I want to make sure I do this right. 'Well, Mrs Macarthur, it's about your late husband,' I say. I notice a flicker of pain pass across her expression and I remember my manners. 'Of course, condolences for your loss,' I add quickly.

She nods in acknowledgement.

'But there's something I've been thinking about for a very long time,' I continue.

'Yes?' she asks quietly.

I wonder if she knows what's coming. 'You remember the mutiny?'

'Of course.'

'It's just that I've always wondered . . . Did you know what your husband was plotting?'

She looks at me straight in the eyes. 'I had a very good idea,' she replies.

'And did you encourage him?' I ask.

She shakes her head.

'But did you try to discourage him?'

She leans forward in her chair. 'No, I didn't,' she replies. 'But now may I ask you a question?'

'Of course.'

'Did you try to discourage your father from doing some of the more outrageous things he did?'

'I did,' I say firmly.

'And did it do any good?' she asks.

I pause. 'No, I'm afraid it didn't,' I have to concede. This conversation isn't going the way I imagined it would.

Her face softens. 'Mary, Mary,' she says. 'Look at us. Two strong women, both living in a world run by men. And my husband and your father were perhaps two of the most indomitable men in this colony. Just as you were unable to sway your father, there was no way I would ever have been able to divert John from his course once it was set.' She pauses, and then puts one of her hands over mine. 'I am very sorry about what happened. I know what a toll that must have taken on you both, and I heard about your courage when the troops marched on Government House. It was a terrible, terrible time.'

I can feel tears starting to slide down my face, and I reach for a handkerchief. She offers me one before I find mine.

'But John . . .' she says sadly. 'You should know that it became a heavy burden on my husband's shoulders, too.'

'How?' I whisper.

'He was away from us for many, many years, away from the anchors in his life that held him steady,' she says. 'His health deteriorated. The British Government never fully trusted him again. Successive governors here harboured doubts about him. In the last years of his life, he was erratic . . . unreasonable . . . unstable . . . He wouldn't even see me.'

I had heard that from Meg but I had never really believed it. Yet now, looking at the sorrow and hurt etched into Mrs Macarthur's face, I could see it was true.

'I'm sorry,' I say, and I mean it.

'Thank you,' she replies, then takes her hand away. 'You have the rest of your life ahead of you, Mary. It's time for you to let your father go, and my husband, and the pain of everything that happened in the past. Make the most of your time here.'

I nod, but I am so full of emotion, I don't trust myself to speak.

She hasn't finished. 'I hear you're in conflict with the governor over land claims,' she continues. 'If I could offer you a piece of advice on that . . . Don't be like your father and my husband and waste your time and passion on fruitless pursuits. We women are masters of compromise, of finding a middle path, and then of moving on with our lives. You have a loving husband, from what I hear, and a good family. We need to count our blessings and enjoy them.'

On the long journey back to Sydney, I have plenty of time to reflect on her words. And when I finally arrive back at Tarmons, I feel strangely lighter and, in a sense, free.

I tell Maurice we should reach a settlement on our land grants, and we drop the claim over Parramatta in exchange for the titles to our other grants being confirmed. Then we sell Camperdown, for a small fortune of twenty-five thousand pounds, and Copenhagen in the Hawkesbury.

A few months later, our daughter Elizabeth gives us our first grandchild, a little boy she names Charles, and Maurice promotes Elizabeth's husband, Henry, to take command of the New South Wales Mounted Police. There's also sadness in the family, however. We receive the news from back home that my sister Anne has died at the age of just fifty-two. Given the fits she always suffered from, and how she was unable to look after herself, it is something of a release. We attend St James' Church on King Street—intended to be a courthouse under Macquarie until he was forced by the ghastly Bigge to turn it into a church instead—to say a prayer for her. I decide to spend more time doing charity work and, as part of my duties, serve on the committee that supports the work of Caroline Chisholm, an officer's wife who's doing so much to help single homeless women, giving them shelter and educating them with skills they'll need to make a living.

It's a busy time for Maurice, too, and I know he gets tired easily. He's under a lot of pressure to send more troops to New Zealand in the hope of putting a stop to land wars between European settlers and the Māori. There's also constant manoeuvring between keeping soldiers in Sydney and moving more to Van Diemen's Land, insubordination among troops on Norfolk Island and rows over the soldiers' rum ration and what can be done about it. My poor husband has the patience of Job.

In June 1846, Maurice and I are summoned to the magnificent new Government House, set in the gardens close to the harbour's edge. We're received by the governor in the drawing room, and Elizabeth, his wife, stands behind his chair. She greets us warmly, but he remains seated, staring at the fire in the grate. He looks terrible: so pale his skin is almost translucent, with his eyes bloodshot and his hands trembling. We'd heard he was sick as he hasn't been seen out in public for weeks. We thought he was avoiding public life because the newspapers keep attacking him, in the way they do all governors towards the end of their time here, but now we can see it is because he is most unwell. The sight of him is a shock. He is only fifty-five, eight years younger than me, and twenty-three years younger than Maurice, but he looks much, much older.

'George!' I exclaim. 'How are you feeling? Is there anything we can do?' I look at Elizabeth, who is gazing at her husband with concern.

'Thank you, Mary,' she replies softly. 'But unfortunately, George has taken a turn for the worse. As you know, Sir Charles FitzRoy is due to arrive in August to take over as governor, but we've decided we can't wait that long. George needs to get home to Britain as soon as possible. We need to be with our son.'

I nod. I completely understand. I know how difficult it is sending children across to the other side of the world for their schooling, and at least I always had other children to console me when we sent young Maurice. They only have Reginald.

'Of course,' I say.

My husband shifts beside me. 'Sir, madam, how can we help with the transition?' he asks. 'Obviously we will do anything we can.'

The governor stirs. 'Thank you,' he says in a voice so thin we both strain to hear. 'We will take a ship to England next month. I will need you to take over as governor until Sir Charles arrives.'

Maurice bows to him once, and then to his wife. 'It will be my duty,' he says. 'My very sad duty, but my duty.'

I'm utterly speechless. Maurice, at seventy-eight, is going to be governor of New South Wales and I'm once again going to be the governor's consort, a full forty years after the first time. It's so strange. Who could ever have seen anything like this happening, the closing of a full circle?

I recover my wits enough to wish the couple well, and to repeat Maurice's words about doing our duty. But by the time we're outside the front gates, I'm back in a state of shock.

'Are you all right, Mary?' Maurice asks, concerned.

'Yes, yes,' I reply. 'It's just that . . . Well, it's just something that's . . .'

He smiles, then gathers me in his arms. 'I know,' he says. 'I know.'

Governor Gipps and his wife sail away from Sydney on 11 July 1846. We farewell them with as much decorum as the governor can stand, which is precious little as he's so anxious to be on his way.

As we watch his ship depart, we wait on Government Wharf, absorbing the reality of our new position. We're now Governor O'Connell and his First Lady, in charge of the colony. It's a lot to take in.

Our children attend the ceremony with us, as well as a few of our closest friends; Meg and Daniel and their children among them. We stand around and chat for a while. Our sons hug me and shake hands with Maurice, while Elizabeth hugs us both. Then Meg and I have a moment together.

'Mary, Mary, congratulations!' she says with a smile. 'After all these years . . . that Bligh girl is back where she belongs. Well, no one would ever have expected something like this to happen!'

'You're right,' I reply. 'Least of all me.'

We embrace and, as we do so, she whispers in my ear, 'Your father would be proud.' And I immediately feel tears spring into my eyes.

We've already decided not to leave our home at Tarmons to take up residence at Government House, as the new governor Sir Charles is expected in August, but after the ceremony our carriage takes us there to inspect the official home. The servants are lined up either side of the driveway to greet us, and we walk between them, nodding and smiling.

Inside, Maurice has an immediate meeting with his Executive Council to talk about the squatting issue he hopes he will at last have the power to resolve, and I wander through the house to the back verandah. There, I sit on one of the steps and look out over the gardens towards the harbour.

In the early days, Port Jackson had only a few ships anchored besides our convoy, but now I can see it's busy with free settler arrivals to the colony as well as so many vessels coming to trade. Governor Macquarie's introduction of a currency has rid us of the scourge of rum and the soldier monopolies on provisions; today, the system is so much fairer. It's something I would have loved my father to have lived to see but, sadly, he was one of the sacrifices made along the way. At least now, thanks to Mrs Macarthur, I can think of him without the pain and anger that always used to haunt his memory.

In a few days it will be precisely forty years since I first arrived in New South Wales as a naïve twenty-three-year-old to be the consort to the governor. Back then, it was to my father. Today, it's to my husband.

I stand up and brush the dust off my hem. It's time to take my place with the men, and to move on to this next stage in my life. When I think of everything I've done, all the remarkable sights that I've seen, the hardships I've endured, and the tragedies I've survived, it seems it was, somehow, always my destiny to end up right here. Where I belong.

AFTERWORD

Mary O'Connell

Mary and Maurice held their positions as acting governor and First Lady until Sir Charles FitzRoy and his wife Lady Mary arrived on 3 August 1846 to take over.

The next year, in 1847, Maurice was succeeded as Commander of the New South Wales forces by Major General Edward Wynyard, and Maurice and Mary made arrangements to leave Sydney to return to Britain and settle in Ireland.

The very day they were meant to board their ship, 25 May 1848, Maurice collapsed and died at the age of eighty.

He was buried with full military honours on 29 May, with a procession of nearly one hundred and fifty coaches carrying the mourners, and more spectators, according to the newspapers of the day, than had ever gathered in Sydney before. His body was interred in the Brickfield Hill Cemetery.

Later that year, the body of Mary's first husband, John Putland, was transferred to the new Camperdown Cemetery—with the land donated from that controversial Camperdown grant.

Mary left Sydney on 5 June 1848 with her son William Bligh and his wife, and settled in Paris, where she lived surrounded by the kind of fashions she'd loved all her life.

She died at the age of eighty-one on 10 December 1864 in Gloucester, England, at the home of her daughter Elizabeth and son-in-law Henry Somerset.

Her eldest son, Maurice O'Connell Junior, was the first to live on the Frogmore land grant with his wife, Eliza. He sold his military commission in 1844 to enter politics and held a number of positions: as an elective member of the first NSW Legislative Council, representing Port Phillip; as the Commissioner of Crown Lands; and, after the colony of Queensland was created, as President of the Legislative Council of Queensland. He was four times deputy to the governor and was knighted in 1868.

One of her twelve grandchildren, William Bligh O'Connell—the child of her second son William Bligh O'Connell—also became a politician and served in the Queensland Legislative Assembly, representing Musgrave, and was Secretary of Lands until his death in 1903.

The former Queensland premier Anna Bligh is descended from Mary's sister Elizabeth, who married her cousin Richard Bligh.

Meg Hill

Meg and Daniel lived together as partners for many years and, despite his wife in England finally dying, the couple never married. Instead, they split up soon after Mary left the colony and Daniel co-habited with another woman, Ann, whom he married instead.

By the time of his death at the age of seventy, he and Ann were living apart.

Meg, however, lived in Sydney until the age of ninety-five.

Three of the couple's four children went on to have large families. Nathaniel married the daughter of a First Fleet convict and had eleven children. Sarah married a convict and had the same number of children, while Ann married another convict and had thirteen children. No record of any children exists for their fourth child, William.

AUTHOR'S NOTE

Mary had a number of different maids during her time in New South Wales, but I've taken the liberty of conflating them into one person for the character of Meg Hill. Meg is based mostly on the character and circumstances of one of Mary's maids in New South Wales, Susannah Harrison, who was transported at the age of seventeen for theft from her employers' home in Old Town, Stepney, London, while the man who'd persuaded her to let him into their house was acquitted of all charges.

While in Sydney, Susannah ended up cohabiting with Isaac Peyton or Payton, the man I've called Daniel Panton. In real life, they also had four children, and thirty-five grandchildren.

FURTHER READING

Cochrane, P., *Governor Bligh and the Short Man*, Penguin Books, Melbourne, 2012.

Dando-Collins, S., *Captain Bligh's Other Mutiny*, Random House Australia, Sydney, 2007.

Daunton-Fear, R., Vigar, P., *Australian Colonial Cookery,* Rigby's Pageant of Australia Series, Adelaide, 1977.

Davidson, H., *Dress in the Age of Jane Austen: Regency fashion*, Yale University Press, London, 2019.

De Vries, S., *Females on the Fatal Shore: Australia's brave pioneers*, Pirgos Press, Brisbane, 2009.

Heney, H., *Australia's Founding Mothers*, Thomas Nelson Australia, Melbourne, 1978.

Hughes, J., Liston, C., Wright C., *Playing Their Part: Vice-Regal Consorts of New South Wales 1788–2019*, Royal Australian Historical Society, Sydney, 2020.

Hughes, R., *The Fatal Shore*, Collins Harvill, London, 1987.

Mundle, R., *BLIGH Master Mariner*, Hachette Australia, Sydney, 2016.

Nelson, P., *Bligh's Daughter*, Trafford Publishing, Victoria, 2007.

O'Brien, C., *The Colonial Kitchen 1788–1901*, Rowman & Littlefield, Lanham, Maryland, 2016.

Prout, D., Feely, F., *Petticoat Pioneers: Australia's colonial women*, Rigby, Adelaide, 1977.

Scott Tucker, M., *Elizabeth Macarthur: A life at the end of the world*, Text Publishing, Melbourne, 2018.

Seale, S., *Mary Bligh*, Riverstone and District Historical Society Inc., Riverstone, 2020.

Walsh, R., *In Her Own Words: The writings of Elizabeth Macquarie*, Exisle Publishing, Wollombi, 2011.

Wilcox, C., 'The Military Command of Maurice O'Connell 1838–1947', *Journal of the Royal Historical Society*, volume 107(1), June 2021.

Williams, S., *Elizabeth & Elizabeth*, Allen & Unwin, Sydney, 2021.

ACKNOWLEDGEMENTS

While I've always absolutely loved historical fiction, I do think it's the hardest genre to write. It always involves so much painstaking research . . . and then there's the constant battle to present it as seamlessly as possibly within a compelling storyline.

But happily, I've had amazing help from others along the way. The biggest thank you, as ever, goes to Robin Walsh, or Wiki Walsh as I have come affectionately to know him, for his incredible generosity with his seemingly endless knowledge of the early colonial era and its peoples.

Robin, the author of *In Her Own Words*, was always so ready to help, advise, point me to sometimes quite obscure historical records and offer continuing encouragement. Along the way, Robin and his lovely wife, Julie, have become dear and treasured friends. Thanks so much, guys.

I'm also immensely grateful to historian Dr Stephen Gapps, esteemed author of *The Sydney Wars: Conflict in the early colony*

1788–1817, and *Gudyarra,* who advised me on the passages of the book that dealt with Aboriginal people in early Australia.

Thanks are due as well to one of Australia's leading naturopaths, the immensely knowledgeable and talented Tania Flack, who advised me on Meg's use of herbs, tonics and remedies.

Editor Christa Munns was a huge help with an unerring instinct for what works—and what doesn't—and suggested some invaluable changes and directions to go along the way. I was very lucky to have had her on board once again.

A big thank you, too, for copyeditor Tessa Feggans, whose sharp eyes missed nothing throughout the manuscript, and who never failed to suggest good alternatives whenever I went astray or repeated myself.

Of course, without my publisher Annette Barlow at Allen & Unwin, I'd never have had the chance to get to know Mary Bligh and her father, and follow their extraordinary lives, failings and achievements. It's been a huge privilege.

The beautiful book cover was a big help, and all credit for that goes to the immensely talented Christa Moffitt. It's another work of art.

I'd also like to thank publicist Christine Farmer who works so hard to make sure these books find as wide an audience as possible. I've known her for a long time now and her vast reserves of energy, enthusiasm and good sense never fail to impress. Thanks to her colleague, publicist Bella Breder, for all her sterling help.

I'm very blessed to have my partner, Jimmy Thomson, by my side, who also spurred me on whenever I flagged and who, after reading the start of the book about the voyage over to New South Wales, delivered the crushing line, 'It's fine until HMS *Exposition* sails in.' Although painful at the time, it became a valuable touchstone for the rest of the book.

My great friend Virginia Addison was also a huge help, reading the manuscript and offering much-appreciated advice, and Clare Birgin's comments were priceless.

Another good friend Raphaela Angelou gave invaluable assistance, particularly with social media, at which I'm hopeless. I came to dread her gentle reminders that it was time to put something online, but I always appreciated them.

I'm immensely grateful too for all the beautiful comments I received from readers of my first historical fiction novel, *Elizabeth & Elizabeth*, which kept me going when times were tough. It was wonderful to be invited to so many historical, social and charitable functions to talk about early colonial history and share the enthusiasm.

And finally thank you to my fabulous agent, Fiona Inglis of Curtis Brown, who encouraged me all the way through.

Thanks so much to you all.